to John

from

MW01226881

BUCKET WALKERS

AND THE ONE HUNDRED QUART RULE

Phyllis Del Puppo

◆ FriesenPress

One Printers Way
Altona, MB R0G 0B0
Canada

www.friesenpress.com

Copyright © 2022 by Phyllis Del Puppo
First Edition — 2022

All rights reserved.

No part of this publication may be reproduced in any form, or by any means, electronic or mechanical, including photocopying, recording, or any information browsing, storage, or retrieval system, without permission in writing from FriesenPress.

ISBN
978-1-5255-8521-0 (Hardcover)
978-1-5255-8520-3 (Paperback)
978-1-5255-8522-7 (eBook)

1. FICTION, FAMILY LIFE

Distributed to the trade by The Ingram Book Company

Introductory Recipe: Huckleberry Grunt
(Serves 15)

4 cups butter or margarine, 8 to 12 eggs, 3 cups sugar, 10 cups flour, 9 teaspoon baking powder, 1 teaspoon vanilla, 8–10 cups huckleberries.

Beat butter, sugar, eggs.
Add vanilla and dry ingredients.
Fold in berries.
Bake in hot oven until firm and golden.

CHAPTER 1
The Storyteller: Julie, 2005

JULIE HAS BEEN CLIMBING through brush for over an hour and at last comes to a meadow, bright with wild flowers.

The sun is warm on her back, filtered through birch leaves, while a gentle breeze keeps any mosquitoes away. Intermingled with the ripple of a nearby stream, the song of a thrush floats overhead. The air is fresh. Julie shimmies with delight.

Obligations, the daily racket, drift far away as she gazes into the blue clear distance, until her thoughts follow a wing of cloud back to Earth, to the West Kootenays.

Julie and her twin, Pink, have one more semester of teaching at the Chagall Art Academy. And then! A year to travel, to celebrate their fifty-five years together. If Pink were here now, she'd throw her hat in the air and whoop, but Julie's the quiet one. She chuckles. Their plans are fluid, but one thing is for certain: racketing around the world for a year with Pink will be a riot.

If they can go. If Pink's operation goes well today. They won't know for a few days.

Julie doesn't want her worries to intrude on Pink; they're so interconnected. Distance is sometimes necessary to keep things on an even keel. This clear blue distance should be just the thing.

Looking around, Julie discovers she's surrounded by plump, black huckleberries. She palms a handful into her mouth, closing her eyes as their tang surges through her. Luckily, huckleberry picking is one of her favourite pastimes. The whole afternoon lies ahead, and by dint of habit, she has a goodly bucket with her.

Some people might contentedly sit in a dark room on a sunny day, watching television ads with the blinds pulled, rather than pick huckleberries. But Julie's in her element as she leans into the bushes. After a lifetime of practice, she's good at this. Ripe berries pull easily from their stems, trundle through her fingers, and roll down her palms into her bucket. Her hands quicken, nimbly shulling the bushes hand over fist.

The clatter of the first berries hitting the bottom of her pail soon gives way to the gentle thud of handfuls landing on handfuls. Her eyes and hands work automatically while her thoughts drift.

They drift to the time, decades earlier, when she and her ten brothers and sisters made the huckleberry trip to beat all huckleberry trips. It was the first time all eleven had been loose on the same mountain at the same time, miles from their parents. Most of them still call it their longest day.

Over the years, a thousand versions of that trip have been sorted and assimilated by Julie. A keen listener and a meticulous observer with an acute memory, she has seen that expedition as clearly through everyone else's eyes as through her own. Julie saw that day gather the Eleven up and shake them out, slightly changed as the summer progressed. She has long planned to write it all down, that summer of 1955. She often carries a notebook with her: she thumbs through it now.

CHAPTER 2
The Family in 1955

THERE ARE FIVE SISTERS and six brothers:

Herald	18
Brick	17
Hazel	16
Fern	15
Ron and Rich	13
Sedge	12
Billy	10
Alvin	7
Pink and Julie	5
and	
Lettuce	the mom
Bob	the dad

That's Herald, Brick, Hazel, Fern, Ron and Rich, Sedge, Billy, Alvin, Pink and Julie. Some friends and relatives write down the list to keep them all straight. Being the youngest, Julie tends to see her siblings in reverse order. That summer of 1955, Julie and Pink are almost six, and up the stepping stones are Alvin, age seven; Billy, age ten; Sedge, age twelve; Rich and Ronnie, age thirteen; Fern, age fifteen; Hazel, age sixteen; Brick, age seventeen; and Herald, age eighteen.

In the early fifties, large families are still popular, and survival in the country means hard work and knowing how to forage. Thrift is as necessary as making porridge thick enough to glue newspapers to the table.

Except for the rare treat of icing on squash cake, porridge and pancakes are the closest thing to umami, the seventh taste after sweet, sour, salty, bitter, roughage, and gristle. Bakery bread is greeted by the Eleven like sliced manna. They still reminisce about when their mom had her appendix out and her sister came to stay. Aunt Hilarity beamed at their happy faces as they choffed peanut butter and jam dagwoods on soft-white-sliced until Moe's cows jangled home. Umami.

Even the wrappers from that bought bread are prized. Brown wax paper from brown bread, white from white, it's all carefully laid in the warming oven to soften, then flattened for wrapping workday lunches.

Old coats are made into snow-pants. Odd gloves are matched. Heavy cotton pajamas are sewn from flour sacks with "Pride Flour Mill" stamped across the buttocks.

As thrift leads the family through the seasons, a warm house in winter means trips to the wood-lot in summer. With much sweat and a little blood, trees are felled and limbed by all the kids strong enough to swing an axe alongside their father. Calls of "Timber!" and "Look out below!" rend the forest. The youngest three play at a safe distance under fragrant boughs, in the cool semi-darkness.

Their laughter interplays with birdsong as their mother opens her sewing box. Lettuce spreads calico scraps over the rusty pine-needles and fiddles out a a new cloche pattern. They all wear her colourful hats.

Around noon, the kids excitedly unpack their food boxes. To Lettuce, her hours of preparation are well worth a few hours in the summer forest. After lunch, she'll be busy on all fronts as the logs are rolled to the trailer hitched to their six-door, Plymouth sedan, which is parked on the shoulder of a narrow dirt road.

Over the summer, the firewood is cut into lengths: the younger kids perch on saw-horses to hold the logs steady while bigger kids take turns on either end of a bucksaw, trying not to jam the six-foot blade. But every so often, they hit a knot or break their rhythm and the blade will bind, bucking the log-sitters on wild rides amid shrieks of laughter, outrageous swearing, and inklings of disaster. In the autumn, they chop the wood and pile it in each other's arms to stack in the woodshed; uneven ranks of cedar, fir, tamarack, and pine await the winter hearth.

Fresh fruit is slurped raw from gardens and countryside: as the season progresses, strawberries and saskatoons, raspberries, red and black currants, huckleberries, gooseberries, plums, apples, pears, and more huckleberries are gobbled and jammed, dried, and canned.

Bright vegetables are harvested from backyard gardens until hard frost, after which installments of root crops and cabbage are bucketed daily from cellar bins. By spring, though still edible, the cabbages are white with black specks. The last potatoes host long, anemic sprouts which have crept from gunny sacks toward the crack of light above the cellar door. Only the Hubbard squash change little over the long winter months. Huge, prehistoric eggs brooding on attic shelves, they maintain meaty orange flesh under rinds like gray rock.

When spring finally shoves aside the clammy embrace of snow, a March thaw keeps the youngsters busy in the streets, engineering huge dams of slush and mud which redirect traffic and flood garages. One call on the party line and half the neighbourhood is grounded, so the kids hurriedly break their dams and clear the worst of the debris off the streets before going indoors, to hunch over Monopoly games and popcorn. On a last scurry before bedtime, puddles are found to be covered with crackle ice, that thin layer which is irresistible to crunch underfoot. In the morning, kids slide through the glassy streets on strips of cardboard.

Eventually, on a warm edge of the garden, last fall's pansies uncrumple; tiny purple faces peer through a mat of vivid mint. Soon lamb's quarter, the delicious weed, is ready for the picking, and the kids hastily pick bushels of the stuff after school, their voices ringing in the quiet countryside:

"Break the roots off, Billy, before you throw it in the bucket!"

"The more dirt you get in, the more we have to rinse out."

"Jeez, Hazel and Fern, don't be so fussy."

"Well, do you like biting on grit?"

"Who moved the bucket? Pink?"

They slosh the greens in a galvanized tub, leaving the hose trickling through. Lettuce patiently does the final cleaning before supper, glad that lamb's quarter is free for the picking. They all crave the luscious greens and it takes three buckets raw to give them each more than a mouthful when it's cooked. At last the snow is gone, the chores are done, and it's time for the kids to run wild over the hillsides in canvas sneakers.

Brick hollers, "Have you seen my knapsack?"

"In the basement," yells Herald.

"Get the marbles," shouts Alvin. Pink and Julie scramble for the skipping ropes. Rich searches for his pocket knife. Ron hefts the football. Billy munches an apple. Sedge, Hazel, and Fern burst out the door, shrieking with laughter.

All over the neighbourhood, children catapult from houses which seem to have shrunk over the winter, while the kids have grown lank as cellar sprouts. Hooting and hollering they push out in all directions at once, spreading and collecting like human amoebae, taking over the streets for rambunctious games of kick-the-can and shinny. Bits of glass are unearthed and tossed into hop-scotch squares that have been drawn with sharp sticks into roadside mud.

Around town and over the mountainside, leafy hide-outs are reclaimed, where meditative souls seek distance from the hurly-burly of the neighbourhood. Young romantics make tentative queries, and a new generation of poets and painters ponders the meaning of life.

Lettuce and Bob's flourishing brood has the luxury of a huge house. Once a rooming home, it's a ramshackle two floors plus a vast attic, a cavernous basement, a back porch, and a front veranda, the whole shebang anchored in bedrock and in reason-ably good working order. The kids have the entire attic to them-selves, with personal fortresses for work, study, and play. Movable partitions are frequently moved, usually after much noisy palaver. The middle floor has a commodious art and project room as well as Lettuce and Bob's own room. The ground floor is allotted to cooking and eating, relaxing, sewing, and visiting.

But no matter how large the house, this large family spends as much time as possible outdoors. Frequently tramping from their backyard into the mountains, they hike miles for the fun of it, often trailing friends and relatives in Wordsworthian "clouds of glory." Life is much more exciting for anyone who gets to know Lettuce and Bob and their eleven children.

Herald, the eldest at eighteen, is feeling cramped at home, in terms of both his size and intellect. He's six foot two and still growing, and his thoughts roam the universe. He wants to see a bit of the world before he's an old man. Herald's afraid if he doesn't get away soon, he'll be stuck for life at the jam factory. He doesn't really have his heart set on going to Victoria for teacher's training, but it sure would be nice. Growing up the eldest of eleven, he figures he's almost ready for the classroom. He has some maturing to do, but in years to come, he'll be loved as a teacher, nick-named Mr. Heron for his height—and, occasionally, Mr. Flight for his verbal flights of temper. His family often calls him "Hare."

Seventeen-year-old Brick, built square and strong, is Herald's stalwart companion. Brick likes to work hard and play hard. A rambunctious competitor in soccer, shinny, and kick the can, he's a kind brother. His calm, patient demeanor belies his red hair. Everyone marvels how Brick works on his stamp collection, with his hands the size of baseball mitts and a half-dozen kids shoving around him asking questions. When he's had enough of their clamour, he stomps outside to chop wood—the knottier the chunks, the better. Brick says that when he graduates, he's going to sea. "When I have my own ship," he says, "I'll sail all of you around the world."

The two oldest sisters, Hazel, sixteen, and Fern, fifteen, act as second and third mother when Lettuce is busy elsewhere. They're sure that chaos would reign without their judicious, level-headed solidarity in the ebb and flow of the household. Fern is quick with remedies for cuts and bruises, liberal with hugs and sympathy, while Hazel is more inclined to stand back and size up the best way to restore equilibrium and get the work done. Like Herald, Hazel is tall, spare, and dark-haired, neat but otherwise indifferent to her appearance—unlike Fern, who pines after lovely clothing. Hazel keeps her luxurious hair in a tidy braid, whereas Fern's peach-blond curls are a frothy nimbus.

The thirteen-year-old twins, brown-haired and brown-eyed Ron and Rich, are rascals. Fern and Hazel dread being in the same room as them at school. If the girls hear an uproar, they usually fade into the background (but let anyone pick on one of their siblings, even Rich or Ron, and the sisters are on the warpath). Ron and Rich can be a sorry challenge to anyone in authority. It's hard to get angry with them, because they're bright and original and often irresistibly funny. For a teacher to reprimand them is to risk bursting out laughing in front of a class, which would not do at all.

Stick-Rich and Robust-Ron are usually in the same class, involved in any shenanigans going on at the moment. They are quite civilized much of the time, but when they decide to turn their class on its ear, they do a good job of it. Like the time they smuggled two Rhode Island Reds into science: the chickens were silent and motionless as long as they were in the dark, stowed inside the box marked "science books" which the boys had set on the teacher's desk. But of course, old Rooster-ella and Butt-Hen flew into hysterics the minute Mr. Nitmust opened the box. The hens had party hats tied on their heads, a truly inspired touch, but when the hats slipped, the hens tripped on the strings. A chicken falling down is not a pretty sight. They flapped over the desks, squawking and cackling, as class order disintegrated into pandemonium. Rich and Ron were all wide, brown-eyed innocence. They were supposed to be studying birds, after all.

Those hens were on lay-off for two weeks after their educational afternoon, with a few feathers missing and still unable to read. Then the boys felt sorry, and Sedge was quite cross with them. She and Fern did their best to re-tame the hens.

Blue-eyed with white-blonde hair, Sedge, at twelve is shy, deep, and poetic. She's helpful around the house, noticing what needs to be done, doing it, and then vanishing. She loves all of her siblings, but she likes nothing better than a solitary hike. Fascinated and contemplative, she observes every turn of leaf and flash of wing. If anyone is with her, let it be Alvin. Peering through gyres of time, they perceive the fleeting beauty of their vast and unknowable universe. Finding a vantage point, Sedge and Alvin will contentedly settle with their sketchbooks for an hour, seldom a word spoken.

Ten-year-old Billy is black-haired, boisterous, and jolly. He's constantly making up stories and annoying puns. His round, dimpled face and brown eyes are almost always smiling. He gets along with everyone and takes an interest in everything. They call him Billy Bridge, because he spans them all and keeps a running conversation amongst them. Where is everybody? Ask Billy.

Blond Alvin, at seven, has a lot of fun in his exploits with Billy. Like when they took apart the old wind-up alarm clock that Herald gave Billy for his birthday, along with a tiny set of screwdrivers: the clock could tick sporadically but no longer tell time. "Can you fix it?" winked Herald. They gave it a good try, ending up with neither the tick nor the time, but a jarful of minute springs, levers and gears. They spent hours tinkering with those parts, especially the alarm mechanism, with Herald taking a keen interest.

Julie and Pink, the family's second set of twins, are almost identically opposite in appearance. Pink has red fizz-hair and brown eyes and Julie has black mouse-hair and blue eyes. Their only identical traits are their skinniness and height… and effervescence.

Pink and Julie have each other, and they can keep to themselves in the crowd of their family. The others are blissfully innocent of much of their goings on. At almost six, they're convinced they can be invisible, which, in a way, they can be. They're will-o'-the-wisps with cores of steel. They don't care if everyone ignores them while they push their boundaries with determination. In one of their private campaigns, they took over a whole dormer of the attic for the expansion of their pixie diorama before anyone noticed what they'd done.

Though the Eleven may seem unpolished, brought up from scratch and often more comfortable in trees than chairs, they are creative and original, known at school as "the clever kids" or "the smart alecks," depending on who's talking. They're all avid readers, immersed from birth in Lofting's Dr. Doolittle, Pooh, and Keats, leavened with the *Scientific American* and the *C.L.C. Chemical Journal*. They're read to or read over any time Lettuce and Bob aren't working on some complicated project, like making paper, concocting a full spectrum of pigments from plants, designing medieval costumes, or conscientiously feeding a growing family.

Lettuce often has one eye on a novel while working in the kitchen, pondering Molly Bloom as she stirs endless batches of apple butter for the Annual Arena Benefit Fall Fair. Edith Wharton and Agatha Christie are handy on top of the fridge, while Proust and Mr. Noddy are wedged into the cookbooks at the end of the counter.

Bob is given more to nature journals, scientific periodicals, and puzzles of all sorts. He has an avalanche of puzzles in one corner of the living room, with a jigsaw generally in progress on a high project table. His rule: if you can reach the puzzle, you can work on it, but if you drop a piece and don't pick it up, you can be sentenced to death-by-sorting-the-vacuum-bag. There is no television in their home. Most evenings, Lettuce reads to the kids or they read to each other while Bob pores over his journals. He often dozes in his armchair with a smile on his face, lulled by their voices.

The family loves to tell stories and write them, as well as read them. Stories are the mesh and modulator of family experience, the gravity-glue which holds them in their proper orbit. Though the rules of thermodynamics might be bent and pummeled, with the help of narrative, the family can all be on one flapjack at the end of the day.

One of the best flapjacks they ever made was their bucketwalk of July, 1955. Julie's family has refined their love of hiking and huckleberries into the art, science and sport of bucket walking. Whether food for the belly or food for thought, there's nothing better than heading out with an empty bucket and coming home with it full of berries—or at least a good story to tell. Her family usually gathers enough huckleberries to keep them in cobblers and pies all winter long, plus a good supply of narrative to feed on. The bucketwalk of their longest day kept them feasting on berries for more than a year and clarifying the story for the rest of their lives.

CHAPTER 3
The Storyteller: Julie, 2005

FIFTY YEARS LATER, FORAGING for huckleberries on the sunny hillside, Julie sends telepathic hugs to Pink. Her twin might be having surgery at that very moment. Their thoughts intertwine much of the time, but they've learned when to give each other space. The last thing Pink needs now is Julie's worries bombarding her like a swarm of rabid mosquitoes. The twins have been known to move mountains when they put their minds to it, but now is not the time.

Julie forces herself to focus on her "Huckleberry Chronicles." It's time that an updated and expanded version of huckleberry lore be recorded, as rural activities give way to urban sprawl and the giant, sloppy handwriting of progress.

The nuances of bucket size, its practical and sociological implications, could be lost to future generations. The importance of spring rain after the flowers are pollinated, as related to the juiciness of berries in July, could be forgotten. Never to be heard again, the clang of buckets over the mountainside, the swish-plunk of berries landing in half-gallon pails, the clink-spatter of small hands filling jam cans.

An important cultural niche could disappear in the slurry of the urban cement mixer, that great leveler in humanity's ongoing attempts to subvert nature's timing and flow and rewrite it in a language that doesn't make sense.

Working on automatic pilot, Julie is so preoccupied that she hardly registers a pair of nuthatches arguing near her head, "Ccha-cha-cha, chi-chi-chi-chaaa." When a fawn scuttles out of her way, she doesn't see it, except for the swing of a low branch.

Can she corral the sparrows of her thoughts and memories into the pages of a ledger? Are small bulbs embedded in couch grass worth weeding, in hopes of a few bright flowers in the year after next?

"Oh for heaven's sake, get on with the job, will you, and tell the story!" That's Herald's voice, nagging her conscience. "You've done enough wool-gathering. Now settle down and spin some yarn."

Fine: she'll try to get some of it down, the juicy parts at least, although it's just as much Herald's story as hers, and he'll no doubt have a say in the editing (he'll tell her never to use the word "whom" because she'll never get it right. Just say "who" all the time!). Okay, Herald. But you can't expect to get every bug out before canning.

"The Chronicles of Huckleberry Picking" has a nice ring to it. It could have a sub-title, perhaps, "The Bucket Walker's Companion: The Arcane World of Huckleberry Picking." It will be a story-bucket, full of the rules and ramifications of huckleberry picking. The Eleven and their parents will be her knit one, purl two; the weft and the woof of her story, their story, their enthusiasm and energy.

With that thought, Julie emerges from the underbrush, munching a handful of prime berries... Hmmmm, good, ripe ones... one patch leads into another... munch... slurp... good and sweet... Mmmmm.

It's very quiet.

An important rule of huckleberry picking is Rule 4X : "Avoid long silences while berry picking. Let the bears know where you are so they don't stumble into you by accident." Julie makes the loud bird-call she uses when out alone like this: "Tradee, tradoo!" Keeping to the task, her eyes never leave the bushes. "Kadee, Kadoo!"

CHAPTER 4
The June Itch

ONE JUNE DAY ON the lead-up to that momentous expedition of 1955, the Eleven are gathered around their large wooden table, on which is a heap of fresh-baked bread and a yellow bowl of forget-me-nots. As the table is jostled, their tiny blue petals scatter over the buttery loaves. "Like sky kisses," says Pink, as she and Julie gently lift them off.

Herald, the eldest, squints at a scrap of paper on which a note is scrawled. He reads out loud:

"Gone for bucketwalk... Back by dark. Love, Mom and Dad. xoxo"

With a collective sigh, the kids fling down their sweaters and bags. The fridge is yanked open; baloney and cheese are wedged between rough-hewn slabs of brown bread. Laughter erupts, arguments flare, water is spilled. "Hasten Jason bring the basin, oops slop bring the mop," sings Alvin.

"How long do you think they'll be gone?" wonders Billy.

"I dunno," says Ron. "At least two hours. Depends what buckets they took. Told you, we shoulda stayed at the ball game."

"They're usually home by now, telling us to get busy," says Rich. "Wanna go down to Chuckie Moozle's?"

"To watch TV? Can we come too, Ron?"

"No, Alv and Billy! TV rots the brains of young children."

"Is that what happened to you?"

"Whaddya mean, Pink? My brain's a powerhouse of knowledge and know-how."

"What about your homework, Ron? School isn't over yet!"

"Homework on Friday, Hare? You gotta be kidding!"

"How come the Moozles can afford TV anyhow?"

"Because they only got two kids, Billy."

"And they got no socks or underwear," says Hazel.

"How do you know? Anyhow, they always got the latest gadget."

"TV's not a gadget, Billy."

"You know what I mean."

"Anyway, Ron and Rich, it's your turn to take out the chicken bucket and get the eggs," Hazel reminds them. "And wash the eggs outside. You got crud in the sink last time."

"We'll do it later. Pink and Julie, it's your turn to pull the chickens some weeds,."

"We know, and it's your turn to peel the spuds, Brick."

Brick peers into the potato bin. "Yar, it's empty. Flapjacks for supper!"

The gang has straggled home hot and tired, still sucking the sweet aftertaste of the free Popsicles and Dixie Cups doled out at the end-of-year school picnic, the highlight of ten months of drudgery.

The total freedom of summer holidays is only two weeks away. Hankering after that freedom in June is like an itch they can't scratch. Giddy excitement, like grass fire, leaps through the house with bursts of laughter and tempers barely held in check. But with final exams looming over them like buckets of curried tripe, the high-schoolers eventually trudge upstairs to pore over their books.

All but Herald. He's just finished grade thirteen, senior matric, and he's whistling as he saunters out to the contraption he's building in the back of the back porch. He can spend hours tinkering with gears, pulleys, springs, and wires, and the wooden handles he's salvaged from worn-out kitchen tools. The family has been puzzling as to the purpose of his machine. Is it an automatic back scratcher? A pea podder? A berry-sorter? Even Herald isn't sure anymore, he's had to move and re-configure it so many times. Since he last examined it, pieces have been added... and taken away. His siblings have many projects on the go, always on the prowl for building pieces. Herald, in turn, has cannibalized every defunct gadget he can get his hands on, and one or two which still worked but were rarely used, like the crank-handled nutcracker and the automatic boot jack. Chuckling, he picks up the rusty eggbeater that Rich and Ron gave him for his birthday. Rusty nails are soldered onto the blades. It's meant to tap a cardboard drum when you turn the handle and angle it just right. Very ingenious. Herald dumps a jar of small nuts and bolts into an old hubcap and begins to sort through them, humming abstractedly.

Their Uncle Ronald had given the Eleven his trunk of erector kits when he retired. He was a bridge engineer and sponsored an after-school Construction Club for many years, specializing in set-ups for model trains, complete with wheel houses, draw bridges, and windmills powered by small steam engines. Ronald's nieces and nephews have personal hoards of his miniature building equipment, an ongoing source of barter amongst them...

"I'm not arguing about it, Herald, this is not your wrench," argues Ron.

"It's not open to debate," says Herald.

"Have it then, but that's my hinge."

"Fine, Ron. Take it. I don't need it anymore."

"What about that clamp?"

"Don't you dare touch it, Rich. The whole thing will fall apart."

"Art, Art, blew a fart, blew the whole dang thing apart."

"Getouttahere you hornswoggling quibblers!" Herald laughs as he tightens the clamp. Even the twit twins aren't going to rile him today.

Herald's aptitude for tinkering and his plans to be a teacher are not surprising, considering the five teachers and three engineers among his aunts and uncles. Right now, Herald needs a few dozen widgets. He rummages in a box under the workbench, coming up with his hands full. He happily sets to work on his invention with one ear tuned to the commotion in the backyard. It sounds like the urchins are raiding the cherry trees.

"Look at the size of these Bings already, Billy!"

"The stones are barely hard. You can't eat those yet, Julie!"

"But these ones in the sun are almost yellow... Mmmm... cherries."

"Wow, some razz-berries are ripe," Pink shouts. "Alvie, are you eating goozeberries already?"

"Mmmmm, they taste sharp," he murmurs. They're the kind of gooseberries that are sour green, even when they're ripe. Alvin munches on them happily.

"Yuck... they turn my mouth inside-out, even when I'm not eating them," says Julie.

"Gad, why don't you try the rhubarb, Alvie? Just don't eat the leaves!" says Billy. "They'll kill you deader than a door nail."

"Hey!" Pink yells, nearly tripping over a chicken half-covered with dirt. "What's Gizzardella doing under the goozeberries? Is she dead? Hey!"

The four gather round the big Barred Rock. She's lying on her side, one black and white wing stretched out, looking dislocated. Her eyes are closed, her white eyelids flickering madly. Gizzardella's in dust-bath heaven. At their laughter, she leaps up squawking and flapping, showering them with dust and feathers. They have great fun chasing her into her yard.

"Eeeeeerp, eeeeeeerrrpp?" the hens iterate, swooping onto the handfuls of grass the kids throw them. "Greeeeeep, greeep, greeeeeens… erip, errrrrp… rip-up-more-or-or-or oooooorrrr."

As Herald sorts through his nuts and bolts, he listens to a wild game of chicken-with-its-head-chopped-off. The ruckus suddenly ends with a chorus of "Oh no!" followed by silence. After fixing a final widget on his gadget, Herald climbs through the tangle of lilac that screens the back porch and asks, "What's up?"

His tattered copy of *Ernest Seton* under his arm, Billy is scrambling from a maple bough to help Alvin, who has shinnied up the rickety clothesline pole and is grabbing for the pulley, detached and dangling out of his reach. At Herald's approach, Alvin drops to the ground with an "Oof!" They mournfully eye the line of towels which has collapsed in the gooseberry patch.

Herald says, "It's a good thing the towels are dry, at least. Julie and Pink, could you run find a clothes basket? Alvin and Billy can help me search for pegs."

They find many loose springs and mismatched wooden parts, which they try to jimmy back together. The girls return with a cardboard box and they all lift the towels from the prickly gooseberry bushes and pile them in the box. A few dirty hand-prints on the clean laundry are inevitable. Julie and Pink will do their best to brush off the loose dirt later when they tussle the linen into the upstairs cupboard.

First they have to hose each other off, to soothe the prickles and remove the sticky webs which cling to them from the tiny worms infesting the gooseberry patch. The kids are a mess of scratches. Herald quickly commandeers the hose before they have it going full-throttle, then chases them into a game of run-and-dry-before-the-sun-goes-down. As they drift into a game of red-light-green-light, Herald reaches down the pulley, yanking out a broken clothes peg and a shred of towel. So much for playing with tinker toys. In the basement, he unearths a hefty chunk of wire, which Billy helps him Jerry-rig to the pulley. Then he fastens the pulley back onto a clamp that will hold it onto the post so that the clothesline will work—at least, until the next time it falls down. Herald shrugs in frustration, tired of the whole makeshift system. Make-do has to be the maxim in a family with thirteen mouths to feed, twenty-six feet to shoe, twenty-six legs to pant, as well as a community in need.

"We should build a new clothesline, Hare,"

"Do tell, Bill. Trouble is, it's one of those jobs that's way more complicated than it looks."

"Like Mom says… things usually get worse before they get better?"

"Yeah," Harald grunts, "so we keep putting it off. If the people who added this porch onto the house about a thousand years ago hadn't used the corner support for one end of the clothesline, the end of the porch wouldn't be starting to pull away. Not to mention, we need a new pole at the other end, too, that isn't an ant hotel for woodpeckers."

Herald dreams of an adult-size Meccano set with enough parts to fix life-size problems. "Next weekend for sure, let's all us guys help Dad rig up a new line… with a pole that will take six-inch spikes and hold up that blasted pulley. Actually, we need a bigger pulley, too."

"And some new clothes-pegs." Billy dreams of buying his mom a new-fangled electric clothes dryer.

For weeks after the incident of the gooseberry laundry debacle, itches and prickles invade the home via the fallen line of towels. Lettuce and Bob wonder if it's mites. The boys are told to dung out the chicken coop and douse it with ashes. There's vigorous scrubbing throughout the house. Eventually the prickles work their way out without medical intervention, and are forever known as the "June Itch."

CHAPTER 5
Canning

IT'S AFTER DARK WHEN Bob and Lettuce finally stagger home on the day of the "June Itch" incident. Their berry buckets are brimming.

Fern and Herald have just mopped up a huge puddle in front of the sink, the result of the spectacular water-fight they'd all had a hand in. Fortunately, when Herald upended a washtub over Rich and Ron, they were outside. A wet blanket has been slung by Rich over a saw horse in the yard. Hazel and Brick are wiping down the cupboards. Ron has been picking up wet dish rags throughout the house, which he surreptitiously flings into the bathtub when he hears the screen door bang. Pink and Julie are toweling their hair. Billy is coming downstairs with a bucket of wet socks. "Hi Mom, hi Dad… We been good."

Lettuce grins. "You wonderful kids, everything's sparkling. You washed the floor!"

"We all pitched in," says Herald.

There's a chorus of: "We made flapjacks!... with raisins!... There's lots for you... a bit burnt... they're still good... with lots of jam."

"We saved you the best ones!"

Lettuce laughs, "I could eat a chair. As usual, we were in the best patch when it got dark—where the berries are always early, at the foot of Mc Coon's hill.

"Lucky we can see in the dark!" says Bob.

Like lemurs, Bob and Lettuce really can find berries well after nightfall, their eyes widening as the shadows deepen, catching the nocturnal gleam of ripe berries, the glint of darker black in the black. Now, in the bright kitchen, their eyes are dazzled and they don't notice the water dripping from the bathroom doorway.

Bob casts a sardonic glance at a puddle under the table but doesn't mention it, groaning as he wrenches his bucket loose, "Whew! I'll be seeing huckleberries in my sleep."

"That's all I can see when I close my eyes," says Lettuce. "Huckleberries and tiger-lilies."

"Please don't close your eyes yet, Let. The kids'll have to help us get these things canned."

"Tonight, Dad?"

"Yes, tonight, Rich. Tomorrow you'll all be loafing around school, entertaining your teachers."

"Ah, Dad."

As Lettuce munches a pancake, she's already organizing the troops. "Julie and Pink, Alvin, time for bed. Hazel and Fern, please get them sorted before you start on the berries. Billy, you can dry sort. Sedge, the supper dishes please, and Ron and Rich, haul up more jars for washing."

There's grumbling and bantering around the crowded kitchen as the first big crop of the season is cleaned and canned, voices running together in a seasonal litany.

"Don't forget, berries shrink when they're cooked. Cram them in," says Bob.

"Whoa, don't squash them," says Ron, "we'll never get a hundred jars."

"Fill in the cracks with hot water," says Hazel. "We want berries and juice, not canned vacuums."

"Stick a knife down the side to get out the bubbles. Gently!" Fern chides. "Those jars are glass, remember. Check the rims for nicks."

"Stuff those jars, boys, tote those pails," teases Sedge as she scalds another batch of lids.

"Take out the inchworms!" yells Pink from the stairs.

Long before they get near the jars, the largest, ripest, blue-black berries meet their demise in the collective belly, yet twelve wide-mouth Mason quarts are boiled and sealed that night. Inevitably, some berries are squashed underfoot, but luckily the stains aren't as dark as they might have been, thanks to that puddle under the table which dilutes the ink. The tiles silently shrug into a deeper patina.

CHAPTER 6
Rule Number One

IN VARYING DEGREES OVER a summer, the Eleven usually bring home enough berries to fulfill their family edict, "The One Hundred Quart Rule."

According to this, the most important rule, when the family has one hundred quarts of huckleberries canned, the kids can sell berries for cash (as noted in Section 11A of the rules).

The sooner they have the jars filled and sealed, the sooner they can start earning their first million, so all of them help with the canning.

"How come they call this canning?" asks Brick. "It should be called jarring."

"Don't jar the canning," quips Herald.

"One more quart for the twelve-jar canner," Fern counts. "Have we got twenty-four yet?"

"Seventy-six to go." Hazel sighs.

Rich groans, "I'm getting beriberi sick of the sight of berries!"

There's dark humour amongst the well-fed Eleven about the deprivation diseases, scurvy and beriberi. At school it takes only one of them to gasp, "Help me, I'm weak, I'm going to die," before three dozen kids are in hysterics, settlers falling and shouting, "I can't walk! My teeth are falling out. Ye scurvy landlubbers, find me a berry! Berry! Not beriberi! Give me fruit, give me rice polishings, I'm dying of scurvy!" All the while, their lean bodies in reality thrum with vitamin C, thiamine, sunshine and sass. One day, Ron and Rich got Alvin and Billy and a bunch of other kids doing this demented routine in a crowded school hallway when along came the English teacher, Mrs. Hortense, a staunch moralist. Everyone froze as her gimlet eyes drilled them.

"I have a good mind to teach all of you a lesson," she said. "You, too, Hazel and Fern, I saw you laughing like hyenas at the end of the hall. And Brick, quit pretending to pull your teeth out. If you actually had scurvy, they'd be falling out without any help from you." Hearing someone snicker, Mrs. Hortense had one of her lightning-bolt inspirations. "All of you are going to perform a ten minute skit at the Arena Benefit Fall Fair."

That included Herald, who laughed out loud in trigonometry when the hallway fiasco made its way into the senior realms. Aw, shucks. He had to pay for his lapse in decorum by horsing around instead of slogging through trigonometry problems.

By the end of the public performance, beriberi and scurvy were thoroughly eradicated and the audience was falling out of its chairs laughing, clattering coins by the handful into the five-gallon molasses cans by the exits. The arena got its roof mended and a thick sheet of ice was laid.

Getting something for nothing, if it tastes better than gooseberries, is a big deal for large families in the fifties. Anything that can stave off scurvy and doesn't make you sick is fair game. If it tastes good, even better.

There's serious rivalry amongst the Eleven and their parents about who can pick the most huckleberries the fastest. Bob is rumoured to have picked five gallons of huckleberries on an evening after work, and Lettuce, with the fierce speed of her hands over the bushes, can pluck a pint in minutes. She knows the intricacies of the sport well, always admonishing her tribe to lift the branches with one hand to expose the berries underneath (should that be Rule 13? 7 or 17? 77 or 37?).

The best expeditions are when the whole family makes a day of it. Setting out early, they pile into their old Plymouth, which is named the Hearse because it's rusty black and it's half a mile long. Crammed with kids, picnic boxes, and buckets, the Hearse scrapes its belly on the mine roads, continually grinding, steaming, and threatening to break a fuel pump or knock off its oil pan. An under-the-breath mantra of, "Please, please keep going" is punctuated by the rattle of rocks in the hubcaps and the occasional, "For crissakes, keep moving!" The big kids walk the steepest parts of the trip to lighten the load, kicking pieces of rusty tail pipe off the road. Iron ore dumps reverberate with the clang of refined metal.

By the time the Hearse finally wheezes onto the top pasture, the kids might be squabbling and barfing, but Lettuce can't restrain her brilliant smile. Escape from the house at last! Idyllic though the ensuing picnic might be, it isn't by magic that a feast accompanies her into the wilderness. They've all hustled and hauled in preparation, but hers is the mastermind behind the success of an expedition. Keeping everyone full of good food keeps them strong—and it prevents them from squabbling and eating all the berries before they get home. One hundred quarts have to be canned.

CHAPTER 7
The Storyteller: Julie, 2005

WITH HER BACK CRAMPING from picking low bushes, Julie's thoughts again mill around Pink. When the twins are creating one of their massive art projects at the Chagall Academy, their interconnection is total and necessary. But now, Julie must let go so Pink can drift free. Julie leans against a bull pine and pulls out her notebook, focusing with determination on her Rules of Huckleberry Picking:

Rule 1: Always carry a bucket when you go for a walk, because you never know. This is such a common-sense rule that it's often forgotten; many a hat has been ruined, many a scarf and jacket indelibly stained during bucketless forays. Lamentable, that the dramatic blaze of red juice on any light surface will gradually fade to battleship gray.

Rule 6: It's never too early to check for berries—or too late.

Rule 32: If you have a compulsion to pick berries, don't fight it. The hunter-gatherer instinct is very strong in some people, and if you are also a bit obsessive-compulsive, so much the better. But it takes all sorts. Some people would never dream of picking berries and other people could pick berries in their sleep.

Rule 9: Have some way to fasten your bucket to your waist. Whatever you use, it has to be strong. A leather belt buckle is fine; an old necktie is ideal.

(The satin binding from an old blanket that Julie is using at that moment? Its strength is questionable.)

Rule 16: There's nothing much worse than picking berries a second time when you've spilt them. The point of fastening your bucket to your waist is to free up both hands for picking… and for hanging onto cliffs.

Some people like to keep a pail on the ground by their feet, but then it's easy to kick the bucket, unless they're kneeling because they've swallowed their pride and worn kneepads (Section 83H, "The Rules of Attire"). At any rate, your bucket should be firmly attached to you at all times (Rule 4D), even though a heavy bucket is an uncomfortable pendulum as you stoop to fill it. Be careful your bucket doesn't swing forward and pull you off your feet when you're leaning downhill (4E). The berry-picker's sporran, several pounds heavy when full, is best secured to the waist while held by one hand as you scramble out of the bush at the end of the day, rickety with fatigue and heavy with plunder.

Section 83H, "Rules of Attire": Don't make yourself conspicuous (except in hunting season). Berry-picking is one sport which does not require making a fashion statement. The best way to keep your berry haunts private is to blend into the landscape, like old Mrs. Orack, camouflaged as earth, flitting through hedges and fences like a bat at dusk as she whisks berries from under hedges.

Rules 83JKL: It's best to get out picking when it's cool enough for long sleeves and pants. If you're young, you may feel it's alright to expose yourself to the elements, but older people need to con-serve what skin they have left. At any rate, your clothes should be sturdy and loose enough that you can climb and bend and even contort, if need be, like when you have to pick berries hanging over the edge of a cliff. Old clothes are best. Boots are recommended, and always wear a hat. Ideally, berry patches are within walking distance of home. If you have to walk past houses, pride in appear-ance cannot be an issue. Don't worry what the neighbours think. Just get out there.

Rule 42A: The "berry-picker's stoop" may develop after tense hours of speed-reading bushes with the gathering instinct in full force, with every sense alert for the bull in the next pasture, or the hound sniffing the hole in the fence.

Rule 36: Rules of numbering: the numbers attached to huck-leberrying rules are typically arbitrary and inconsistent, more symbolic of order than order itself.

Julie sorts through her rough copy, evoking her family fifty years earlier. In this secluded landscape, her recollections are clear as spring water: she hears the yelling, singing voices making their way into the berry bush on that long ago day, in the third week of summer holidays.

CHAPTER 8
Eleven on the Mountain

IT'S THE JULY MORNING of the Eleven's unforgettable 1955 huckleberry expedition. At first light, the sun is a narrow dazzle on the horizon. The high pasture is shrouded in mist when their father drops them off before he goes to work. It has been a feat of determination, co-ordination, and organization, but there they all are, with their heap of buckets and packs, looking like a herd of troglodytes in multicolored hats. They yell and clatter, hugging Bob through the car window, shouting "We're off to seek our fortunes!" Bob shouts above the din, "I'll meet you at Stooge's Mill around five-thirty. Stick together and take care of each other!"

He would've given his back teeth to be going with them.

The rattle of the Hearse dies away as the urchins get organized for their day of roaming the mountainside picking berries. The younger ones feel a breathless excitement in the chilly mist; it's their first time to be aloft so early. As Billy helps Alvin cinch up his pack and Hazel and Fern get Pink and Julie sorted, Ron and Rich chase gophers.

Herald, Sedge, and Brick are already hurrying out of sight when Hazel calls after them, "Meet us for lunch at Stooge's Mill." The old mill foundation is usually their base camp on trips like this. A well-worn cow trail leads past it and beyond. They will follow that trail intermittently, but trying to fill their huckleberry buckets will lead them far and wide.

Pink and Julie have one-pound strawberry jam cans to fill. Hazel and Fern have five pound Silver Leaf lard pails, with a three-gallon Malkin's Molasses tin to empty into. The older the kids are, the bigger the buckets. Herald and Brick have their mom's biggest soup pot to empty into. All the containers are metal, whatever can be fitted with a wire handle. They clank and clatter as the children ramble. Any self-respecting bear knows exactly where the kids are.

Within an hour, the sun has burned off the mist; the day is warm and fragrant. Fern pushes her curls under the green brim of her hat and gazes into the sky, where cirrus clouds are unfurling like shadowless feathers. Everyone but Herald, Brick, and Sedge are within earshot of each other in a vast patch of berries near the foundations. A flapping scout hat catches Fern's eye: it's Ron, swatting flies. Suddenly, there's a loud crash not far off. She shouts, "Hey Ronnie, what was that crash?"

"Where, Fern?"

"Over there! What was it?!"

"Just."

"Just what, Ron?"

"Just you being a scaredy-cat."

There's another crash. Closer. Ronnie yelps, "Maybe it IS a bear. Rich, are you over there? RICH?

"It's me, Billy. Rich took off. So did Brick."

"Shoot!" Ron gasps. "Brick's got my grub. It wouldn't fit in my knapsack. I'm going to look for him and Rich. I just gotta finish this bush first."

(Rule 17: Don't put all your food in one pack, especially if it's someone else's pack.)

(Rule 46: Don't send out too many search parties at one time.)

"You just want a smoke, Ron."

"Bubonic plague, Bill."

"Don't be an odoriferous rodent, Ronald!"

"Bilious big baboon, Bill."

"Obstreperous buffoon," chips in Fern.

"Don't step on yer leopard-ass with yer rotten sass, Ron!" shouts Billy.

Billy wins that round. Vocabulary War is a sesquipedalian game (Ses-qui-pe-da-li-an: involving big words.) It was invented by Fern and Hazel on a rainy ten-day trip across the prairies with their Aunt Anne, Uncle Will, and a dictionary: with nothing else to do, they played with words. The object, according to Hazel, is: "to out-do each other's long words, puns, synonyms, and zany associations. There are bonus points for alliteration and double meanings. Vocabulary Wars: the last word often wins the round."

Some of the kids go so far as to memorize complete dictionary definitions, showing off by spouting them at opportune times. Their friends think they're daft and hilarious and their teachers think they're verbally precocious, possibly even brilliant. (And sometimes hugely annoying.)

Pink says, "Dad says it's claptrap about us being gifted. He says it's poppycock and balderdash."

Billy says, "He just doesn't want us to get conceited."

"Why not?" asks Ron. "What's wrong with being conceited? Seems like the conceited kids get all the prizes at school."

"Dad says we'll get lazy if we think we're too great," says Julie.

"'Cause we'll rest on our laurels," says Pink.

"And end up stupid like Floyd Porge, even though he taught himself to read when he was two," says Billy. "By grade ten he was flunking, 'cause he never learned how to study, 'cause his mom told him he was a genius... and he was lazy."

Hazel harumphs as she pushes back her bright orange tam. "And her without two brains to rub together. She thought he was reading when all the time he was sleeping with a book propped on his belly, so's he could stay out all night and do petty thefts."

"But though," says Fern, "when he had to actually figure things out for himself, he couldn't do it. Like when he couldn't unlock the bathroom where he was hiding with a bag of loot in that house he was robbing, and they caught him red-handed and he ended up in the clink for two months." They all laugh.

"So the moral of the story is, don't get conceited?" asks Billy.

"But what's laurels, Haze?" pipes Julie.

"Nothing any of us need to worry about."

"Well anyhow," Ron says, "I'm going to vamoose. Please don't pick your noses while you pick!"

"Eee-ew!"

"Don't go too far, Ronnie. Don't get lost!" Hazel calls after him.

"Don't kick the bucket," he shouts back.

Billy stares after Ron, shaking his head. "Why wouldn't Ron leave room in his pack for the most important thing... food! I hope he finds Brick fast. He could starve in ten minutes."

With Ronald gone, that leaves five of them, Hazel, Fern, Pink, Julie and Billy, by the tumbledown foundations of Stooge's Mill. Hazel gripes that everyone has scattered without making a plan. "As usual, Sedge and Alvin are probably off philosophizing, Ron and Rich will get up to no good together, and Herald and Brick have loped off, leaving you and me, Fern, in charge of the changelings."

"But though Billy's with us. And this is the best patch." Fern looks warily at her tall older sister, whose face, except for a deep scowl, is all but obscured by the downward crease of her tam. Fern sighs. Surely Hazel can't have the curse, today of all days.

Billy has buckled down to a good bush. Hazel and Fern join Pink and Julie along the concrete footings, where the branches are damp and laden.

Fern hums. Buckets clank. Mosquitoes whine.

Time passes. The sun blazes.

The cirrus feathers are slowly matting together in the west.

Pink and Julie cool off on their bellies in a damp gully. They're closely watching a toad... How its silver throat pulses ever so gently, how its eyes glitter gold... Suddenly, there's a splintering moan overhead and the toad jumps right in their faces. They clamber into daylight, disheveled and slightly frantic. One of Julie's shoes is off and Pink's hair is falling over her eyes. "What? What was that?"

"Just trees complaining," soothes Fern. She helps find Julie's shoe while Hazel sweeps Pink's red mop back under her aqua-flowered hairband. She reties their matching yellow kerchiefs. Pink tucks a daisy into Fern's buttonhole. Julie offers Hazel a large, ripe, slightly squashed berry she's been saving in her hand. Hazel eats it. The twin ragamuffins huddle, grumbling quietly to each other, "My knee hurts." "I scratched my face."

Fern hugs them. "It's okay. Help pick this bush, then we'll find a place for a rest. Let's stick together."

Hazel says, "Ha! A bit late for that! Billy, do you know where Alvin went? And Sedge?"

"I think Alvin took off after Brick. I don't know about Sedge," answers Billy.

Hazel, in her role as second-mother, throws her head back and yodels, trying to locate her brood. Her "whoo-hoo-oo-oooo" resounds over the hills. It's sent back and forth through the woods as the kids respond, still fairly close. The noise is a cross between the noise that Missus-Up-the-Hill makes to call her children home, and what they imagine a hoot-owl to sound like. It works, as far as calls go, but the echoes can be confusing. At this point, all eleven believe this will keep them in touch for the rest of the day. One by one, they'll learn this is not to be.

Pink tugs at Billy's arm. "Do you think there is a bear around here, Billy?"

"If there is, it's prob'ly scared-er than we are."

Julie hiccups. "Can you tell us a story, Fern?"

"Wait till I get a few more layers, then we'll have a picnic. (Rule 5: Always pack a snack.)

"Just skim the big ones for now," advises Billy.

"But Billy, Dad says to pick clean." (Rule 16D.)

Billy munches a handful of black orbs. "Well, Pink, we're not going to stay here all day, are we? Anyhow, we should leave some good under-berries to get on the way back." (Rule 15H.)

"Make sure you remember which bushes you've left berries on," says Fern. (Rule 18 X.)

Hazel flings off her sweater. "Cripes, I'm getting hot!"

"Billy, will you tell us a story?" pleads Julie.

"Sure." Billy climbs onto a tree stump and cracks his knuckles. "One day the big fat toad had a picnic and he ate and ate watermelon until he was so round he rolled to the beach and he did the toad-stroke in the Red Melon Sea."

"That wasn't much of a story, Billy."

"Well then… what do you call someone who likes to eat fancy melons while riding a horse? Can't anyone guess? It's a galloping *gourdmet*! Ha, ha, get it, gourmet?"

"Ha ha ha," says Hazel. "You and your melon jokes, Billy. You've really been working on them, haven't you!"

"Keeps the bears away, anyhow! " Billy nearly chokes, he's laughing so hard. There's nothing he likes better than a ready audience for his verbal antics.

Hazel breaks into song, her voice slightly off-key, "Hmm, hmm, laaaa, let the sun shine in…"

Fern joins in with her melodic alto:

Let the sun shine in,
Face it with a grin
Open up your heart
And let the sun shine in!

"And face it with a grin..." Billy thumps on a log with a stick, munching berries. "My bucket's already half-full!"

"Is not!" Pink is indignant. "I can still hear them rattling on the bottom." (That's metal buckets for you.)

"The odd time one makes it past your mouth!" adds Julie.

Hazel snorts, "Come on, give Billy a break. When you girls get snipping, you're like a pair of scissors."

The five-year-olds giggle. "Sorry, Billy."

Some of the Eleven follow the rule about not eating berries while they pick (number 17B.); some don't; and some fill their buckets and wear juice to the eyebrows.

"Mmmmmmm," hums Billy, "these berries are scrump-dilli-icious!"

"Really sweet!" agrees Julie.

"Don't eat the berries while you pick!" says Pink.

"Who says?" asks Julie.

"Dad says, once you start eating you can't stop and that's how come Great Uncle Eldridge's cousin always brought home an empty bucket," explains her twin.

"With his mouth stained purple," adds Fern.

"Then he'd eat all the pies and junk that Grandma made out of everyone else's berries!" continues Pink.

"Too bad he ate everything but the curried tripe!" says Fern. "Anyhow, you'll never fill your bucket if you fill your belly."

"Dad says an empty bucket is an insult to industry," quoth Billy.

Pink giggles, "Mmmm, those were good ones."

"Mom says, eat them if you're thirsty," says Julie.

Billy likes to eat the ripest berries hot from the bush. There's nothing like that tart nectar on the back of the throat. Rich calls it "vitamin jazz." Some like them raw, some like them cooked. A family favourite is huckleberry buckle. Much easier to make than pies, Fern and Hazel know the recipe by heart.

Even better is literary buckle, a hasty pudding for the mind. Whip up a rich batter: add a pinch of this, a pat of that, some descriptive leavening, some plot thickening, and cook it well. Something savoury usually pans out, but thickening "to consistency" is the tricky part of any pudding.

"Mmmm," murmurs Billy. "Fresh huckleberries are delectable... hmm... hum... and collectible... Mmm."

Cow bells jingle as the dairy herd winds its way to higher pastures. The sound is musical from a distance, and reassuring to children who followed time-worn cow trails out of the high meadows in early light. Perhaps to the cows, the children sound like another sort of herd, a family spreading out to canvass the wild fringe of the countryside, their buckets jangling.

Further up the mountain, Alvin has been climbing toward the clang of buckets, but he gradually falls behind Brick, who doesn't know his little brother is trying to catch up as he heads toward Herald and Sedge.

Alvin mostly just wants to get away from the baby twins. He often feels like a reluctant triplet when he's with Pink and Julie. Inveigled into their schemes, he usually has to clean up a far worse mess than he'd ever make on his own. Like that egg-mustard-flour painting on the kitchen wall, for instance, which did NOT look like the smiling sun. There's still a stain to remind Alvin every day that he got blamed for "egging on" the little twits.

Things like that weigh on Alvin. At seven, he feels half-responsible for Pink and Julie but he gets treated like one of the little kids. His eight older siblings are constantly hovering, instructing, and interrogating, with the little twits always in his way. Yet he can feel lonely, surrounded by family. Is he the only one who feels this way? The older kids know things about him that he doesn't know himself, like ridiculous things he did when he was a baby, and they expect him to remember events before he was born. There's so much family history he was never part of. No one understands him, except maybe Sedge.

Alvin follows a deer trail.

CHAPTER 9
Lettuce at Home

MEANWHILE, IN THE EMPTY house, Lettuce clears away breakfast, assuring herself the kids will be fine on their own. They have lots of food. Fresh water is abundant on the mountainside. They're responsible. The older ones will look after the youngsters. Lettuce had thought to keep the three youngest at home: she would have let them build a fort in the living-room. But being masters of twin tenacity, Pink and Julie have gone on the expedition. Alvin, of course, would not be separated from his big brothers.

Not even old Perth is with them today. It's their first summer hike without Perth, their lovable, loyal, good-natured Australian heeler hound, bred to herd cattle, trained to herd kids. Saddened by his demise, they can barely talk about him, never mind contemplate replacing him. Perth had filled an important role keeping track of everyone on hikes. None of them want to miss the peak of the July berries on a day in the mountain without parents, but they will miss Perth.

Lettuce hauls out the laundry bins. She's hoping Bob won't be late and can drive straight out to Stooge's after work, and she hopes he's wearing his lab coat. His shirt has to last another day... His other one needs its collar turned. But not today. Button-down white shirts be damned! Let the bureaucrats do the laundry!

That young lab trainee better not have another nervous accident with acid, like the one that burned a hole in Bob's nice green tie. Lucky he had it on though, to save his hide. Fern embroidered a gray rat over the hole, with Sedge adding some yellow lazy daisies. Bob grins every morning when he puts it on. What can you do with a family like that? Lettuce tries to keep them looking respectable, but.

When the birds are singing, listen.

Lettuce props open the kitchen door to let in the communion of robins, the fragrance of honeysuckle draped over the lintel. Gazing into the sky, she pictures the children. They'll be getting their feet wet in the tall grass heavy with dew. Mist will be rising from the morning pastures, where meadowlarks are likely singing. Lettuce watches iridescent puffs of cloud in the blue distance.

Then she picks up a stray sock and sorts the wash. She'll have the wringer washer going all day, with no one underfoot. First, she wants to sort out her boxes of Rit, though, and get the kitchen curtains washed so she can soak them in a dye bath. That'll be fun. And when she has the towels on the line and the kids' clothes agitating, she'll get a stew on to simmer. The gang will be ravenous when they get home.

Then she'll have a cup of tea and read a few pages. Thus Lettuce manages to avoid being totally smothered by housework, the specter of death-by-detritus which stalks all homemakers. The kids are trained to do chores, though they often make things more complicated and take a lot of straightening out. But they're learning.

Lettuce is luckily not house-proud. She has creative distractions.

Her family is always curious when they see her hunched over her battered ledger. But they keep a polite distance because of her aura of solitude, and the fierce expression that appears on her face if they come too close.

A vase, if carelessly touched while wet on the turning wheel, is quickly misshapen.

CHAPTER 10
The Storyteller: Julie, 2005

THE VOICES OF HER brothers and sisters accompany Julie through the woods decades later, blending with the susurrus of poplars and the manic laughter of woodpeckers. It's the woodpecker time of day where she is. A flicker swoops through the poplars, flashing its orange under-wings as it lands to dig for ants in a tussock of grass. A pileated woodpecker gouges chunks from a pine, its head a red crest on a pneumatic chisel, its long pink tongue eeling for ants.

It's moments like this, on a blue-sky afternoon in the height of summer, which make life worthwhile. Julie's struggle through the sharp branches of a broken spruce, the scrapes and bites, the ripped shirt, the narrow avoidance of mine holes overhung with loaded branches, all are worth the taste of ripe huckleberries in the wild. Their dulcet sting recharges her spirit. She's inspired to capture the moment's beauty on paper, sending ripples of encouragement toward Pink to ease her ordeal.

A page and a half later, an ant bites Julie's ankle.

"Rule 36B," she jots, "Keep moving while berry-picking."

As she hauls herself further up a rocky bluff, the foliage isn't promising. Orange and red snake-berries and unripe elderberries are plentiful. It's the kind of hillside where you keep thinking you've reached the top until you find another bluff rising off the back of the last one. As she scrambles upwards, Julie's hands sink into bird's-eye, a mat of tiny blue flowers.

On a rocky flank she finds mostly boxwood. (Her treatise will mention that hills covered in snowberry and boxwood seldom produce huckleberries: Rule 59L.) Continuing along the rocky spine, hoping for good picking along the flank, she heads toward some trembling aspen. She rests a moment under their spinning yellow discs. A robin softly ad-libs, "Twee dee, deedle tweet."

Julie's thoughts drift again to earlier times. The voices of yesterday's children still carry on the breeze, chattering and laughing.

CHAPTER 11
Watch Out for Mine Holes

UNDER THE MID-MORNING SUN, still near the foundations and as yet untouched by the clouds fledging in the east, colourful hats bob over the berry bushes: green, that's Fern's, Hazel's orange, Billy's bright blue and Pink and Julie with their yellow kerchiefs. Billy and the older girls are busy foraging; the twins are having a break.

Clove Pink has both shoes off and is puddling her toes in wet moss. Julie Cosmos is lying on her belly, face submerged in twin-flowers. "Mmm, they smell like spices."

"They're twins, like us," says Pink. "Clove Pink and Julie Cosmos. A clove is a spice from a flower bud of a tropical tree."

"A cosmos is harmony, which means no fighting. And it's a magenta daisy," murmurs Julie. "Cosmos Clove and Pink Julie."

"Two on each stem… twin-flowers, just like us," smiles Pink.

But unlike twin-flowers, Pink and Julie don't look alike, though they have an uncanny similarity. It's as if sparks dance between them and set them into co-operative action. When at play, their expressions are transparent; you can see their thoughts moving across their faces. "Like watching sunlight flicker over pebbles in clear water," as Sedge puts it. Except when they stonewall. The imps can keep their expressions absolutely blank when it serves their purpose. Rich says that when he tries to understand them, he feels like he's looking through the wrong end of binoculars.

Pink and Julie chatter as they collect twigs of a particular size and once more study the tiny pink bells carpeting the earth.

"Julie, how come we don't look the same, like these twin-flowers? Aren't twins supposed to look alike?"

"Yeah, but neither do Ronny and Rich, and they're twins... Stocky-Ron and Sticky-Rich. At least we're both skinny," says Julie.

Having overheard her youngest sisters, Hazel blats out a short lecture about fraternal twins and splitting zygotes. Fern throws in some tidbits about genetics and how twins are likely to have twins themselves when they have kids.

Pink and Julie look at each other and wrinkle their noses, falling over giggling.

"All ginger cats are male," mentions Hazel.

"So what about Pink?" Billy asks. "Her hair's red and she's a girl."

"But she's not a cat."

Billy looks speculatively at his younger sister. "Are you sure?"

Pink snatches his blue fez, tossing it to Julie, who puts a lump of moss in it and tosses it back to Billy. He puts it on without removing the moss, saying, "Now that we're on the topic of genetics, don't forget about chromosomes. Do you want to hear about the chromosomes and the melon?"

Fern groans, "Okay, Billy."

"Well, see... these chromosomes say to the melon, 'Hey, can you give us a ride?' The melon says, 'Sure, hop on,' so the chromosomes find comfortable niches on the vast green melon-back...'"

"Billy, is this a very long joke?"

"It's not actually a joke, Hazel, it's a short story. Quite short."

His sisters plunk themselves down to listen as the verbose ten-year-old continues in his radio voice. "The chromosomes are just dozing off when, suddenly, the melon rolls over. You'll never guess what happens next."

At this point, Billy deliberately stretches and wanders away. He's thinking like mad, making up his story as he goes along. Hazel chucks a pine cone at him. "Billy! What happens next?"

Billy shrugs. "Well, that's how chromo-melons are made. Chromo-melons, you know, those shiny silver melons made into things like car bumpers, roasting pans, kettles, and your bucket... it used to be a chromo-melon, see."

Fern pulls Hazel to her feet and they chase Billy, threatening to kiss him, whooping and singing, "Can she bake a cherry pie, Billy boy, Billy boy, can she bake a cherry pie, charming Billy?"

Catching her breath, Fern, third-mother-in-charge-of-food, announces it's time for their picnic. She doles out bread and jam on a clean hanky. Hazel takes a spare bucket to the nearby spring. (Rule 28: always camp near water.)

(Rule 30: If you're camping near water, make lots of noise so the bears and bobcats can hear you over the noise of the water. They'll generally stay away if they know where you are.)

Noise is a safe constant for large families traveling in droves, although Rule 8Y, never travel alone, is often ignored because everyone in a large family needs time by themselves.

Hazel returns with a pail brimming with icy water and plunks it down, soaking her shirt-front. She perches on a rock near Fern. "I'm glad we packed our own food. But I wish Sedge were here. We're supposed to stay together."

Fern hands Hazel a slice of bread and jam. "Don't worry. Sedge'll be alright. She likes to keep up with Herald."

Billy hoots, "Ha! Fat chance. Herald's prob'ly never stopped walking the whole time we've been out here. And he'll come back with his bucket full. With only about fifteen berries in it, they're so huge."

Hazel agrees, "Herald and Brick won't stop until they find the best berries in miles and have had a good, long hike. I could use a good, long hike myself."

"Why waste energy tramping around if you don't have to?" asks Fern.

"And it's bad luck to skip around and not finish picking a bush," adds Julie (Rule 18C).

Pink frowns. "Who says it's bad luck?"

"Dad says."

"He also says the worst thing is getting the seeds in his teeth," says Billy, "and small berries have the same number of seeds as big ones. So I'm not going to pick the small ones!"

"But Billy, we'll prob'ly end up picking them on our way back."

"Just because you go in circles, Pink."

"Speak for yourself, Bill. But though it's not fair to cream the crop!" (Rule 49).

"How come, Fern?"

"Because the only thing worse than picking what someone else leaves, it's picking what you leave" (Rule 17D).

"Mom calls it 'gleaning your rejects,'" says Hazel.

"Dad calls it 'mining the tailings,'" says Billy.

"A berry in the bucket's worth ten in the bush," says Julie.

"Well, my dear sisters," says Billy, "see this here big handful of huge, scrumptious, purple huckleberries? Slurp! Ah. That's called 'recharging my batteries.'"

Fern packs away the food, saving the applesauce cookies and raisins for later. "I'll bet Ron's getting hungry, but if he's found a good patch, he won't leave till he's picked every berry on it."

"Well anyhow," says Billy, "I'm going to find a better spot."

Hazel looks up anxiously, "See if you can find Alvin!"

"Watch out for mine holes!" Pink yells after him.

"Watch out for whole mines!" With a hoot and a jangle, ten-year-old Billy sets off on his own.

At last. Much as they love Billy's easy-going company, the girls feel a need for a bit of decorum around any boy. Now, finally on their own, they can piddle without hiding.

Hilarity sweeps over them. Pink and Julie blow rude noises on their arms and Fern belches loudly. Hazel adjusts her riggings and gives her backside a long thoughtful scratch.

But, as they keep within earshot of each other, the four sisters wish Sedge were with them. The five-year-olds skip around, looking for toads and finding luscious berries in every damp hollow. Their voices run through the woods like a cascading brook, refreshing and merry.

Their "old" sisters work side-by-side. Fern and Hazel like each other's company and don't care who gets the most berries, as long as they fill their buckets between them. Anyhow, at the end of the day, all the berries get dumped together until One Hundred Quarts are canned. Until.

Hazel sighs. "It all seems so hopeless. I'm glad Dad gives money to those families-less-fortunate-than-ours. The Mine Disaster Fund and all that. And I know we're so lucky to have a dad, and… at least we're out in the fresh air, not washing dishes or mopping floors. But."

"I know, Haze," says Fern, "but though, you just can't lose hope. And I know it's ridiculous and evil to fret about superficial things, but it wasn't fair when Mom gave Liz and Annette those pretty dresses from Auntie Anne. Mom says she'll make us better ones, but when will she ever have time? And we never get a big enough piece of cloth to make anything but trimming and patches."

"The seamstress's kids have no seams," says Hazel.

"And those darn flour sack pajamas I made?" continues Fern. "They're softened to perfection now they've been washed ten million times, but that printing on the back-side never seems to fade. After I wore them to my class sleepover, half the girls in school started calling me 'Pride Flour Ass.' In one way, I think it's hilarious, and in another way, I wish they'd been someone else's pajamas. Is it wrong to want something brand new and store-bought for a change?"

"It's easier to give up on clothes," says Hazel. "You just have to shorten things, but I always need them longer. If girls were allowed to wear pants to school, I could wear Herald's hand-me-downs. But I know what you mean. Like, I don't usually care if my sardine sandwiches are wrapped in Star Bakery paper, but when Miss Prizz is the lunch monitor, I notice things like that... the way she wrinkles her nose, shaking out her lace hanky with the very tips of her perfectly pink fingernails. And then it infuriates me that it bothers me."

Fern shudders. "Miss Prizz... always making little noises, dainty but definite. You always know when she's lurking around by her inhalings and exhalings... her little squeaks and sighs... her whispers that aren't quite audible. Miss Prizz and her glee club girls, skin soft as lard. They never get their hands dirty. Do they even go outside?"

"The Priss sisters," Hazel snorts. "Their only exercise is polishing their nails. I wouldn't be one of them for the moon. All that rah rah and never grit your teeth in public. Billy calls them the 'Piss Sisters.' Ha!"

Nearby, Pink and Julie pat down the moss displaced by their romping as they sing, "Emerald and leafy green, pine green, mint and lily-stem green." They've just discovered five new shades, plus chartreuse, which is Auntie Ben's favourite colour. Carefully they transplant sprigs of twin-flower, making tiny gardens and twig tepees and bridges, entire villages in the miniature moss-forest. They have an ongoing game of mapping out fantasy lands, with imaginary paths that only they can follow. They are quiet and thoughtful at the moment, but their moods can change suddenly and simultaneously, responding to currents only they can feel, which gives them the nick-name the Quick Silvers—or just the Silvers, because of their ongoing quest for all things bright and shiny.

Julie and Pink watch a chipmunk stuffing a bread crust into its cheek and creep after it, hoping to find its hidey-hole.

CHAPTER 12
The Storyteller: Julie, 2005

ALONE ON THE MOUNTAIN years later, Julie cringes with a spasm of worry.

"Please be okay, Pink," she whispers.

"Oh, Pink. Please."

"Bracken green, boxwood green, Solomon-seal green," she murmurs to calm herself.

With determination, she pulls out her notebook, plunks herself on a mossy log, and tries to focus on her huckleberry rules.

Clarification of rules for sticklers:

Rule 48C: Always pick the bushes clean. This means never leave good berries on the bush. It's not the same thing as Rule 48D, be a clean picker. Being a clean picker means be careful not to let debris drop into your bucket, like leaves, needles, rotten berries, stink bugs, etcetera.

Rule 62: If you're passing beneath trees that are losing their needles, hold your hat or your shirttail over your bucket. Rule

62B: if you're passing through tall grass hold your bucket up high, because grass seeds are the worst things to clean out of berries. Almost as bad as stems that stay in the berries, but there's not much you can do about stems except pick them out.

Being a clean picker is a delicate art.

Rule 48H: Whenever you sit down, dry-sort your berries.

Dry-sorting is the initial removal of large debris. It's a lot of work, and that's why being a clean picker is so important. Dry berries can be kept for three or four days in a cardboard box, even longer if they're in a fridge. Eventually, the berries will be immersed in water to skim off small debris, then run through your hands for a final inspection and placed in a strainer to await bottling or baking.

Rules of kitchen etiquette: It's very uncouth to grab a handful of cleaned berries to eat unless you've done the cleaning. Even worse is dropping clean berries, because not only do they have to be picked up again, they have to be washed again. Even worse, that terrible thing, waste, could occur; a squashed berry is nothing but an indelible stain.

To the novice huckleberry picker, these rules no doubt sound like a lot of blather. The best way to learn any game is to play it, so get out there and practice and you'll be surprised how fast it all makes sense.

CHAPTER 13
On the Subject of Twins

IN THE WHITE PINES above Hazel and Fern, ravens cough and complain, squabbling over their look-outs. They knock down heavy cones that glance off the girls' shoulders, dabbing them with pitch. A hot gust of wind blows needles into the buckets and when the wind subsides, deer flies attack. As the girls work over a sprawling bush, they talk about their obnoxious twin brothers and their perplexing twin sisters. Their voices join the arguing and cackling of the ravens.

"All year, Ron and Rich were hoping to get expelled," says Fern. "But though Dad and Mom would've made them work ten times harder at home. Mr. Nitmust was so mad, he gave them a two-week detention with only four days of school left. They'd tweaked his scroll map once too often so's it wound up with a big racket and fell on the floor. You can imagine pens and books went flying all over the room when everyone jumped. Mr. Nitmust gets so red in the face, it's scary."

"Well," says Hazel, "he shouldn't have ripped up their map homework. Confiscating their bag of jaw-breakers was bad enough, just because they outlined the oceans with red instead of blue. Again. Not that I'm sticking up for them, but outlining all water on maps in blue is ridiculous. What a waste of time. In grade three, okay, but not grade seven."

"They deserved the strap for their weight-volume project in Mr. Ego-Evanomalosovitch's class," says Fern, "He was so flabbergasted, he didn't even know what happened."

"That racket when I was writing my math exam?" Hazel asks.

"Yup. You know Auntie Ben's gallon jar of marbles? Well, Ron and Rich accidentally on purpose spilled it in the middle of Mr. Ego-Evanomalosovitch's class, right when everyone was handing in their homework. But though, they said the chaos would've been worth every marble they lost even if they had got a detention. The marbles were mostly pale cat's eyes anyhow, 'cause they kept all the best ones at home. "

Hazel cackles. "It drives their teachers crazy, how they ace their exams after fooling around all year... talking slang and writing perfect English exams!" She suddenly clutches her side and clanks down her bucket on a hunk of concrete. "Jeez Fern... you got any rags?"

While the girls ransack their knapsacks and get themselves re-sorted, the heckling ravens are joined by more of their ilk, causing a treetop ruckus as Hazel says, "Don't you wonder what's the point of our little lives when big hunks of metal and concrete can rot into the ground? What will we leave behind? A scorch mark?"

"Like when we leave the hot iron down too long?" laughs Fern. "But though, maybe we'll get famous for something."

"Like what, Fern? Mopping the same floors fifty trillion times? Or feeding six brothers and their friends ten-kazillion sandwiches? And making sure Pink and Julie don't levitate the house?"

"Speaking of those little witches," says Fern, "where have they gone? Girls! Come back near the path!"

"We're pikas," yells Pink. "Behind the big rock!"

The older girls scan the mountainside of big rocks and glimpse the twins dodging from one to another, now chirping loudly. Pikas discovered. Hazel shrugs with exasperation. "What gets me," she says, "is that when the boys come up with a project, our plans get swept out the door. They always have to do something important, like moving a big boulder so they can build another wall where we don't need one. Or digging a huge hole for someone to fall into. And when they come in starving after their earth-shattering hard work, guess who has to feed them? And we have nothing to show for it, just more mess to clean up."

"But though, Haze, even with just the six boring ingredients to work with, I'd rather cook than clean up after their cooking. Herald's pretty neat and Brick's not too bad, but when they all get in a feeding frenzy, it's horrible. Yesterday Alvie was gouging peanut butter out of the tin with the corn tongs."

"That's nothing," says Hazel. "I found a spoon stuck to the wall behind the kitchen door! Brick threw it full of porridge at Rich two days ago and he was supposed to clean it up. But of course, he forgot. I had to soak it off. This porridge war has been going on way too long. Just when I thought they'd smartened up, I saw Billy flicking some mush at Herald. Herald made him scrub it off his sleeve, but neither of them noticed globs of it on the floor, and then of course they walked in it and of course it was my turn to scrub the floor. Next time it's one of their turns, I'm going to make an extra batch of porridge and spread it all over the floor to dry nice and hard. —Except I wouldn't, because waste is evil and they'd never clean it up properly, and we'd have to do it or get overrun with ants and evil weevils. And they'd do something worse back. Like squeal on us for putting porridge in Nasty Nitmust's thermos, our one stroke of rebellion all year."

Fern groans. "Of course Ron and Rich *would* be on chalk-brush detention and see us doing it... and tell their dear brothers. But though, I swear I get stuck with the porridge pot whenever I do dishes. I even put porridge in my ethics essay. 'There's the porridge pot, scum and lump it, should you wash it, should you dump it?'" Mrs. Hortense gave me a C."

"If you ask me," says Hazel, "writing essays is like pushing words through a sieve... all I end up with is a worthless mash."

"Oh yeah, Hazel, that's why you always get an A. But anyhow, when Mom was running six ways getting stuff ready for the relief hamper? Pink and Julie were splatter-painting Dad's white birth-day hankies with wet crepe paper! Nothing's been the same since they decided they're colour scientists. I thought Dad would have a fit, but he just laughed."

"If they get their hands on my white scarf," Hazel mutters, "I'll throttle them."

"Sure, Haze, you're the worst one for laughing when they do something outrageous. Mom and Dad have no idea half the feuds going on under their roof. They're so trusting, and so busy. Sometimes I think our parents are like forgotten houseplants on a dark windowsill. They're starved for a bit of sunlight and atten-tion, but they faithfully burst into bloom every so often, just for the fun of it."

"Sheesh... that's poetic, Fern! You should write that down for Mrs. Hortense next year. But we don't ignore Mom and Dad that bad, do we?"

"Mom hardly ever sits down!" Fern exclaims. "She even stands up to read, 'cause if she sits down, someone plunks on her lap right away or she has to jump up to stir something. If women live long enough, they get so they stand up all the time from one day to the next, until they fall over dead!"

"And men build mills," says Hazel, "to grind ore to get iron that'll rust away when they run out of ore to grind. Or sawmills that will go to ruin when there's no more trees to grind."

"And all that's left is a few steps to nowhere," shrugs Fern.

"Steps to oblivion!" shouts Hazel. "Steps to doing exactly what we want because who cares anyhow! Sawmill, ore mill, turkey mill! Oogle, hoogle, groogle!"

Fern and Hazel belt out the song "Stranger in Paradise" with mock passion.

Pink and Julie hear the wailing. They make faces at each other and giggle. "Sounds like they got belly cramps," says Pink. "Hope we never get like that."

"We won't," Julie assures her, gulping a handful of berries. "These top ones are the sweetest 'cause they get more sun. And the ones underneath are juiciest 'cause they get more rain."

"But don't eat too many," gobbles Pink, "or we won't have enough for the long long dark winter. And our wicked step-parents will eat us."

"Fiddle, piddle... taradiddle."

"...the little hog coughed..."

"...and the hyena jumped the baboon."

"C'mon. Let's cut pipes, Ju Ju. Here's a big elder."

Julie and Pink can hear the older girls yakking but can't make out their words, and that's quite close enough for them as they search for thick elderberry stocks.

Fern wonders, "Where do you think Herald and Brick are, Haze?"

"Miles away," says Hazel. "Scouting a good place to make some moolah."

"They're not picking for money already?" shrieks Fern.

"Yup," says Hazel. "If Mom doesn't snick them all into jars. City Locker pays ten cents a pound... pretty good deal for someone too lazy to pick their own berries... ten cents a pound, picked, sorted, cleaned, weighed, and delivered. How many berries does it take to make a pound, do you think, Fern? About sixty thousand? By the time we risk our necks scrambling over kingdom come, our work is worth about minus two cents a pound."

"We better watch the boys don't sell theirs and ours go into jars," says Fern. "We should all get some money. But though Haze, don't we have to can a hundred quarts before anyone can sell any? The One Hundred Quart Rule!"

"All for one and one for all? Folderol!" says Hazel. "Dad's still mad at Mrs. Broom for re-weighing her order last summer. Brick said it was five pounds and it was five pounds, plus ten extra berries. Mom called it an insult to integrity. I think the boys were just glad they got paid, after that dog snozzled on the berries. Anyhow, I hate it when everyone goes haring off in different directions like this. We might not see Brick and Herald for hours. Do you think Alvin's with Sedge? "

"I hope so," says Fern. "But though, I don't blame Sedge for taking off any chance she gets. She says she feels like baloney, sandwiched between Billy and Alvin on one side and Ron and Rich on the other. But Alvin usually keeps her or Billy in sight, when he can get away from Pink and Julie. Really, we're one big Dagwood sandwich. Speak of the imp twins, here they come."

"What do you mean," squawks Pink. "Why would Alvin want to get away from us?"

"You know you're always getting him in trouble," laughs Hazel. "He's leery of your mad ways."

"Huh!" huffs Julie. "Alvin likes us."

CHAPTER 14
Fern Tells a Story

MEANWHILE, BILLY IS CLIMBING up the ridge above the foundations, intermittently calling for Alvin as he scrounges berries. Although he often finds himself 'alone with the girls', he likes to keep track of everyone, and his brothers and sisters increasingly expect this of him, especially now that Perth is gone. Billy dreams of being a shepherd, paid to wander from one reading spot to another, although Herald tells him wool-gathering is no longer a viable profession. Too bad no one keeps sheep anymore, except old Sam with his one sheep, Mandy, who usually has a hen nesting on her back. Sam always checks Mandy's back when he needs an egg. But what Billy really wants is to have his own radio program. He has a quip to try out on Alvin, and he hollers, "Alvin, where are youooooooooo?"

No answer.

As for Alvin, he's far off on his own. Like thirteen-year-old Ron and Rich, he's decided to lose the rest of his family. He doesn't want to be stuck with the girls all day.

Alvin's a bit of a brooder, and he finds much to ponder in his family of thirteen. Since that rainy afternoon when he and Billy dissected the wind-up clock, Alvin has thought a lot about what makes people tick. How can Julie and Pink rearrange a whole room without anyone noticing them do it? When Herald's so mad you can see his hair smouldering and he finally lets loose a word storm that so discombobulates everyone, ka-whooosh, that the air's cleared without Herald swearing or hurting anyone... how does he do it? Does Brick really plan to be a sea captain some day? He seems such a homebody, content to play board games with the kids for hours. And Sedge, when she gazes into space with her gentle smile, what is she thinking? Alvin notices her separateness, but when he asks her if she's lonely, she seems startled by the question.

Deep in thought as the sun nears its zenith, Alvin clambers onto a stump and eats some peanuts. A Steller's jay inspects the shells he drops and screeches triumphantly as it flies away with a morsel of nut. Alvin breaks up a nut and drops it. Soon another jay joins the first, and he studies them, absorbing the exquisite blue of their feathers. He'll concoct that colour with his paints at some later time.

Back near Stooge's Mill, Pink and Julie empty their pound jam cans into a Malkins bucket, disappointed their berries make hardly a layer. They're sleepy. They've been working industriously for almost an hour and have purple splotches on their cheeks.

"Fern, will you tell us a story now?" asks Pink.

"Maybe we all need a story," she answers. "Let me have a drink first and get this bucket off before my back breaks."

Hazel works on a knot in her shoelace, while the twins pick pine needles out of her long, brown braid. Fern twists her peach-blond mop into a bushy up-do. She gazes into the clouds as she rummages through the five-and-ten of her imagination, gathering colourful images to take their minds off their aches and itches.

Any old thing will do; it's the spirit of the telling that matters, and the dollops of humour.

They've all practiced concocting stories during rainy camping trips and epic waits when the Hearse has broken down. Stories can make waiting part of the picnic. Lettuce says making a story is like making candy. You get fudge when you cook the syrup to soft-ball stage. If you cook it too long, it reaches hard-ball stage and turns into toffee. If you want toffee, that's fine, but if you want fudge, hard ball won't do. Bob and Lettuce sometimes start a story which is stretched back and forth like pull-toffee from one kid to the next, often from one day to the next, until it's a tasty confection, flavoured to everyone's taste and chewed to nubbins, a lasting sweetness.

(Occasionally one of the kids has to be reminded not to confuse fact with fiction. Sedge and Rich once had to write a piece for Mrs. Hortense called, "The Difference Between a Story and a Fib." It contained many fine lines.)

While Fern gathers her thoughts, the twins help Hazel clear dead branches from the base of an immense cottonwood, and voila! A mossy chesterfield. She and Fern lean against the tree, with the twins settling against their knees. Fern's melodic voice comforts them. "What's been happening lately with Mr. and Mrs. Ornery Peevish?" she asks. "Well, let's see."

Mr. and Mrs Peevish and the Huckleberry Bucket

Het-Up Peevish is one of those people who's always agitated about something, and right now she's fed up with her husband, Ornery. Het is a worrier, one of those people who is constantly preparing for the worst. It's a passion with her. Her tragedy is that the worst never happens, so she wastes most of her life getting ready for nothing. She takes her frustration out on her husband.

Now it just so happens that Ornery Peevish is a complainer. He and his wife are quite a pair. He isn't loud about it, but he usually has some plaintive little problem he's fussing about. Very annoying. Lately, he's all the time complaining about his huckleberry bucket. He says the top half always takes longer to fill than the bottom half, so the top half of the bucket must be wider. Het-Up points out to him, impatiently, day after day after day, that his bucket is absolutely straight-sided all the way down and all the way up. It's only because he's more tired by the second half that it takes longer to fill than the first half. But oh no, in his tiresome way, Ornery insists that the shape of his bucket is at fault.

"Ornery Peevish, Het screeches,"If I hear one more word about your bucket, I'm going to teach you a lesson."

"My bucket…" he said.

So she did.

She taught him a lesson by secretly making him a bucket with sides gradually slanting outwards, so that it *did* take him much longer to pick a top layer than a bottom layer. "Ha, ha, that'll teach him," she thought.

But Ornery didn't notice the change. He just kept worrying about filling the top half of his bucket as fast as the bottom half. Finally one day he was too exhausted to complain. In the subliminal way that an earthworm might sense the presence of thunder, he knew that his wife was about to wrap the whole fan-dangled thing around his neck if he didn't shut the heck up about it.

Het watched Ornery stew for a couple more weeks until she finally took pity on him. She made another bucket. This one was narrower at the top than it was at the bottom.

He didn't notice the difference, but he was very happy because now he *could* fill the top half faster than the bottom half.

Then one day, Ornery got new glasses and he could suddenly see that his bucket was brand new and shiny… and maybe even a different shape. But he decided not to mention it.

"Was he mad?" asks Pink.

"No, but after that, he insisted on using the bucket that was wider at the top, just to show he was a good sport, and he never complained again. He had learned his lesson."

"What was his lesson?"asks Julie

"It's useless to complain about your fate?" suggests Hazel.

"How did Mrs. Het-Up Peevish make the buckets?" asks Pink.

"Let's all have a short nap," says Fern.

CHAPTER 15
The Storyteller: Julie, 2005

FLASH FORWARD TO JULIE almost fifty years later, where she's crawling up a ridge glimmering with heat waves. She's glad she's remembered Rule #3: wear a hat. But there's a persistent horsefly dive-bombing her. The idyllic shade and the huge, ripe berries on tall bushes under a fringe of birch trees where she started out? Long gone.

That first lavish spread of grape-sized beauties has petered out. Even the best patch wears thin eventually. Julie is sieged with bug bites and prickly heat. It's not the first time she's been lured into a wild huckleberry chase and ended up high,dry, and far away. Fireweed fuzz gets in her nose, its magenta bloom already gone to seed on this hot granite outcrop. Mountain laurel tangles her feet as she searches a threadbare gully with the callow hope of finding another berry banquet.

Rule 18X: A partially full bucket is not full enough to take home.

Julie navigates scree, brambles, and osier, ending up on the back of a cliff. That's the trouble with bucket-walks. You never know. There might be good berries close by or none for miles. She picks a red measle out of her bucket, a stink bug, pine needles, an inchworm. Fireweed fuzz sticks to her fingers. Aaarg. She gives her shoulders a good stretch and crawls upwards. The view is worth the climb.

Mountains overlap one another. Layer after layer of tissue-paper shades of blue merge with a steel-wool smudge on the horizon. Puffs of cloud drift overhead. She whispers, "All will be well, Pink, all is well. Leaf green, moss green, stem green, chartreuse."

Julie turns down a stream half-hidden by hazel and ocean-spray brush until it widens into a steep meadow, and hey, presto! A veritable tapestry of dark green bushes lies before her, adorned with purple berries. Although she has to stand awkwardly with one foot higher than the other, her hands fly into action and her thoughts turn philosophic once more.

Julie reflects that the ancient Taoists found an enlightened path by free and easy wandering. Long rambles in nature are good for the soul, giving thoughts a chance to swim out of their murky back-eddies into fresh water. It doesn't hurt to carry a bucket and a notebook, though, in case you find yourself smack-dab in the middle of berries too numerous to eat, or an epiphany too long to remember. If not recorded, bright ideas can so quickly drift away, never to be found again. You can end up with nothing for your mind to work on, except the back and forth of the daily wash.

Sometimes, a few bright thoughts can be reeled in before they dart away, like glittering fish in a downward flash of sunlight.

Which puts Julie in mind of Rule 3H: when you can't bring home berries, you should at least return with a good line or two.

(But don't try to keep her rules in any sort of logical order, because they have none.)

Rules 82–86, the Rules of Bucket Size, are complex. A whole chapter could be written on them, but suffice it to say, it's a tricky business. Over-ambition is offensive. That's what makes it so embarrassing for anyone coming home with a few berries rattling in a large bucket. Yet, Rule 2H clearly states: any huckleberries are better than no huckleberries.

An ideal bucket would expand, possibly made of macrame or canvas. It would be rigid enough that the berries wouldn't squash, as they would in a plastic bag, and flexible enough to fold into a pocket if not needed. Ah, but it's far from a perfect world. Sometimes you have to take your chances. Rule 31J: those paltry, under-ripe berries in the first places you check don't mean there aren't lots of beauties further on.

A two-quart bucket could be considered a minimum size (Rule 20B). If you stumble upon a really good patch and you have only a one pound honey pail, that's a serious problem, as bad as having a serious brainwave with no pencil or paper on hand, and a really short memory.

Rule 19R: an imperial gallon (five litres) is a good-sized pail. And Rule 65: better to be caught out with an empty bucket than no bucket at all.

Rule 19S: if you don't want to carry a bucket, wear a dark hat that won't be spoiled by berry stains.

Rule 19C: don't take more than a twenty pound container on a solo hike because, according to Rule 31, you should be home by dark.

The most insidious Rule is 4F: don't come home till your bucket is full.

A lot of endurance and pride is involved in bringing home a good load of berries, so the full-bucket rule is common sense to the everyday avid berry picker. But to some children of legend, it had an ominous note. On the doorstep in the early-morning mist, sleepy faces up-turned, their mother clanged huge buckets into their out-stretched hands, warning, "don't come back till your buckets are full." It's a myth the Eleven like to tease their mother about, laughing as she hugs them good-bye.

CHAPTER 16
Sedge, Herald, and Brick

NOW RECALL THAT THE Eleven, on this rare occasion, are spending a full day on the mountain with no adults. Are the older ones looking after the younger ones and vice versa, as their parents in good faith believe they will? They've promised to stay together and meet their father at five-thirty PM to get a ride home. But Brick has the only reliable watch and he's forgotten to wind it. As the sun climbs the sky into afternoon, the Eleven are scattered far and wide.

Sedge has kept pace with eighteen-year-old Herald, hiking up the main trail for over an hour, neither of them saying a word. At twelve, Sedge is strong, athletic, and keen to get away from the knot of younger kids. She finds Alvin's seven year old perspective interesting, and he's a good listener. Billy's a lot of fun but too noisy; he could talk the arms off a windmill. Pink and Julie are fine in small doses, and she has good times with the older girls when they're not trying to fix her. But when it comes to dragging along with all of them, Sedge just has to get away from the racket.

Respecting each other's need for solitude, Sedge and Herald gradually veer off the trail and go their separate ways. "I'll come back
this way," Herald says, "after I scout around further uphill." His red
beanie quickly disappears in the trees.

Much as he likes hanging out with his brothers and sisters,
Herald's been feeling very crowded at home lately. He'll soon be
working full time and, without realizing it, he's already distancing
himself from his boyhood. The plan is for him to earn enough at
the Phoenix Jam Factory to pay for college in a year or two, living
at home in the meantime. But Herald has itchy feet. Victoria seems
like a distant beacon, a three day trip from home. He knows Auntie
Ben and Uncle Al would hardly charge him for room and board.
Heck, he could help out around their place. He can fix almost anything and he could help lots with his younger cousins. Bob and
Lettuce, of course, are urging him to do the practical thing and get
his training closer to home. They know he's saved every penny he's
made, but Victoria will have lots of expenses he can't anticipate.
Anyhow, they'd like the pleasure of his company for another year,
and they insist there's lots of room for him at home.

Ha! He has to duck to go down the basement stairs as it is.

Herald kicks a fallen pinecone and watches ruefully as a family
of brown wrens scuttles into the bushes, upturned tails flicking
in agitation. He sighs. As things stand, he'll be stuck at the Jam
Factory until at least next fall, stirring bubbling vats and jamming
jam into cans. At the mere thought of it, he feels a wave of cloying
heat wash over him. (One good thing about his work is that the
cavernous fug of the factory strengthens his resolve to further his
education, lest he be jammed there the rest of his life.) But first, a
glorious day of hiking, a chance to stretch his legs more or less free
of responsibility (or so Herald thinks).

Meanwhile, not far away, seventeen-year-old Brick has been
pushing through dense soopalallie. He pauses to wipe cobwebs off
his face and grimaces at the nastiest of rural flavours: huckleberry/

bug repellent. He takes a long slug of water. Steaming, he fans himself with his blue ball-cap. He shucks off the wooden pack-board and spare buckets which inevitably become his responsibility on trips like this. He gives his shoulders a good scratch and adjusts a strap where the pack-board has been digging in. The pack-board is a relic made by their Uncle Will in his prospecting days and should have been thrown out years ago. Herald was always going to make a new strap for it, but Brick had rigged it together with an old belt and some rope and loaded it up. He takes pride in hauling for the younger tribe, but he sure gets hot. He has a guzzle from his water canteen and gets back to work.

Brick was ten pounds and twelve ounces at birth, with a shock of red hair. (Or fifteen pounds, depending who you ask.) His dad has every colour of hair and his mom has black hair with red highlights. Anyhow, Bob had taken one look at his ruddy son and called him "Brick". The name had stuck. Brick doesn't mind. In fact, he'd be mortified if his friends learned his real name. Percival Howard. Uncle Percival never liked the name either, and has always been called Purse, while his great-uncle Percival had been known as Satchel. Satch for short. Purse, Satchel, Satch, Hand-bag. Heck, Uncle Percival's ears will pick up even at the word "suitcase." Brick chuckles. It's a good thing his dad broke the cycle by giving him a good, solid nickname.

Brick finds a plot of marble-sized berries and hunkers down, the juicy orbs rolling into his hands almost of their own free will. He continues to muse about names. One person with an even worse name than Percival is his Social Studies teacher, Mr. Ego-Evanomalosovitch. Poor guy. With his hairy Adam's apple sticking out and his big schnozzola, it's hard to take seriously someone who looks like they walked out of a Goofy comic. Some of the seniors call him Mr. Id, or Mr. Libido-Evanomalosovitch, but not to his face because they like him, really.

Aunt Hilarity's name is sure weird, too. She always says it full out, doesn't want them calling her Auntie Hill or Auntie Larry—except their dad, because he's her brother-in-law, can call her Larry and, occasionally, Larry Hill. She says her name is worth a good laugh, ha ha. He says Larry is a Hill of a good name and she says at least Hilarity's not boring, like Bob. If she wants to make him mad she calls him Bob-a-link. Herald one time called him that and he got a glare that sizzled him to the ground.

As for Herald, he's named after Uncle Harald, but spelled with an "e" to mean messenger. Did his parents know he would herald ten brothers and sisters into the family? Brick ponders the mystery of a family in which the boys are named after uncles and the girls are named after plants. Which apparently is in honour of their mom, whose name is Lettuce. Not Leticia. Just plain Lettuce, because that was her own mom's favourite food. Sometimes their dad calls her Let. Even Julie is named after a plant, because her middle name is Cosmos, which is a purple daisy, and Pink says she's named after that flower that's called Pink that smells like cloves. But their Mom says it was her bright pink face and pink cotton-candy hair at birth that named her. Brick thinks it must take a lot of imagination to name eleven children, especially when they come in twos. Anyhow, he likes being Brick. He's sturdy, confident as his name, and indifferent to his terracotta hair.

He has a guzzle from his water canteen.

CHAPTER 17
A Narrow Escape

BACK NEAR THE MILL foundations, Julie and Pink are napping. Fern has just finished telling them a story about Mr. and Mrs. Ornery Peevish. Its moral is that fussing and worrying are a major waste of time, but that doesn't stop the older girls from worrying.

Heavy-lidded, the sky glowers like a parent needing a nap, blue-hot, with clouds closing in from the east and west. Hazel and Fern stretch and yawn and wonder where Alvin has gotten to. And where are Herald, Brick, Sedge, Ronnie, Rich, and Billy? Hazel hoots like a ululating loon, "HooooooooOOO hoooOOOOooodle oooOO." When no one answers, she slings on her pack. "I'm going to look for Alvin," she says.

Fern says she'll keep Pink and Julie with her near Periwinkle Pool, where the berries are plentiful. The twins soon wake up, lively and talkative, and join in picking berries. Fern finds their chatter entertaining and quite informative if she keeps quiet.

"'Remember when we found Mom's thimble?" Julie asks Pink. "When she was going crazy looking for it, 'member, when Dad's pants split open? And he had to hold a towel around him while Mom mended them?"

Pink laughs uproariously."Burt was waiting for Dad to help with his busted water pipe... and the shoe mending machine needed a needle, so Mom had to fix Dad's pants by hand, so she needed her thimble 'cause they're canvas."

Fern and Hazel had puzzled how the twins had found the thimble in the nick of time, after it'd been missing all week. Now Fern learns they'd stashed it in Auntie Ben's silver teapot, which they were plotting to sneak into their "secret" trove in the attic. So that was why they suddenly decided to polish the teapot... it wasn't an uncanny coincidence, it was a twinge of twin conscience. But next thing the imps had found a needle for the shoe-mending machine right under the treadle, and that did seem miraculous.

"And 'member when we found the old silver medallion under the chicken coop? Sometimes we sure are lucky," Pink crows.

"Nobody but us would crawl under the chicken shed looking for treasure," chortles Julie. "We just knew we'd find something exciting under there."

And nobody else would have the gall to take Dad's flashlight under there, thinks Fern. Lucky for them it didn't get broken.

Next the twins start giggling about the "Fabulous Spring Dance" and Fern shudders.

It had seemed like such a nice, big-sisterly thing to do, taking the little girls with them to the dance, when they'd promised they'd strictly stay with Hazel and Fern and behave. They'd been so cute in their matching silver tunics, which Mom had magicked from a scrap of remnant. Too cute, teaching everyone how to do their silverfish dance, sashaying around the stage with that cute singer. Fern and Hazel were so embarrassed they just wanted to run home. But of course they couldn't without the twins. The worst of it was they seemed to be the only ones not under the silverfish spell. Fern glumly picks berries while her little sisters gleefully re-enact their dance.

After what seems like hours wandering around the same area, picking smaller and smaller berries, Fern and the twins hear a sudden loud snapping of branches. They look up to see something tall moving towards them, with branches swaying overhead.

"Aaaacckkk… what?"

"It's Hazel! It's Alvie!… It's Billy!"

It's Hazel with Alvin on her shoulders, with Billy whistling at her heels, lugging Alvin's pack as well as his own. The three of them are muddy from head to sodden feet. Hazel deposits Alvin unceremoniously on the ground near the twins and lunges for the water can, throwing it at her mouth while Billy and Alvin take turns at a flask. Alvin drinks the longest of all, as if he's been thirsty for days. Then he sits mute. His eyes are huge in a stricken white face. Julie and Pink drop on all fours in front of him, watching him intently. Pink gingerly touches Alvin; his hand, his cheek, his knee, his ear, as though he's a peculiar specimen that she's always been curious about.

Julie is staring at the black toenails sticking through his socks. "Where's your shoes, Alvie?"

Billy is still panting, "Ooph… we barely made it back, Fern… Alvin was in a mine… Me and Ronnie, we heard him hollering… we could just see the top of his head… I had to crawl on my belly to get to him, 'cause I'm lighter, and Ronnie held my legs… Then Hazel came along, and her arms were long enough to grab hold of him and I held her legs and Ron held mine. Ron was the anchor."

"So where's Ronnie?" Fern wants to know.

"Gone to catch up with Rich."

Fern's shock turns to relief and then anger. She and Hazel glare at their youngest brother even as they gently pull dirt and twigs from his hair. "Alvin Bartholomew! How could you go in a mine!?"

Alvin has still not uttered a word, which, for him, is rare. His eyes are unfocused and huge, fixed on Billy. Pink and Julie back off, almost as if they're afraid of him now. This is not the Alvin they know.

Fern tucks a jacket around Alvin and finds a band-aid for a scrape on his wrist. Hazel rustles food out of her knapsack, muttering in agitation, "God, Alvin, if anything had happened to you…"

Alvin croaks, "It did happen, Hazy… I fell in a hole…"

"And you put Billy and Ron and me in danger getting you out! Mom would die if she knew! You know you're not supposed to go in mines, Alvin!"

"You won't tell Mom… will you Haze… please… Billy, please don't tell… I was only exploring, I only went a little way."

"You went in a mine!" screeches Hazel.

Billy has flopped on the ground by Alvin, finally catching his breath. "Good thing you've got a strong set of lungs, Alv… if I hadn't heard you hollering, you could be half-way to China by now… it's not so bad, looking in a mine… but you can't go past the light… those old timbers are rotten… you could be falling still!"

"You sound like you know all about it, Billy!" says Fern. "How do you know so much?"

Billy jumps to his feet. "I'm going to start a fire, Alvin's wet and cold. Anyhow, Fern, I've never been in that mine."

"THAT mine!?"

Clouds have stolen the sun. A nervous breeze scuttles around them. Glad to have some line of action, the kids start scrounging kindling. Alvin's grateful to get away from everyone's scrutiny. He tugs off his tattered socks, drapes them over a rock, and starts snapping twigs. The promise of a campfire pulls his thoughts away from the deep, haunted, endless black tunnel.

Quickly, a pile of kindling is assembled on a rocky ledge above the pond. Rocks are built around it and matches are struck. The kids are adept at this. Since early childhood they've had campfires in the mountains. Survival means matches tucked into pockets, bits of paper for fire-starter, hoards of food, and emergency wads of linty gum for when the grub runs out.

"We'll have to keep the fire small," warns Hazel. "I'll get a bucket of water."

Well aware of the hazards, the Eleven have never yet started a forest fire, although one summer after a neighbourhood cook-out, a root fire had smouldered under a rocky knoll. Wisps of smoke had fingered their way out of crevices for days afterward.

Soon a squiggle of smoke struggles out of the pile of twigs. They cluster around, adding twigs, talking in subdued voices.

"Too bad Herald has the hot dogs in his pack," says Billy wistfully.

"Too bad we don't have steak and corn on the cob," says Hazel.

"Let's roast some apples," suggests Fern.

"Hey, do we have a can opener for these beans?" asks Pink. "No? I'll bash them open with a rock."

"Don't even try," says Hazel. "Brick has an opener in his pack, if we ever see him again."

"Well anyhow, we've got lots of cheese and bannock... and hard-boiled eggs." says Fern.

"Ack! Choke!"

"Jeez, Bill, take the shells off first."

Hunks of bannock are roasted on sticks and warm, softened flesh is sucked from charred apples. Fern makes a clover flower concoction. Despite the pine needles and ashes floating in it, it's the best tea they've ever tasted.

Finally sated, the kids sit back on their haunches, returning to the subject of Alvin and the mine hole.

Alvin still doesn't have much to say. The horror of being stuck with his legs hanging in mid-air is too vivid, too real—the sound his shoes made when, untied as usual, they had fallen off his pedaling feet, too hideous—the barely audible sound of them landing far, far below, followed by a trickle of rocks—a larger rock crashing, and another, until it had sounded like the whole Earth was giving way underneath him.

How long had he hung there, afraid to move, wedged in a jumble of boards, hollering for help until his throat tore? Trapped in the dark, Alvin's imagination had conjured "Deady-White-Eye," the nightmare chicken, but he knew he was screaming much too loud to be dreaming.

* * *

(Alvin doesn't know that his clamour reverberated through the mountain. Unknown to any of them, far below on a treeless slope, a tall shaggy form heard his cries and peered up the mountain, listening intently.)

* * *

Alvin shudders even though he's safe now, on solid ground, in broad daylight. He remembers the scrape on his chest and unthinkingly lifts his shirt to inspect the damage, which sets off another barrage of recriminations from the girls.

Billy takes pity on him after a while and playfully punches him on the shoulder. "I think I know why you went in the tunnel, Alv… because you knew darn well you weren't supposed to, plain and simple."

Hazel snortles, "You should know all about that, Billy, you and Ronnie!"

Alvin has to turn away to hide his tears. The shining in the tunnel had been water, of course he'd known that, but just for a minute he'd played prospector, investigating the mysterious glimmer of gold, iron pyrites in rusty water. "We need more kindling," he mutters, breaking sticks with vicious energy. He knows Billy's right. He'd wanted to do something exciting without older boys bossing and girls jabbering. He stifles a sob. "It's not fair being the youngest boy! I wanted to go with Brick and Herald, but they said to stay with the girls. I never get to do anything exciting."

Fern sighs. "Trouble with you boys, your idea of excitement is doing something risky. Why can't you be safe and sensible like us?"

"Oh yeah?" scoffs Billy. "What about Hazel doing her cartwheels on the train trestle? One of these times the train's going to surprise her."

"Never mind," says Fern. "It's a good thing Hazel can do gymnastics or Alvin might be in China by now."

"And he doesn't know any Chinese," Hazel laughs. "Anyhow, I can hear a train miles away when I'm on the trestle. Let's get back to picking berries. Alvie, can you stay and look after the fire?" (That should assuage his pride.)

Begrudgingly, Alvin stays by the "stupid" fire on condition they won't tell Mom and Dad on him. Worse almost than anything is imagining the hurt in his mom's eyes when she knows he's done something dangerous. He won't think yet about what his dad might say in his quiet voice-of-reason, with logic that makes your head feel like sawdust. Alvin knows about gravity, he knows about the dangers of mine tunnels and he knows about the perils of pretending, but he still did what he did. Sometimes he wishes his dad would yell and wave his arms like other dads. If anyone does that, it will be his mom; she's never convincing at it. But first, he must face his brothers. He dreads seeing scorn or pity in their faces. As if it's not bad enough he got scared out of his wits, he also lost the shoes that his best friend, Pepper, gave him. They were a bit used, but at least no one in the family had ever worn them. Alvin tosses pine needles into the fire and watches them spark for an instant before turning to ash. Ashes falling into ashes. His feet are full of prickles and rock bruises. He's chilly and damp, but inside he burns with humiliation.

Billy has a fair idea how Alvin feels. It's hard being your own man with so many brothers and sisters telling you what to do. They put you into a little box and expect you not to change for the rest of your life. He sees the closed-in, mournful look on his younger brother's face and spies an opportunity to try out a melon joke. "Hey you guys, listen up!" he says. "A melon and his friend Gordon Gourd walk into a bar and ask for a drink. The bartender looks at them and says, 'I'll serve the melon but I don't serve gourds in this here bar. So the melon says, 'What's the matter? Ain't my friend gourd enough for you?' Get it?"

Billy chokes, he's laughing so hard, and Alvin blows a humdinger and begins to feel like maybe things aren't so bad after all.

Ravens chorkle in an overhead pine snag, then hurl themselves into the air with a raucous "Blook! Bloook!" Billy and Alvin answer back, "Brroook... bloook!"

"Scrack, scrook!" shout Pink and Julie.

Another raven answers—or is it one of the older boys, croaking further up the mountain?

Buckets clank.

CHAPTER 18
Sedge

ONCE ALONE, SEDGE FINDS a good berry patch and gives a happy skip. Made it! Peace and quiet at last. No noisy brothers, no Pink and Julie asking questions, no Fern and Hazel talking their heads off and trying to mother her. Is she the only one who craves a chance to hear herself think? Probably that's why Herald dashes up the mountain any chance he gets, and definitely why she's at his heels. Solitude isn't for everyone, but those who need it feel it like a thirst. Sedge watches a hummingbird buzz an orange tiger lily, a jewel on a rampage. In poplars overhead, a small bird queries, "Trill-a-trill?" "Lilt-a-trill," another answers.

Intent on filling her gallon honey can, Sedge nestles into the shade, where the berries are lush. As her hands keep a steady rhythm, her thoughts take wing, like the red-shafted flicker which swoops near her.

She works steadily for over an hour before she pauses to watch a flurry of swallowtail butterflies. Alighting on the damp earth, they uncoil long proboscises that probe the clay. To drink? To suck up minerals? To catch a taste of what has been and what will be? Sedge watches the folding and unfolding of their wings, the bold patterns of black on yellow alternating with subtle gray and brown. Open, shut, alight, and lift. Why do they fan? To keep their balance? To cool themselves? To dry their wings? To circulate their green ichor? To send messages in semaphore to other swallowtails? "Come join us"...or..."Stay away, this selenium is ours."

It's very quiet now. Almost too quiet, even for Sedge. A bird call emphasizes her solitude: the muted whistle of a varied thrush, followed by an answering whistle in a lower key, a flutter of disappearing wings. Her isolation is complete. She can no longer hear a stream. She can no longer hear Brick clanking around. Where is Herald? It's been a long time since his red beanie bobbed away through the trees. Sedge has wandered further than intended in this maze of ridges leading off ridges, like wrinkles on an elephant's back. It's easy to ramble from one hill to the next without noticing, following the random flow of a berry patch, especially when preoccupied with bucket-thoughts and fragments of verse.

Has Herald missed her on his way back? She is quite camouflaged, with her gray sweater and tan bucket hat. There's an unwritten rule: don't leave something (like her) by the trail to pick up on the way back because usually you'll forget about it, or go back a different way, or miss it even if you do go back the same way.

Sedge would like to stash her heavy sweater somewhere. Bundled around her waist, it's getting in the way of her bucket. She scrambles onto a granite boulder to get her bearings and scans the treeline. Is that the stump where she'd retied her laces? She feels a fleeting terror. Even worse than being lost is the embarrassment of being found. She gives herself an impatient shake and is about to let out a where-are-you hoot when she finally spies Herald's red cap in the trees. He's loping toward her from quite the opposite direction she'd expected.

Herald's grinning, tipping his bucket to show that it's half full of cherry-sized huckles. He hollers for Brick, who answers with a gruff bark. Sedge and Herald each scurry down an elephant leg to meet him, topping up their buckets on the way.

Brick has his pack on again and clangs toward them with his two-gallon pail and the five-gallon soup pot. They decide to empty their buckets into the soup pot and leave it with Brick's pack in a safe spot between two boulders on Third Ridge. They can pick it up later, after they refill their buckets on the easy pickings up Third Creek.

Rule 37: Never leave your huckleberries unattended.

Sedge wedges her sweater between two rocks near the soup pot and she and her brothers continue on automatic pilot, stooping, scanning, reaching, plucking, scooping, shulling berries hand over fist. They'll worry later about how to haul them all back.

CHAPTER 19
Ron and Rich Up to No Good

RICH IS ON HIS own mission. He's done a fair bit of earnest berry-picking, but what he really wants right now is to meet up with Ron and have a smoke. He knows Ron has a cigar that Chuckie Moozle nicked from his old man, but Rich has the matches. He's been zig-zagging up the mountain, purposely veering away from the noises of Herald, Brick, and Sedge. He keeps wondering where Ron is. He climbs onto a boulder to see if he can spot his slow-poke brother.

What Rich sees is Brick's pack and the walloping big soup pot, large as life, all by its lonesome, heaped with monstrous berries. Chortling, he swoops down and scoops out a handful, sitting down for a good munch. Very good. He has a few more and a few more. Wow, it takes a while to eat a layer off this cauldron. He rifles the pack, has a feed of cheese and bread, and then, with a belch, he stretches out in the sun. He dozes, vaguely musing how the aroma of cheese and berries might attract a bear.

Twenty-five minutes later, Rich hears a loud thump. He jumps to his feet on high alert. An alder moves violently, there's a snort and a snuffle, and Ronnie blunders into view, swatting a horsefly. Ronnie is as startled and relieved to see Rich as Rich is to see Ron, and they burst out laughing when Rich gestures to the potlatch at his feet.

Ronnie's eyes bulge. "Holy succotash, what have we here?" He slurps down a big handful of huckleberries.

"Herald and Brick must have stashed them," marvels Rich.

"Aren't they the trusting souls!" says Ron. "Are you thinking what I'm thinking?"

Two pairs of brown eyes gleam.

"Let's hide them!"

Soon Ron and Rich are hauling their booty into a gully, narrowly missing catastrophe as they hoist it through a tangle of Oregon grape. Twice they have to scoop up berries that have toppled out.

"Shoot, we should eat more off the top so's we don't waste any more spilling them."

"Yeah, it's way too full."

Slurp, choff, choff, gulp, slurp.

"How 'bout we leave it by this stump?" says Rich.

"Sure, we can come back for it soon's we pick the bushes around here. We can leave Brick's pack right beside it... soon's I dig out some of the grub that I didn't have room for."

"Jeez, Ron, why'd you take up half your pack with your football?"

"Well, you never know when it might come in handy... Aha, the cheese!" Ron rips off a hunk and wolfs it down with a slab of bread and another handful of berries.

Satisfied with their hiding place, the brothers hunch down out of the breeze to light the tattered cigar which Ron has extricated from his pocket. It takes a few matches to get it going, but it's one fine cheroot. They choke, they gasp, they laugh, and they nearly die of asphyxiation having a heck of a good time until they have to lie down on the rocks to recuperate.

"How much did you pay Moozle for that butt, Ronnie?"

"Five cents."

"Just think, we could've had a whole roll of Lifesavers for that much. Or enough jaw breakers to last us all day."

"And we wouldn't've had the joy of getting green-dizzy."

"Ack."

As they lie on their backs contemplating life's complicated choices, they don't yet know how in-the-soup they're going to be by the time their caper with the soup pot is played out. They are unaware of the burden of nemesis and irony that looms over them as they enjoy their wooze.

"Aah, this is the life!"

"Yeah… intense! Ack, herack. Eeeep."

"It's a good thing we got out here today. I was starting to panic, seemed like the summer's half over and we haven't done anything yet."

"Yeah, I know. Next thing we'll be digging spuds again."

"Cripes, we haven't even finished hilling them yet and before we know it, school will be starting again."

"Anyhow, how come you took so long to get up here, Ron? I was about ready to head back down to find you."

"Well, I was on my way when I heard all this hollering. At first I thought it was Fern, but it was Billy shouting his lungs out, 'Help, help, help!' And then I could hear Alvie hollering, 'Billy, Billy, come back!' It turned out Alvin was stuck in that mine tunnel, you know the one where we found the rock pick… except the boards in between have rotted out. Alvin just about fell right through."

"Holy crap!"

"I know," says Ron. "So we hauled him out, Billy and me, and Hazel happened along so she helped a bit too, and I piggy-backed Alvin part way back… He was, like, in shock… You never heard Alvie so quiet… Then Hazel took him 'cause I wanted to get up here."

"Alvie'll be mad to get stuck in camp with the girls… scared we'll call him sissy."

"Camp, Rich?"

"You know, where the girls hang out near Stooge's Foundation… They call it Gurgle Springs or something stupid like that… 'course they might not be there, but they usually more or less stick together. And they're not hard to find, they make such a racket."

"Yeah, like old man Horkalinki's guinea fowl, 'Geeble, weeble, greeble!'" laughs Ron. "Anyhow, Alvie lost his shoes down the hole, so that'll sure slow him down,"

"Poor old Alv," says Rich. "Too small to keep up…"

"…and too big to keep down. I'd hate to be in his shoes… which he doesn't even have anymore."

"Billy'll cheer him up. Good old Bridge… keeps everyone's spirits up with his corny jokes."

"Do you think Herald and Brick have realized yet the soup pot's gone?"

"Haven't heard any hollering… we'd better give them awhile," says Ron. "I gotta find more berries… I really want that bike… one hundred quarts, here I come."

The twins work at the same patch for a while.

Ronnie soon finds a promising spot and settles down to methodically work his way across it. He's thorough, is Ronnie, the sort of guy who decides what he's going to do and does it with determination, whether it's a homework assignment or a bicycle wheel that needs re-spoking. Even when he has to write lines in detention, once he accepts that he can't get out of doing it, he settles down and gets the job done. Though his writing may be too large and smudged and changing in slant every couple of words, it's legible enough, and of adequate amount. As for huckleberry picking, he can stand mindless work as long as he can be outside, free to pursue his noble thoughts. Like how he's going to soar like a condor on that bike Joe wants to sell him. It's got most of its spokes and a nifty headlight. Maybe he can get a few bucks from the jam order if he works hard. Before long he's singing at the top of his lungs:

> …I will make you fishers of men,
> fishers of men, huckles of men,
> hmmm hmmm I will sell your huckles
> to men if you follow meee…

Rich, on the other hand, doesn't like picking berries. He can't stand wasting so much time and dexterity on something uncreative. He prefers whittling and painting, while Ron is more comfortable with wrench and pliers. But Rich, too, is a diligent worker. He takes pride in his MacLean Method hand writing and erases sometimes to the point of wearing a hole in his paper when he's in a conscientious mood. But put a paintbrush or a jack-knife in his hand and his touch is unerring.

It's a family joke how Rich "spills his berries" on huckleberry trips, coming back with hardly any in his bucket and his lips dark purple. That's because he subscribes to the often forgotten rule:

98C: Eat as many berries as you can while you're out there.

Cooked berries have a flavour that scrapes his inner chalkboard. Licking the juice from a corroded tin pan when he was three turned him off huckleberry pies for life. Great Uncle Eldridge's cousin is welcome to his share of huckle-tin-oxide. But fresh berries! Rich eats them constantly on a day like this.

Ron sighs. "It'd sure be nice to both have bikes at the same time for a change, eh Rich? I hate borrowing Fern's girly bike. Last time she made me wash my face and comb my hair before I could use it… and then I had to tighten the chain. She wanted me to wash it afterwards, but that's when I said maggots and she ran away."

"Ha!" says Rich. "And Brick's old bike is getting so dilapidated. I don't know how many more times I can patch that back inner-tube. I don't mind no brakes, but that wire Herald rigged up to hold the seat on? It keeps snagging me arse. I'll have to wrap some more rags around it."

"Maybe you should wrap some rags around yer arse."

"Shaddup Ron! Anyhow, if Herald got a new bike… then by the time it got to us it would still be half-decent."

"Yeah, but his bikes are already third- or fourth-hand when he gets them. If he didn't keep out-growing them, we'd never get any change-over… Do you think he's quit growing yet? I hope not, but he's over six feet now."

"Too bad the family didn't start with twins," muses Rich. "Then there'd be two of everything to pass on."

There's silence for a while as the boys ponder the juggernaut of fate.

Rich yawns, scratches his arm, ties his shoe, tightens his bucket tie, then blurts, "Do you ever wonder did Mom and Dad want so many kids?"

"No," says Ron. "I mean, they seem to like us well enough, but. They'd be so much better off without us. As far as money goes, at least."

"Yeah… Dad's glasses are soldered together… and Mom's sewing machine is skipping stitches. You know what," says Rich, "I don't think they planned on so many twins."

"Hazel says it was statistically unlikely," cackles Ron. "But one moonless night, lightning flashed, like… sending mumbo-jumbo electricity crackling over the homestead… and although Mother didn't realize it at the time, she had been hit by the Twin Curse! "

Rich stomps his feet, "Ba-da-boom, ba-da-boom, doom! Two sets of twins!" They both sing, "Ta-rah-rah-boom-dee-ay":

my wife had twins today,

she has them every day
and twice on Saturday…

"Ah, but we'll never get new bikes," moans Ron. "The newest thing we ever got's that hockey stick blew off someone's truck. Uncle Ronald was so lucky to be an only kid. He must've had new everything.

"Except he never had a brother," Rich reminds him. "Only kids are lonely kids."

"But," says Ron, "the killed-miners' kids? The three families whose dads got kilt in the mine collapse? I know it's rotten to say, but I wish I got half the handouts they got."

"Yeah," says Rich, "everyone gives them stuff. Except most of it's stuff they prob'ly don't want. Like Luke's family? All boys, and some church sent them a box of dolls. Hoo ha!"

"Is that why they say 'cold as charity'?" asks Ron, "'Cause half them dolls got no clothes? Ha. I found a doll leg down the road the other day, and then I found an eye, so I fastened the eye on the toes with a rubber band and put it in Fern's pencil case. You shoulda heard her screech."

"Cripes, me and Luke were looking all over for that eye, Ron! Me and his brothers had a doll fight. His Mom chased us down the block with a broom, said those dolls were for Buddy's sisters and us pilfering weasels better put them back together or else. So. We ended up with three dolls with half their parts on backwards, and Luke traded them to Buddy's sisters for a bike with one wheel."

"One wheel, Rich! What happened to the other one?"

"It got away from Ralph, you know, at Hilltop Garage? When he was helping Luke change the tire? It didn't stop rolling till a truck ran over it two miles down."

"What use is a bike with one wheel?"

"'Bout as much use as a doll with no head!"

The boys break up laughing.

"Hey," says Ron, "maybe we could rig the bike up like with some other kind of wheel."

Four brown eyes light up as Rich and Ron simultaneously picture the ruined baby pram in Amegrotto's back field.

"They prob'ly wouldn't even notice if we nicked that old pram,"says Ron. "It's been sitting that same spot since last summer... brand new until it got run over. Why'd they leave it in the middle of the road, anyhow?"

"They didn't,"says Rich, "Joe and Annette rode it down the hill and got tired of pushing it back up... so they ditched it in the grass... and it rolled round the corner, right into Mr. Horkalinki's truck coming up."

"Good thing Darling Toddy wasn't in it."

"He was, but on the first bump. he rolled into a patch of clover... hardly even woke up."

"Hey," cackles Rich, "maybe we could look after Toddy for Mrs. Amegrotto in exchange for the pram!"

"Yeah right, she'd maybe pay us to get us off her doorstep... or more likely call the cops."

"Just because we ate all those Girl Guide cookies," groans Rich. "How were we to know? But hey, Mrs. Amegrotto might give it to Luke. She likes him. We could rig a buggy wheel to his one-wheel-marvel, and we'd be in business!"

(As it turned out, many kids rattled that 'go-go-mobile' down Ralph's hill before it finally disintegrated in a patch of thistles at the bottom, while the two-wheel pram in Amegrotto's back field eventually sprouted a luscious huckleberry bush.)

Ron and Rich have been moving in opposite directions around a big huckleberry patch, their progress marked by the bobbing of their scout hats. They've been getting out of shouting distance and then meeting on the other side to pick up the ends of their conversation.

"You know what, "says Rich, "we may never have two decent bikes, but we're way better off than those killed-dad kids no matter what they get… unless it's measles. "

"Yeah, no dad," says Ron. "Cripes. The worst off is Donny… Only child, no dad, and someone gave him his very own TV. His own TV! But the picture tube was broke. When I saw his sad face, I gave him a handful of marbles, like. Mostly pale-ies, but a couple beauts."

"Blind me with your halo," says Rich. "But Buddy's even worse off; no dad, no brother, and a pack of sisters!"

"Is that why he wears his hair like that?"

Rich hoots. "Two of his sisters want to be hairdressers when they grow up, like, and they can't get enough of making pin curls. Too bad they can't afford Beauty School." After Ron's guffaw dies down, Rich continues. "So like you know what, Dad and Mom are giving to the Fund for Fatherless Mine Children another year."

"So no electric sewing machine for Mom or new glasses for Dad," says Ron. "Good thing we don't have to go to Beauty School! Those kids just better not get better bikes than us!"

"Think of poor Pink 'n Julie," says Rich. "The tag-end of every-thing. They get the orphans' hand-me-downs."

"They seem happy enough," says Ron, "like they don't know any different. Yet. But the Kludges… ten kids and their dad's gimp after the mine explosion… and their mom's got the Arthuritis so bad her hands're gibbled up like chicken feet. They don't have an indoor toilet even, and their upstairs got no 'lectricity."

"Yeah," says Rich. "Their house was like only half-built when the mine blew to smithereens, so. Their old man can't stand the sound of a hammer or like any kind of loud noise, and he near jumps out of his britches every time the boys shoot their potato guns."

"Sometimes at recess all's they got to eat's raw potatoes… peels and all," says Ron. "I guess spuds is one thing they got lots of.

Anyhow, there's no decent berries left here. I'm going to look for a new patch."

Rich and Ron wander off in different directions without deciding what they plan to do about the soup pot. Neither of them take a backward glance at it.

Rule 32: When in the bush, look behind you frequently to keep track of where you came from and notice some landmarks for when you go back.

Rule 33: Things always look different from the other side.

If Perth had been with the Eleven that trip, he would have been back and forth to that soup pot a dozen times. keeping track of it all day.

CHAPTER 20
Thunder

HAZEL, FERN, BILLY, PINK, Julie, and Alvin are downhill from Ron and Rich, near the main trail and the fire they built to warm up Alvin after his harrowing rescue from the Yellow Sea. Alvin has lost interest in feeding the flames. He's playing along Periwinkle Pond. He's watching periwinkles, the larvae of caddisfly, extend their long arms from shells they've built from silk and sand. He wishes he could make shells like that for his feet.

The fire is spewing acrid smoke. Even the sky seems to smoulder. Julie coughs, and then Fern. Alvin clears his throat and spits. Billy spits. They both hork.

"Ack. Let's put this fire out of its misery," says Hazel.

They douse it and stir the ashes with sticks until it's a cool slurry, which Billy happily plasters on his legs. Alvin follows suit and soon, they're all dabbing the soothing paste on their mosquito bites. It feels good—for a while.

"We look like neanderthals" laughs Billy. "Argg!"

"'Ugh, ugh, oogah-goo-goo,' says Alvin.

Hazel lifts her head at the sound of distant thunder. The cirrus clouds have given way to stratus and cumulus in the west. "I wonder where Ron and Rich and Herald and Brick are," she mutters.

"I wonder where Sedge is," sighs Fern. "I wish she'd stayed with us. I hope she's okay."

Alvin scowls. "I hope she isn't all by herself. She likes being on her own, but we haven't seen her for hours."

Fern drapes her arm over his shoulder. "Don't worry, Sedge knows this hillside like the back of her hand. "

After a thoughtful silence, Hazel asks, "How well do you know the back of your hand? Like, if a thousand hands were put in front of you, could you recognize your own hand?"

"Well Haze, that's way too deep for me," says Fern.

"A well's a deep subject; watch you don't fall in," quip Pink and Julie.

"But look," insists Hazel, "this mountain's like a giant's old, gnarled hand, with ridges and gullies running off bigger ridges and gullies. It's easy to get mixed up and be out in no-man's-land before you notice."

Fern lets out a whoop, hoping someone will answer. "OooOO wahoooooOOO..ooooOOOOoooooo!"

They hear no response but echoes... especially after Billy and Alvin start yodeling like demented roosters.

Unseen, a bear looks nervously over its shoulder, peers up the mountain towards them, and shambles downhill at a fast trot.

Half a mile away, Sedge listens. Is it Rich and Ron she hears, or coyotes? She can see Brick's blue cap, but she can't see Herald's red one. She joins Brick, who looks up and grins.

"How ya doin' Hedgy?"

"Pretty good. Have you seen Herald lately?"

Crouched behind low bushes, Herald stretches to full height, "Errrr! I'd rather have a badger gnawing my foot than keep picking these puny berries. What say we head down the creek a ways?"

"Yeah, we've more or less cleaned out this area. They'll be good in the lower meadow," says Brick. "We could probably pick there for hours. When is Dad coming for us?" He flicks his watch and winds it.

"Didn't he say he'd pick us up at the foundations after work? Around five?" asks Sedge. "Or did he say he'd meet us where he dropped us off?"

"Well," says Herald, "if we're not at the field he'll come to the foundations, won't he? I just hope the Hearse doesn't die."

"Don't even think about it," groans Brick.

Sedge feels uneasy. "We better not leave the soup pot too long."

"Or the other kids… let's pick down Third Creek," says Herald, "and be back here in half an hour."

Herald, Brick and Sedge head for richer pastures.

CHAPTER 21
Watch Out For Devil's Club

SO, RON AND RICH have wandered up Sasquatch ridge, while Herald, Brick, and Sedge are heading down Third Creek. (They each have their own names for these places, names not necessarily recognized by anyone else in the family in that vast, complicated landscape.)

Hazel and Fern, Pink and Julie, Alvin, and Billy have gathered up their paraphernalia after putting out their fire near Gurgle Springs. As they fan out on both sides of the main cow trail, buckets clanking, they wonder if they'll ever again be all together.

Alvin kicks his socks under a rock. They're more hole than wool now, with only a vaguely sentimental value to him. Billy doubles back to give the ashes one more stir and discovers, by way of steam, that the rocks were still too hot to pee on. No one notices Pink's aqua-flowered hairband fall from her rat's nest updo and cling to a branch. Nor do they notice Billy's magnifying glass, left where he'd been scorching lichen on a granite ledge near the campfire.

Alvin is determined to keep up with Billy, hopping over sharp rocks. Billy pauses often for his stalwart younger brother, knowing what it's like to tramp in bare feet. His own feet are none too comfortable in Sedge's hand-me-down boots. They're long enough, but way too narrow for his chunky feet. He pulls them off and asks Alvin if he wants a turn, socks and all. Alvin gladly clomps along in them until blisters rise on the tops of his big toes, where he has to press them upward to hold the boots on. He gives the boots back to Billy with a sigh. "My feet are so scrawny, Pink calls me Chicken Foot."

"Sometimes Pink doesn't think."

"Sometimes Pink stinks."

Alvin is happy when he and Billy go larking off together. Billy lets Alvin do pretty much whatever he wants without harping at him, and Alvin knows Billy will always look out for him. The boys now thwack mosquitoes with cedar branches, yelling at the top of their lungs, "It ain't the 'eavy 'auling that 'urts the 'orses 'oofs, it's the 'ammer 'ammer 'ammer on the 'ard 'ighway!" Thwack stomp, thwack stomp! More mosquitoes swarm, drawn by the fug of hot boy blood.

A bear lifts its head and woofs. It rises to its hind legs. Sniffs. Dropping to all fours, it lips berries from the bushes as it lumbers deeper into the forest. Too many humans in the woods today.

Julie and Pink are keeping Alvin and Billy in sight at the same time as they track their big sisters, orange-hat and green-hat. They skip ahead and fall behind, their bird voices shrilling in their own crazed lingo as they collect soft pink roses in their kerchiefs.

Fern and Hazel drift toward the shade below the trail, their voices unspooling behind them, sometimes like multi-coloured ribbons, sometimes like yittering guinea fowl. Climbing through briers, Fern gets a thorn in her finger. "Can you pull it out, Haze?"

"Ugh, Fern, your fingernails are like coal scuttles."

"No matter how I scrub them... Yours aren't any better, Haze. Huckleberries are like ink under our nails."

(Rule 54: You can't pick berries with gloves on.)

Hazel slaps her tam at a horsefly, shouting, "I'd rather be a slob than a dandy!"

"No way. You're like Herald, you always look tidy."

"Because we're ten-foot bean poles," sighs Hazel. "You'll always be curvy and petite. You're the lucky one."

"But though," says Fern, "Mrs. Hortense says, be glad we're not kids in Wales clawing coal out of tunnels too small to stand in, hardly seeing the light of day. Even their eyes are covered with black dust."

"I guess we're supposed to see our sweet lives out-lined in black so's we don't take them for granted," says Hazel. "It's bad enough when we get our winter's coal dumped by the back door."

"We're lucky we have fresh air. I love being out here in the mountains—but though, it's embarrassing when the mountains go to school with me."

"I know, Fern. Like that day I had burrs in my hair and my face was scraped from that trip up Crag Leap? I got so fed up with Dick asking me if I fell down the outhouse, then Hodge came up and said I look like I got dog turds in my hair. I hauled off and slugged him in the guts."

"Ah, Haze. Is that what happened? But at least Dick and Hodge got in trouble too."

"Yeah, but apparently I was the aggressor, because they never touched me, they just drove me nuts all day. Then I had to serve detention with them, writing lines about deportment. They kept asking me how to spell "apologize." And on top of that, Miss Prizz kept flitting around getting ready for glee club. She never said anything, but you know her little sniffs and twitters. Lovely Miss

Prizz, with hands as white and soft as whipped cream, she said we should be well-mannered like Sedge."

"It's just that Sedgie's shy, and always looks fantastic with those rosy cheeks and white hair, even with twigs in her hair and her bangs too long. Some boys call her 'Hedge.'".

"They're only trying to get her attention," says Hazel. "She just walks away when they tease her. Hardly anyone gets to know her."

"But though," Fern adds, "those who do never forget her. She's beautiful, even bushwhacking and wearing Rich's hand-me-downs. She's so natural. It's that inner beauty, like Mrs. Hortense was yakking about in Guidance Class?"

"If anyone knows about inner beauty, it should be Mrs. Hortense," says Hazel. "Too bad her looks go against her. Ron calls her Mrs. Horse-ass."

Fern gasps. "Rich says she has a face like a turnip... plain and stumpy with little hairs. But, she's nice. Most of the kids like her, but they won't admit it... The main reason Ron and Rich don't like her is she sent them to the office for putting wheels on their desk chairs. Ron always has tools in his pockets."

"Yeah," laughs Hazel. "They stole the wheels off the portable chalk board. I was handing out notices at lunch and I heard the whole thing. It was hilarious. Mrs. Hortense in that precise voice, you know, like... 'I commend your ingenuity and industry, boys, but you will have to arrange time with the principal to put things back to rights after school. It's hard enough keeping track of you whipper-snappers without you having wheels.' I just about died laughing... But hey, I haven't heard the imps for a while."

Fern hollers, "Yoo-hoo! Julie! Pink!"

"We're over here, catching a snake."

"Well, catch Alvin and Billy and never mind the snake," Hazel tells them. "Hey! Alvin, Billy! Get away from those cows! They'll never let you ride them! Pink and Julie, stay off the path. Can't you see the cow-pies?"

Alvin, Billy, and the small girls gather to examine the cow-pies with sticks. They are avid young explorers in a fascinating world.

Hazel and Fern turn their backs in disgust. The more attention they pay to the younger kids, the worse they'll get.

Hazel reaches around a fallen pine to the plump berries amongst its branches, still on the topic of teachers. "I think Mrs. Hortense and Mr. Ego-Evanomalosovitch would make a good pair. Her in her baggy tweed skirts and him in the same baggy tweed suit every day."

Fern crouches to reach handfuls of colossal berries underneath the pine. "Actually, Mr. Ego-Evanomalosovitch has more than one suit. I watched him pace past my desk every day in Social Studies. Sometimes his sleeves hang over his first knuckles and sometimes they are half way up his wrists."

"Maybe some days his arms are longer," suggests Hazel. "You never know."

Fern laughs. "And another time, I noticed one shoe was brown and the other was black. So I got in the habit of checking, and quite often his shoes are different colours, or different styles and the same colour."

"Hopefully they aren't both for the same foot."

"Ha ha. Another day one of his pant legs had a cuff on one leg and not on the other. So, he does have more than one suit, but they've all got some weird mismatch about them."

"Maybe he has fashion dyslexia," says Hazel.

"Maybe. I don't think most of the kids notice, they're so busy watching his Adam's apple bop up and down. What are Adam's apples anyhow, Haze?

"I dunno… Something to do with Adam when he bit the first apple? A big chunk got stuck in his throat, and forever after men have a lump in their throat to remind them not to be hogs? But Herald says it's to do with big deep voices… Big voice, big voice box. "

"Mr. Ego-Evanomalosovitch does have a beautiful deep voice," agrees Fern. "He's one of those people it's best not to look at when they're talking."

"Maybe he just needs a wife. Someone who can trim hair and sew. Can Mrs. Hortense sew?" Hazel asks.

"Probably. She can do everything else. She used to be married, you know, for a couple years. Her husband was killed in the war. She told us in Guidance. And that's why she wears that red scarf all winter, red like the poppies in Flanders Fields. Hers is a life blighted by war. She says it's only luck we were born here in freedom and fresh air, with lots of food... and not Ethiopia, or Cuba, or down the States. And we'd better appreciate it. She almost makes you feel guilty for being lucky, but what's the point of that?"

"No point," says Hazel. "Mr. Nitmust says World War Two isn't over yet, and the A-bomb is just a new phase of an old war. And we're on the brink of World War Three. And a nuclear war will kill us with radioactive fallout if we don't get blown to bits. Strontium 90. Life will turn to dust. Forever. And no matter how much we want to be with our loved ones when we die, we all have to take that last journey alone. Does he have to tell us stuff like that?" She suddenly feels like a heavy, dark cloth is smothering her.

Fern gulps. "Mr. Nitmust says too much gloom and doom. I get so scared, like hyenas are ripping out the back of my head. Then I repeat the twenty-third Psalm, the one we memorized for choral reading?... 'He maketh me to lie down in green pastures'..." She looks hopefully at Hazel.

"Nah, all that religious guff gets me nowhere, Fern. When someone tells me that we'll get our reward in heaven, *I know* I'll never get mine."

"Oh Haze, you're incorrigible!" Fern swats her year-older sister with her hat, then straightens its lovely green brim.

"Yep, a true heathen, that's me," says Hazel. "Who wants a silly halo anyhow? But I *would* like to fly."

"Well then, you'd better pray. Anyhow, it calms me down if I picture the green pastures and still waters. I don't really care what the rest of the Psalm means, it just makes me feel hopeful instead of scared."

"Anyhow," says Hazel, "we'd better catch up with Billy and Alvin and Pink and Julie before we fall down the pit of despair. Pink! Julie! Where are you?"

There's a high-pitched noise and two small heads duck out of sight. Aha. They're playing their stealth game, darting into Hazel and Fern's line of vision and darting away. They're quite naked, with thimbleberry and bracken wrapped around them, and they're making weird noises.

"Watch out for devil's club!" Fern shouts after them. It's not easy to miss the sprawling, eight-foot shrubs with their giant leaves and spikes of red berries, but it's easy to accidentally grab a prickly handful when bushwhacking.

"And don't lose your clothes!" Hazel yells. "…Although I doubt they'll lose anything. It's amazing how they manage to keep their stuff together. Some kind of twin system."

As Fern and Hazel mosey along the berry bush, Fern says, "First time I wore my yellow sweater, Billy spilled huckleberry jam on me and permanently ruined it. The worst of it was that I didn't know till I got to school and Dick and Hodge started telling everyone I had monkey shite on me… until Ron told them to stop or we'd skin them and hang their hides on the clothesline."

"If we had alchemy," muses Hazel, "we could make huckleberry ink that stays bright purple instead of sludge… Instead of scrubbing that stupid kitchen floor ten times a day, we could dye it gorgeous, never-fade purple. And squash cull berries on it to keep the colour up… the ones too gross to eat."

Fern likes that idea. "We could call it Wormy-Berry-Blush, or Mauve-Mildew… with mordant of stink-bug."

"Navy Inchworm," laughs Hazel.

Fern and Hazel are startled by shrill laughter. "Pink! Julie! Where did you suddenly turn up from? Fully clothed, I see."

"We need more pretzels to feed to our chipmunk. See, she's coming right up to our feet!"

"You should save those pretzels for yourselves. It's a long time till supper."

"But Fern, they taste like dirt."

"Well anyhow," says Hazel, "either help us pick these or catch up to Bill and Alv and head back to the foundations. We'll join you there soon as we can."

"Yes, Ma and Ma. See you next summer, Mommers."

"Imps! That chipmunk is following them. I tell you, those kids are already giving me gray hairs," says Hazel. "My luck, my hair will turn gray by eighteen and then fall out."

"They can't manage without us for half an hour when we're busy, but when we want them, it's catching fish on a plate. Like at the spring dance."

"Don't remind me."

"What's really strange," says Hazel, "is how we mix them up. They don't look the least bit alike.

"They have the same voice," says Fern.

"Yes!" agrees Hazel. "Their voices are interchangeable. They can take each other's places if we don't keep track who's talking." Hazel thinks for a while and asks, "Did you study symbiosis yet in science? How two organisms need each other to survive? Could Pink and Julie survive without each other, or Ron and Rich?"

"Hmmm," ponders Fern. "It's like tearing burrs off socks, trying to pull Pink and Julie apart. Like they want to be one person. And Ron and Rich, too?"

"Bravado and buffoonery, that's Ron and Rich," agrees Hazel. "But when that tiny mouse was dragging its broken foot? They were nearly bawling. They're like inky-cap mushrooms, you know, that dissolve when you touch them. Nothing left but a splot of ink."

"It must be weird being stuck with a twin," says Fern, "getting lumped together all the time, whether you like it or not. You know how we usually say Ron and Rich, not Rich and Ron? And Pink, then Julie? Maybe we should switch it around and see what happens, instead of always saying Pink first and Ron first?"

"It's usually Pink or Ron in our face doing the blabbing, so we focus on them. Domination by conversation. It's usually Ron or Pink who jumps into the fray when there's an argument going hammer and tong. Rich tries to change the subject, or Julie bumbles around doing something silly... singing into a spoon, or measuring everyone's hands, or blowing bubbles in the middle of the melee. Whatever clownish thing she can think of, until everyone's laughing or leaving in disgust."

"Do you think Julie gets sucked into Pink's aura, and Rich into Ron's?" asks Fern. "Probably nothing like that, but you know what I mean, they're just weird. Canny and uncanny. Hammer and tongs, feathers and bananas. Marshmallow hand grenades."

"That Pink just loves to get everyone going," says Hazel. "In her confidential little voice that everyone can hear. Like, 'What were you grinding in your workshop, Herald?' And, 'What was in that little dish, Rich, the one you didn't want us to see?' What was that all about? Something to do with Herald's science experiment? All those planters of marigolds?"

"I don't know, but though, an argument's still flaring between Herald and Ron. And the flowers stink worse than a bag of rotten socks."

"Mom told Herald to give Auntie Ben's wheat grinder a thorough scalding after he scrubbed it," muses Hazel. "What was he grinding? Pink knows something, but she can button up like an acorn when she wants to. And Herald and Ron and Rich keep giving each other the chicken eye."

"Heckle and Jeckle, that's Ron and Rich," laughs Fern. "I bet they'll grow up to be politicians."

"Or lawyers," says Hazel. "And Pink and Julie will join a circus and tour the world as acrobats and fortune tellers." (Actually, they'll travel the world as art teachers.)

"Herald will be a good teacher," says Fern. "He's always nice Mr. Right. Except when he's wrong. Then he's nice Mr. Wrong. And Alvin's the thinker, trying to figure everyone out. Our psychiatrist. Just think, our very own shrink. But though, Sedge and Alvin are way too deep for me."

"Sedgy's our poet," adds Hazel. "And our nature expert. And Billy's our entertainer. Let's see, have we left anybody out? Alvie's the shrink, Sedgie's the poet laureate. What about Brick?"

"Brick's everyone's kind uncle," answers Fern. "The uncle everyone wants. A professional uncle?"

"Maybe a school counselor or something like that. So we've figured out everyone except us. Who are we, Fern?"

"Let's face it, Hazel, we're second and third mother, whether we like it or not, always serious and at all times conscientious... and models of deportment... Booga booga looga!"

"Hoohoooooodle oooooo hooooooo heloooooodle!" Fern and Hazel fall together laughing, then look around for the younger girls.

"Pink? Julie? Pink and Julie!"

"We're here," they squeal, "right behind you." (Eavesdropping.)

"You'd better get your kerchiefs back on," Fern tells them, pulling a stick out of Pink's mop.

Hazel scans the mountainside. "Billy! Alvie! If that cow stands up, you're going to get kilt. There's no way she'll let you ride her! Leave her alone!"

"Are your buckets full, you guys?" calls Pink.

"Just about," fibs Billy. "There's great ones below the trail. Come on, Pink and Julie, come and help us."

"We'll come as soon as we can," yells Pink. She and Julie have other plans, singing loudly as they skip away:

Yankee Doodle went to town
Upon a painted poooony,
Stuck a feather in his cap
And called it macarooooooni!

"What about that cow?" worries Fern. "Is she alright? The poor thing must be sick, the way she's still laying there."

"All the more reason to stay away from her, Fern. Don't get any of your nurse ideas," warns Hazel.

Pink and Julie run off the trail, a safe distance from the others. They have some matches. They want to smoke some elderberry punk and they want to do it alone, without the boys bossing them how to do it, or their sisters telling them *not* to do it. (Some time in the distant future, they may shake their heads at the foibles of their own children and think, what's the use? They'll do what they do regardless of what we try to teach them. They'll wonder if the monkey-see-monkey-do mystique of fouling the lungs is some primitive instinct, like fire worship... Those who can make and control fire and smoke have heap-big magic. At the moment, smoking holds the thrill of hijinks for both sets of twins.)

At any rate, some of the Eleven, while not exactly together, are at least within calling distance of each other. Hazel, Fern, Billy, Alvin, Pink and Julie are in the same draw below second ridge, where they more or less illustrate Edict 11: Stay together when you're out in the bush.

Cow bells jangle as the dairy herd ambles across the mountainside, their bulging udders rumbling. A sultry haze has settled over the afternoon, the miasma that often precedes a thunderstorm. The kids look around restively. The bugs are getting vicious. Thunder grumbles closer.

Alvin can now be heard buzzing on a kazoo while Billy shouts in sing-song doggerel, something along the lines of:

Melon, rebellion, gourd, manured
a bright felon named Melon,
a bright yellow fellow...
fat-headed scallion...
dum-dee-dum...
He sat on a cigar and blew very far...
blue manure, gourd,
gourd melon... rapscallion...

* * *

(In a ravine on the back of the mountain the tall dark form listens, motionless, as the boys' racket catapults down a riddle of forgotten adits, mine shafts, and tunnels; through chasms shiny with mica; along gnarled roots in ancient creek-beds; past granite, quartz and iron pyrites, filaments of gold and lichen; through a crevice in a cliff-face, to a shaggy ear far below.)

* * *

CHAPTER 22
The Storyteller: Julie, 2005

TO THIS DAY, JULIE ignores the rules about not hiking alone and enjoys it immensely. Alone in the back country, past the end of the road and the tumbledown farmhouse, the world is quiet. Not even a dog barking. In the mid-afternoon heat, she wanders into a birch grove. A towhee flits along the ground ahead of her. The shade is soothing. Her retinas feel singed by the bright orange, yellow, white, and purple flowers she can see even with her eyes closed: hawkweed, buttercup, daisy, vetch, and everywhere, the overlay-underlay of ripe huckleberries.

A mosquito whines in her ear.

Time to get moving. Her bucket is only half-full and, though her shoulders are starting to feel like a bag of knots, she tightens her bucket tie. There are a lot of berries waiting to be picked. She wades into the bushes.

As she settles into the task, huckleberry stories flutter through her thoughts. She's kept her school habit of thinking out compositions while hiking. Pages settle randomly into her mind's files as she picks berries, hand over fist, fist over hand.

Random files. No index. The pursuit of the wild berry is far from a linear journey. In fact, people have been known to go in circles for hours on the chase. That's why the sport of huckleberry picking has some important rules, some of which are straightforward and some of which need explanation.

For instance, Rule 16 is neat and to the point: All rules are subject to change. Whereas Rule 76 is complex and convoluted: Don't knowingly pick berries on someone else's property. This rule has undergone numerous changes over the years, especially around that word 'knowingly.' Huckleberry rights are a complicated business, and must be looked at in the context of the countryside in which they evolved.

The meandering edges of rural properties have historically spilled onto crown land to make room for woodpiles and extra garden space. More than one potato patch has thrived on railroad right-of-way. Dairy cows have run open range on well-packed trails throughout the countryside, while old fences, gradually bowed down by snow and trespass, have permitted handy shortcuts through the valley bottoms. "Frank" fences are not uncommon, named after the man who was notorious for gradually replacing tumbledown wire and posts with bed springs and gutted dressers, stove pipes and bedsteads, lashed together with vetch. Such haphazard barricades sprout wonderful huckleberry bushes in sheltered nooks. There's nothing a huckleberry likes better than taking root in a drawer full of birch leaves.

In old rural landscapes, there's seldom a clear marker where one property begins and another ends. If, perchance, there is a post, it's likely not in line with actual surveys. At any rate, berry patches have never known boundaries. The unmown edges of property absorb rain, shelter roots, and produce berries which are extraordinarily plump and nectarous.

Uncertainty about boundaries may account for the skulking behavior of some berry pickers, like batty Mrs. Orack and grabby Aggie Turkle. When they see large, over-ripe berries dropping to the ground, untended in a back lot, they pick them covertly. Waste is a terrible thing.

An important rule for people like that is number 2: Tell no one where the berries are. (Except next of kin.) (In an emergency.)

Some rules are innate and subtle. For instance, Rule 47M: When near a road, hide if a car comes. And Rule 47J: Avoid making tracks in damp sandy soil.

There are some hard-core rules, like Rule 11K: If you're under duress and have to give information about the location of a patch, be vague or prevaricate.

A rule that is seldom employed but important to remember is Rule 86: People who know too much may have to be done away with. Aggie Turkle is lucky to be alive.

Rule 79: If you're truly to be successful at harvesting wild berries, you need to be a bit rough and tough. You can't let the toxic prickles of devil's club, the insect bites, or social niceties divert you.

CHAPTER 23
A Plot is Laid

RON, RICH, BRICK, HERALD, and Sedge are scattered at random over the mountainside. Half a mile away from the kazoo duet, Brick has decided it's time to reclaim the mother-lode soup pot. He clambers up one ridge of elephant-hide onto the next and looks around. He back-tracks, scratches his head, scratches his arms. A horsefly nips him between the shoulder blades and he jumps with a bellow. Sedge and Herald whoop in reply, climbing toward him.

Brick is swatting flies like a madman, shouting as they approach, "Didn't we leave our stuff here?!"

Herald wipes his glasses on his shirt, scowls at the smudged lenses, and slaps them back on his face. "It sure looks like the right place."

Sedge grabs her gray sweater, camouflaged where she'd stashed it in the rocks near the soup pot. "It *is* the right place! Here's my sweater, right where I left it!"

Herald looks at Brick with horror. "Where are Rich and Ron? Is this one of their nitwit stunts!"

"Har! They wouldn't dare!" replies Brick. "But who else could?"

Sedge gasps, "You think Ron and Rich took the soup pot?"

Brick ponders a moment, then emits a long, blood-curdling roar, his eyes glittering with fury. Sedge shoves her hair under her brown bucket-hat, bracing herself for combat. The three of them huddle. Muttering and scowling, they slap mosquitoes and make a plan.

First thing is to find the soup pot.

This task is annoying, but it's not difficult to locate Brick's pack leaning against a stump near a trampled area that reeks of cigar smoke. Beside the pack, the soup pot is not very subtly hidden.

Next, Brick guards their belongings while Sedge and Herald skulk around to locate the teenage renegades. Without their packs, Sedge and Herald are light-footed, moving quickly and quietly. Before long, they hear breathy whistling. They peer around a massive bull pine, and there's Stick-Rich twenty paces away, looking like a skinny beaver as he industriously whittles a chunk of pine, whistling a repetitious little stick-beaver song. Good old Rich, so sweet and innocent. Sedge and Herald stifle laughter and creep away.

Next they track down Ron. They hear him, too, before they see him. The sound of sliding rocks draws their attention to his robust figure climbing on all fours across an ore heap a quarter mile away, fleecing stray berry bushes on his way across. He's sending cascades of small rocks down the slope behind him. Look out below!

Sedge and Herald hurry back to Brick, who is sacked out against a tree, dry-sorting. They tell him where Rich and Ron are and they plot their revenge while they pick sticks and leaves out of the mother pot. (Their words could use a little clean-sorting too.) It would be too simple to merely wait by the soup pot and ambush the twins when they come back for it. Instead, they'll haul it back to the foundations, rather than abandon it again. That will scare the rascals worse than an ambush, if they go to retrieve the soup-pot and it's gone. They plan a route that will skirt around Rich and Ron back to Stooge's, where they're counting on finding Hazel and Fern. It will be a slow hurry through thick brush, because they'll have to avoid the trail. They had hoped for more help when the time came to lug back all the berries. Brick and Herald will carry the soup pot between them, with buckets in their other hands, and Sedge will carry two buckets. They hope to leave their bounty with Hazel and Fern, then back-track and, if all goes well, surprise their poaching brothers.

Before setting out, Brick, Sedge, and Herald let loose loud, wicked laughter which echoes horribly, intended to strike fear into the hearts of their foe. It does. Even the innocent feel a tremor of alarm. The dreadful duo is soon to witness the glorious revenge of this conspiring trio.

Meanwhile, Hazel and Fern and the younger kids are nervously wondering what that furious roar was about.

"Was it Brick?" asks Fern.

"Yup. I'd say so," answers Billy.

"He sure sounded mad," says Pink

"Maybe he spilled his berries," suggests Hazel.

"I'm glad I'm not over there," says Fern.

"Me too," says Alvin.

Brick normally has lofty patience for his mischievous siblings, but they all know, when he blows his stack he means it. His hair isn't brick red for nothing.

As the mad laughter ricochets and fades, Pink and Julie giggle nervously, scuttling closer to their big sisters. Billy gazes up the mountain with a worried frown. Alvin thwacks a rock with a stick. The whine of mosquitoes is loud in the gloomy silence, until another peal of demonic laughter shatters the air.

"Sounded like Herald and Brick, didn't it, Haze ?" asks Billy.

"Yeah, and Sedge."

"Sounded like they're all going nuts!" says Alvin.

"Scary nuts," says Julie.

Fern shudders.

"Anyhow, it's nothing we did, is it?" asks Pink.

"They got no reason to be mad at us, have they?" asks Julie.

"Well, not that I know of. Not this time, anyhow," says Billy. Seeing everyone's anxious faces, he scratches his head. "I got a question for you, Haze. What word do you use to describe a mean melon?"

"Oh, what, Billy?"

"Melon-evolent... get it? Like malevolent?"

"Billy, that's kind of lame. Kind of nil, Bill." says Hazel.

"Kind of willy-nilly, Billy," adds Fern.

"Silly Billy," giggles Julie.

CHAPTER 24
A Little Remorse

A QUARTER MILE AWAY, Stick-Rich makes another serious effort to fill his four pound Phoenix Jam can before he once more finds a good chunk of pine to whittle and a warm rock to sit on. Occasionally he gives his bucket a rattle to keep up appearances, and it hasn't taken long to get his hands stained enough to pass inspection. (His carvings often have a purple overcast.)

Rich knows he won't deserve any cash from the jam order, but heck, he can make enough for an inner-tube by carving miniature dolls and birds. Julie and Pink sell them on the playground for a share of the profits, which keeps them in embroidery thread and seed beads. Four kids want birds. Dabbed with paint and coloured thread, they'll sell for five cents each. He can buy a nineteen-cent tube of red oil paint at the paper office. Cardinals sell well, especially in a used and redecorated penny match box. The girls will spend ages decorating boxes—even Hazel and Fern, when they're in the mood. They have a family business, ha ha. Ron and Herald can carve whistles. Sedge specializes in stick puppets dressed in bright ribbons. "Oops!" Rich's thoughts are getting carried away and he's decapitated a finicky doll. He roots in his pack for a larger project... a palm-sized bird he's been working on for a couple weeks. He brushes off crumbs and burnishes it with a candle stub, then carefully notches more details into the feathers.

When Brick roars, Rich drops his knife. He desperately searches the bushes to retrieve it. Hurriedly stuffing his carving into his knapsack, he climbs a rock pile to have a look around... just when Herald, Sedge and Brick release their crazy laughter. "Oh, oh. That didn't sound good," he mutters.

A chill creeps up his legs from a crevice in the rocks under his feet. He jumps to more solid ground, listening for his twin, filled with foreboding.

Ron is eating a handful of berries when Brick yells. The berries stick in his craw. Craning forward to listen, he jumps half out of his boots when he hears the manic laughter, clouting his head on a branch. "Blast!"

Rubbing his head, Ron listens to his own voice echo, mingling with the echo of the demonic laughter that is fading, falling, disintegrating, gone. A sinister lull pervades the mountain. He tosses another handful of berries down his throat, then trots off to find his twin. He hears Rich's low hoot not far off and skedaddles towards him.

The boys collide in a hazel thicket, falling over each other with relieved cackles that they quickly stifle.

"Did you hear Brick?" gasps Rich. "Holy catswallop! I guess they noticed the berries missing!"

"Serves them right for being such know-it-alls, " says Ron. "Time they had a good shock treatment. But that laughing was creepy... or was it howling? Sounded demented, whatever it was. Out of control, like."

"Like when we play monkeys-in-the-zoo, but for real," agrees Rich. "Like, not just yelling our heads off, jumping at each other in the dark in Mom and Dad's room when they're not home."

"Way worse, Rich... out in the wild... no mommy to stop them if they try to murder us... Sounded like they might. Brick sounded real mad. And that laughing was way too weird."

"Shoot, I didn't think they'd go totally bonkers... Now what, Ron?"

Another burst of hideous cackling ricochets across the mountain. The pranksters stop in their tracks.

"We'd better lie low for a while, Ron."

"Yeah, like maybe a few days."

The thirteen-year-olds fling themselves on the ground, truculent but with inner quaking. Ron and Rich often find themselves threading a fine line through the loopholes of sibling demography.

Like many in large families, Ron and Rich compete fiercely for territory. For them, as for Pink and Julie, it's a dual struggle for identity as a unit and also as individuals. In the middle of the muddle, they often find themselves in the soup for unknowingly tramping on someone's sensibilities. Singed and surly, they quickly get over it by laughing their heads off at no one knows what. Who can blame them if at times they purposely ruffle feathers just for the fun of it? The older kids don't know how hard it is being them. Grumbling, they sit and wait for the dust to settle.

"We have four older kids telling us what to do, plus Mom and Dad and all our teachers," says Ron. "And five younger kids and all their friends who *we* have to tell what to do. It's a lot to keep track of. Did you ever think how many rules we're supposed to follow in a day?"

"Rules, Ron?"

"Yeah, Rich, like the right way to do things... you know... Hold your pencil properly, don't spit, keep your feet to yourself. Don't talk back, don't talk, think about your future, what are you going to do with your life if you can't get paid for tomfoolery?"

"Yeah," agrees Rich. "Like what I had to write one hundred times: 'I will not slouch in my desk with my head on the back of my chair and snore loudly during grammar.'"

"And write in proper sentences, not just columns of each word done one hundred times, yak yak yak."

As Ron and Rich crouch on a log grumbling, they get onto the subject of sister rules. Bouts of being "straightened up" by Fern and Hazel keep them on edge, defensive about their slovenly ways. Even neat Herald cringes when he hears that particular high screech of the older girls after he's been in the kitchen. Ron and Rich now start mimicking girls' voices in falsetto.

"Wring out the mop before you put it away… Stand it with the strings at the top so it'll dry before next century."

"Put down the toilet seat. Always flush the toilet. Except when we're low on water in the summer, then don't flush if it's only number one."

"Wipe your feet, hang up your clothes!"

"Wipe the cloth all over the dishes, don't just wave it over the sink… and rinse them! And feel with your hand to make sure you got all the muck off. A clean dish is a smooth dish."

"And wash the handles and outsides of pots, not just the insides."

"Don't flick water, you're getting the window smeary."

"Wash the sink, wash the taps. Wash the soap!"

"Don't put a serving bowl in the fridge with only a few peas in it so's you don't have to wash it."

"Don't use the dish rag on the floor. And don't use the floor rag on the dishes! Nag, nag, nag."

Some individuals are like chunks of ore with hidden seams of gold. They resist the daily rub of families trying to bring out the best in them. In spite of the exertion of school and society to make them conform, Ron and Rich have strong minds of their own, like everyone in their family. They don't suspect that through the instruction, criticism and conflict of school and home, through the alembic of rules, they're gradually being polished to bring out the best in them, whether they like it or not.

Rich and Ron happily resist domestication as far as possible, feeling it's not in their best interests to learn how to clean toilets and sew on buttons. Even so, the niggling complexity of family life gets them down at times. That's why they have to cause havoc every so often: to maintain their integrity.

In a larch tree overhead, a squirrel unzips a tirade of abuse. A raven makes a noise like a sweaty armpit and chuckles.

Ron laughs, "Ah, shaddup!" He kicks a rotten log, eliciting the attack of a zillion flying bugs which the twins slap with their scout hats. He lights his cigar stub to make a smoke screen and they cough and snort until, dizzy again, they grow pensive. They start to think. A trifle belatedly, they realize their mischief with the soup pot may not have been their brightest idea.

"Herrackk," coughs Rich, "these skeeters are like eating me alive. Let's get moving. That filthy cigar didn't keep them away for long."

"I guess we better get the soup pot," croaks Ron.

However, now that Ron and Rich decide to retrieve their booty, they find they're heading in opposite directions.

"It's over this way."

"No way, remember, we put it, like, by that stump."

"Yeah, but we were above the Second Ridge, weren't we?"

"That one over there?"

"Uh. Crap."

They stare around them at the many folds on the elephant-hide mountain. "Or was it that ridge over there? Uh oh."

Rich and Ron trudge back and forth, up and down and around and back. Their nonchalance soon turns to irritation verging on panic.

"We can't have missed it… It's big as a cow."

"Even if the pack's fallen over, it should be easy to spot."

Mosquitoes attracted by the twins' frenzy are a scourge in their faces. The boys are bone-weary, thirsty, and hot. The air is windless, heavy with an approaching storm. A sick despair steals over them as they realize they've lost not only Brick's pack, but the mother of all buckets, the five-gallon soup pot full of huckleberries. They've lost the family fortune. Furtive partners in crime, back and forth they clamber across the hillside, dreading the moment the older kids catch up with them. Exhausted, they slump into the shade of a pine tree, only to leap up, swarming with red ants. They're bitten on their bites. Once more, they tramp over the last gully.

The jokers are beginning to feel pangs of remorse.

They know their brothers and sisters each have inner longings, just as they do, for things they can't afford. The list is long: an inner tube, silver trinkets, a radio, a watch, an electric mixer, chocolate, binoculars, hiking boots, gum, books, soft slippers, a pair of pliers, a lacrosse ball, something nice to wear: things for which they hope to get a few coins from the sale of their berries.

After perhaps half an hour of getting more and more desperate and tired, Rich looks at Ron and shakes his head. "Somethin' ain't makin' sense to me."

"Yeah, like how come we can't hear those guys hollering anymore?"

"Right… It's way too quiet out here."

They perch on a couple of boulders under a bull pine, heads hanging.

A raven coughs. It peers down at them with an eye like a steel bearing and cackles.

"Anyhow," complains Ron, "I'm starved and the rest of my grub's in Brick's pack. I didn't have room for it."

"You didn't got to bring that football, did you Ron?"

"Yes I did have to, 'cause Shwartzy wants it back, and if he went to our house and asked for it when I'm not there, Mom'd give it to him sure as shootin'... 'cause she hates it after it broke the crock lid and like now she has to use a board over the rotten cabbage. And the trade was fair and square. I gave Shwartzy fifteen comics for it and now he's read them all and he wants the football back, and he ain't gonna get it."

"Here, you can have some of my spits," offers Rich. "But cripes, that thing's not even a regulation football."

"Better than nothing. We can play catch if we ever get back to the field. We need to practice if we want to make the team. Anyhow, it makes a great pillow!" Ron tucks it under his neck and lays back, pretending he's comfortable until a mosquito flies up his nose and he chokes on a sunflower seed shell. A deer fly bites him on the cheek; he slaps his cheek too hard and jumps up. "Zip-blasted ass-pissers! Let's get outta here!"

Ravenous flies and mosquitoes are now joined by a tightening web of midges. On another flank of the elephant back, a bucket clanks and someone curses. There's the sound of someone running through bushes, then running back.

A pair of nuthatches harangues over a clump of thistle seeds. "Cha cha cheee... nag nag nag neee!"

CHAPTER 26
Good-bye, Pink

A MILE AWAY, PINK and Julie start one of their long, quiet arguments. They know if they disagree loudly, they'll quickly have a few brothers and sisters butting in, complicating things. Corrections and criticisms are not required. The twins see eye to eye most of the time, but when they don't, they can't rest until they do. Like the inner workings of a single organism trying to maintain equilibrium, the twins are best left to sort things out on their own.

"You can't go without me, Pink!"

"But I have to. I won't get lost, Julie!"

"Yes you will, Pink. You can't help it."

"I won't, I promise. Anyhow, I don't get lost, I get sidetracked," Pink insists.

"Sometimes it's the same thing."

"Is not, Julie!"

Pink and Julie move further from Fern and Hazel as they get more agitated. The problem is, Julie has just noticed that Pink's hairband is missing under her kerchief. This is not a trivial matter.

The aqua-flowered hairband has talisman status for the twins, cherished by both of them. It's not only their favourite colour, it's made of shiny new plastic in an era when plastic has not yet infiltrated every aspect of human life, an era when the children in a large family seldom get anything that is not homemade or hand-me-down. It's a gift from the Fuller Brush Man, along with a red plastic frypan spoon-rest that sits in state on the windowsill with only one small dent. The aqua hairband is not only brand new and unmended, it's an item of personal vanity, even more precious.

Pink is determined to find the hairband by herself because she's the one who lost it, and Julie had practically begged her not to wear it berry-picking. It's a matter of honour. She knows the sacrifice it took for Julie to give it to her in the first place, because Julie most wanted it herself. In twin logic, the ornament had been bound to meet with disaster because they had not agreed on when to wear it.

"You better let me come with you, Pink!"

"No! If we both leave, Hazel and Fern will notice and make us come back. You need to stay here and keep singing! I know where to find it."

Julie eventually accepts Pink's reasoning and begins to sing half-heartedly, "La, la… la…"

Pink tightens her pack straps, gives Julie a quick hug, and tramps off on her quest, with Julie anxiously watching after her. "La la la la la la la…"

Fern and Hazel have no idea Pink has left. As usual, they're deep in conversation, currently about the best way to get burrs out of hair, pitch off pants, and more profound things… such as what makes otherwise sensible, responsible people like Hazel want to scale tree-tops and do acrobatics on cliffs and railway trestles. Fern admires Hazel's "agility ability." But "wouldn't Auntie Ben's cat, Purrfect, have eventually come down from the roof without you balancing on the chimney ledge to rescue it?"

Hazel won't admit even to herself that she especially pushes her limits when a certain tall classmate is around. She now stretches her arms wide, says, "It's about getting beyond the humdrum… I want my own space to myself, to live my own ideals. I could live in a little cabin on a mountaintop, with nothing around me but air. I'd never come down except for food… and books…"

Fern ponders this and unconsciously takes the role of second mother as she asks, "Wouldn't it be cold up there, and windy?"

"I'd be okay. But actually… if you're on the very top, on a pin-nacle, you're confined to just a tiny foot-hold… even though you can see forever… Freedom is a state of mind."

Fern says, "If you have imagination, your mind can go any-where, even if you're inside a box. If you can think of anything besides getting out of the box."

Hazel says she'd die in a box. "I have to have space around me. In my next life, I'll be a bird… A raven, because they're big and strong… They can soar and they can eat anything… and they can cuss the whole world at the top of their lungs. I want to transcend."

"Well… transcend what?" asks her practical sister.

"Oh, I don't know. You're looking at me as if I've grown a beak!" says Hazel. "I'd transcend the ordinary, the washing dishes and minding kids, the same walls, the same boring schoolwork. I'd get away from all that."

Fern thinks it would be wonderful to have her own room, but she wants it snug inside a house. That would be ample space for her. She likes safe, level places, home and comfort. "I want my life to go along evenly. Like rolling fields or a calm lake. I like moun-tains too, but I want to always have a level place to come back to. I don't understand people wanting to be on the edge."

Hazel tries to explain. "I don't think it's really the edge I like when I think of high places… Really, I would like a summit to myself, more than a pinnacle; an alpine meadow with a clear view, where I would have no responsibilities but my own survival.

Where I'd be free. It's hard trying to set a good example all the time. Everyone expects me to mother them, even Herald sometimes. But you're the one who's a natural born nurse, Fern. I never want to be a nurse. Maybe I'll be a pilot."

(Years later, thanks to scholarships, Hazel and Fern will have professional careers, but not what they anticipate. The Hazel who approached challenges like a rolling barrel of rocks will emerge sophisticated as polished granite, an anthro-archeologist flying the world to study cliff people and their dwellings, modern and ancient. Hazel will never have children of her own, but she'll dote on her many nieces and nephews, swooping into their midst at every opportunity for fun and laughter. Fern, to everyone's surprise, decides she doesn't want to be a nurse. Ever the domestic one, she becomes a household electrician instead. Her editor husband will stay home with their five children alternate weeks, while Fern works where she loves to be, in the heart of homes, wiring them for washers, dryers and entertainment centers. But that's far in the future.)

In the meantime, Hazel and Fern are so caught up in their conversation that they barely register Julie's repetitious monotone: "Found a peanut, found a peanut, found a peanut last night…" At any rate, Alvin and Billy are making enough noise for five kids, Alvin humming like ten kazoos and Billy shouting limericks. He's got one just about nailed and he's pounding it home.

A gust of wind sends a fir branch clattering to the forest floor.

A squirrel rewinds hysterically.

Ravens shout, "Bloook! Brack, Broook!"

Further up the mountainside, Ron and Rich are still anxiously searching for the soup pot and Brick's pack, their faces streaked with sweat, juice, and dead bugs.

"Rich stops in his tracks. "I just had a horrible thought. What if the Kludges took it?"

"Pig shite!" says Ron. "I never thought of that. Do you think they're out here?"

"I dunno, but seems we should of found it by now. It'd be just like those idiots!

Thunder rumbles.

CHAPTER 25
A Belt Slips

FAR AWAY, SEDGE RE-POSITIONS her buckets while Herald and Brick switch hands on the soup pot, steeling themselves to cross a scree slope. The steep morass of small rocks slips and shifts under their feet, sending more rocks cascading behind them. Their legs feel like over-stretched rubber bands by the time they find a solid place to rest. They gloomily gnaw on hard pretzels that smell slightly rancid and automatically dry-sort their buckets.

"Ouch! I think I broke a tooth," yelps Herald. "These pretzels are hard as rocks."

"Maybe the yeast was too old… maybe that package that fell in the sink?" wonders Sedge. "But it didn't get very wet."

"Did Ron n' Rich help make these pretzels?" Brick wants to know.

"They helped stir for a while."

"Hmmm… I hope there's no bone dust in them," mutters Herald.

Sedge chokes. "Bone dust? What d'ya mean, bone dust?"

"Oh, nothing," Herald coughs. "You know, elbow grease, bone dust, sweat of the brow, the hard work that goes into making things. They're salty, at least. And we need salt to replenish our sweat factories."

"Lovely," murmurs Sedge.

"Only thing is, I'm getting thirsty." says Herald. "Sure is getting hot. I hope the other kids are closer to a creek than we are. How much water we got left there, Brick?"

"Not much, Hare. But we've got about a hundred pounds of plums. Kind of mashed up but juicy. Let's eat some, eke out the water."

Sedge doles out handfuls, laughing as the red pulp slides through her fingers, "I feel like a mother Sasquatch with a fresh kill."

Herald and Brick hunch their shoulders, snorting, drooling, grunting, "Urf, ulk, glup."

Sedge, Brick and Herald get ready to pack up, but can't quite get the volition to move on. They continue to dry-sort, tipping their buckets from side to side to pick out debris.

"Did Billy tell you what you get when you cross a plum with a rock?" asks Sedge.

Herald sighs, "No, what?"

"A plum-a-granite. Get it? Pomegranate?"

"Yuk!" groans Brick. "He says he wants to have a radio program when he grows up. I wouldn't put it past him; he's sure got the gift of the gab."

"He'll do it," says Herald. "He's making friends at the radio station already, trying to get a slot for the school in the fall. 'The School on Air', with guess who as emcee."

Sedge is rooting around in Brick's pack again. "We could prob'ly live out here for a week with all this."

"Heaven forbid," says Brick. "I just wish Rich and Ron were hauling it. Some of it's their stuff. I've got Ron's grub, although why he trusted it with me, I don't know. Ronnie needs food every fifteen minutes. He could starve!"

"What if it wasn't them that hid the soup pot and the pack?" worries Sedge.

"Oh, it was them alright. Just their kind of thing. Anyhow, no one else ever comes out here," says Herald.

"What about the Kludges?"

"Nah, their turf's way over the Dorsey Bluffs."

Sedge, Herald and Brick pull each other to their feet and plod onward, trying to keep their minds off their sore hands and backs, with the niggling hunch that their detour is a bit of a mistake that will be way harder than they expected. What ordinarily would have taken a half-hour is becoming a long, grueling trudge.

"I hate to say it, but we've got too many berries." Herald is exasperated. He'd kind of forgotten they'd have so much scree going this way.

"It seems like there's way more gravity when you have to go slow," muses Sedge. "The slower we go, the heavier these buckets get and the slower we go."

"That darn Ron and Rich, putting us to all this trouble." Brick and Herald start inventing horrid ways to punish the twins... Make them eat cow pies... Ants in their soup... Lock them overnight in the chicken coop.

"Come on you guys," laughs Sedge. "They were just playing a joke. As if you guys never do."

"Us? Dear old Brick and Herald? They're worse hooligans than we've ever been," says Herald. "Don't they realize what barbarians they are? Especially Ron. Rich specializes more at being ridiculous, like Julie, hamming it up so nobody knows what's going on. Why can't they be sensible and gentlemanly like us, eh, Brick! But that's half the problem. They *can* be perfect gentlemen when they want, Ronald Henry and Richard Harvey, with their 'yes sirs' and 'no ma'ams.' Contrite looks and sweet smiles, convincing everyone they're misunderstood angels. Ha. Dad says their antics will catch up with them some day. Something tells me this is the day!"

As it turns out, it's also Herald's day—for a lesson in responsibility and forethought. He will grow up three notches during that long day in the wilds, with the ten younger kids and no one older to pick up the slack.

"What gets me is when they laugh at themselves," says Brick. "Like donkeys on their hind legs. But next thing, we're laughing and forgetting to be mad at them. That's what makes me maddest, when I stop to think about it."

"Better not think about it," suggests Sedge.

"We wouldn't have to think about it if we didn't have to take this horrible detour," says Herald. "If we didn't have to pay them back for stealing the berries."

Justice can be a heavy burden.

"The worst punishment for Rich and Ron will be looking for the soup pot, thinking they've lost it," says Herald. "And worrying what we're going to do to them! Like when Uncle Percival made us cut our own switches, eh, Brick? When we put slugs in his gumboots? Who would've thought a few slugs could make such a gluey mess?"

"Haven't you ever had to clean one off the bottom of your foot when you're going barefoot?" asks Sedge.

"Big banana slugs. Yar. As soon as I saw his socks I knew we were in for it, but I didn't really think Uncle Purse would whip us," says Brick. "Not till I saw he was furious. Worrying about the whipping was the worst part. And then he barely flicked us with the switches."

"Flicked us with switches, witched us with twitches. Frisked us with stitches… Arg, I need a rest." Herald and Brick stagger to a halt, wedging the soup pot between two boulders, their legs feeling like rubber.

Sedge, who's been suffering in silence, thankfully collapses on the ground. "I feel like my arms have stretched about ten inches!"

Her brothers give her a concerned look. Sedge is tall and athletic, but her face is crimson and one shoulder's twitching. They're used to her quietly carrying on, and forget she's only twelve. Herald unbuckles a canteen from his pack and passes it to her. Brick puts his hand on her shoulder and says, "Rest all you need, Hedge. We've got all day." Brick finds her an apple. She eats it, core and all.

Their water is lukewarm, but they're glad of a swig. They can hear the tantalizing sound of a creek cascading high above them where it funnels into a rocky gorge, unreachable until it spills into a dozen glittering streams on the lower flanks of the mountain. They've skirted the main trails, encountering no one and no water. The sky is flickering with heat lightning.

Eventually, they struggle to their feet. "We've just about got it licked," says Herald. "Now if we can only make it across this last ore heap without breaking our necks. We'll have to be slow and careful."

Were those words a jinx? After one last slurp of tepid water, they've gotten reorganized and Brick is shrugging into his packboard when disaster strikes. The belt that holds it together gives way. The pack swings sideways, knocking Brick off-balance, and the rock he's standing on tips over, hurling him headlong. He lets out a groan as he tries to hoist himself to his feet.

"Ow… My arm… It's twisted."

"Oh no!"

CHAPTER 27
Mayhem

HERALD, BRICK AND SEDGE, Hazel, Fern, Ron, Rich, Billy, Alvin, Julie, and Pink have gotten thoroughly scattered across the mountainside, having long ago abandoned hope of staying together. The clouds are heavy, hanging low as cow's udders at milking time, ruminating, preparing to let down.

Herald and Sedge are trying not to tumble down the scree slope as they help Brick to his feet. It's hard to keep their balance on rocks which keep shifting under their feet, but they manage to improvise a sling for Brick's arm. Most of the first-aid supplies are in Fern's pack, about a mile and a half away. But with the ingenious use of a smooth piece of wood, a scarf, a spare bucket tie, and some helpful suggestions from Brick, they splint his arm.

Far away, Ron and Rich are behind Second Ridge, wandering in ever more lop-sided orbits, searching for the soup pot. They have only a shred of hope now of surviving the day. They have lost not only the soup pot but all their bombast and most of their bravado.

As for Hazel, Fern, Billy, Alvin, and Julie, they're still finding lush berries scattered within a half mile radius of the old mill site, where rusted chunks of machinery lie abandoned like mammoth bones. Their buckets are getting heavy.

Only Julie knows her five-year-old twin has gone off by herself.

On her solitary quest, Pink has gotten lost while looking for what she lost, as people often do. She'd been sure she knew where to find her hairband, picturing so clearly how it must be caught in the alders where she'd chased Alvin. Or did she lose it when the hawthorns ripped a chunk out of her hair? She'd been so busy trying to hold her scalp on, she hadn't given a thought to the hairband at the time. The treasured strip of brand-new aqua-flowered plastic glows in her mind's eye. She has hunted through a lot of brush of all sorts since she left Julie, and her only glimpse of bright aqua was a scrap of robin's eggshell.

Pink is used to being with her twin and having older sisters and brothers keeping track of her when she's not keeping track of herself. It's quite a while before she admits that she's lost.

Julie had been right. Pink should never have gone off by herself in this hinterland of mine pits, bears, and thirst. Not that Julie would have kept her on the right path, necessarily, but at least they would have been lost together. They usually stay near one of the cow trails, sure they can follow the cows back at the end of the day if need be. But Pink hasn't heard a cowbell for a very long time, nor seen a cow plop.

Her path has suddenly dwindled to nothing, the way deer trails do. In the forest there are endless trails leading off trails leading nowhere.

A pitiful image flashes before Pink, of Alvin with his skinny chicken feet caked with mud, socks in shreds, his ankles scraped, his shoes probably still falling to China. She imagines how far away those shoes must be. Thinking of the infinitely stretching distance makes her dizzy.

She shakes her herself. Alvin's okay now. She'll be okay too. She won't be gloomy. She can be brave. She remembers Hazel telling her it's best to stay in one place when you're lost. Trouble is, she doesn't know where she was when she got lost. If she sits down right now and waits, will someone find her? They're all somewhere on the mountain, Herald and Rich and the rest. But not here. Pink crouches on a mossy log, brushing her fingers over the miniature forest. Kelly green, jade green, sage, Logan green, emerald, moss and clover green. If Julie were here they'd make fairy towns, but there doesn't seem much point in it by herself.

Pink begins to focus on the sound of water trickling. It's not far off, a splashing sound, tantalizing to one as thirsty as she is. She needs that cool sweetness. She has to have some. Raspy with thirst, scratchy with thirst, she pushes through thimble-berry and bracken and skids down a steep bank like a wild creature, where water sparkles over smooth rocks. She lies face-down, slurping and lapping her fill, then sits back on her haunches to watch a dipper. Pushing off with its short legs, the small black bird plunges into the icy stream and jumps out on the other shore, bouncing on a rock. Dip and bob, dip and bob. Its song is a delightful burble, whistle, tweet.

Pink has another long drink, face-down, before she has a good look around. The place where she'd slid down the bank looks too steep to climb back up. She wades upstream, looking for an easier route. The bank gets steeper and is hung with loose boulders. She comes to a wide spot and hops across the creek, rock by rock, to a sandy place where she can climb out easily on the far side.

With a thrill of discovery, she's sure she's the first person to ever stand right there. An explorer's mantle gently settles on her shoulders with a whisper and a shimmer. She runs to investigate a patch of shooting stars, more than she's ever seen in one place. She kneels to memorize every detail so that later, she can recite them to Julie; how the magenta petals curl back from the golden crowns.

Is Julie patiently waiting for her to come back? She wouldn't have told Fern and Hazel. Would she? Pink wishes Julie were with her now, another pair of eyes to take it all in, and sends out a silent message... Come and find me, Julie. Come and find me.

Led by curiosity, Pink slowly walks along the creek bank, brushing her hands through asters, timothy, and vetch. The nicely spaced trees provide intervals of dark green shade. The ground is pleasant underfoot, springy with fir needles. A smidgen of bright red catches her eye. It shiny. But it's nothing but a candy wrapper caught on a thistle. She picks up another one, and a bit further, another. Yuck. Litter in this special place. That means she's not the first one here.

She shoves the wrappers into a pocket. Hazel teases her and Julie about coming down with "Magpie-opia," colour blindness brought on by too much admiring of bright objects. She wonders if Hazel has seen the corner by the attic window, where she and Julie have created a glittery bower. Another shiny wrapper finds its way into her pocket.

Pink hears boys' voices. Her brothers? She walks around what looks like a natural fort of gigantic boulders, some taller even than Herald. Behind one of them there's a lean-to of branches. All around, there's a jumble of old boards and chicken-wire, a burnt-out wood stove, rusty stovepipes, smashed bottles, a rotten sock, and more candy wrappers. The voices are not her brothers'. They wouldn't dare litter in nature's beauty. Pink creeps closer as she hears hoots of laughter... mean laughter... and a funny grunting sound that she can't identify. She peers around a boulder and sees four boys poking at something with sticks. They don't notice her as she skulks forward to get a better view. What she sees is a porcupine, curled up half under itself with fear while the boys harass him. He's the one grunting so pathetically. She watches with breathless horror.

An instant later, mayhem ensues as Pink hurls her forty pounds of outrage behind the knees of the tallest boy. His legs buckle and he staggers, knocking over the boy next to him, who tries to regain his balance by grabbing the next guy. Like gangly dominoes they fall over each other into a heap around the porcupine. The only one left standing is Pink. She watches anxiously as, indignantly, the porcupine waddles away, swatting its tail from side to side, dragging his heavy armour through the tangle of arms and legs. There is screaming.

Pink throws her head back and laughs. "Serves you right, you big bully sissies, tormenting a poor little innocent porcupine!"

The boys stare at her, open-mouthed.

"Where did you come from, Squirt?"

"Don't call me Squirt, and how dare you throw your trash on nature?! Take that!" and she chucks a wad of candy wrappers at the nearest gaping mouth. It squawks.

When Pink has a conniption fit, you want to get out of her way. She was already furious with these guys before she even set eyes on them, and now she's really mad.

As for the boys, they are totally thrown off-kilter by her temper and by the excruciating pain of the quills piercing their thick hides. None of them is free of the black and white needles, which dig deeper into their flesh with every move. The biggest guy clenches his fist in anger, then yowls as the quill in his wrist reminds him it's there. He tries to pull it out and yelps. Some of the nasty barbs will be removed by the doctor later that night; others will take weeks to resurface.

A creature which cannot travel quietly, the porcupine has, with much scraping of claws and rattling of quills, hauled itself into a pine tree. It settles into a crook of the top branches to have a leisurely gnaw of bark.

One of the bullies is starting to blubber, his arm bristling with quills. "It's your fault, you stinking little guttersnipe!" he hollers at

Pink. His buddies huddle around him, shouting and arguing and scowling with menace at the little girl.

Pink's eyes fly open in shock at language she has never heard the likes of, but she stands her ground, stamping her foot. "It's your own stupid fault for being mean and stupid, and... you're all so stupid... and... and I'm... lost." Suddenly she runs out of steam and bursts into tears, which makes her even angrier. "How would you like it if some big huge moron porcupines started poking sticks at you?"

The gang hulks around her, jeering and mocking, "Oh boohoo, little spitfire ain't so brave now... poor baby's lost... ouch, ow, ouch these things hurt like snake bites."

Pink covers her ears at the foul words that follow.

CHAPTER 28
A Wild Time

MEANWHILE, ABOUT THE TIME Pink first crosses the creek, Julie is overcome with an urge to find her. A twinge in her belly pulls her on an automatic-pilot beeline toward her twin. She doesn't veer from her path except to have a drink of water and to investigate something she sees flashing in the sunlight on a rocky outcrop. Billy's maggot-frying glass! She stows it in a pocket and then refocuses on the magnetic pull from Pink. It's as though she's pulled by an invisible line that winds through the forest and through the creek. Eventually she hears the bullies' loud voices. She prowls closer, hovering and creeping, until she gets a rough idea of what's going on. Then she jumps into the fray, hollering.

"Leave my sister alone, you big bully cowards! Don't you dare touch her!"

The bullies look at each other in disbelief. Two of them! It's like a nightmare. Are they midget aliens? The boys start a hasty retreat, tossing their bottles and chip bags on the ground as they trip over each other in a panic to scram.

Pink and Julie shout at them, "Don't you dare leave that junk here! Pick it up!"

Unfortunately, that stops the boys in their tracks and one of them sneers, "Oh yeah, who's going to make us?"

"We are… and our big brothers and sisters!"

"Well there ain't none of them here, so tough on you!"

"Anyways, little foo-foos, who are these brothers and sisters?"

"Herald and Brick, and Ron and Rich and Billy and Alvin, and we'll sic Hazel and Fern and Sedge on you too!"

The boys' eyes bug at mention of the girls. "Let's get outta here! Have fun being lost, pipsqueaks! If you're not back by next week, we'll send a search party, but there won't be much left of you by then."

The oafs stumble away, yelling and whingeing. As soon as they're out of sight, Pink and Julie babble twin-talk. They'll give the gang a few minutes' head-start and then maybe follow them. Julie picks up a porcupine quill and examines it. "It's hollow. Maybe we can dye these… and cut them up for beads."

"Or stick them in plasticine to make hedgehogs… for paper weights… for birthday gifts," enthuses Pink.

The girls scurry around picking up more quills and carefully tucking them into a pill bottle. They also collect the candy wrappers that Pink threw in the boys' faces. Shiny bits are shiny bits.

They peer into the lean-to and step back abruptly, holding their noses. "What a pigsty!"

"Don't insult pigs! Pigs don't drink beer!"

"They prob'ly would if they could. Can't you just imagine hogs in greasy undershirts, holding beer bottles and cigarettes?"

"…Wallowing on couches full of magazines and dirty dishes… and babies."

The girls gather up armloads of ripped magazines and toss them into the lean-to, along with tin cans, a moldy sweater, and a bag of rotten apples.

"They prob'ly won't even notice. It would take a month to clean this up."

"Let's come back sometime with Fern and Hazel and do it. We'd better get going. Jeepers, it sounds like those porcupine bullies are blubbering."

It also sounds like the sky is clearing its throat. There's a flash of lightning.

Pink and Julie stare into each other's eyes with dismay. "I'm glad I found you," says Julie. "It's a good thing you had your magnet turned around so I could get here before the storm."

"Yeah," nods Pink. "If we'd been looking for each other at the same time, we would've both been positive and pushed each other away. And you would've never found me... But doesn't it sound like those guys are going in circles?"

"Poor babies are crying," Julie marvels. "They don't know whether to jump or lie down and die. I hope that porcupine taught them a lesson once and for all."

"And doesn't just make them more meaner," says Pink. "Those quills are driving them crazy."

Julie and Pink half-hoped the gang might lead them to a good trail, but when the yelling and swearing get more and more vicious, they decide to go their own way. The adventurous five-year-olds gaze at the creek. They know if they follow it, they'll eventually get down the mountain. They'll have to wade across first. They solemnly stow their sneakers and socks in their packs.

More than one stream has joined forces here and the water thrashes wildly through rocks and fallen trees, but it looks like they'll have easy going for quite a ways if they can get to the other side. Anyhow, Pink hopes to show Julie the shooting stars.

"Let's pretend Fern and Hazel are with us. And Sedge. They could get us across easy if they were here."

"Let's pretend they're on both sides of us with their hands on our shoulders."

Thus invoking the aide of their big sisters and using a fallen cedar to hang onto partway, they skither across the slippery stones. When they fetch up on the other side, wet and scratched but undaunted, they triumphantly fling themselves on the grassy bank to rest a minute.

Sunlight suddenly torches the clouds, turning them molten. The girls feel touched with glory. Delighted with the glistening world, they watch a mourning cloak's brown velvet wings flick over a mauve aster. They plunge their faces into a golden spread of arnica, breathing in the spicy petals. In the shallows where the creek has widened and calmed, they watch water striders and periwinkles.

"If I was a periwinkle, I'd make my shell out of arnica petals."

"I'd use emerald moss bits."

"Moss green, arnica leaf green, pebble green."

But as they stare into the limpid pool, the water darkens and starts to ripple. As suddenly as the sun had appeared, dark wings of cloud blot it out.

Tall grass blows flat against the ground; the sky rains twigs. The explorer's mantle which had settled so comfortably on Pink's shoulders and automatically enfolded Julie now flaps in the wind. Pink shivers. Then she lifts her face defiantly to the wind and shouts, "Oinky! Doinky! Boinky!"

Glad to hear her above the thunder, Julie whoops with laughter and they laugh and laugh, chattering loudly to hear each other above the storm. They climb over logs polished smooth by ceaseless washing and over root tangles taller than they are. The creek once again narrows and grows unruly, rearing up to plunge through rock bluffs. The girls veer away from it, skirting tall rocks like the ones around the gang's lean-to.

They stand shoulder to shoulder between two giant boulders, awestruck.

"Monsters."

"Monoliths?"

The solemn aura of nature's Stonehenge permeates the dank air. Uneasily the girls step away.

There is no denying that cliffs have overtaken the meadows. Julie and Pink might have to cross the creek yet again. They can see a clearing on the other side. It looks ferny and inviting.

Thunder sounds like a distant giant rattling its shackles. The flibbertigibbets take each other's hands, trembling, and stare into the crashing water. They can no longer hear the nearby uproar of the bullies.

CHAPTER 29
The Storyteller: Julie, 2005

ADULT JULIE IS KNEELING to pick some low bushes. Her knees are telling her she should be wearing knee pads. She does her best to ignore them by keeping a steady flow of berries tumbling into her bucket. As they roll through her fingers, she automatically shunts the undesirables aside, food for chipmunks. She marvels at the agility of her hands, nimbly plucking the bushes while hauling herself up the mountain. She muses that huckleberry picking is like touch-typing, a skill involving mental and manual dexterity and great powers of concentration. It's mesmerizing work.

She's so preoccupied by such lofty thoughts, Julie scarcely registers a rustling sound on the other side of her berry patch.

A branch snaps loudly. Something bigger than a squirrel. She lifts her head. Looking at her a few feet away, dense black with a light brown nose, is a bear. *A bear!* An electric jolt zaps through her. In a fluster she leaps to her feet just as the bear rears onto its hind legs, standing twice her height. (Rule 29: Never look a bear in the eyes.) The bear woofs. Julie staggers backwards, falling. Black silence.

Julie expects the bear at any second to clamp its jaws on her neck. To rip her arm off. She can't see anything. Her face is smushed against a rotted stump. She waits. Can't see. Can't hear. The bear snorts. She waits, cringing, not breathing, heart slamming. And waits.

She's not playing dead: she's too scared to move. After a minute which seems like hours, Julie lifts her head in time to see the bear drop to all fours and bolt. It disappears in seconds, leaving behind a rank smell, some swaying branches, and Julie untangling herself.

She's gratified the bear has run from her, but she's trembling. Three hundred pounds of brute strength had flexed its muscles a few feet from her. How had that much bulk gotten so close so unobtrusively?

Rule 29A: Never underestimate the speed and subtlety of a bear.

Rule 29B: All wild animals can disappear instantly in their natural habitat.

Rule 8: Don't forget to look around you occasionally, no matter how good the berries are.

Rule 8B: If the berries are really good, remember that bears love berries even more than you do.

Rule 46: Announce your presence; sing, rattle your bucket every so often, even if you're taking a break from picking.

It's a moment before Julie discovers she's torn the satin blanket-binding with which she had so blithely tied her bucket earlier in the day, and her berries are half-spilled. So much for dexterity and co-ordination. Nervously glancing around, she scoops up some of the berries, but it'll be hard cleaning the debris from that layer in her bucket, so she leaves many scattered under the bushes. Help yourselves, bears and chipmunks!

"I'm over here, bear! Ka-reee! Treee-do! Ka-deee!"

Rule 65: The only thing worse than going for a walk with no bucket, is coming home with it half-empty.

Rule 85: The only thing worse than that is a bucket half-empty because you've spilled it.

So, Julie proceeds cautiously on her berry quest.

She's always wondered what would happen if she discovered a bear on the other side of her berry patch. The bear bolted, this time at least, and if she hadn't been spread-eagled by panic, she likely would have bolted too, which might have triggered the bear to chase her. She wonders how long the bear had been there. It was never "her" patch, of course. Good thing she and the bear seem to have gone in opposite directions.

If it's true, as some people say, that to ward off the attack of a black bear, you're to act large and aggressive, and to ward off a grizzly you're to be meek and submissive, then how do you decide which kind of bear it is in the five seconds you have before you jump out of your skin?

There are many more variables in any situation than one realizes. Deciding whether it's a grizzly or a black bear is only one problem. Are there cubs? Does the bear have an escape route? Is it a very crabby bear? Whichever kind it is, it's probably best not to enrage it by throwing a rock in defense. The situation is challenging enough without the bear thrashing wildly in a fit of temper.

Rule 73: When you see a bear staring at you, the most important thing is to stay calm.

The only way to learn calm is through practice. Ha. It's amazing what a passion for huckleberry picking can get you into.

Rule 74: If you're in the same huckleberry patch as a bear, it's the bear's patch.

Rule 75: Let the bear have it.

Rule 76: Never argue with a bear.

Rule 76C: Never hurt a bear.

Julie's reminded again of the rule about making noise while picking berries and wishes that bears would stick to the same rule.

In summary: Let the bear know where you are. Stay calm. Don't corner the bear. Make noise. "Kadee, kadooo!"

CHAPTER 30
Slow and Steady

A GLOOM OF THUNDER rends the air as Herald, Sedge, and Brick get reorganized after Brick's fall. When they worry about how rapidly his hand is swelling, he makes light of his injury.

"Well, at least it's just my arm that's busted. Nothing serious, like spilling the berries, or breaking my neck. Good thing I didn't have a bucket in my hand when I fell."

"Yeah," says Herald, "and you look quite jaunty. Lucky no one ever wore that pink and orange tie, so it's strong enough to hold your arm together. Mom prob'ly hid it in the rag bag so Dad wouldn't wear it to work... Auntie Anne's off-colour joke."

"That stupid dress code at the lab," says Sedge "They were complaining about his rat tie. The gall! He should wear that purple and blue polka-dot dress Auntie Anne gave us and see what they do about their dress code!"

"Lucky she hid this hunk of tent in your pack, Brick, because you're shivering. Maybe we should wrap it around you," suggests Herald. "You must be in shock."

Brick hadn't realized he was shivering. He tries to sit down but finds it awkward with his arm trussed up, so he takes a few steps and clenches his teeth. "I've gotta keep moving. But I can't carry more than a bucket."

"You shouldn't pack anything."

Sedge gingerly puts Brick's ballcap back on his ginger head and Herald tightens his boots for him. He leans against a stump, where he impatiently waits to regain his balance.

Now what to do?

Having his seventeen-year-old, strong-as-a-truck brother busted makes Herald more anxious about the younger kids. "How 'bout Sedge stays with you, Brick, and I'll pack as much of this down as I can, and round up some of the other kids to come help?"

"Okay. But we can make it partway back. I might be slow, but I gotta keep moving."

Sedge is replacing one of her shoelaces with string. "We can carry stuff a ways and then come back for more. Oh, but. The soup pot!"

They all glower at the engorged cauldron. It glowers back.

"Is it getting bigger?"

They're starting to wish they'd never had a soup pot, had never seen a soup pot. They're even starting to dislike soup.

Herald decides he'll haul it down. Hopefully the others will have set up camp at the foundations. Sedge helps him reinforce some spare socks with electrician tape to keep the wire handles of their heavy buckets from cutting into their hands. Herald sighs, "I never meant to stay away from the other kids so long. I'm the oldest; I'm supposed to keep an eye on everybody."

"Impossible" says Sedge. "Pink and Julie are like keeping track of hummingbirds."

"No kidding!" says Herald. "They're energy personified. Like how did they move that big bookcase upstairs with none of us knowing they were doing it? It must have taken them hours to take all the books and junk out of it and put it back again. It had to be them, no one else wanted it moved."

Brick shakes his head. "They're relentless when they get a mind to do something. Last week after our bonfire, when they were supposed to be in the house getting ready for bed? I heard them jabbering behind the woodshed. They had a whole camp set up, complete with two cats in a box of shredded paper and a can of Prem!"

"Cats? Whose cats?"

"Dunno. They were big, healthy looking critters, so they must have good homes somewhere. The girls were planning to smuggle them into the house during the night. I told them they could get arrested for catnapping… only way I could get them in without the cats."

"They're getting that darned mind of their own, like all you kids at that age," says Herald.

"Well, Hare," teases Sedge. "Isn't independence a survival trait? Isn't it the whole point of growing up?"

"But those little scalawags are so elusive."

"They're good practice for when you're a teacher."

"Yeah, thanks, and good practice for all of us losing our minds. Okay, Sedgy-Hedgy, thanks for the help with my mittens. I'd better get going."

They have another rummage through their packs so Herald can take back what Sedge and Brick don't need, including Pink and Julie's spare socks and sweaters, five harmonicas, Ron's bag of lunch, several comics, and the hunk of tent. What Herald can't stuff into his pack, he ties onto it. Looking like an itinerant peddler, he gives Sedge a gentle push on the shoulder, brushes a mosquito off Brick's ear, and trundles down the hillside, stopping before he's out of sight to switch hands on the Big Pot and wave his red beanie. Sedge and Brick call after him, "Watch out for bears!"

Brick grimaces. "This is going to be one long afternoon."

"I'm sorry you're hurt, Bricky."

"We're kind of all in the soup now that I can't carry much. There must be a moral here somewhere. Like, don't pick more than you can carry."

"We should have known better than try to out-prank the pranksters. Ron and Rich better not be laughing right now."

"I should have listened to Herald when he told me the pack-board needed mending properly. I think I permanently wrecked it when I fell. We'll have to haul stuff in relays, I guess. We better not lose any buckets in the process!"

"Or should we stay here with everything in one spot? I hate leaving our berries unprotected. Look what's already happened today."

"We can take it in small trips, so the ones we're leaving behind are still in sight. Let's make it to that bull pine down there. And then have a rest and come back for more. When everything's collected at the pine, we can pick another spot to aim for."

They make two trips. Sedge can see the pain in Brick's face, and he can see the determination it's taking for her to keep going. They claim a rocky ledge where they can swing their feet and lean against the corky bark of the huge Ponderosa pine. It's comforting to rest against, solid and dependable, perhaps two hundred years old. They have a thick cushion of dry needles to sit on. Overhead, the wide branches sigh. Brick pries out a nugget of golden pitch to chew, while Sedge hunts out a sack of spits. She unearths a small bottle of Aspirin. "Here's what Mom would give you for your arm, Brick: Aspirin, her cure-all!"

"Good old Mom, thinks of everything. I wonder what else she's got in there. No jars of Jello, I hope. Sure, I'll take an Aspirin."

He swigs it down with a gulp of water. There's only a few swigs left. It's a good thing they know how to sublimate their thirst on long hikes. The muggy air presses on them, hot and itchy as a woolen army blanket. They munch on sunflower seeds and share a couple more handfuls of squashed plums. Brick laughs, "Can you imagine eating this mess at home and thinking it's okay?"

"Plum à la pine needle and pack grit? Not your everyday appetizer. But it wets the whistle. A bit."

Brick whistles Sedge's favourite song, "Mockin' Bird Hill." She sings along, "Tra-la-la, twiddle dee dee… With peace and good will, to wake up in the mornin' on Mockin' Bird Hill." She looks at him in a new light. He's brave and good, so much more than just another smelly boy.

Brick catches her sweet look and clears his throat. "You're some beauty, Sedge."

She almost falls from her perch.

Brick's as surprised as she is at what he's said. They never have that kind of conversation. But it's not the first time he's thought it. It's not just her speedwell-blue eyes. It's their clarity. She's not poised, not posed. She's beautiful partly because she doesn't know it yet. Brick knows it's risky to tell her, but he might not get another chance if he dies on the mountain, so he decides to risk it.

"I hope telling you that won't make you snooty and fancy, Sedgie. Like some of those girls at school. One in particular. If she'd just go back to the way she used to be before she started her act…"

Sedge tips the brown brim of her hat over her eyes, concentrating on braiding the long pine needles that cover the ground in ready-made threesomes. "I didn't realize you noticed things like that, Brick. I mean, we hardly ever talk, really. It's usually everyone blathering at once. And we don't really say anything."

"That's us. You'd think all we knew were radio jingles and how to crack demented jokes. Just a bunch of smart alecks."

Sedge groans. "I had to write the definition of 'smart aleck' ten times on the board for Mrs. Hortense. 'Someone who is sarcastic or funny in an obnoxious or arrogant way.'"

"Very good! How come you had to write lines? Oh, never mind. We're all good at sass."

"Thing is I wasn't meaning to be a smart aleck. It's just sometimes I see the humour at the wrong time, when nothing's meant
to be funny."

"Some people have no sense of humour. None. It's fun making
people laugh. But I've had more than my share of being the class
clown. It's brilliant until you want to say something serious and
everyone laughs. Once you get pegged, that's what you're supposed to be. It's hard to get past stereotypes. Sometimes, when I
go back to school after a holiday, I feel like maybe I can start out
fresh. Everyone's changed a bit, and they don't notice so much if
you try something different."

"Like if I actually got a proper haircut they wouldn't make a
huge joke of it?" asks Sedge.

"Yeah. Or if you wore that fabulous coat from Aunty Anne, the
one you love? That bright purple one that you stroke and try on
every day and it fits you perfectly?"

"Brick! Anyhow, I like to fade into the background."

"No kidding. With your brown hat and gray sweater. If you'd
wear that purple coat, they'd get over it in two days, when they finished talking their heads off about the shock of it all… and you'd
feel happy."

"I can't stand the yak, yak, yak."

"Neither can I, Sedge. What happens to me is I usually dig
myself into the same old rut each year. Once an ox, always an ox."

"That's not true! "

"Well, I'm solid, right? I'm Brick. I'm proud of being strong.
But I get fed up with people treating me like a stupid ox. That
one girl… I'm not subtle enough for her. And I can't make myself
subtle. I'm not subtle at all. When I sweat I, sweat buckets. When I
fart, everyone chokes. End of lesson."

"And when you laugh, everyone laughs, Brick! Everyone likes
you. That girl is probably one of Miss Prizz's pink and white fluff-
brains. Everything so la la la and pretty precious, they make me

feel like a piece of cardboard. But Brick, you're kind and generous and smart."

"I don't know about that. But what about you, Sedge? What ticks you over?"

"Me? I'm in another world half the time. I get so absorbed in nature, everything that's growing and living around me outside. Then when I get back with people, it's like I can't find my place. I can't place myself. I'm too subtle. Especially around loud people."

"Like me and our brothers?"

"Sometimes it's as if my edges give way. I lose my outline. I feel invisible, until I gradually get back into people mode. Does that make sense?"

"Sure. Like that lost feeling after I see a really good movie or finish a good book. When you want everyone to be quiet, because you're not ready to come back? So that's why you're quiet a lot of the time."

"Thanks, Brick."

"Yar. I hope that Aspirin kicks in. I gotta get moving. Let's make another haul. How 'bout to that Douglas fir?"

CHAPTER 31
Cartwheels on Trestles

FAR BELOW, HERALD IS hitching along with the five-gallon soup pot, feeling awkward as a beetle with a dung bundle. His thoughts have been circling over each of his brothers and sisters, getting more anxious as the western sky blackens with cumulonimbus. He hadn't meant to abandon Hazel and Fern with the small fry. His legs had just carried him away, once they got a chance to stretch, and one thing had led to another.

Herald admits that his outrage over Ron and Rich's prank got him way side-tracked. The rotten varmints. They live to make him fume. His "ignoring-it muscles" are getting stronger, but obviously they're not strong enough. The little caper today was too soon after what the twins had done yesterday, messing with his porch contraption. He'd known they'd sabotaged it because he'd heard muffled snickers behind the lilacs, where they were lurking to hear his reaction. He managed not to say one word when he discovered they'd pilfered a crucial part, substituting a broken potato masher for a sprocket, as if that would work. And they'd soldered a bunch of wires and Meccano parts to it. He'd considered leaping out and chasing them through the neighbourhood. But they would love that. Big reward. Getting chased is one of their favorite things, even in snow. Bare feet? So what. Even if his own legs were to buckle, his feet freeze off or shred, a good chase was well worth the effort.

But this time, his mind has turned to revenge of the carefully planned variety. Is it time for the totally unexpected bucket of water that drops from one of the maples along the driveway? Are the boys still routinely looking up before walking under the trees, after the last deluge? He can wait. The great thing is Ron and Rich don't know when he's hatching one of his cunning plots. They think they've gotten away with their latest antic. It's all a game to them. Usually he can ignore their teasing. But for them to risk losing the berries! And now Brick is badly hurt as a direct result of their fooling around. Well, an almost direct result.

Herald knows he occasionally flies off the handle a little bit. He has a fleeting image of himself as a black disc of burnt porridge, hurtling through space. But the screw that holds the handle that prevents the whole batch from shlucking across the kitchen has so far held, if only by a few threads. Mrs. Hortense calls it, "practicing dignity under duress." It's a hard study. Most of the time, he no longer indulges in the porridge wars, tempting as it is. There was that one time he let a spoonful of congealed oatmeal splat against the wall, but he had cleaned it up, reaching behind the stove with a rag clamped in the corn tongs... wearing Fern's daisy apron. Thank goodness Hazel had laughed. Crisis turned to comedy. He doesn't fly off the handle often, but when he does, it's impressive enough that the kids smarten up for quite awhile. It's his love of horseplay that he has the hardest time curbing.

Speaking of being without a handle, the soup pot feels handle-less at this moment, because Herald's hands are too numb to feel it. He lowers it between his feet. His arms seem to float at his sides. He flexes them a few times as he worriedly surveys the sky. Thunder is rolling closer as clouds from the east join clouds from the west, looking like a great, writhing hawk overhead, sending out flickers of lightning. Herald hoists his burden and carries on down the mountain.

To take his mind off his troubles, Herald begins reciting grammar in a guttural monotone. He's practicing for the upcoming Provincial Parsing Competition. "Noun, verb, adjective, adverb, preposition, gerund, participle, conjunction..." The competition is like a spelling bee, except each person is given a card with a fifteen word sentence to parse. They have two minutes to study it, and another five minutes to orally give each word its proper grammatical designation and purpose. Those who win that round go on to more complicated challenges, such as lines out of Thoreau or Milton, fifty or more words. The kids like to tease Herald about his parsing practice. Julie and Pink call it his parsnip fracas and ask him if he ever has to practice carrots or corn. But what the heck, he's good at grammar and it's a chance to go to the National Literary Symposium in Toronto! A chance of a lifetime to travel past these mountains. And if he wins there, it could mean a scholarship for college.

Meanwhile, far below, there are sounds of alarm near the foundation.

"Julie?... Pink? Pink and Julie!!?"

"WOOOOooooo-hoOOot-hoooOOOOooo-oo-oooOOOO...

The absence of the young twins has been noted by Hazel and Fern.

"Billy, I thought they were with you and Alvie."

"We thought they were with Fern and you, Haze... They usually are."

Fern and Hazel look at each other in guilty alarm.

Alvin is beside himself. Usually his younger sisters tell him before they take off, even if they don't tell anyone else. It's a strict rule. They know he won't squeal on them. He knows they need time to themselves, just the way he does. The youngest kids get more than enough attention in a big family, but mostly they just want to do their own thing. Sure, they get more lap time, but that's usually because there's nowhere else to sit. Alvin still has to sit on someone's lap in the Hearse, which is okay if you don't mind being tickled and told to move your head. (Where are you supposed to put it, under your knee?) And sitting on a lap is slightly more comfortable than getting squashed between a jump seat and the tool box. But it's embarrassing when you're half grown up, like Alvin. Anyhow, Pink and Julie have gone in secret, and that's not common sense. They should have at least told him.

Billy, too, blames himself for not paying more attention to his little sisters. He tries to bridge the gaps between everyone, but sometimes they're just too far apart. He'd been too busy trying to keep Alvin's mind off his lost shoes and working on his limerick to notice when the twins had disappeared.

Suddenly it feels like they're all doing cartwheels on trestles.

There's a sense of urgency. The sky is rattling like an overwrought snare drum in a school play, the one that fills in time when you've forgotten your lines.

They decide that Fern and Alvin will stay at the foundations in case the twins turn up there. They could be anywhere. Hazel and Billy will search along the main trail. They'll check back in half an hour. Not that anyone has a functioning watch or any great sense of time.

Alvin and Fern organize camp, pulling together rock shelves and stacking firewood. Then Alvin discovers that his bare feet fit neatly into the knurls of a bull pine trunk, and he finds a lookout twelve feet off the ground on a wide first limb. He's up and down that tree a dozen times, but he can't spot Julie and Pink anywhere.

CHAPTER 32
Like Wounded Bears

A COUPLE OF MILES away, Ron and Rich are making ever-widening circles around where they think the soup pot should be. It seems hopeless. They're stumbling with fatigue.

"You know what, Rich?"

"What, Ron?"

"We ain't never going to find that crap-cursed kettle. We might as well head back and face the music."

"Yeah, like I been thinking the same thing. This bushwhacking is crap. Mosquitoes flying up my nose so I'm seeing spots."

"But wait a minute. Did you hear someone holler?"

They stand still and listen. Sure enough, they hear shouting. Fighting. Loud fighting. They climb onto a knoll and gaze down on the source of the racket. Cripes. It's the Kludge gang, carrying on like imbeciles. There's Crick and Squat and the tall one with the yellow hair. Yellow-Mane. And a couple guys from the Gulch. Ron and Rich also see a deep pool hidden from the gang by a screen of alders. Leaving their heavy packs, they scramble down and wallow in the icy water, the best thing in the world for dire thirst and scrapes and bites. Drenched, they creep back to their spy rock. The gang is stumbling around like ballistic baboons.

The gang can't see two other pairs of eyes watching them from close proximity. Peering between two trees, Julie and Pink are watching with fascinated horror. The bullies are shoving each other and yelling obscenities. Yellow-Mane, the biggest and fiercest, falls into a ditch and bawls with pain. Pink and Julie stifle nervous giggles, covering their ears. For some time they've been watching closely for a chance to sneak past the gang to the other side of the creek. But now, as Yellow-Mane crawls out of the ditch, they spy something bright blue sticking out of his shoulder pocket. Their eyes lock on that object with astonishment.

"That's the exact colour of... that's got to be it!"

"Our hairband!"

"We have to get it off that porcupine tormentor."

"How can we? It's on the hairy beast!"

"We just have to. There's no point asking him for it, now they hate our guts for no reason. What use is an aqua-flower hairband to a caveman?"

"We'll just have to wait for our chance and grab it."

And so they wait. They wait, getting more and more desperate as the boys argue and push each other around.

"It'll get broken!"

Meanwhile, Ron and Rich, watching the gang from their perch on the other side of the creek, have come to a nasty conclusion. The Kludges must have stolen their soup pot.

"They've prob'ly eaten all the berries."

"And kicked the bucket to Timbuktu."

Rich and Ron are already in a foul mood, and it's getting worse by the minute. Seeing the gang on what they consider their turf... well, actually not their turf, but still, seeing the gang acting like such idiots has ramped up their tempers. They're going to get those berries back if it kills them.

"But hold on, Ron. Why're those guys acting so weird? Do you think they're drunk?"

"Wouldn't put it past them. Lookit!"

The gang keeps blundering every which way, tripping and flailing. Sounds like the one who crawled out of the ditch is crying. Bawling his head off! And Squat is holding his arms out straight, causing him to bump into Crick, who gives him a vicious shove and then howls as if he's been stung by a dozen bees. Very weird.

"Like wounded bears. Could be dangerous."

"We better stay out of reach. Let's holler down to them. There's no way they can get at us, the way they're acting."

Rich and Ron yell at the top of their lungs, "Hey! You down there, what's the matter? Did you drink too much Kickapoo joy juice?"

Startled, the ruffians gape up at Ron and Rich, hollering back, "What's it to ya, pips? Ya got a problem or summat?"

"You're the ones with the problem. How come you're blubbering?"

"You would too if you had a zillion porkypine quills stuck in yer arse!"

Ron and Rich look at each other and burst out laughing. "Quills? How come? Did you sit on a poor little porcupine?"

"No, wise guys, the critter shot them at us!"

"Porcupines can't shoot their quills, everybody knows that... except you! You have to be awful close to get quills stuck in ya... Usually only happens to dogs."

"Well it happened to us, and if you don't stop yer laughing, we're going to come up there and thrash ya!"

"Oh yeah? So what did you guys do with our pot of huckleberries?"

"We didn't see no pot of berries, and if we did, tough luck for you."

"You did so take it! Admit it, Scum-bags!"

Yellow-Mane lunges up the rocks towards Rich and Ron, waving a cudgel and bellowing furiously, but he stumbles back, screaming when his rump hits the ground. Some quills have gone way deep! His buddies crowd around him and jeer up at Ron and Rich, throwing rocks and insults.

Meanwhile, with unified tenacity, Pink and Julie have taken full advantage of their brothers' distraction and crept closer to the gang, peering from behind a rock. Their eyes are fiercely riveted on that one shoulder pocket, where the band of turquoise plastic beckons and twinkles. While the gang has their backs turned, Julie nudges Pink. Pink darts toward Yellow-Mane's bulging shoulders, jumps up, grabs the hairband, and skids back behind the rock, fast as a silverfish. The brute doesn't even realize she's been there— none of them do, they're so busy hurling abuse at Ron and Rich.

Ron and Rich's eyes pop at the sight of the imps scurrying towards the creek. What in tarnation? They continue to harangue the gang, taunting and yelling to keep them busy while their quicksilver sisters slink from boulder to boulder, across the creek, and into a poplar thicket.

"Ah, come on Rich, let's go, these guys are hopeless! I don't see the berry pot. It'd be kicked over empty if they did have it. Let's vamoose!"

"Yeah, I've seen enough of these morons."

"Bye-bye, darling babies! We're so sorry you're having a bad day!"

Rocks clattering at their heels, Ron and Rich scurry out of reach, half-expecting Squat and his minions to come hurtling after them, but quickly the yowls and growls fade in the distance. Ron and Rich find their sisters sprawled in the grass under the poplars downstream, laughing and chattering and whooping with excitement when they see their brothers. A jolt of double-twin energy surges through the four and they run down the creek to get a safer distance from the gang, yodeling and nose-singing and carrying on like orangutans until they collapse with laughter.

"Well, little tatterdemalion sisters, it's a good thing we found you!"

"Same to you, big spindle-shank brothers!"

It's a relief for all of them to be back with family. Julie and Pink had been nearly exhausted from their journey and their perilous vigil. Miraculously safe and re-energized, the girls dance around Ron and Rich, giving them hugs and swinging on their arms. They're confident their big brothers will save them from the thunder and a lifetime of being lost on the mountainside.

This boosts the boys' morale, brought low by their lost-soup-pot dilemma. They feel brave and good again, rescuers of little sisters. They genuinely admire Pink and Julie's daring-do. When the clouds break and rain finally begins to pour, the big twins lead the little ones to shelter in a cedar grove. They share the sweaters they've begrudgingly dragged along all that hot afternoon. Julie hauls out a bundle of peanuts in the shell from Buddy's sister Pam's birthday peanut-scramble. They fall hungrily on the peanuts, but not before Julie carefully divides them. The aqua-flowered talisman is safely nestled in peanut shells in Pink's pack. Rich delves out a bag of cooked macaroni à la ketchup, which he passes around.

Ron contributes two sticks of gum, which they divide up. His baloney sandwich and bag of macaroni are still in Brick's pack, wherever that is. He spins his football on the palm of one hand as he contemplates his priorities.

Crouching under the trees, enjoying their weird meal, they ignore the first rain splattering around them. Pink and Julie shriek with laughter as Ron and Rich, in screechy high voices, elaborate on the household rules they were going on about earlier:

"Don't use the dish rag for washing eggs. If you do, don't put it back on the counter."

"Or someone will wipe dishes with it and get chicken kak on the dishes. Put it under the sink."

"Don't put it under the sink dripping wet."

"And don't wash the eggs in the house anyhow! Haven't you ever heard about salmonella?"

"Who's that? Cinderella's sister?"

"How many times have I told you not to eat out of the chicken bucket?"

"And don't leave your toenails in the sink."

"Mmm, toe jam."

"Eeew!"

CHAPTER 33
Lettuce at Home

BACK AT HOME, IN a lull before the storm, Lettuce has escaped the fuggy kitchen to pull in a line of laundry.

The cool breeze feels good on her face. It's a peaceful reward, bringing in the clean, fresh clothes. The children feel close despite their distance. Uninhabited, their garments seem mysteriously like the children when they're asleep: close but unfathomable in their dreams; there but not there.

Lettuce pulls in a skirt pieced by Fern from the backs of denim pant legs, embroidered with bold daisies in yellow and green yarn. Fern will spend an hour at the ironing machine flattening it. Her friends now want pant-back skirts. Lettuce un-pegs two bright pop tops hemmed by Pink and Julie. Their stitches are getting smaller. She folds Sedge's brown sweaters and gray flannels. With her tanned rose complexion and platinum hair, Sedge is shy and hides herself. She satisfies her love of colour with kaleidoscopic embroidery that she pins on the curtains. In comes Hazel's favorite shirt. She's lost a blue button from the middle and replaced it with a bright red one, sewn on with yellow thread. That Hazel. If her cuffs are frayed, she finds just the right scrap of fabric to bind them. She claims not to care about clothes, but Fern and Hazel's answer to anything shabby or out of style is to re-invent it, sometimes with striking results. They salvage every scrap of new cloth that falls from her own hands; yellow, green and blue for Fern; hot colours like red, magenta, and orange for Hazel. Their everyday clothes might be faded as a moth's under-wings, but their trimmings are rich.

Lettuce is reminded of her mother and her sister Hilarity in her children's diligent handiwork and artistic eye. She would love to indulge them with bolts of fabric, but the National Drama Society has a strict budget for their seamstress. She has three or four main commissions a year and several smaller ones; she has just sent off a fifteen-person magician ensemble, in fifteen different colour schemes. She scarcely has time to sew for her kids, but they do well enough on their own.

Their main source of fabric is the school's yearly White Elephant Sale. They obsess about the sale for several weeks before the big day. The way it works, the classrooms get a wooden white elephant to hang above their door for each box of rummage they collect for the sale. There is a prize, usually a jumbo box of chocolates, for the class with the most elephants. Competition is fierce.

Before school on the day of the most recent White Elephant Sale, Lettuce had been busy with other parents sorting the donations onto long tables in the hallways. Everything was there. Piles of comics, books, and toys of every description (including a collection of wind-up toys that no longer worked but were too nice to throw away), puzzles, mountains of clothes, tools, and gadgets. Amazing stuff.

Lettuce was nearby when her five girls swooped noisily onto the rare pile of clothing donated by the glee club. After a moment, there was a loud snigger. As one, Hazel, Fern, Sedge, Pink and

Julie had looked up to see the Priss girls coolly appraising them, tittering behind their hands. It felt to the sisters like their pride had been smacked in the face by one big cow dollop.

Pink was the first to revive. She gave the Prisses a haughty look and returned to digging for the silver buckle she could glimpse under a twisted crinoline. With defiance her sisters dove as a team into the clothing, Fern waving the crinoline in the air with a crow of triumph. Lettuce chuckled to herself from across the room. Her girls knew what they were doing. The fabrics were to die for.

When they got home with their armfuls of loot, the sisters flew into paroxysms of unstitching and restitching, concocting new clothes that were nothing like the hand-me-downs. Other girls eyed their outfits with envy. Bob resurrected a couple of old treadle machines; Velma dragged her aunt's portable hand-crank machine over on a worn out toboggan and a sewing club was born. Bob and Herald, Ron and Fern are kept busy tinkering to keep those old machines running.

Only Fern, Hazel, and Sedge are allowed beyond the semi-partition of their mother's sewing area, and then only to help with the hand-basting and gathering for her projects. Lettuce's treadle machine is too temperamental for anyone but her to use. She has a pause now between sewing projects. Ahhh. It's a light-hearted feeling. But she has a lot of catching up to do around the house, and the garden. Once again, she hears her half-read novel calling from the kitchen shelf in a voice like a muted harp.

Back indoors, Lettuce tosses a blanket into the wash machine to agitate and pushes the socks through the wringer. No one seems to care if their socks match, which is a good thing, since seventeen odd socks typically come out after a dozen pairs have gone in. But after soaking them in the left-over dye water, they're all more or less the same gunge colour. Another unifying experience for the family.

Little does she realize just how un-unified her family is at the moment.

CHAPTER 34
The Storyteller: Julie, 2005:

FAST FORWARD BRIEFLY TO grown-up Julie, still out in the wilds, looking nervously over her shoulder under a grove of poplars. Her left hand is clasped as though holding Pink's right hand, as it often is when she's troubled.

It's hard to hear anything beyond the rustling leaves.

"Koo-karee! Koo-karee karoo!"

Is that bear anywhere close? There could be other bears, too. If you're in berry country, you're in bear country. (Rule 23.) The problem is, her bucket is half empty because of the spill. Her gathering instinct overrides her instinctive fear. Before launching into a dense berry patch, she takes a careful look around and calls again, "Kadee kadoo! Taree trado!" Julie has to fill her bucket. She continues to call out every few minutes, feeling idiotic but safer. The mosquitoes are coming on strong. She doesn't waste time on any skimpy bushes.

Rules 31, 18, and 72 are in play here. That is to say, you can't go home with an empty bucket. When there are berries available, you have to pick them, even if it causes you serious discomfort. And the odds are that, usually, you can have only one bear incident in a day.

Rule 85: If you feel like you have been stung, it might be just a horsefly bite. If it is, it will go away faster if you ignore it.

Rule 86: Stay calm. If it is a sting, getting agitated will only make it worse. (Staying calm is a good rule in most circumstances, and the hardest one to follow.)

Julie finds a promising bush of ripe-reds. These large, flat, glossy huckleberries are burgundy red, even when they're fully ripe.

Some say there are over forty varieties of huckleberries, and it may be so. Whether this variability depends on location, exposure, soil type, root stock—who knows? Within a few acres, ripe huckleberries can be found in a palette from wine-red to blue-black, drop-shaped, oval, round, or domed; on bushes shoulder- or ankle-high, with soft, thin leaves or firm, thick ones, abundant or sparse. There's even a variety of tasteless scarlet huckleberry growing on high bushes with small leaves, usually close to sea level. They're all huckleberries, as long as they have that tell-tale ring around the blossom end.

If the berries are orangy-red and taste like snakes, they're snake-berries (soopalallie). If red, slightly sweet, and growing in twins on waist-high bushes, they're honeysuckle twinberry. These varieties are neither poisonous, nor worth eating unless you're starving.

With steely determination, Julie can almost ignore the onslaught of biting insects and thirst and backache, her worry about bears and fears for her twin. She tries to remember the bright promise of the early afternoon, when the sunlight was filtered through birch leaves and a gentle breeze kept any mosquitoes away; when a stream rippled in harmony with the singing of thrush.

There's no water here.

A coven of ravens on a dead tamarack alternately cough, snore, and argue.

The back of Julie's neck is getting fiercely sunburned. But, for the time being, the berries are really good, and she keeps on task.

CHAPTER 35
Downpour

THE LONG-THREATENING RAIN FINALLY cuts loose. Billy and Hazel are getting drenched as they search the main trail for Pink and Julie. Their throats are raw from calling. The trail is slick with mud. Whistling through his teeth a repetitive three notes, Billy is working hard to keep up with Hazel as she slogs along, her face drawn into a fierce scowl beneath the sodden clump of her orange tam. They stop suddenly when they hear the tintinnabulation of cow bells further up the path.

They hadn't counted on the cows heading home. But sure enough, the head cow is sashaying down the narrow path towards them, an uncompromising, steaming, straining bovine hulk, swarming with flies. Hazel and Billy stand their ground as she comes to within a few feet of them, where she stops, lifts her tail, and lets fly a noxious stream. The other cows crowd behind her, stretching out their necks, mooing and bellowing.

"I guess they're not going to go around us, hey, Billy?"

"Nope. I'm climbing up the hill."

Hazel soon gives up trying to out-stubborn the cows and joins her brother on the steep bank above the trail. The herd lumbers past just below them, broad backs swaying, swollen udders swinging from side to side. The cows have done their day's work and are heading back to their barn to be milked, their bells clanging, "Get out of our way, we want our hay, end of the day, get out of our way." When the last cow has belligerently tramped past, Billy and Hazel scramble back onto the trail. Then splap! Hazel slips in a cow pie. The slimy mess is all over her. Billy reaches to help her up, and down he goes too, landing on his back, his blue fez narrowly missing the muck. "Oorf."

"Are you alright?"

"I guess so. Yuck! Peee-ew!"

They sit in shocked silence for a moment, then Hazel yells, "Stinking cow muck!"

"Yucky gut crud!" hollers Billy.

"Squishy poop slop!"

"Disgusting smelly cattle dung crap dump!"

Then Hazel and Billy look at each other and burst out laughing.

"Now we're really in a mess!"

They wipe the worst off with bundles of thimbleberry leaves. The rain will have to do the rest.

"How long do you think we've been looking for those girls, Haze? We told Fern we'd check back in half an hour."

"It must be longer than that by now. The cows are already heading home, so it's getting late."

Ron and Rich and Pink and Julie are still half a mile away, well hidden by a wall of cedars, their voices absorbed by the rain and thunder.

Billy and Hazel gaze into the mist. Hazel sighs. "You know what, Bill, just yesterday I was thinking it would serve Pink and Julie right to get lost, the way they're always haring off. And now I feel guilty. As if I tempted fate."

"I know what you mean," says Billy. "When I was trying to keep track of them this morning, I lost track of Alvin and look what happened to him!"

"Near scared me out of my wits, seeing him down that tunnel," Hazel sighs. "Trouble is, we all like blazing our own trails. Dad always says we're too darned independent for our own good, which would be alright if there weren't mine holes. Or cougars."

"Do you think Alvin was looking for gold?" Billy wonders.

"Who knows? I hope Pink and Julie aren't looking for silver! Them and their shiny things. They had a fit yesterday when I wouldn't let them make silver wizard capes out of Mom's roll of foil. Let's go to that next switchback, Billy, and hang out there for a while. If we still can't see them we'd better go back to camp, in case they've headed back another way."

Pink and Julie are on their way, at least, with no cares in the world now that they're escorted by Ron and Rich. The imps are ragtags of laughter, buffeted by the wind. Ron and Rich feel a lifting of spirit in the company of their merry sisters, though they trudge toward their doom.

While Hazel and Billy are getting a close-up understanding of cows and the twins are starting to head back toward the mill, Herald is unfolding himself from an overhang of rock where he has kept most of the deluge out of the soup pot. Even so, he has to cautiously drain off water, holding back the berries with his red beanie. The last thing he needs is a gallon of water to haul. He's about twenty minutes from the foundations of Stooge's Mill, where Fern and Alvin are also waging damage control. They've huddled over the berries behind the old foundation's steps to nowhere, but two buckets are swamped. Alvin frantically scurries after spilled berries while Fern ladles out handfuls of water, accidentally spilling more.

It's hard enough, toiling up and down mountains for miles to pick huckleberries, without spilling them and having to pick them up a second time. Some rules apply:

Rule 3X: If you drop one berry outside, you can let it go.

Rule 3Y: If you drop several berries outside, try to retrieve them.

Rule 3Z: If you drop even part of a berry in the house, pick it up immediately, on penalty of death-by-scrubbing.

Re-picking is the bane of any berry picker, and it doesn't get much worse than Fern and Alvin's wet, cold mess of pine needles and moss bits. Good thing they scooped the escapees into Fern's hat and not the buckets, although her pretty green cloche is sadly stained. "I should take these berries to the spring and rinse them," she says. "Can you stay here and keep an eye on things, Alv?"

"Sure, Haze. Here's my tuque to sort them into." (Faded purple, it, too, will soon have dark stains.)

Alone at camp, Alvin rolls a boulder closer to the fireplace and sits on it to sketch the large black beetle that has crawled out from underneath. He snacks on a handful of unripe huckleberries— not as sour as gooseberries, but pretty good. Hearing a whistle, he looks up. A red cap is bobbing towards him above the alder brush. "Herald!"

"Ahoy, Alv! Wanna give me a hand?"

Alvin runs to his biggest brother. He gapes at the brimming soup pot and helps Herald lower his pack. He hoists it onto his own shoulder, nearly pitching sideways with the weight of it. Herald steadies him. "Easy does it, Alv, don't strain your gizzard."

Alvin drags the pack, its assorted tie-ons bouncing every which way while Herald wrestles the soup pot the last hundred yards to the concrete abutments.

"How long've you been here by yourself looking after every-thing, Alvin? Where's everyone?"

"Huh?" Alvin hadn't really thought of it that way and fluffs his feathers a bit. He explains in one breath, "Well, Fern's taking forever at the spring washing berries, but yeah, me and Fern's been taking care of things 'cause Pink and Julie are lost and Hazel and

Billy've been gone for ages looking for them and we don't know where Ron and Rich are and we ain't seen Sedge and Brick all day, or you either, Herald!"

"Whew, worse than I expected. And Brick's arm's maybe broken. Sedge is with him up the mountain."

"Oh! I'm glad Sedgie's with him. But what happened to Brick?"

"He fell on the rocks. He's in bad pain. And we've got tons more berries to pack down… And I've got to get these clodhoppers off my feet before they ignite."

Herald pries off one boot, but a knot in the laces of the second one defies his cramped fingers. Alvin works at the knot with a pointed stick until he can yank off the boot. Herald sighs and stretches out on the ground, leaning against the steps to nowhere. "Thanks Alv! You're a life saver. How's your day been?"

"Me and Billy had fun… and this morning, I… I…"

"This morning, Alvie?"

"My shoes fell off, Herald."

"Oh?" Herald looks quizzically at his small brother. By the pinched look on Alvin's suddenly down-turned face, and his bare feet, Herald knows he'll have to wait for the story, and it won't be a happy one.

Fern finally reappears with the hats full of berries, firewood tucked under her arm. Alvin shouts, "Fern, Fern! Brick's maybe broke his arm and he's up the mountain with Sedge!"

"Say what? Brick's hurt?"

When Herald explains to Fern about Brick's arm, she nearly starts to cry. But she quickly swings into nurse mode at the sight of Herald peeling his socks off his blisters. "Your heels are bleeding, Herald. I'll find some gauze. Now where's that tape? Gad, what a day! I hope Hazel and Billy have found the little twins. And I don't know where Rich and Ron have been all day."

"Pink and Julie?" Herald asks with panic.

As Fern explains about their disappearance, Alvin fleetingly wonders if Pink and Julie really could have vanished, like, supernaturally.

Herald tapes up the holes in his feet, as well as a scrape on Alvin's knee. He switches his socks for the ones clinging to the soup pot and levers his boots back on as Fern and Alvin try to explain how they lost Pink and Julie. Then Herald fills them in on the details of Brick's fall and the soup pot fiasco—how Ron and Rich stole the berries, and how he and Sedge and Brick stole them back.

Fern is shocked into silence. Alvin hops around laughing as he carefully hides the soup pot under a flour sack and some slabs of bark. "Ha ha, they'll think it's still missing."

Herald grins. "Serve them right! We might as well prolong their agony, worrying what happened to it. We thought we could out-fox the foxes, but that sure backfired. They just better get back here to help haul down the rest of our stuff. Six full buckets and Brick's big pack."

Herald scrounges more wood while Alvin and Fern snap a pile of kindling and cover it with chunks of bark. Before the afternoon is over, they'll be glad of a fire. Alvin clambers up to his lookout in the ponderosa for the umpteenth time. Mist is creeping in.

Still no Pink and Julie.

"I don't know which way to turn," says Herald. "We have to find Pink and Julie. And Sedge and Brick will think I've deserted them if I don't get back to them pretty quick. And I need to take Ron and Rich up there to help haul everything and give Brick a shoulder to lean on. How long ago did Billy and Hazel take off to look for Pink and Julie?"

"Seems like ages." says Fern. "They said they'd check back in half an hour, but I think it's been a lot longer. Oh, here they come!… without Pink and Julie."

When Hazel and Billy finally reach camp, wet, disgruntled, and smelly, they're happy to see Herald but dismayed that Pink and Julie are still missing and Brick is hurt. They anxiously discuss the dangers that surround them: mine holes, cougars, bears, cliffs, lightning, and the tumbling streams which have turned wild with a storm that won't stop rumbling.

Fern calls to the heavens, "Please help those little ninnies get back safely!" and then, "Surely they can't be too far? They've probably been waiting the storm out somewhere."

"Maybe they're with Ron and Rich!" suggests Alvin.

"At least they'd be a bit safer. Those guys have good enough heads on their shoulders," says Hazel. "When they use them for something besides holding their brush cuts."

"And trying out Mom's hats," adds Fern.

Herald says he'll rig up the hunk of canvas that Brick was hauling around all day. "It's just what we need right now to make a bit of shelter over the stairs. Can someone hold that corner from blowing away? And I'll hook this hole over that pine snag."

Billy grabs the canvas and holds it taut, saying, "Next time, let's set up camp when we first get out here."

"Our stuff would be easy pickings for the Kludges or whoever else comes this far. Someone would have to stay around camp all day," says Fern.

Alvin's ears perk up at that. "I was here my myself, but I didn't even think about the gang. I was busy picking up glass. Anyhow, I'm not scared of the Kludges. I just laugh and they think I'm dim-witted and leave me alone." He spots a shard of milk-of-magnesia cobalt blue and adds it to his stash. "Darn stuff is everywhere."

It's good that Alvin, with no shoes, is aware of glass underfoot, though his feet are tough as cow hide. He keeps thinking about his lost sneakers. He seldom wears shoes in the summer, but losing stuff is the worst thing, he's been told many times. Technically, he hasn't lost his shoes. He knows where they are. They're plummeting end over end toward the center of the earth. He heaves a big sigh. Fern gives him a hug. "I'm glad you built up the fire ring, Alv. Wouldn't you think the rocks would still be where we put them last year? It's as if some under-the-snow trolls roll them around during the winter, hey, Alv? For a game of ogre marbles?"

"Or boogie-man boccie," he laughs.

Hazel has her own thoughts about how ice and snow, spring thaw, gravity, and ground tremors can move rocks, but for a change, she isn't in a mood to expound and says, "Maybe it was a game of troll pool."

Fern says, "What's weird is how we all want to be here amongst these old hunks of concrete. It would be smarter to be under the trees, out of the weather, wouldn't it? It's like we feel a little bit at home here, because at one time it had walls and a roof."

"Pathetic. The babes in the woods find a home," Hazel says.

"Even if only a symbolic one. Anyhow," says Herald, "this is where Dad is supposed to meet us at five o'clock, isn't it?"

"I thought he was coming at six," says Fern. "Well, after work, anyhow. What time is it, Billy?"

Billy pulls out his dented pocket watch and snaps it open. "Two o'clock? Oops, I guess it stopped."

He winds it carefully, gives it a gentle flick with his thumb and holds it to his ear, listening contentedly to its tick, tick, tick, tick. Like a small animal purring, it's almost like a pet, the way it responds. Billy doesn't care much what time it is. But he sure likes the Roman numerals on his watch and the smooth, round shape of it in his hand... and the fact that it was his grandfather Bob's watch, engraved with Billy's own initial. He likes the way it shuts with a smart click as he tucks it back into his pocket. Some day, he'll pass it on to Alvin.

"What time do the cows head home?" asks Herald.

"Around five, I think," says Hazel. "Depends how long the days are."

CHAPTER 36
Four Twins Singing

HERALD PACES THE HILLSIDE behind the camp. His thoughts rage, "Fire burn and cauldron bubble!" Two little sisters and two middle brothers, gone. Double trouble. They might turn up any minute. Or not at all. What to do?

Hazel is prowling around the edge of the clearing, listening and craning through the trees. Now Herald catches sight of her orange hat frantically waving. She is shouting, but her words are scattered by thunder. Herald lopes toward her, joined by Fern, Alvin, and Billy as Hazel dodges back into the misty forest, disappearing as though she'd never been there.

Then, on a gust of wind, shrill bird voices can be heard.

"Pink and Julie!" shrieks Alvin.

"Rich and Ron!" shouts Fern. "I can hear them singing!"

"All the twins!" Hazel crows, bounding triumphantly before them into the field.

Jubilation!

Pink and Julie rush about, hugging and dancing, their voices swirling like bright pennants in the wind. It's almost as though their excitement brings on the lightning, which suddenly flashes overhead. All nine race to the foundation to huddle under the canvas in the fresh torrent of rain. Lightning strikes closer with a roaring crash. The tallest brother holds up his tent, leaning over the younger eight with arms outspread, a kindly heron with glasses askew. As water gurgles over the rim of the canvas, their excited babble all but drowns out the steady thrum of rain, so that it's a minute before they realize when the cloudburst is over.

Untangling themselves, they stumble into the watery sunlight, taking tentative steps into a fresh new world. For a moment, the whole land glistens.

A meadowlark fans its wings. An arpeggio of clear notes fills the air as it takes flight.

Herald, Fern, and Hazel are so glad to have all the twins back, they can't be angry yet. That will come later. They don't know yet just how alone their littlest sisters had been for a big chunk of the afternoon, separated from each other by a mile of wilderness, not just alone together, but *alone* alone. Everyone assumed they'd at least be together, the invincible inseparables. It would be a long story, how they survived that afternoon, a story which would not be fully unraveled for days—years, in fact.

Herald and Ron shake puddles from the tarp;Rich tightens the rope while Julie, Pink, Hazel, and Fern do a crow dance in the field.

Reluctantly, Herald halts their festivities to break the news to the twins about Brick's accident.

"Jeez!" yelps Ron. "Will he be alright?" asks Rich. Pink and Julie clasp hands in alarm.

"He's tough as barbed wire, but he's not alright," says Herald. "Now, we've all got to band together to help him... and make sure no one else gets hurt in the process."

Nine heads bow in consternation; nine faces look solemnly up the mountain, unable to see where Sedge and Brick are waiting for help. Remorse weighs heavy. They hadn't stayed together. Worse, most of them had known darn well that they wouldn't stay together; from the first mention of the trip, they'd planned to go their separate ways. That's one reason they'd all been so keen on going. Brick is hurt because of them not looking after each other, not sticking together. They're all to blame. Hazel and Fern know that Alvin's near-disaster and Pink and Julie getting lost would never have happened if they hadn't been gabbing all day, or if the older boys had helped keep an eye on them. Pink and Julie are momentarily too shocked about their strongest brother being hurt to even glance from their interlocked hands. Herald regrets the joy he'd felt at stretching his legs that morning. Grim reality darkens Alvin's eyes. Billy sighs, looking around at all of them, mentally shoring up his bridge.

Rich and Ron cringe. Not only had they abandoned their brothers and sisters for most of the day, they've lost the family's biggest potful of hope and hard work. Their collective conscience is like a rotten tooth, probed by a restless tongue of guilt.

Clove Pink and Julie Cosmos seem to hover inches off the ground. Now they wish to go help Brick. They want to make him some arnica mush to heal his arm. With high-pitched voices, cheeks bright red, they gibber in twin talk. Hazel finds their excitement a bit frightening; she prepares a nest for them under the tarp. Fern gathers the small girls, one under each arm, and settles them in the nest under a flannel shirt. Almost instantly, they're asleep. Hazel and Fern grin.

Why is it that the elation of release from worry so often turns to anger? Is it anger at having been made to worry? Fern and Hazel link arms now, a formidable wall of banked-up angst and vocabulary. Pink and Julie had been naughty, taking off on their own, but that will have to be sorted out later. They turn instead on Ron and

Rich, who are play-acting the rescuing heroes, having plucked their wee twin sisters from the jaws of destruction in the wilds of the forest. They're also working very hard at deflecting suspicion from what they've really been up to for the last few hours.

Fern stomps her foot. "Stop it, you two! You're acting like nincompoops! Listen! Where were you all day? Hazel and I've had to be second and third mother ever since Dad dropped us off this morning, haven't we, Hazel?!"

"Yes!" Hazel agrees. "Since it was still half-dark out. It's time you guys took some responsibility for the younger kids in this family. It's time you were second dads for awhile. Tomorrow, Fern and I are going to take off all day. With Mom. And you can hold the fort all day and make supper. It'll probably take a week to get the house clean afterwards, but it'll be worth it to see you on your knees scrubbing! Now, we're finally going to get out of camp for awhile. We're going to hike up to Brick and Sedge."

Hazel gives Fern a big wink and she plays along with Hazel's whim. "You boys can be stuck in camp, getting bored out of your skulls keeping a fire going, while we take off on our own for a change!"

Herald splutters on his mouthful of water, says, "Okay, if that's what you want, girls. But I'm the only one who knows exactly where Brick and Sedge are. And I think Ron and Rich deserve to do some heavy hauling for a change after shirking off all day."

"Well, alright," Hazel shrugs. "Anyhow, Pink and Julie are sleeping. And Billy needs to keep Alvin company, so we'll just stay around here. So enjoy your junket up the mountain, guys."

Herald hasn't said one word about the soup pot, but he can tell it's tormenting Ron and Rich's minds as the praise for their rescue mission fizzles out. No rest for the wicked.

Alvin is hovering in front of the hidden mother-of-all berry buckets. He looks at Herald and makes a small gesture towards it. Herald shakes his head emphatically, "no," then slaps a mosquito to camouflage his head shake. He wants Ron and Rich to feel the pang of guilt a while longer.

Alvin has to keep his head down looking for glass to stop from laughing out loud, while Fern and Hazel busy themselves filling water bottles and finding cloth and safety pins to make a proper sling for Brick when he gets back.

Ron and Rich mutter about the Kludge gang likely up to no good, stealing things. Herald makes a skeptical "aaherm" sound, and Fern says if the Kludges are around, then she and Hazel definitely have to stay to guard camp, because the gang is scared of them.

Herald has filled the canteens and water jars for Ron and Rich to carry and proceeds rapidly up the mountainside, calling for them to hurry up. He's soon way ahead, which gives them a chance for a quick debate as to whether Herald knows they've lost the soup pot. They don't have breath for more than a few words as they hustle to keep him in sight. No more bellicose blather from those two.

Fern watches them go and shakes her head. "Stick-Rich and Robust-Ron. They look to be on their last legs."

Alvin calls after them, "Skinny legs and barrel legs, keep up with Heron legs! "

"And be gentle carrying Brick," calls Hazel.

"Good thing Brick is so brave," says Fern.

At that moment, Brick is feeling like overcooked cabbage. While Sedge is making one last trip to make sure they haven't left anything behind, he gives in to misery for a few minutes. As a person might feel remorse at the hour of death, Brick wishes he had stayed with Perth on the dog's last night alive. Perth was most often near Brick, and had fallen asleep with his head on Brick's knee that evening. But Brick had slipped away to meet his friends for a stupid, boring game of scrub, and when he'd come back, Perth was dead.

CHAPTER 37
The Feckless Way of Fate

AFTER HANGING AROUND CAMP for half an hour, Billy says he knows where there's a patch of whopper berries that he and Alvin should clean up at the edge of the pasture. Hopeful sun rays are slanting under the cumulus that billow on the western horizon. Billy saunters away with his arm over Alvin's shoulder, a skein of doggerel unraveling behind them:

> …We need to find more huckles
> so we can buy more buckles
> for the dog named Chuckles
> who can bark in the dark
> at the sharks in the park, hark!

Hazel checks on Julie and Pink, who are snuffling contentedly, sound asleep. She chortles, "Well, here we are, right where we want to be, just like Br'er Rabbit safe and sound in his brier patch after begging Br'er Fox not to throw him there."

Fern deals out a game of rummy. "I'm glad Herald figured out we were bluffing, but though, I feel kind of sorry for Ron and Rich trudging up there instead of goofing off here. I hope they don't conk out part way and need packing down."

"I know. Trouble with Ron and Rich, they're so fun to tease… because they're always teasing us and making us more work. So don't feel too sorry for them, Fern."

"I was a bit, but then I remembered the Scouts are making soap at our place on Saturday. It'll be chaos. Last time they made it outside, but they kept running in for things. And of course the whole pack was there, with Herald being Akela. And Brick being Baloo." Fern lays down a queen.

Hazel picks it up. "Them and their making everything. Last time, their soap had dirt in it. They were stirring it with their staves! How can you get anything clean with dirty soap? Anyhow, some of the worst stains are the ones you can't see."

"Oooh, Haze. You sound like Miss Hortense."

"Do you think an alchemist could unmake something they make? Sort of reverse Midas touch?"

"You've lost me, Haze." Fern sets down three tens.

Hazel pretends she's lifting up a big dictionary, reading out loud: "Alchemy is the process of transforming something common into something precious. Like turning floor dirt into marzipan."

"Or turning filthy tea-towels into snow white silk?" laughs Fern, laying down two runs. "Silk for dresses, just imagine!

"Silk or serge? We must be practical," teases Hazel.

"Practical shmactical," says Fern, "Mom has shelves of fancy fabric and we have to be practical. The trouble with linen, it wrinkles like hags and never wears out. Fifteen years on sink duty, and our towels look like floor rags even when they're clean, but they still work. When they actually get holes, they get floor duty for a few years. If I ever have my own kitchen…"

"Ah Fern, you will one day, I'm sure of it. I won't though. I plan to cook over a campfire most of my life and live in a shack. But back to alchemy." Hazel hefts the imaginary dictionary again and recites in a highfalutin voice, "Alchemists use alembics to get rid of impurities. An alembic is something that refines or transmutes by distillation."

"Like filtering wormy-berry-juice through an alembic and presto! Fabulous Fern-Hazel-Permanent-Pastels! Swirls of pink and lavender, pale yellow and soft green," sighs Fern.

"Crimson and orange for me," Hazel laughs. "But I wonder if an alchemist could make an alembic?"

"Next time I get heck for daydreaming in Math class," says Fern, "I'll say I"m being transmuted by an alembic for a better understanding of algebra."

"Ha!" Hazel slaps down three queens and four threes.

The sun is sinking into a horizon that is bundling up like winter coats. As day recedes, heat rash will give way to shivering.

After a far-reaching look into the sky, Hazel heads to the forest to round up more firewood.

Fern busies herself sorting spoons and tin plates, the all-purpose flour sacks, an odd sock for a potholder. She builds a tepee of small wood in the fire ring and shakes the match tin. Not many left. She carefully transfers berries into a clean sack to free up a bucket for more water. The little girls haven't stirred. They won't miss her if she hurries to the spring. She'll be back in a jiff.

But wouldn't you know it!

In the feckless way of fate, just when Fern pauses to admire a throng of stars of Bethlehem, their white petals shimmering under the cedars, an intruder blunders into camp.

It's one of the Kludges. Crick is on his way to his aunt's house on the upper-outskirts of town. Crick has inherited a reputation from his cousins for being a hoodlum, a hooligan, and a bully. Maybe he is, maybe he isn't. He has fared better than some of his buddies, but he has a couple of porcupine quills stuck on the inside of his elbow and a few in his ankle, and he's grouchy as a badger. He stops in his tracks when he sees the sweet little camp. It looks deserted.

He has a quick snoop around. He nicks an apple. Aha! Berries. His eyes bulge with greed. He's snaking out his arm to grab a full bucket when Pink and Julie suddenly wake up and scramble out of their hide-away. Crick takes one look at the wild-haired harridans and shrieks, flailing head over heels into the bushes.

Fern and Hazel, approaching camp from opposite directions, sprint forward when they hear Crick's inhuman shriek and see him running for dear life.

"Julie! Pink! Are you alright?"

"Yes! Did you see that guy run?"

"What on Earth did you do to him?"

"Nothing, we just looked at him!"

"...You do look a fright."

The twins laugh hysterically and dance in circles, shouting, "Who's afraid of the big bad Kludge, big bad Kludge, big bad Kludge, who's afraid of the big bad Kludge, not I, not I, not I!"

CHAPTER 38
Thoughts of Poltergeists

MEANWHILE, WAY ABOVE CAMP, Brick and Sedge have sheltered from the rain as best they could, wrung themselves out, and then worked up a sweat hauling buckets and gear. Their base this time is on the last elephant flank between them and the foundations. They rest against a massive Douglas fir and spread out their belongings to dry.

It's been a day of constantly shifting moods, sun to storm, incredibly dry to wet, burdensome to footloose. There's been dismal misery and also moments of sheer joy, such as when Hazel glimpsed an indigo bunting, and when Ron plunged his hot face into leaping water. Those near a creek are the lucky ones. Brick and Sedge have to soothe their throats with rainwater and plums and are still thirsty, though the air feels like a wet veil.

"How far do you think we still have to go, Brick?"

"As the crow flies, a quarter mile. Too bad we're not crows, eh Sedge? For us, about a mile I guess. I sure hope Herald's made it back to the foundation in one piece, with that blasted cauldron of berries. And I hope Fern and Haze are there, and the rest of them."

Sedge clears her dry throat. "And I hope he comes back with someone to help us. And I hope he brings some water."

A breeze rattles twigs and cones and an old bird nest falls from overhead branches.

A robin stammers a rain song, then abruptly flies away.

Sedge yawns. "Last night, I was too keyed up about today to get much sleep. How about you, Brick?"

"Off and on. Hey, did you hear Hazel shouting last night?"

"I thought it was Fern."

"Someone was carrying on. Must have been a nightmare."

"I think Alvin was sleep-walking again, too. And then Ron and you were muttering, Brick. Practically telling a story if I could've understood the language."

Brick yawns. "Sometimes I get the weirdest feeling there's a whole other life going on in our house that none of us know about when we're awake. Not a malicious spirit exactly, but something Other."

"More than us just making rude noises in our sleep?" asks Sedge. "Like maybe other people are living in the house who we don't even know about?"

"Yeah, something like that," he says. "Like a whole other act. We each glimpse different bits and pieces of the puzzle, but never enough to put the picture together. Act 3, Scene 5. Sustained irony that only a fly on the wall can understand."

"A fly on the wall with a notebook," she suggests.

Brick searches his sister's face. "You must think I'm loony, talking like this. But you'll tell me, won't you, Sis, if anything bad happens?"

Her eyes flick away from his and then return to meet his steady gaze. "Okay, I will. And I don't think you're loony."

Whatever else is going on, some of the confusion in their home is because of Julie and Rich's ventriloquism. Though they're opposites on the twin scale, (boy/girl older/younger), Julie and Rich seem to share some of the family's weird twin wiring. They can throw their voices, which is bad enough when they decide to clown around. But when they're unconscious in sleep, their talent can run amok without them meaning any devilment. If Julie sighs in her sleep, it can float a long distance, the disembodied sound quite spooky if it hovers over someone. If Rich groans in his dreams, the sound seems to come from nowhere and everywhere. A laugh can fall eerily from the ceiling or trickle from under a bed, without Julie or Rich even knowing.

"Sometimes our whole house seems like a loony-bin, Brick."

"When isn't it?" he sighs. "With thirteen of us living in that old ark with only about three doors we can close and two dozen passageways, and stairs up and down all over the place, we're like rabbits in a warren."

"Or a colony of pack rats.

"That bad, Sedge?"

"I never really thought about the doors, but it's true. Jeez, even our six-door sedan has more doors than our house does."

"It used to have scads of doors," explains Brick, "when it was a rooming house. But the next owners tore everything out for studios and didn't put it half back. It's great we have those extra sinks and toilets upstairs… and a good thing Uncle Bob brings his plumbing truck every so often. But we really need more solid walls, not partial partitions that're always getting moved… especially when Julie and Pink have the place to themselves for awhile."

"Maybe we're all of us moving things a bit everyday without noticing it," says Sedge, "just by rushing around, and over a month or two, everything has moved quite a bit."

"Like a bunch of small earthquakes, us being clumsy, stomping around?" Brick asks. "Or just shifting things out of our way without thinking about it. Then one day we notice and say, 'How did that get there?' I guess that's bound to happen when all the walls and doorways are movable."

"And then Pink and Julie renovate every so often. I'm worried about those will-o-wisps right now," frowns Sedge. "I usually help keep track of them when we're out like this."

"Me too," Brick sighs. "Those fluff heads are more will and less wisp than most five year olds. I never know what to expect from them. The other day they had the upstairs landing half buried under scraps of catalogue and they got mad at me when I had to get through. They had Dad's three-hole punch and were filling little jars with the punchings."

Sedge grins. "They were under the back porch making the weirdest noises, and said they were singing to their sow bugs. They showed me some sow bugs in one of Mom's best teacups full of confetti. Nothing is too good for their weird pets."

"Pathetic. But I don't blame Mom and Dad for putting their foot down about no more cats after that flea epidemic when Billy was a toddler Remember that cat named Tortoise, Sedge?"

"Was she slow?"

"No," laughs Brick. "Her name was short for tortoiseshell. She was actually the fastest stray on four legs. When Fern opened the door to see what was yowling, Tortoise catapulted upstairs so fast, she was having kittens in a bottom drawer before anyone even knew she was in the house. Unfortunately Miss Tortoise Truffle was infested with at least 600,436 fleas, which immediately hopped onto her kittens, and so on. Long story short, no more cats... and anyhow, no room once Pink and Julie came along. Then poor old Perth died. We'll never find another dog like Perth."

"No, and so Pink and Julie are trying to make Mom and Dad feel sorry for them not having a pet. They were pretending those sow bugs were Pixie larva, can you believe it, Brick?"

"Yes I can. They were singing their Pixie Larva song at bedtime last night."

Sedge looks at Brick thoughtfully. He always seems to ignore the chaos around him, like a rock in a river. But he's a lot more tuned in than he lets on. His calm manner is due to will power more than oblivion. Right now his face is screwed up with pain but he doesn't complain. Sedge offers him her last stick of Juicy Fruit.

He tears off a piece and hands the rest back. "Thanks, Sis. You know what, I was already mad at the boy brats before their stunt today. They like to meddle with my stuff, you know, just to bug me. Something small, like putting my books upside down in one shelf. It might take me a day or two to notice, but I know they've done something in my room because of their sly looks. Really annoying. Did I say 'my room'? Is that wedge of the Ark my room, or is it a hallway through the house that I don't know anything about?"

"Sometimes I wonder about poltergeists," says Sedge.

"Or if one of the former occupants still lives in the house," says Brick.

Sedge paces. "Ron says there's evil spirits coming through cracks in the bedrock, connecting the basement to the mine tunnels. Mr. Nitmust says we should find a mine hole to live in when the A-bomb blows. I wish they'd keep their creepy ideas to themselves."

"Me too."

"You, Brick? You always seem so steady and sure about everything."

"We all have overactive imaginations, Sis. Especially at night when we can't go to sleep."

"I know Alvin has a hard time with creepy ideas," she says. "Sometimes he talks to me about things."

"He's a thoughtful guy. Too thoughtful for his age," says Brick. "He takes everything to heart. He's compassionate, our Alvin. But Ron and Rich… They get on everyone's nerves on purpose, as if their special mission in life is to figure out the best way to do it. It's a game for them. I don't think they realize half the conflict they cause. But when they catch on to someone's weakness, they're like horseflies between your shoulder blades when you're picking berries. Last week I caught them red-handed, messing with my stamp collection. They think it's sissy, fussing with little bits of paper, but I find stamps interesting. You can learn a lot of geography from them, and history. Those guys have no respect."

"They're just brats."

A chipmunk examines the brother and sister, stares long and hard from a safe distance, then scampers forward to nibble a plum stone near their feet. It darts away and comes back, darts away, comes back. They drowsily watch him.

Brick yawns, "Erf, I'm sleepy."

"Me too. My eyes keep shutting."

Sedge and Brick lean against the big old Douglas fir and doze.

CHAPTER 39
Bob and Lettuce

HOME FROM WORK, BOB has changed into his tramping clothes and pulled on his boots. Lettuce has rice pudding and tea waiting for him, which he sloshes down while standing. He's late. Some high-paid ignoramus had to pick his brains about tungsten just when he was heading out the door. His work is all very interesting, but he'll be glad when his research contract winds down and he can start up as a pharmacist when the local drugstore opens in the fall. That will be a happy day. Ten minutes' walk instead of a forty-five minute commute on a rickety bus. More time to spend around home. No more white shirts.

"Why don't you come with me to get the kids," he coaxes. "Can't you leave all this for a while, Lettuce?"

"If only. You know I'd dearly love to. But supper's on the stove and there are still the blankets to wring and rugs to wash."

The washing machine has been thump-a-lugging throughout their conversation and is getting louder, as though to remind them of its whereabouts five feet away.

"Sounds like a sluggish boxing match," says Bob. He tightens the agitator and tweaks the wringer bolt. He takes a quick side-trip to his puzzle table and plunks three pieces of ocean into place one after another, plink, plink, plink. "It would be nice if problems in the lab would solve themselves that easily!"

"Maybe you're all just trying too hard, Bob."

"Too bad they pay us to work. Otherwise we could play chess all day and solutions would fall into our laps, plink, plink, plink," he laughs.

"That usually only happens in poetry."

"And chemistry."

Smirking, Bob gives Lettuce a swinging hug. She gives him a quick back scratch and hands him a gallon jug of water and a bag of pretzels and apples for the kids. He grabs a couple of buckets from the porch and crunches the Hearse into gear, even as he's banging his door shut a third time and waving good-bye to Lettuce.

She checks the laundry on the line. Rain-rinsed, it might have a chance of getting dry if the breeze continues. It's been a capricious day. Prisms suddenly dance along the clothesline.

Lettuce steps quietly into the garden, trying to spot any birds before they fly away. Swallows darn the verdant mist between garden and sky, where myriad tiny wings are swarming. The air is vibrant; everything is in motion. She tries to see the garden as if for the first time, as though she has nothing to do with this place she's happened upon, not responsible for the weeds in this haphazard extravaganza of radiant petals and sun-drenched leaves. The pea vines lean over their fences, gossiping with the hollyhocks, whose red petals brush her shoulders. The delphiniums are taller than she is, enveloping her in their blue hush, heavy with wet blossom.

A gust of wind shakes the trees. Lettuce ducks under the cherry branches to find a plump Bing and delightedly crunches it, the ripe juice reddening her lips.

At the foot of the garden, crackerjack marigolds are slumped with rain, rapidly becoming a slug warren. Having gumboots on, Lettuce wades in to tie them off the path. She skirts around the squash patch, where lumpy shapes are silently gestating.

For the ten thousandth time, she hopes the kids have found shelter. When they're all around her, she doesn't need to think about them constantly, because she's part of their goings-on. But today the eleven have never been far from her thoughts.

Lettuce can hardly imagine life without them. They're worth all the effort. She could never do it all without their help. Of course, without them there wouldn't be so much work.

Eleven children! If she had known years ago that this would be her lot in life, would she have welcomed her fate? Yes. Yes. It annoys her when people ask her that kind of question, often with a tone of pity. How could she have too many children? She and Bob always wanted lots, and they came easily, even two at a time. They've all been blessed with rugged good health. They're fascinating, every one of them, and they pull their weight much of the time.

Life would be boring without children.

If only they wouldn't argue, but they seem to thrive on it. It's the pitch that gets to her when they squabble. It's not the boisterous racket of their voices in harmony, which she quite enjoys, but the roar, as if more than one of them is falling off a precipice. That's hard to take. They each want to get in the last word, that's the problem. And they mostly think they've had the last word until, sooner or later, someone disabuses them of that idea, which leads to another spiral of argument. And then just when she thinks they're done, someone puts an oar in and spins the boat around again, whether through lack of tact, orneriness, or sheer mischief, she doesn't know. Luckily, someone usually takes the role of diplomat and peacemaker, or someone sees the funny side, which sets them laughing again.

It's actually a bad sign when there hasn't been an argument for a day or two, especially if they've been cooped up in the house. Domestic conspiracies proliferate in boredom. Brooding puts three and four together and comes up with fifty-six. Sure as anything, tinder builds up in some quarter and an angry spark sets it flaring. The uproar then is phenomenal.

Occasionally, Lettuce or Bob has to be the wet blanket that subdues the flames. No point trying to get to the bottom of things when there's usually no bottom to get to. Housework is the best dampener. By the time they finish a day's worth of chores, the kids are too tired to fight anymore and united by common suffering.

Lettuce sincerely hopes they've not been having some kind of fracas up on the mountainside, playing that game where they toss jackknives at each other's feet, or being careless with the hatchet.

Even at the best of times, does every mother see fleeting images of her children in peril, plunging from roofs, running into traffic, choking on strings of Swiss chard?

The chickens are whining. Lettuce throws them some weeds and they screech in a frantic game of keep-away. She finds six eggs in the middle of the floor and two more behind the food bin, takes them in, and returns to the delphiniums, her face washed with raindrops as she gathers a luscious armful.

She hurriedly wrings the blankets. She wants to iron and rehang the kitchen curtains before the kids come home. She's pleased with the knock-your-socks-off lime green they've turned out. Three packs of turquoise and eight of yellow have done the trick. Eat your heart out, sunshine.

But the wash isn't done yet. A blanket has jammed the wringer and Lettuce has to release it, one agonizing inch at a time.

CHAPTER 40
Quills of Conscience

ABOUT THE TIME BOB is leaving the neighbourhood with a clash of gears, his eldest son, Herald, is slogging over the brow of the hill where Brick and Sedge are sacked out under the Douglas fir. Herald wipes his steaming glasses and looks around at their colourful sweaters and socks laid out to dry, their packs and buckets strewn around. "You look like a gypsy story," he says, gently waking them. Their faces light up when they see the jars of water. They drink and drink, while Herald has a foul-tasting swallow from Uncle Al's tin canteen. "Whew, thank God you guys are alright," he says. "I never thought you'd haul everything half this far."

"It wasn't easy," grunts Brick, "but it gave us something to do,"

Herald shoves Brick's pack behind the tree. "Those twin twits will soon be here," he says, "and they think the pack and the soup pot are lost. Let's keep them in suspense as long as we can."

Sedge, Herald and Brick put their heads together. "Let's... mumble, mumble... ha!... grumble, murmle, mumble... hee hee ha."

The Terrible Trio has just enough time to plot their confrontation with the Dastardly Duo before Ron and Rich at last stagger into view. They look like whittled-down versions of themselves, a pair of Rich's stick carvings. Are those dried tears on the sun burnt cheeks? No more bombast and bravado? Poor boys.

Sedge feels sorry for the rascals, while Herald is clearly delighted to be a few steps ahead of them for a change. Brick coughs like a coffin. He stares at the twins without saying a word until they start to shift nervously from foot to foot. Do a few quills of conscience begin to penetrate their tough hides?

Ron blusters, "Why're you three looking at us like that?"

"Yeah!" says Rich. "Like... demented meerkats!"

Herald, Brick, and Sedge say nothing.

Ron and Rich are covered with scratches and bruises and look parched. Ron has a welt the size of a walnut below one ear. Rich has blood on his cheek, and running down one knee where a chunk of pant leg is torn off. They're filthy. But ever the gentlemen when they wish to be, they pass around the water bottles they've lugged up, patiently waiting with their tongues hanging out for their turns to guzzle. They glance furtively around the camp. One question is on their minds. Where is the soup pot? Of course it's not here, how could it be? And yet, they'd had an irrational hope that it might be, that it might mirage itself into existence at any moment, or that suddenly everyone would have total amnesia about its ever existing. But no such luck.

Herald peers over his glasses at the twins and asks in a stern voice, "Do you know where our soup pot is?"

They flinch.

Brick clears his throat in an ominous way.

Sedge paces to hide her smirk.

Herald glowers.

"What the…" Ron starts a belligerent retort, then thinks better of it. The twins look at each other, confused, unsure, and exhausted. Losing their last shred of swagger, they blurt, "We lost it!"

Brick croaks, "You lost it?"

Sedge laughs, "How could you lose something that big?"

Herald holds them in his best practice-teacher glare, with raised eyebrows and sizzling eyeballs. The twins shrink as they look up at him towering over them. Herald stretches out his long arms and swoops at them so suddenly they yelp. He wraps one heron-wing around Rich and the other around Ron, then firmly pulls them towards a log where he sits them on either side of him. Held in his unyielding embrace, the thirteen-year-olds at last break down. They recite the sad litany of their afternoon, their interference with the soup pot, their conviction that the Kludge gang has stolen it, and the Kludges' vicious attempt to kill them. Sedge, Brick, and Herald listen without interrupting. By the end of their sorry tale, Ron and Rich are limp as overcooked noodles sliding down the drain. Yet they feel slightly better than they did before. At least they're still alive, although they still believe the soup pot is missing. Ron and Rich have been given plenty of time to cut a worthy switch for themselves. The twins don't even notice a flicker of sunlight penetrating the rain clouds. They're too busy wondering if they'll still be alive at the end of the day.

Down at the foundations, Fern and Hazel are puttering around camp, doubting that all eleven of them will ever again be in one place at one time. Billy and Alvin's voices are drifting further and further away. Hazel shouts, "Billy! Alvin! Come back!" She can't decipher their reply.

The oldest sisters have two buckets of water heating. They have sorted the food caches and are playing rummy in between tending the fire and keeping watch over Pink and Julie, who are forbidden to leave camp. The five-year twins have discovered Alvin's glass collection and are inventing a game they call "hop-marble." It involves them screaming "Hop-marble glass-startle!" as they hurl themselves from the crumbling steps, trying not to land on the pieces of glass they've strategically placed in the mud. Luckily it's old glass, mostly worn smooth.

"Jeez, when are Herald and those guys coming back, do you think? The sun's almost down," frets Hazel.

"That's just because of where we are," soothes Fern. "The sun's prob'ly still high in the valley. We can see only a little wedge of sky from here. At least there's a little break in the clouds."

"I know… but the cows went home ages ago. Dad should be here."

"Let's make tea."

On a high ridge of the elephant back, Brick, Herald, Sedge, Ron, and Rich are progressing cautiously across the last ore heap on their way down to camp. No one is talking. Herald keeps expecting Ron and Rich to ask him why they were up this bald part of the mountain in the first place. But the teen twins are concentrating only on carrying Brick's share of the load so he can lean on a stout pole to steady himself.

Brick feels like he has a rat-trap clamped on his arm and he's trying not to think about it. Instead he wonders why his knee feels like it's got a stiff chunk of rubber wrapped around it.

Sedge is the first to notice the rainbow. "Look!" They stop in their tracks, quietly watching the vivid colours shimmer into a full arc.

At the foundations, Hazel and Fern stand transfixed, voices muted as they watch the colours unfurl. Pink and Julie lie on their backs, their faces smudged with rainbow light, licking it as though it's cotton candy.

Alvin and Billy stop their racket down by the creek for a moment and watch the rainbow slowly drop away.

Bob, driving the Hearse into the valley, glimpses the rainbow in his rear-view mirror and thinks of Lettuce.

Lettuce, at last pegging out the blankets, watches the rainbow paint the valley richer green, the mountains deeper purple, the garden more vividly every colour, and thinks of all her family.

Seeing that rainbow from thirteen different vantage points, it briefly shines in all of their faces, uniting them without their knowing it. Except for Rich and Ron. A rainbow usually holds them spellbound till the last glimpse, but they can't enjoy this one, they feel so unworthy. If an angel were to swoop out of the heavens right now to give them a lifetime achievement award, they'd say they didn't deserve it.

As the rainbow fades, Sedge and Brick, Ron, Rich, and Herald share bottles of water and shift their packs and buckets. Brick passes around a pouch of Sen Sen he's kept for just such a time. The licorice tidbits refresh them momentarily and they move on.

Herald and Sedge banter as they trudge down the mountain, trying to get a rise out of Rich and Ron. They drop hints about the soup pot of berries, "the dark blue treasure at the end of the rainbow."

But Rich and Ron aren't listening. They're concentrating too hard on putting one foot in front of the other.

CHAPTER 41
Crick to the Hospital

MEANWHILE, AS BOB STEERS the Hearse down the last bend into the valley and past the dairy, a glance at his watch tells him it's almost six. The cows are heading, single file, into their milking barn, moaning loudly enough to be heard above the groaning vehicle.

Damn, he's late, with another half hour's drive ahead of him. He'd better get a move on. He coaxes the Hearse up the first hill and over the top.

Hold on. Who's that staggering down the middle of the road toward him?

It's Crick, limping.

Bob cranks down his window, slows to a rough idle and leans out, hollering, "You look like you need help."

Crick looks pathetic. His face is red with scratches and his tongue seems to be stuck to his bottom lip. He holds his matted hair to one side so he can look up at Bob, his eyes glazed. He's sniveling. One foot is bare and badly swollen, its shoe and sock clenched in a muddy fist.

"Do you want a lift?" asks Bob.

Crick can't talk and Bob doesn't have time to dawdle but it's obvious the kid needs medical help, so Bob stomps on the emergency brake, hauls himself out, yanks open a back door, and hauls the boy in. Twenty minutes later, Bob's explaining to the night shift at the hospital how he found the boy, the boy needs help, and he doesn't have time to wait around with him because he's got a bunch of kids waiting for him up on the mountain.

A tall nurse who looks like an agitated leghorn rustles out a form and clucks by Bob's elbow as he signs it. As he heads out the door she's cackling at the boy, who is staring with a look of terror at her when Bob turns to call good-bye.

When he restarts the Hearse, it has an attack of asthma, alerting Bob to the fact that it's trying to run on empty. Good thing it's only a couple blocks downhill to get gas; he can coast if he has to.

Finally, gassed up, he's once again jouncing over the pot holes by the dairy, while the cows are straggling into their night pasture. It's almost seven o'clock.

The Hearse once again begrudgingly grinds up the first rocky hill on the way to Stooge's Mill. It bucks and balks up the next hill, wheezes, flounders around a hairpin turn and then... of course, what else?

There's a cow lying in the middle of the road.

CHAPTER 42
Eleven at Camp

IT MUST HAVE BEEN about the time Bob was taking Crick to the hospital that Herald and Brick, Sedge, Rich, and Ron at last stagger back to the Stooge's Mill foundations. They'd never thought they'd be so glad to see the steps to nowhere. Alvin whoops like a banshee from his lookout tree as they approach while Billy and Fern, Hazel, Pink, and Julie run to meet them, clustering noisily around Sedge and the boys. Brick holds them off with his good arm.

"Whoa, stay back, girls, don't touch me, I'm fine. I'll just set myself on this rock by the fire and try not to burn myself."

Brick is shivering. Herald helps him sit down without jarring his arm. Julie and Pink gently snuggle up to him, crooning. Hazel tucks her jacket around his shoulders and Sedge brings him a cup of hot cocoa. Alvin straightens Brick's ball-cap and helps Hazel and Pink make up another batch of cocoa, going easy on the dwindling sugar and powder milk.

They gather around the fire.

Brick won't let Fern fuss with his arm and she sadly puts away her neatly folded regulation Girl Guide sling and pink diaper pins. He will have to stay wrapped in his pink and orange tie and blue scarf. Fern and Sedge carefully tuck a sweater under Brick's head. Brick has to admit he's slightly comfortable once they have him settled, and he sighs. He can't really feel his arm anymore. He's starting to notice that his knee hurts but he keeps that to himself. Saying it out loud will only make it worse. Instead he says, "Thanks for all the attention! I feel like I have four moms and it sure is great."

Hazel playfully tosses a handful of tiny hemlock cones at his feet. Alvin feeds them into the fire one by one, watching them quickly turn to neon ash.

Brick looks around and asks, "Hey, where's Billy?"

"Search us!" says Hazel. "He said he'd stick around but next thing, he's down the gully, hollering he's found some good berries. And you know how that goes, we might not see him till tomorrow."

"Right," Fern sighs. "Next thing it'll be two days later and we'll still be wondering where he is. I don't know why he had to take off right when we finally were all going to be together."

Alvin shoves a stick into the fire and mutters, "I went with Billy a long ways but I got sick of picking berries. And I was cold." He has his feet buried in dirt and ashes. Everyone's tired. No one has much to say. While they wait, itches are scratched and scrapes are inspected.

Herald slurps noisily from a bucket, asking, "Anybody got the time?"

"Seven-thirty, more or less," mutters Brick. "Dad's sure late. I wonder why it's taking him so long to get here."

(They would be amazed if they knew that at that moment, Bob is making the acquaintance of a cow named Sweetgrass.)

Hazel makes a megaphone with her hands and shouts, "Billy! BILLY! Come back! NOW!... What a day. Someone's always lost."

"Or just not found," says Julie.

During this conversation, Billy is not far away, as the crow flies. But he has to climb down a ravine and back out again and then the reverse.

It's peculiar how a person can suddenly know they've lost something, even when they haven't been thinking about it. Billy has nonchalantly been plunking some good-size berries into his bucket when it suddenly hits him that he doesn't remember putting his magnifying glass away after he'd gotten that moss smoking where they'd had their lunch. He hopes he didn't leave it where it could start a fire. Good thing it rained. He checks his pockets a second and a third time, knowing it's not there. Well. But. He's not that far from where they had lunch. Billy decides to make a quick sweep around there to see if he can find it. He hears Hazel calling him and hollers, "I'll be back in a few minutes." His words are garbled by distance, but Hazel knows it's Billy's voice and he sounds okay.

It takes a bit longer than a few minutes for Billy to accept that he's not going to find his magnifying glass. He does find some laden bushes when he stumbles into a ditch alongside a fallen tree. No rules about picking clean or clean picking apply at this stage of the day for Billy. Skimming the whoppers off the top of the bushes is entirely legal under the circumstances. His search for his magnifying glass has not been a total waste of time. Determined not to lose any berries, he holds his heaping bucket with both hands, cautiously making his way back to Stooge's with eyes straining to pick out the easiest route. He calls greetings as he nears the mill site; everyone's glad he's back.

"At last! Hooray! You're here!" shouts Alvin.

"We're all here, finally!" says Fern. "Where've you been, Billy?"

"Where have you been, Billy boy, Billy boy? Where have you been, Charming Billy?" sing Pink and Julie. "Have you been to seek a wife?"

"Or did you get lost?" Hazel asks. "Wow! Look at all your berries, Billy!"

"Yup," Billy smiles. "I just found too good a patch to leave behind. My bucket's nicely rounded, eh. I went further than I planned, but..."

Julie shouts, "Billy! Billy! I found your maggot-frying glass." She hands it to him proudly.

"Holy smokes! Thanks! I went looking for it where we had our lunch, but..."

Hazel snorts, "So the truth comes out. That's why it took you so long to get back to camp after everybody else was here, Billy! As if we needed one more person getting lost while they looked for something they'd lost."

"I didn't get lost... it was just further than I thought. I got lots more berries. And Julie, it's a *magnifying* glass. I magnify things with it, not fry them... except bits of lichen and straw."

"And maggots," says Ron.

"Eeeewww!" Julie is disgusted.

"But though, you're here safe and sound," cheers Fern.

"Woo-hoo! Everyone's here at last!" shrill Pink and Julie.

Before they get too carried away with excitement, Herald does his finger-whistle to get everyone's attention. "Let's really stay together now, hey, gang, it'll soon be getting dark! I'm serious. If anyone takes off without saying so, they're going to be in big trouble."

"Sir, I need to wee," says a small voice.

"Take one of your big sisters with you, Julie."

Hazel agrees to go with her.

Sedge and Pink go in the opposite direction, to the creek for fresh water. Unsentimental Pink rushes back to camp with her water, while Sedge stops to watch the last shred of mauve leave the sky. She lingers in the falling light, already longing for the day that's passing. She imagines pulling back the beauty, strand by strand: the shimmering morning of anticipation, the twirling swallowtails, the bird song, her time with Brick. The rainbow. Then she picks up her bucket and hastens back, where she dips her scarf in the icy water and crouches by Brick to hold it against his forehead. The chill water gives him agonizing relief and he brushes his cheek against her hand.

With heavy clouds in the west, darkness is coming early. They settle in around the campfire. Fern doses Brick with another Aspirin. Ron tucks his football under Brick's shoulder for a cushion. Brick's glad of the comfort and wonders vaguely where the cushion has come from. Alvin seems to be the only one who enjoys unsweetened Kool-aid, but even he is drinking it very diluted. He takes a cup to Brick, who sips it questioningly. Fern riffles through her first-aid book, consulting with Sedge and Herald about arm injuries. Is it a sprain, is it a break of the ulna or radius, transverse, compound, spiral, a distal radial metaphyseal fracture? Will he need surgery, a cast? They won't know until tomorrow.

Accustomed to being the strong one, Brick's poleaxed by his accident. He gives up trying to figure out what else he can do and falls into a jumpy slumber. He's comforted by the familiar voices around him as they mingle with his dreams.

Pink and Julie sing rounds of "The Bear Went Over the Mountain," then intone a new chant in voices like chickadees:

I wish for a dish
and in the dish a fish
and in the fish a wish
that I can wish once more
that behind the kitchen door
I will find a dish
and in the dish a fish... and so on and so on, ad nauseam.

Billy caterwauls "Oh Susannah" on a harmonica and Alvin keeps time by thumping on a log. The girls pinch their noses, tap their throats and hum loudly, gurbling a sound like Horkalinki's guinea fowl on whiskey.

To Brick, it sounds just like home, and he slips into a deeper sleep, snoring gustily. His snores are a soothing sound for the rest of them and they gradually grow quiet, which causes Brick to wake with a start, sit up, and groan. Julie brings him a jar of water and after a long drink, he says he feels a bit better as long as he holds his arm still. Herald asks him if he's up to helping tell the Saga of the Missing Soup Pot. Brick stretches, has another drink and mutters, "Sure, I'll have a go at it. Let me see now. My bucket was almost full. It weighed a ton, so I decided to empty it into the soup pot. I was hot and the mosquitoes had been eating me for lunch…"

Ron and Rich fidget. They've had a few hours to stew and chew over their side of the story. If they could get away with it right now, they'd hightail it into the field to kick the football around. Rich scoops it up now that Brick isn't using it and passes it to Ron, who steps into the shadows.

"Hey, where do you guys think you're going?" asks Herald.

"Nowhere."

They slip into twin zone, deftly tossing the ball back and forth. The others expect it to fly out of control at any moment, but it doesn't. It looks like it's connected to the two boys by invisible elastic as they effortlessly volley it. In tune to every feint and spin of the other's hands, they never drop the ball until Brick, resuming his narrative, gets to the part where he and Herald and Sedge realize that the soup pot is missing. The football jerks suddenly into the field. Neither Ron nor Rich dares take after it.

Sedge speaks of their outrage at finding the soup pot gone, their anger, their fury. The Terrible Trio asks the Dastardly Duo, in solemn voices, "Do you admit *you* took it?"

"Um, erm, uh yes, we took it."

"Are you sorry?"

"Of course we're sorry. Cripes! Our day's been horrible ever since."

"You'll never fool with other people's berries again?"

"No, no, no! Now will you leave us alone! We said we're sorry."

"Sometimes sorry isn't enough."

The boys no longer personify smug superiority. Abjection and Dejection would be better names for them now than Bravado and Bombast, with their heads hanging, their exhausted faces streaked with dirt.

Herald gives Alvin a signal that it's time to make his presentation. Alvin jumps up and with a hand around his mouth he trumpets a fanfare. "Ta-da-ta-do! Hey everyone... ta-do-ta-do! Lookee here!"

With a flourish, he whips the jacket off the soup pot and waves it like a magician's cape. "Ta da!" He pulls the bark away from the pot and pulls off the flour sack to reveal the heap of shiny berries, "Ta-doo-ta-doo!" Herald drums on the water bucket, taradiddle, double diddle flam!

Ron and Rich tread in midair as they rush to the soup pot, gaping. They expect it to disappear before their eyes, or shapeshift into some other kind of pot. They can't believe it's there in front of them and not only that, it's full of berries still. Everyone else is shrieking with laughter. Automatically, Ron reaches out to grab some berries and pulls his hand back, before lightning can strike him dead. Rich shakes his head in consternation. "How the heck? How did you guys? What the... Where did you? How? Why dint you tell us?"

"Oh. I get it. You wanted us to worry," says Ron. "Like waiting for Uncle Percival's switch?"

"You mean, you guys have been worried?"

"Yeah, we been worried. Halfway to puking."

Herald, Brick, and Sedge laugh wickedly. Not all the others know the whole story yet, but they realize that some kind of huge joke is playing out. Billy is beside himself with delight as the drama unfolds.

Ron and Rich stammer, "We would've put the pot back if you'd just given us half a chance."

"We didn't know that," says Herald. "And never mind trying to put the onus on us! You're the ones who tampered with the berries we'd been slaving over since the crack of dawn. Good thing we're not bears or you would've been cuffed long ago, hey Brick?"

"Yep. Sure is a good thing we're civilized human beings, and we decided to teach you boys a lesson. Instead of killing you. We thought we'd make life easier for you, by smartening you up a bit so's you don't have to be in trouble for skulduggery all your lives."

Sedge chortles at the twins' indignation. "Do you think you've learned a lesson, Ron and Rich?"

"Uh, yeah… We learned not to uh… what lesson did we learn, Ron?"

"Uh, I dunno… not to trick people? And not to tamper with the family hoard?" asks Ron.

"Even if it does look like a soup pot full of pesky sour purple blips. I've got cankers so bad! I don't think I'll eat another berry my whole life," Rich complains.

Fern hoots. "You poor little innocent boys! This reminds me of that time Miss Hortense was teaching us choral reading. That time you switched the words?"

"Tell us, Fern! Give us the story!" shouts Billy.

With animation, Fern begins, "It was when Miss Hortense brought Ron and Rich's class into our room to practice our choral reading for the community assembly. Of course, our boys were right up front, volunteering to hand out the word sheets. We were supposed to read "The Rime of the Ancient Mariner" by Coleridge and everybody was so sick of his "glittering eye" and "not a drop to drink" that we were ready to drop dead. Well, lo and behold, what do Ron and Rich hand out but the words to "Jabberwocky" by Lewis Carroll? So Miss Hortense lets the class stumble along for about ten minutes, trying to read the impossible words, none of us ever at the same place.

"Finally, she bangs her pointer on her desk and we stop. She's got her words all thought out, you know the way she does, and she says in her precise way, 'Ronald Henry and Richard Harvey! By what sleight of hand you have accomplished this miscarriage of decorum I do not know and I do not care to know. But I believe you planned to create havoc in this last practice by purposely handing out the wrong word sheets.' She glared at Ron and Rich for about five minutes, with everyone too scared to move. Pretty soon you could see Ron's shoulders twitch, he was trying so hard not to laugh, and Rich was one big tic from his feet to his eyebrows. Even Mrs. Hortense had a hard time keeping a straight face looking at their poor little dumb innocent faces."

"Yeah, and then she told us we had to recite the whole six verses of Jabberwocky for assembly, with only three days left to memorize it," groans Rich.

"And then," says Ron, "after we'd almost worn out our brains getting it perfect, she gave us word sheets just before we went on stage. I guess she was afraid we'd spoil the show by messing up."

"Plus she wanted us to suffer first, trying to memorize it," adds Rich. "But by then we knew it by heart, so we chucked the word sheets on our way up to the stage and stood up there and said the whole thing easy as counting to ten."

"Yeah! But it damaged us," says Ron. "We still can't get Jabberwocky out of our heads. It's bonded like glue to our brains."

Ron and Rich recite perfectly:
'Twas brillig and the slithy toves
Did gyre and gimble in the webe…
Beware the Jabberwock my son!

214

The jaws that bite, the claws that catch!

Beware the jubjub bird…

"So Mrs. Hortense boosted our F in co-operation skills to a B minus," says Rich.

"But then," adds Ron, "we accidentally called Miss Prizz a 'frumious bandersnitch' and she gave us an F in social skills."

"You called her that?" shrieks Hazel.

"In unison."

Everyone roars. Ron and Rich can finally pull their heads out of the noose that's been around their necks all afternoon. They're free, and the berries are safe! Wild with new energy, they run into the field with Billy, Alvin, Pink, and Julie, laughing and clapping and turning cartwheels in the meadow, oblivious of cow pies and gopher holes.

Brick watches them and shakes his head. "How can those guys get away with it, not breaking their necks in their circus act out there, when I just have to stand on a rock wrong and I get busted?"

Herald, Sedge, Fern, and Hazel move closer to him, near the fire. Herald shrugs. "Accidents are never fair. A tipsy rock could have pitched anyone over, especially with a pack the size of yours on their back. The waist belt broke and that's what sent you off kilter. It's my fault. I should never have let you take that load, and especially I should never have let you use a broken pack-board."

"It's okay, Hare, it's my fault for being macho. And now it's really wrecked."

Herald tears the board off the pack and cracks it over his knee. "That ornery old frame sure didn't give much resistance. It didn't deserve to be mended, it's about a century old. I've got a good idea, let's burn it!"

Fern and Hazel cheer. "A sacrificial fire! An appeasement to the gods to make Brick's arm better. Come on, everybody, we're going to burn the pack-board!"

They salvage buckles and bits of canvas and Rich saves a piece of the well-seasoned wood for carving. Then they shove pieces of the board into the fire. Brick pokes it with a stick, turning it until it catches. Hazel says, "We took you for granted, Brick, carrying so much weight. We're sorry, Bricky."

There's a chorus of apology.

Brick is embarrassed by their concern and turns to watch as Ron and Rich continue their acrobatics in the field. "Those guys must have some kind of twin protection, doing handstands in the dark like that. Invisible nerves of steel that run between them, keeping them safe."

"A twin connection?" asks Herald. "It's as if they can see with each other's eyes and hear with each other's ears, as well as their own... so they're doubly connected to the world."

"That sounds very complicated. But maybe that's why they do so well on exams when they hardly seem to study," suggests Hazel. "They can study in half the time, because there's two of them working on it. And they can pick each other's brains."

"And still have time for all their bluster and blather," says Brick.

"Pink and Julie have something weird like that going on, too, some connection that defies logic," Hazel puzzles. "Though none of our twins are even identical. It must be a weird family twin gene."

Herald laughs. "Sounds like a good essay topic. Fraternal twins with brain-links. How common is the phenomenon? Nobody knows."

Bored with the conversation, Julie and Pink help Alvin retrieve his glass collection so no one's bare feet will get cut in the dark. They save a chunk of cobalt blue and a small vial turned mauve with age, which they take turns holding up to admire in the fire-light before Alvin stows them safely away. Ron and Rich roll up another log to sit on. Fern ransacks Brick's knapsack to find the can opener. "Ah, jeez, not this one."

"Whatsamatter with it?" asks Rich.

"It's the one you and Ron took the do-ma-hickey out of. For one of your cockamamie contraptions," says Herald. "There ought to be a law against tampering with important things like can openers, it could be a matter of life or death. Hand it here, I'll see what I can do with it." Herald has a screwdriver which, smacked with a rock, could open the can, more or less, but that might damage the screwdriver. He searches his pockets. He comes up with a Meccano slat and piece of wire. He Jerry-rigs the can opener, Uncle Ronald style, and soon has the family-size can of pork and beans ratcheted open.

Ron has finally located his baloney sandwich and macaroni. They're nicely blended, squashed together all day in one bag in the bottom of Brick's pack. He passes the bag back and forth with Rich. Mmmmmm. Umami with grit. They cram their mouths, making it sound so delectable with their slurping and smacking that they have to dole out morsels to Alvin and Billy. When Julie and Pink want some too, Rich says snot and that's the end of that. He reaches for another handful of "mac-aloney." "How come you girls don't like the snot word?" he asks innocently.

"You don't like snot worms, snot webs, snot spiders?" taunts Ron.

"Eeeew, tell them to stop teasing us," whines Pink.

"Fight your own battles. Just ignore them," advises Hazel.

"How come you couldn't ignore them when you had the stomach flu and they kept showing you pictures of rabbit intestines?"

Hazel scowls, "Please don't let's have another argument. Ron and Rich, stop teasing. You may think it's fun, but nobody else does."

Herald jumps up and takes the boys by the scruff of their necks. He's beside himself. How can he get through to them, short of banging their heads together? Has nothing he's said or done made the slightest difference? He usually vents his temper with an explosion of words, but he's close to imploding. Herald is speechless. He pushes them away.

Perhaps it's the way he looked right through them as he weighed his thoughts. Perhaps it's his total loss for words. Rich and Ron see something in their eldest brother they've never seen before. Despair? They realize they've come close to breaking him. And that's scary.

They sit down quietly by the fire. Herald yanks the bark off a birch log.

Fern and Hazel have been taking turns stirring the beans and deem them hot enough. Ron grabs the sock potholder; with the help of his pliers, he hoists the can onto a concrete slab. Billy supervises as Pink and Julie dole their beans onto one plate, then the rest of them belly-up to the five other plates. Then the highlight of the meal is ceremoniously roasted and assembled: hot dogs! With lots of mustard. Finally, potatoes are raked from the coals to cool slightly, then eaten out of hand, the charred remains scraped clean and tossed back into the fire.

"Mmmm, delicious."

"This is the life."

A few more plums are eaten. Fern once again tucks away the applesauce cookies and raisins for later. She looks around at all of them in their haphazard, mismatched jackets and trousers held together with belts, suspenders, buckles and twine, and their one-of-a-kind beanies, berets, cloches, ball-caps, bucket hats and tuques. They look like an illustration from a story, and she ponders the story.

As their hunger eases, they gaze into the convoluted patterns in the flames, beginning to piece together the events of their long day. The where and when take some sorting out. Their story is basted together at first by long running stitches, like Pink and Julie's hems, which tend to pucker, and are frequently torn out. Parts are rearranged again and again and still never seem to quite fit. Other pieces are quickly feather-stitched in rainbow detail. Eleven individual accounts are sewn together thread by thread, like one of Fern's crazy-quilt skirts, which must be pressed again and again by the ironing machine before it will hold its shape.

They all have something to add to the theme of the "trick-that-back-fired." There's Pink and Julie's elaborately detailed recital of exploring a new land and finding their hairband and saving a porcupine. There are several versions of "getting caught in a lightning storm." There are demonstrations of almost dying on a scree slope and disappearing down a mine hole and of shoes falling half-way to China. There are overlays and underlays about the mother-lode soup pot and the mother of all pack loads, which are seen as both salvation and burden. There are various episodes of lost and found, discovery and concealment. The rainbow is reviewed from all angles and bird songs are imitated.

It's a story that will be folded and refolded, expanded, refurbished and embellished, again and again, over the next hours and days and years. It will become a family legend, whittled and woven, hemmed and darned, re-enacted in skit, pantomime, painting, limerick, lyric, and long-winded anecdote.

Outside the circle of animated faces, the trees are black silhouettes against a gunmetal sky. Brick has dozed off again and no one wants to disturb him to look at his watch. Their Dad should have come long ago. A feeling is creeping in from the shadows that something is very wrong at home.

* * *

(Far below them on the back of the mountain, a dark, shaggy form is sniffing, eyes glowing.)

* * *

CHAPTER 43
Lettuce and Bob

MEANWHILE, FOR THE UMPTEENTH time, Lettuce gazes out the kitchen door, ignoring the large gray moth which flutters inside. The mountains have faded from green and blue into a rich infusion of all the colours of the day. The wet air is saturated with lilac, the garden is deep in shadow. The blaze of nasturtiums on the western edge, which held the day's sunlight in their petals, has long since faded.

Lettuce pulls on her gumboots and soon discovers the back clothesline has collapsed with its load of rugs. It was bound to happen, shredding on a splice after too many heavy loads over too many years. She has half a notion to bury the old rugs, which have flopped into a fresh Grand Rapids patch. She eyes the shovel, handy under the eave. She could get rid of the rugs and replant lettuce at the same time... She would have to dig a very big hole, though, to bury the miserable rugs. Maybe she should just scatter seed over top of them where they lie, making a sort of lettuce hill? The rugs look as much like dirt as dirt itself. Rinsing them in the dye water hadn't improved their looks. Oh well. At least they haven't landed in the gooseberries. Lettuce dutifully slings the heavy lumps over the tire swings and the bottom limbs of a maple tree. The kids can hose them off in the morning. They'll love that job.

Bob and the kids should have been home hours ago. But Bob did take an empty bucket with him, and he can pick berries in the dark. As Lettuce mopped the floors, she was glad they didn't come tromping in—but that was ages ago. The peace and quiet is getting her down. Supper's ready. The wash is finally done. Lettuce puts down several layers of newspaper by the backdoor, determined to keep back the felted Aunt Hilarity rugs for special occasions. There's nothing more she can do but put her feet on a kitchen chair and give in to the suspense of Donald Hyer's *Amazon Intrigue*. Howard Spring will have to wait a while longer with his piping, "Read me too; I'm almost due."

* * *

Far away, barreling up the mountain, Bob has barely managed to stop his menace-on-wheels in time to avoid the cow sprawled across the road. The Hearse backfires a few feet from her and she lifts her head with an earsplitting, "MMMMOOOoooooOOooo!"

Bob climbs out and cautiously approaches the startled animal. She's obviously panic-stricken, but she doesn't rise from the ground. Is she injured? What can he do to help this mountain of flesh? The cow must weigh at least a ton more than he does. She looks at him with huge, dark eyes, sweeping her head back to lick at her hind-quarters, and Bob realizes with a shock why she's lying there. A calf is about to be born in the middle of the road. Wouldn't you know it, just when he's in a rush.

Bob paces. What else can he do? He envisions playing the role of country vet and immersing his arm to the shoulder, navigating blind internal alleys, untangling unborn limbs. No. He's not going to try that. Nor is there room to drive past the cow. In her precarious state, he dares not harass her into moving. He stares at the cow glumly. As though offended by his lack of delicacy, she stretches her neck and moos long and soulfully, "Mmmmmoooooooooooo."

Bob peers under the hood of the Hearse, where he feels a little more capable. The kids would have been teasing him to check the flambulator. He tinkers with the spark plugs, adds water to the radiator and tightens the cap, and then, without thinking, he slams the hood shut. The cow groans dreadfully, lurches forward as if to stand and collapses with a gurgling moan. She's panting and licking. Not much he can do for her. Bob finds a map book, digs in the food box for a pretzel and, leaving the door ajar, walks down to the switchback to study maps and watch for traffic.

He thinks fleetingly of hiking up to see the kids. It's almost eight. Do any of them have a watch? Brick, maybe. Billy's hasn't worked for ages. They'll be getting worried. But it would be pointless to go up without the car. And the last thing he needs is another vehicle rear-ending the Hearse in the dark. There's nothing to do but stay put until the cow finishes what she's doing. He can't see the map properly in the thickening dusk, but he gnaws on his pretzel.

He feels like a bag of nails turning to rust.

CHAPTER 44
Rootbeer Ants

THE ELEVEN ARE GETTING bored and despondent. The first stars are hidden by skittering clouds. A nervous breeze flicks the fire this way and that, stinging their eyes with smoke. They're tired of playing camp for what is starting to seem like three or four days. Glum voices drift, disembodied, in the dark.

"The Hearse has prob'ly died once and for all."

"Is a flambulator sort of like a gizzard?

"If the Hearse had either one, it'd prob'ly be broken."

"Maybe some of us should hike down and see if Dad needs help."

"No. It's too dangerous to go blundering off in the dark. We've had enough danger today."

"We have to stick together. Safety in numbers."

"At least we're finally together."

"We might as well resign ourselves to staying here."

"For the rest of our lives?"

"No, but maybe till morning."

There's deep silence in which Pink and Julie snuggle between their big sisters. Sedge tries to think of a cheerful topic. "Mom said Auntie Anne might come with Auntie Ben and Aunt Hilarity later this summer to make plans for next year's Summer Art Camp for Cousins."

Pink and Julie spring up in excitement. "They might come to our place? That would be so fun! Tell us again about Aunt Hilarity's, please, Fern and Hazel. You're so lucky you've been there." And one of their favorite topics unfolds.

"One whole wall was tapestry," begins Hazel. "Three dimensional flowers and birds and dragons. The house was enchanting… but to tell you the truth, it was a bit much for me. All those colours! I felt dizzy half the time."

"How can colours make you dizzy, Hazel, but climbing on roofs doesn't?"

"I don't know, Rich. I was mostly watching birds and roaming the fields, or in the barn building bird houses and stilt puppets. But you thought the house was heaven, didn't you, Fern?"

"Yes!" Fern enthuses. "Skeins of every colour of embroidery thread, wool, and ribbon hanging on racks. Shelves and shelves of fabric, and paper, every texture and colour you could imagine… Little cabinets full of beads and buttons and shells and sequins. Aunt Hilarity slept and made her meals in just a crowded little end of her house. Her huge embroidery hoop took up half the living room… like a rainbow harp."

"And her loom took up the other half," adds Hazel. "I pitched myself a tent in a barn."

"Wasn't that kind of scary and lonely," asks Julie, "sleeping alone in a barn?"

"Not at all," laughs Hazel. "I could lie with my head out and see an owl looking down at me in the moonlight. A barred owl. Early early in the morning, I could hear her shwoosh out the window to hunt."

Pink and Julie have been dancing in smaller and smaller circles until they fall in a heap.

"Let's pick up our stuff before it's pitch dark," says Herald.

There's a general pulling on of sweaters and jackets and rolling down of sleeves, and pant legs for those who have any. No one is bare-headed, at least.

Gear is tossed into packs, firewood is organized, and more wood is scrounged. Ron, Pink, and Billy follow their ears to the spring and refill the spare bucket and canteens. Water is set to heat in the cocoa pan. The fire is carefully fed with branches that are quickly devoured.

"It's like we're feeding a pet," muses Billy. "In return, it gives us warmth and light."

A pitchy branch makes a loud snap, sending up cascades of sparks to the delight of the youngsters and concern of the elders.

"It starts out small and cute but keeps growing," says Ron. "It'll eat us alive if we overfeed it."

"Like the cute little Hobyah that swallowed the dog?" asks Billy

"Hobyah, hobyah, hobyah, I'm coming to eat you," growls Rich.

"Stop it!" cries Julie. "I hate that story."

"Why do you always have to say it in that scary Mr. Nitmust voice?" asks Pink.

"You know why I do? 'Cause if I don't you'll pester me until I do."

"Not now. Anyhow, Hobyahs aren't real," soothes Fern.

"We don't know that for sure. They could be somewhere we just haven't looked yet," says Pink.

"In the bottom of mine holes?" asks Alvin.

"Stop it, you guys. No more scary stuff," warns Herald.

Stories which promote hysterics are the last thing they need now. No good can come of kids falling over themselves with nightmares on a remote mountain. Hazel matter-of-factly says, "You have a choice. You can either dwell on creepy things and scare yourselves to death, or you can decide it's nonsense and get over it."

Alvin says it's hard when the pictures are stuck in your brain. Brick groans in his sleep. Fern says they should all try to think happy thoughts. Hazel tries to change the subject, and she succeeds by talking at great length about an article she read about the sleeping habits of moles. The mood shifts from tension to boredom, which is an improvement.

In the backs of their minds, they all have ghastly tales they'd like to tell, as if by sharing them, they'll dilute them. But even harmless sparrows released by day can come back as vultures at night.

Alvin and the little twins have more than once crouched behind the attic door to hear the older kids' muffled discussions of war and death, of strange happenings between twilight and dawn. And later wished they hadn't listened.

But haven't we all struggled to hear the stories we dread?

Cranked up the world news?

Hobyah hobyah?

At any rate, when a pitchy chunk of tamarack shifts on the flames, it's as if a twister of bad luck spins through the group. Julie yelps when a spark lands on her ankle, quickly scuffling it out in the dirt, while just then, Billy, breaking up sticks for kindling, gets a chunk of pine under his thumbnail. "Bull bollocks!" he yells.

Startled, Brick jumps, dislodging the football supporting his injured arm. He stifles a moan, which Hazel sustains off-key as a cramp twists deep in her innards. Herald shudders, the hair bristling on the back of his neck.

Could a hostile outside energy be having sport with them? They know in their heart of hearts it can't be true, but they feel in their bones that it is.

Cause and effect get complicated when eleven siblings interact day in and day out, year after year. And when two sets of twins play mind games, switching things up and turning things around, no one can be sure what's for real. Add to that the fact that Rich and Julie are untrained ventriloquists and it's no wonder some of them believe in ESP and UFO's.

Herald and Hazel can debate this kind of thing by the hour. Can they ever really know what's natural and what's supernatural? What's coincidence? What's fate? What's chance and what's the result of persistent meddling? If we look up in surprise at a sudden change, maybe it's because we haven't seen the infinite small changes which have finally breached our threshold of awareness.

On Chuckie Moozle's innocent black box with knobs and rabbit ears, some of them have watched *Crypt of Horror* and *Executions In the Abyss* The supernatural is a topic which they try to laugh off. It's just entertainment, isn't it, like comic books? Pretend stuff. Or not. They have an inkling of things which can dissolve the filter between make-believe and reality. On Friday nights, when compelled by the flickering in Moozle's window, when poor reception adds to the lure of journeys into the Twilight Zone, they'll watch, spell-bound, though they swear off the show after each episode. The creepiness gets to them in different ways, at different levels.

Much of the time, the Eleven are at peace together, but sometimes a restless current short-circuits them. It's as if a haunting breath enters their collective imagination.

"Ouch, my ankle hurts from that spark."

"Here's some icy water for it, Jule."

"Hey Sedge, you poured it on my knee."

"Well, Rich, get your knee out of my way."

"You think you got problems, I got half a consarned tree stuck under my nail. Shite! Ron, can you hold that candle so's I can operate on my thumb?"

"Ouch! Ron, you dripped wax on me!"

"Well, get outta of my way, Pink. Would the rest of you get back so's me and Billy can operate? Now you blew the candle out, Jule!"

"I got a wad of gum you can use to pull the sliver out, Bill. I'll dig it outta my pocket. And chew on it awhile to soften it up."

"Naw, thanks, Alv. I'll use pitch. Last thing I need's hoof and mouth."

"Don't break it off or you'll have to wait for it to fester out," warns Fern, ever the nurse.

"Thanks, Fern, I can feel the gangrene setting in already."

"Can anything else go wrong? It seems like we're jinxed right now," says Rich. "Maybe we are. Maybe there's a crack in the safety shield between us and dark space."

"Har!" says Brick. You've been reading too much science fiction, Rich. Too much Isaac Asimov and not enough Scrooge McDuck."

"It kind of feels like we could be in space right now, doesn't it?" asks Sedge. "You can see the round edge of the sky when you tip your head back."

"Do you think there is life out there?" asks Billy.

"Nobody knows… but lots of scientists think it's possible. It would explain lots of the strange things that happen," says Herald.

"Oh boy, here we go," groans Alvin.

"Dad always says there's a logical explanation when things don't make sense," says Fern.

"A logical chain of events. A chain reaction," says Hazel. "Cause and effect of seemingly unrelated incidents."

"Way too deep for me," sighs Fern.

"Remember the rootbeer ants?" asks Billy.

"Oh yeah," says Rich. "Me, you, Ron, and Alvin. And Luke. Five of us."

"And two dozen bottles of flat pop with ants in it," moans Ron.

"Chuckie asked why it tasted like ka ka," remembers Alvin, "which was pretty rude. And Ron told him some ants mysteriously got in the rootbeer after it sealed. Big mystery."

"And poor old Chuckie's superstitious," laughs Ron. "The reason the ants got in, was we had to find the bottle-capper. We should've had it ready... but Mr. Evanomalasovich called and we got sidetracked..."

"...'cause we thought he was phoning about that trouble at school, but it was only about his lost puppy," continues Rich. "And we forgot about the capper until the pop was ready to bottle."

"And us five all went down the basement to look for it," says Alvin, "and Billy caught his toe in the mouse trap under the work bench and he screeched and that made Rich jump..."

"And smash," says Rich, slapping his knee, "I bumped into Luke, he fell against the canning shelves which knocked out a support..."

"And, five jars of peaches hit bedrock ," says Billy mournfully. "We not only wasted a year's supply of sugar for our pop... but also the peaches... no Scout badges for that effort."

"You'll never pick enough berries to make up for wasting those golden peaches," sighs Hazel.

"Imagine if we could turn gooseberries into peaches!" says Fern.

"Then we'd have too many peaches... and they wouldn't be special," says Alvin. "Anyhow, I'd rather have gooseberries."

"Too bad it wasn't the gooseberry jam that smashed," rumbles Brick. "Why do we have to make that stuff every year? There'd have to be crop failure for ten years for us to run out."

"And gooseberries are the one crop that never fails. Too bad the jam factory won't buy them," says Fern. She especially does not like gooseberries and she very much doesn't like picking them, with their icky, sticky caterpillars.

"How come," asks Rich, "we always have to use up the what-ever from ten years ago, so we'll never find out what fresh stuff tastes like?"

"It's true," says Billy. "As a rule, we save the best for last. We have to eat the scabby apples first, before they go rotten, and the Bings that got the bad parts cut off have to be eaten before the nice, whole, dark purple crunchy ones. What cherries we haven't already filched, that is."

Herald laughs. "When we're finally allowed to eat the best from the year before, it's June, and the new fruit's ripe and the old stuff isn't the best anymore."

"Anyhow," says Fern, "How exactly did the ants get in the pop?"

"By the time we got that mess half-cleaned up in the basement," explains Rich, "a herd of ants had found the rootbeer. In the rush to get it capped before Mom and Dad got home, we didn't notice the ants until we opened the first bottle."

"So there was a logical explanation for the rootbeer being flat and full of ants… and tasting like ka ka," says Hazel.

"Not extraterrestrial ants, like Luke said… crawling through glass and all that," concludes Billy. "…So it all goes to show… there's no mysterious aliens that can take over our lives without us knowing it."

"As far as we know," says Alvin.

"I wonder if that rootbeer will preserve the ants or dissolve them?" wonders Brick, with a mind to his grade twelve science project.

Billy's thumb throbs. "Still though, it's weird I got this half a tree under my nail the exact moment a spark burned Jule's ankle and Brick moaned like a werewolf. Gave me the heevy-jeevies."

"Superstition," tsks Ron. "Supercilious superstition."

"Superstition-station for supercilious suspicion," adds Rich.

"An angry emission by someone trapped in submission by a mouse trap reaction," quips Ron.

"You would've blubbered, you had a trap clamped on your bare toe! It was a startled screech, not a temper screech," Billy defends himself.

"Anyhow," says Ron, "tantrums are kind of fun when someone else is having them. And fun to set off."

"But it's mean," says Fern. "Like Hodge teasing his cat until… pffffst… he has to jump out of the way or get his face ripped off… because he's driving the cat wild."

"It's like lighting a firecracker and tossing it before it explodes in your hand," laughs Ron.

"Remember when Hodge slammed the classroom door so hard and it startled Mr. Nitmust?" laughs Rich. "Nitmust was hunting for something in his desk and he screamed so loud they could hear it up the block. But Hodge skedaddled down the stairs so fast, by the time Nitmust got the drawer pulled off his head, Hodge and everyone else was long gone. That was fireworks but no one got burned. "

"Sometimes we're one big pile of firecrackers," says Fern.

"Please, no fireworks tonight. We have to get home in no more pieces than we already are," warns Herald.

"Well, at least now we know how the ants got in the rootbeer," sighs Fern, pulling the gray-green brim of her hat over her ears.

"Speaking of ants," says Billy. "There's about fifty ants per square inch on this mountain and fifty ka-zillion mosquitoes. I'm making a grass smudge."

"Erf, gag, retch. Great idea, Bill, no more mosquitoes, but now we can't breathe." Brick coughs like a sepulcher.

"Sorry, Baloo," says Billy.

Julie and Pink leap up with a loud, "MmmooOOOooo," which sets off a very loud group "MmmmmmmooooooOOOOMMMMMOOOOO!"

Which cheers everyone immensely.

CHAPTER 45
The Storyteller: Julie, 2005

DECADES IN THE FUTURE, Julie is thinking about heading home from her afternoon's berry picking. The four o'clock sun is fierce and she's getting pretty tired. But. Her bucket's only a little over half-full.

It seems like days since she started her climb into the morning-blue distance, where she discovered berries in the lambent shade of birch trees and contentedly listened to birdsong, far from workday stress. She had experienced, for a time, the Taoist joy of free and easy wandering. But then her quest for material gain took over in a grueling determination to fill her five-liter bucket. The going was pleasant enough until the bear incident. Spilling her bucket was an annoying set-back and she's been a bit nervous ever since. Her bear-calls have gotten lots of practice.

"Koo-roo, koo-ree!

"Karee, karooo. Kadoo! Kadee!"

She's picked more measly berries than she normally would, because that's all she could find for quite a while. She had to refill her bucket with some kind of huckleberries, (Rule 5), in spite of the sultry heat and the depredation of mosquitoes, black flies, deer flies, horse flies, and no-see-ums. And mites.

Julie can either scoot down the face of the mountain in full sun and be home in an hour, or meander down the other side of the creek and continue her berry quest in the shade. She opts for the creek, where she can soothe her bites and quench her thirst with icy water.

One thing's for certain, Julie has somewhat quelled her anxiety about Pink's hospital stay while hiking and searching for berries. Taking the long way home, she can fill her bucket while continuing to re-live the expedition, fifty years earlier, when she and Pink and their nine older siblings had survived their countless hours on the mountain. The day their dad had a jinx of a time trying to fetch them home.

CHAPTER 46
The Sowbelly-Smith Swine

THE ELEVEN ARE VALIANTLY trying to entertain each other in between getting on each other's nerves. Stories stretch back and forth. "Remember the time we got stuck in the woodlot after dark, and Dad wouldn't let us have a fire?"starts Ron. "Because we were camped under trees!" reminds Hazel. "And Dad had to walk ten miles to borrow Newton's truck," continues Herald, "because that decrepit Neolithic chunk of cantankerous corrosion on four wheels conked out."

"Yar, the Hearse," says Brick. "But at least Mom was with us, for the small fry. Not that the twin-imps are much trouble so far," he says, glancing at Pink and Julie sprawled in sleep, faces hidden under grubby yellow kerchiefs. It's a family mystery, how those girls can sleep anywhere, as long as they're together. When Julie was in the hospital with tonsillitis, no one got any sleep until they let Pink stay in a cot close enough so they could hold hands.

Alvin has his arms wrapped around his knees and is peering into the encroaching forest. He sees black holes that look like eyes, and when he looks at the fire and back at the trees, he sees white dots. White eyes. Alvin knows Deady-White-Eye isn't real, but still, if he drops his guard, it haunts him, rustling closer and closer. A chicken can flap around quite a while with its head chopped off, a gruesome sight they'd all witnessed at Mr. Horkalinki's farm when they helped butcher his broilers and more than one headless hen flapped down the creek. (Lettuce had tried to keep the younger kids at home, so of course they'd gone.)

And, Alvin muses, a chicken can be barely alive for days, and then twitch or squeak when you're sure it's completely gone dead. That's what supposedly happened with Deady-White-Eye. She wasn't buried deep enough and, because of reflexes, she stood up after she was buried, with just her eyes peering out the top of her grave, like two shining white marbles. Deady-White-Eye would hypnotize you if you looked at those eyes and suck out your eyeballs so it could see again.

Pink and Julie suddenly wake up laughing, startling everybody. "We dreamed that Alvin's shoes made it to China," says Julie, staring at Alvin's red, muddy feet in the flickering light. She nudges Julie and they giggle. They pick up Brick's wool gloves he's not using and tuck them over Alvin's feet. He sighs.

Herald drapes his arm around his small brother, saying, "Hey Alv, you're all tied up in granny knots."

Herald's arm is heavy and warm and Alvin yawns, feeling like a bag of ice turning to slush. He burrows his face momentarily against Herald's woolen sweater, then turns away brusquely. Alvin picks up a burning stick and draws neon ferris wheels in the dark. Pink and Julie feed small cones into the flames to spark, flare, expire. Soon they, too, are preparing sticks for neon-writing.

Herald pulls Alvin a little way from the group. "Your shoes fell off, Alv?" he asks.

Alvin's throat hurts with words that he doesn't want to say but has to say. He coughs. "Thing is, Hare, they fell down a mine hole."

Then Alvin quietly tells his biggest brother his whole mine story. Herald says, "You're safe now, Alv," and he gives Alvin's back a thorough scratch, after which Alvin feels ninety-six percent better.

Sedge smiles at Alvin, glad to see his face brighten. "How many quarts do you think we've canned?" he asks.

Fern laughs, "Mom's always cagey about it. She's treading that fine line… between not getting our hopes too high and keeping them high enough so's we don't give up."

"One hundred quarts is a cruel rule," Ron groans. "It would be nice to make a bit of moolah before summer's over."

"Yeah, like twenty dollars split eleven ways," says Hazel.

"Share and share alike. We could go together on something," suggests Fern.

They stare into the fire, collectively despising the One Hundred Quart Rule. But doesn't every family have some over-arching goal, accepted or rebelled against; success in sports, or high marks, civic duty, political ambition, material wealth, one hundred quarts of huckleberries?

In the flames, the Eleven visualize bike tires and knives, silver bracelets, a pulley, a new car, fluffy pillows, kites, a telescope and ice cream, a bottle of Friendship Garden cologne, new shoes, new glasses for Dad and an electric sewing machine for Mom.

It's a comforting fire at the moment, a steady flicker over red-hot coals with very little smoke. The breeze has gentled. Their voices murmur.

"Remember Aunt Ben's cat, Purrfect?" asks Pink.

"Of course. Purrfect Purrfection. And her kittens? Purrpetual Purrsistence and Purrcival."

"And Purrfidious Purrsuit."

"Purrloin. Purrpendicular. Purrsnickety. "

"Catatonic. Catapult. Catastrophe."

"Does anyone have another story?" asks Brick.

Pink perks up, saying, "I was alone today. All by myself. I was alright, though. Julie was alone too for a while. And we're both still alive! Aren't we Jub Jub!"

Julie hugs Pink. "Yup. I could hear Pink calling me as soon as she went off by herself."

"But I wasn't calling you then, Julie!"

"Yes, you were. Not with your voice. With your magnet! I knew you were going too far and I could feel you pulling me. When I felt the twinge, I knew it was time to come. I could follow your path like iron filings. We're okay being separate until we go too far."

Herald looks skeptically at Brick. "Are these girls actually magnetic personalities?"

Ron and Rich jump into the narrative and the two sets of twins start re-enacting and untangling their afternoon.

Hazel laughs, "I can't believe you girls risked your necks for a piece of plastic?!"

"It's our hairband, Haze!" yell Pink and Julie. "And aqua-turquoise is our favorite colour!"

"Har," guffaws Brick. "The Kludges must have an attack of the prickles a thousand times worse than the June itch."

The Eleven drift back into silence, huddled in the cold dark, wondering where their dad is. Waiting.

"Maybe there's something wrong at home," Hazel worries.

Fern claps at a mosquito. "Maybe Dad's sick, or hurt, or... I hope Mom's alright!"

Herald looks at the small white faces around him and mutters, "Probably just car trouble. Maybe the fuel pump. We'll be alright."

Billy sees a chance to try out his latest melon joke. "Hey everyone, listen up. What do you get when you cross a melon and a cauliflower?"

"I dunno... What, Billy?"

"You get a meloncauli-flower!"

"Oooh, that's melancholy."

Giggling ensues. It's not just Billy's corny jokes, it's the way he tells them that cracks everyone up. Brick's guffaw turns into a croak. Fern gently adjusts his pack so he can lean back more comfortably. "Yowtch!... ah... That's better," he sighs. "How about a bedtime story."

"Can you tell us your Sowbelly story, Fern?" ask Pink and Julie.

"Um," she answers slowly. "Let me think... Do you mean the one about Sally and Stewart Sowbelly-Smith?"

They all laugh. Sedge has told the story so many times they know it by heart, but they still love it, even more so because Miss Priss gave her only a C for it. She didn't see the humour in it, as an essay on the importance of good manners.

Sedge has a long drink of water and begins:

The Sowbelly-Smiths

It's a sunny July day when Sally and Stewart Sowbelly-Smith take their darling swine-babies to the turnip parade. Bluebell and Sunshine are trippling along in their little yellow hock cozies, knitted by Sally for their precious feet. Sally twirls her parasol as they splatter along, and Stewart swings his acorn-tipped cane. They are a fancy family, happily full of swill as they stroll across the meadow to the annual Rutabaga Parade.

All four Sowbelly-Smiths are decked out in their matching yellow and blue sweaters that Mrs. Sally knitted for them. It had been a challenge getting the shape just right to fit over their wide swine shoulders and short necks. But it was worth it, because they arrive at the parade looking proud and splendid. Well, just about splendid. Mrs. Sally Sowbelly has to bustle around her lovely darlings, tidying them up from their various small trippings and splattings on the way. She murmurs in a melodious whisper,

"Please remember, darlings, don't put your front feet on the ground. That would look so very very common."

Soon the Sowbelly swine are nodding and smiling with everyone else gathered around the rutabaga stalls. The drums are ka-ditta-booming just around the corner. A uni-cyclist in a peacock costume is weaving this way and that as he plays pan pipes. Next comes a throng of children on decorated bicycles. All is excitement and glee.

It's an innocent boy with a peashooter who spoils everything. Ping! Ping! Ping, ping! When dried peas bombard little Sunshine's tender loin, she lets out a terribly loud, rude shriek of cuss words. She flails and kicks and knocks over Bluebell. When Bluebell falls, she knocks over a keg of ginger beer which is being sold from a wagon on the edge of the parade. Well! Now both Swine-babies are on all fours.

But it's what Sunshine and Bluebell do next that really mortifies their mother. She has never been so embarrassed. Because, in full public view, down on all fours, squealing with delight, her pampered darlings are slurping up the spilled ginger-beer, pushing and shoving people out of their way to get to the deliciously sweet puddle.

They're acting like swine.

They're acting like hogs running amok in the muck.

They're an ad hoc performance of swine slumming in hock-cozies.

As for the boy with the pea-shooter, he hadn't meant to hurt anyone, he'd just innocently wanted to try out his new peashooter. He didn't get a second chance, because when Sunshine uttered her ear-splitting squeal, his mother grabbed the toy from him in a fit of panic and beat him over the head with it. The splintered peashooter flipped out of her hand and landed amid the heap of rutabagas in the Odd Fellows' float, never to be seen or heard from again.

Poor Mr. and Mrs. Sowbelly-Smith. All they can do is wait for their little lovelies to have a thorough wallow in the sweet mud they've churned up. Everyone else starts hurrying down the road to get away from the revolting scene of piggery. But, pigs will be pigs.

When the Sowbelly-Smiths finally head home, Bluebell and Sunshine are waddling on all fours. No more tip-tapping. They trudge along with their hock booties hanging in muddy tatters and their yellow sweaters mere rags of muddy string hanging around their shoulders. Mrs. Sally Sowbelly flings her broken parasol under a hedge. She's chuffing and flartulating several steps ahead of Mr. Stewart Sowbelly. Stewart has lost his cane but is chewing contentedly on a large turnip. As soon as they get home, they'll have a long, snoring Sowbelly siesta.

"There's an important moral to this story. Don't get too fancy with your swine. Remember! Don't get too fancy with your swine!"

CHAPTER 47
Bob and Moe

BOB IS WAITING FOR the cow to finish her drama in the middle of the road, and he's very thankful when eventually a battered pick-up clangs into view. The driver leans out and shouts above the racket of the engine, "What the dang-blam! Why're you sitting in the middle of the road, Bob?"

It's Moe from the dairy. Bob explains the situation. Moe scratches his gray bale of hair and apologizes. "Sorry she's in your way, lad. I been looking for that dern bovine half the day! She was supposed to stay in the barn this morning but she got out with the crowd. Stubborn old fool."

With Bob directing him away from the edge of the narrow road, Moe backs down to the next wide spot, turns around, and backs back up to the Hearse. He hauls a rope and a shovel from his truck and trudges up the road with Bob to investigate the situation with the cow.

The cow, by this time, is rolling her eyes, her back arching and her sides pumping. Bob is sure she must be close to death-by-convulsion but Moe mutters, "She seems to be doing alright. You keep right on going there, Sweetgrass, you'll be just fine. We'll stay right here and it'll calm you real good to hear our voices so close." Moe gives his hayrick jowls a good scratch and leans comfortably on his shovel to wait, regaling Bob with lurid anecdotes about the finer details of animal husbandry, such as castration, cow colic, and rooster culling.

Bob explains about the whereabouts of his children, his anxiety to get them and his worry that he won't get his car re-started, because when it stalled it sounded like a garbage can full of rocks. Moe casts a baleful look at the Hearse and says he'll stick around in case it needs a jump.

Much later, the cow is finally ready to move on; the calf's been born and suckled. Bob scrapes some dust over the road to clean up while Moe secures the rope around the cow's neck, leading her past the Hearse, with the calf tottering behind its mamma on pathetic stilt legs. Bob helps Moe lift the struggling calf onto the hay in the back of Moe's pick-up. Moe ties the cow to a tree, "So's she won't try climbing into the pick-up with her bairn." Sweetgrass bellows her outrage and a second rope is needed to secure her. Her newborn, which she'd been cursing when its legs were stuck in her innards an hour ago, is now the most precious thing in the world to her and she won't be separated. It's bawling for her udder. She will continue to bellow until she's reunited with her calf once she can follow the truck to the barn. It's with the ear-splitting bawling and bellering of Sweetgrass and her offspring that Moe and Bob finally tramp back to the Hearse. Bob can barely see the dial on his watch. It's almost ten. He yanks open the hood.

CHAPTER 48
Gristle

THE ELEVEN STRETCH AND rearrange themselves around their
fire. Sedge finds her shrunk-wool spare socks and hands them to
Alvin. "Thank you!" he croaks, and pulls them up to his knees,
handing back Brick's gloves, which he has kept warm by the fire.
Sedge helps Brick get one glove on and tucks the other across his
swollen hand.

Fern and Alvin wail on harmonicas, while Pink and Julie sway
like cobras around a broken shoe lace which Herald dangles in
front of them. Hazel and Fern sing "Swanee River." As usual, Fern's
voice is clear and true, while Hazel's is that little bit off-key, which
makes everyone laugh when she stretches out every note in high
vibrato. Four harmonicas are played in shrill cacophony until
Sedge plays one sweetly while Herald and Fern sing "The Skye
Boat Song" and "Greensleeves."

Off to one side, Ron and Rich juggle pebbles, keeping four in
the air, until Herald, watching closely, joins in with another one
and then Pink and Julie creep into the circle and patiently follow

the rhythm until, for one magical moment, the five of them are juggling seven pebbles. Then one hits the billy can and knocks it off the fire with a clang and a whoosh.

Brick plays a one-handed dirge on a harmonica while Alvin and Hazel sing:

Whenever you see the hearse go by
don't you feel like you're going to die?
They put you in a big black box,
and cover you up with dirt and rocks…

"Let's sing something nice," suggests Fern.

Pink and Julie chime in, "Nobody loves me, everybody hates me, going to the garden to eat worms, long fat squishy worms, short thin icky worms, itsy bitsy ishy squishy worms worms worms worms…"

Then Rich and Ron belt out, "I'll tell you a story of Martha and John, Martha and John, Maaaartha and Joh-o-o-o-on," ten verses in all with Alvin, Billy, Pink, and Julie droning along.

The shadows deepen. The talent show has taken up a small portion of what is becoming a long night. They gnaw on dry pretzels, washed down with very diluted, unsweetened Kool-aid. Hardly better than nothing.

Herald says, "Try to remember what Uncle Al says. When life is a trudge, you just have to keep your head up and believe there's something good up ahead, and you have what it takes to get there."

"Har," says Brick.

Alvin and Billy rustle out comic books to squint at. Hazel, Fern, and Sedge lean close to the fire, trying to play rummy. Julie and Pink are unraveling a sweater cuff to make dresses for their matchbox dolls. Hangman is scratched in the dirt. As Ron and Rich guess letters, Herald scratches them off with a smirk and adds another leg to the man. Sporadically everyone plays twenty questions. There's one question that repeats itself.

"When do you think Dad will get here, Hare?"

"Any minute, Pink."

"You said that hours ago."

"I hope it's not a broken axle," worries Brick.

"Or the flambulator falling out."

"I don't think so, Jule." Herald tousles her hair. "I'm sure Dad's on his way."

Ron impatiently drums on a log and soon they're all drumming on wood, on rocks, hats, laps, buckets and one another; the night is a drum.

A fine drizzle descends on camp. The Eleven feel like they've never been dry. Billy stirs up a batch of very weak, sugarless cocoa. It's warm, at least. Only Alvin enjoys the sugarless Kool-aid. In boredom, Fern crunches a last hard pretzel and spits out a lump of gristle. "Gristle? In a pretzel? Yetch!"

"Mine has something hard in it too," complains Hazel. "Like gravel!"

"Gristle? Gravel? Why would that be in a pretzel?" Sedge wonders.

Rich whispers to Ron, "Next time we'd better sift the bone dust, eh, Ron?"

Ron and Rich guffaw and Herald gives them a shove so they roll off their log into the pine needles, cackling.

"What's going on?" Hazel demands.

"I'm not sure," says Herald, "but I think it might have something to do with my science project."

Hazel jumps to her feet. "Bone dust? Out with it, Herald."

"Well, you know I was growing those flowers and green beans? I wanted to see if bone meal would make them grow better. So I ground up a bunch of bones."

"Eew, I don't like where this is heading," says Sedge. "But I remember… Mom complaining about Auntie Ben's grinder being clogged."

"Yeah, well, I did the grinding when no one was home. I knew you girls would have a fit. And I had to rush clearing up the last batch before you came in."

"What kind of bones?" asks Fern.

"Well, pretty much anything I could get my hands on. From dinner scraps mostly. A couple of Perth's bones."

"Har! You ground up Perth's bones?" croaks Brick.

"No, cripes, I'm not that demented. Just a couple he never got round to burying. But don't worry, I scrubbed them and dried them in a pot on the back of the stove… that rainy week when most of you were sewing."

Fern gags. "I wondered what that smelly mess was in the old roaster. Why didn't you tell us?"

"You never asked. Anyhow, I knew you'd be disgusted and make a fuss. Pink was the only one interested in my project."

"Yeah," Pinks chirps. "I knew sort of what you were doing, and I saw Rich and Ron spying on you."

"Us? Not us."

"Yes, you, Ron." Herald says "I knew you and Rich were behind the lilac when I was working back of the porch… You guys with your tuques pulled down, muttering and snickering. But I chose to ignore you. That was sure a mistake."

Four brown eyes gleam in the firelight, as Rich and Ron remember when they'd figured out Herald's project and what to do about it. Ron can't resist bragging. "We'd pinch only a smidgen at a time, Hare, so's you wouldn't notice, and we saved it up."

Julie chortles, "Pink and I saw you putting white stuff in that little jar. But we didn't know what it was."

Rich explains how one day they put some bone dust in the cornbread.

"You brats! You horrible, conniving brats!" shrieks Hazel.

"But no one noticed," continues Ron, "because, you know, cornmeal is a bit gritty. So then we put some in the bread."

"Eeeew! We'll never eat anything homemade again!" Fern squeals.

"You'll starve, then, around our place. Anyhow, it was perfectly harmless. A bit more calcium or whatever," laughs Rich.

"It's the principle of the thing!" shouts Sedge.

"Actually, it's the phosphorous and nitrogen that plants thrive on," mumbles Herald, inwardly admiring the twins' planning and execution.

"Anyhow, we all ate the bread and we're healthy as swine," says Ron. "Only we didn't know we'd be so starving we'd eat the pretzels ourselves. Problem was, by the time the bread was made, we'd used up the fine bone dust and had to use the chunky stuff for the pretzels."

At this Hazel, Sedge and Fern pounce on Ron and Rich and grab them by the wrists. Herald and Billy quickly grab their ankles, swinging them by their arms and feet, giving them the bumps until at the count of four they wriggle free and there's a clown act in the field, with Alvin, Julie and Pink clapping and shouting, "Yo ho, tie the man down!"

Brick hollers from his couch by the fire, "Bring me a bone!"

* * *

(The mountain trembles in the uproar. Eleven voices echo, slide, tumble, telegraph their location to the tall, shaggy form plodding uphill. The heavy head lifts, startled. Now it falters, and takes several shuffling steps deeper into the shadows.)

* * *

CHAPTER 49
Bob

THE ELEVEN WOULD BE shocked if they could see their dad now, trudging down the road back to town. He's sure-footed on the wet rocks, but his night vision is hampered by the drifting mist and he has to walk cautiously.

After Sweetgrass gave birth on the road, if you recall, Bob helped Moe settle the calf in the back of his truck and tie Sweetgrass nearby. Moe had assured Bob his wife would ring Lettuce, let her know Bob would be late. The calf had squealed and the cow had bellowed the whole time Bob was labouring under the hood of the Hearse. Trouble is, it stalled in reverse, thanks to dear old Sweetgrass. Moe impatiently whistles under his breath, holding a flashlight. It shines in Bob's eyes every time Moe turns to look down the hill, where Sweetgrass is trumpeting to her new-born. Will her ropes hold?

With the help of wire, wrenches, and Moe leaning on the right hind bumper with his belly on the fender—and with absolutely no co-operation from the Hearse—the car finally coughs into gear and lurches forward. Finally, Bob is on the way again. He beeps the horn to thank Moe and rumbles uphill, holding his breath. He tries to calculate how many times his metal Lazarus has been resurrected. Chunks of rubber and wire, strong hands, and heart-felt swearing have once again caused a miracle.

"Steady on, Plymouth," Bob prays as the car judders over the ruts full of loose rocks. "Was that clang the oil pan? Blast!" At the lip of the next turn, there's a moment when the back wheels are kicking like a donkey in quicksand. But whew, they make it up another switchback.

The rain has settled the dust but also washed a lot of dirt out of the washboard. Swashbuckling around the next hairpin, Bob can almost see the back far bumper through his side window, as if the car were bent double. And then, kapow!

A blown tire. The Hearse ricochets sideways with Bob barely managing to steer onto the bedrock shoulder, stopping with a crunch. He cautiously edges out his door and peers down a fifty foot drop. Bob shoves a few loose boulders behind the wheels, although it isn't likely the car will roll with a bent axle and a trashed oil pan.

"What to do?" Bob half-wishes he could push the ornery contraption off the cliff. Some things are worse than nothing. (Is that the same current of rebellion that had tempted Lettuce to bury the rugs where they'd fallen in the mud?)

Bob is stuck with the same conundrum that faced him a couple of hours earlier when the labouring cow was blocking the road. It would be pointless to hike up and check on the kids without having some way to haul them down. So, he's hiking back to town to get help, trying not to trip on the sharp ore chunks with which the road is surfaced.

CHAPTER 50
Lettuce at Home

ON THE FAR SIDE of the valley, within what would be a pin-prick of light if the kids could see it, Lettuce winces as an icy pang scuttles up her spine. The cap she's been rick-racking falls from her hands as her worries travel out the window in ever widening circles. She opens the curtains and sees only reflections of the cupboards and her own white face.

Outside, as her eyes adjust, the pitch dark fades into a murky gloom. The Earth and sky are one and the same. The valley is obscured by heavy mist, which separates her from all vestiges of her family.

"Are you still out there?" she whispers. "Hello?"

She can hear the p-zeet p-zeet of nighthawks, until Hobart's cougar hounds start their baying.

Where is her family?

Lettuce walks down the road, straining for a glimpse of the valley. No sign of the Hearse. Should she start walking out that way? Should she ask a neighbour to drive her? Pete's always good about the odd time they've asked for help. He's had his share of fretting about boys skitting around the hills at night, and they've all survived. But it doesn't look like anyone's home.

Back in the kitchen, the clock seems to be standing still. Are the hands moving at all? Lettuce half-thinks she's worn it out, looking at it so many times. The fun of rehanging the curtains is beginning to wear off. They are crisp and clean and lime green, just as she envisioned. But where are the kids?

She adds a parsnip to the stew. She mixes up some dumplings to add later. She finally finds the lid she's been looking for and plunks it in the rack. Why was it on top of the fridge, along with the potato masher and the strainer? She tidies the cupboards. The kids claim the pots and pans have a "more or less spell" on them. A few things are like that. When you want more of them, there's less, and when you want less, there's more. And why is Auntie Ben's gallon jar of marbles taking up half the bottom shelf? No wonder things are stacked on the fridge. Putting things back is haphazard in a kitchen that's run much of the time by eleven kids and their Dad.

Lettuce enjoys feeding her family, but she doesn't have time when she's galloping her treadle through an emergency order, like the fifteen magician costumes she's just sent off. The kids have been chief cooks and scullions for a couple of weeks, making bread, concocting soup, pitching in with the canning, and trying out all manner of experiments in the process of feeding thirteen people.

Bob says cooking is a necessary evil, and for some reason the kids think that sounds like killing pack rats. But he's efficient at whomping up large, delicious meals, and he's good at organizing the kids, while Lettuce is dedicated to training them. They'd rather learn to cook than leave meals to chance, anyhow. They can be quite capable in the kitchen, though their methods are sometimes quite unusual. She keeps finding marbles and putting them in their jar, wondering what they've been used for. Rolling pastry maybe?

Looks like bits of dough stuck on them. She'll have to remind the kids that ground glass in food is deadly. She buries a few chipped marbles in the garbage, then hauls the gallon jar upstairs, coming back with an armful of laundry... and the rolling pin!

Lettuce glances at her book, but can't relax. Should she wash more jars? There's a dozen already clean and alert, lined up on the counter. They might have to can berries tonight, if they're too wet. Assuming the picking's been good. She'll haul up more jars and scrub them.

When she's rooting around in the basement, Lettuce finds a vast sticky patch in one corner. What the... ? Oh. The golden peaches. The boys had taken shifts cleaning up that mess, but now's a good chance to do a final scrub. Typically, they'll come trooping home when she's in the middle of the job.

She can only hope.

CHAPTER 51
An Interrupted Story

ON THAT HIGH, NIGHTTIME flank of the mountain, in the clearing where a once-working sawmill is now a ghost mill, amongst the disintegrating concrete foundations, around their small campfire, the eleven brothers and sisters impatiently wait. And wait.

Pink and Julie have woken up again and are jumping around like crickets. One of their saving graces is their ability to nap and wake up unerringly happy, tiring though it is for those who have not napped. It's far past their bedtime. They chatter, settling down to draw pictures on each other's backs. Herald explains calculus to Ron and Rich, who get twitchy and start playing slap. Herald joins in their game, slapping hands and getting slapped and wondering why they think it's fun. Alvin hums into his kazoo. Fern braids Sedge's hair as best she can without a comb. It shines silver in the firelight. No one can braid Fern's curly up-do, which is stuck together with pitch. Hazel stares balefully into the fire.

"I'm so hungry," Ron sighs. "Let's double-check our packs for food."

One by one, they itemize their findings.

"Here's two peanuts and a jaw-breaker with a few layers sucked off…"

"There's bits of peanut shell on it, but here's part of an apple."

"I've got a lump of something, I think it's cheese with fuzz on it."

"Here's a few squashed plums."

"Jeez, doesn't anyone have anything decent? All I got's some soft hard-tack."

"Wanna trade for a squashed hard boiled egg?"

"Is the shell still on?"

"More or less."

Brick rouses himself. "I remember Mom muttering about "no sense taking an empty pocket." What's that lump on the back of my pack, Fern?"

"Hey! A bag of something. Looks like… bannock mix! With grated cheese in it! "

"Yar! Deluxe! Thanks Mom!"

They're quickly roasting bannock on sticks and munching contentedly. All's right with their world again.

Rule 93: Starvation's held at bay when umami saves the day.

Satiated, they stare into the fire. They don't see the stars flashing through the skittering clouds, but they feel a breeze.

Silence, except for the eerie yipping of coyotes in the distance.

"You shoulda brought your transistor radio, Bill."

"Nah, I didn't wanna rattle it around."

"Anyhow, why do you need a radio when we have you around?" asks Brick.

Billy doesn't need much encouragement. He adjusts his fez, untucks its crimson tassel, and walks around the fire, using a knot of wood for a microphone. He pulls a wad of papers out of his jacket and shuffles them. "Ahem, ahem, listen up, folks! A special broadcast from station JXY is about to begin. The Barred Rock sisters have made the news again." Billy takes a bow.

"Yay! Billy's got a story!"

The Three Barred Rocks

This story is about Fright P. Hen, Frightella Dot Hen and Egglantine Hilda-garble Hen. They are relatives of Mr. and Mrs. Fluster Havoc.

The sisters are feeling optimistic after a sunny morning of scratching. Garble and Fright flop into their dust baths, fluffing the dust through their feathers. It feels so good. They stretch their wings and roll their eyes.

Frightella suddenly lets out a startled squawk... Arrrrk! She tips her head this way and that, trying to figure out what's what... Awk, erk... ack! The gate's open!

Soon the three hens are bustling and shoving around the gate, peering anxiously at the wide, green, wonderful world outside. Chickens cannot resist an open gate. Wherever they are, they have to get to the next gate. That's a no-brainer.

The problem is, Garble has to take the first step out, because she's the head hen. But she's chicken. And when the head hen is chicken, no one gets far in a hurry. They give the juicy bits under the gate a thorough going over. Peck, peck, peck. Erp, eeerrrrp.

Nattering and nibbling, they don't notice the garter snake until it suddenly darts in front of Frightella. She screeches in panic and accidentally flies ahead of Garble through the gate. This really upsets Garble, so now there's a great fuss.

Another problem with the three sisters is this: Frightella is afraid of bright light and shadows; Fright is afraid of the sky; and Garble is afraid of everything, because she's the smart one. So they spend a lot of time up in the air, not coming and not going.

Garble tries to help her sisters get organized, but it's pretty frustrating. She's the only one whose brain is in the middle of her head, where it belongs, instead of rolling from one side to the other. Garble tries to talk some sense into Fright and Frightella, but it's hopeless. "Don't be such ridiculous foolish idiotic cluck-brain neurotics,"she squawks, "Quit running around like chickens with your heads cut off; help scratch, help scratch some lunch up, scratch! Scratch!"

At this point, Billy starts dancing from foot to foot and says, "Ladies and Gentlemen, your program will now pause for station exlaxation. Stay tuned to JXY for more about Fright, Frightella, and Garble after a ten minute break."

"Billy, can't you finish the story first?" begs Pink.

"No, I have an appointment in the bushes."

"Rich, could you go with Billy?" Herald asks.

"See you in the funny papers!" Billy calls as he and Rich melt into the darkness, the crunch of twigs fading behind them. Nine brothers and sisters fidget around the fire, poking at it, adding in wood.

"I like Billy's stories," Sedge laughs. "I like how he always has that wad of papers he refers to. Can he really read them, do you think? They look like a big smudge to me."

"His hieroglyphs make sense to him, I guess. He's really coming along with his radio voice, too," Herald says. "He's getting good."

"Sure is," agrees Fern. "What do you think the moral of his story's going to be? Don't garble while you scratch? He prob'ly doesn't know yet. But he'll come up with something that'll make us laugh, count on that."

"I hope Billy and Rich don't break their necks out there," worries Hazel after a few minutes.

"I don't hear any hollering," says Ron. "Maybe I should go look for them."

"Don't you dare." Herald grabs his arm. "The last thing we need is you wandering off."

"When I'm rich, I'm going to buy sixteen flashlights. One for each of us and Mom and Dad and three spares," says Ron.

"Yeah, sure," says Hazel, "when we've sold two thousand pounds of huckleberries we can buy all sorts of things."

Glum silence.

"Shouldn't they be getting back by now? Billy! Rich! Hurry up! Woo-hoo-oo-hoooo!" yodels Fern.

"They haven't been gone that long. Don't get your shirt in a knot, Fern."

Fern hates being told that, especially by Ron, when her shirt's already in a knot. Everyone else seems to be half asleep, so someone has to worry. Hazel puts her arm around Fern and they stand staring in the direction the boys have gone.

Rich and Billy were out of earshot almost immediately on their expedition, and the campfire's glow is suddenly cut off from them when they walk down a dip behind a big pine tree. Next thing Billy, in his ill-fitting boots, stumbles on a low-lying juniper branch. Rich trips on Billy and they land with one loud "Whoomp!"

They sprawl, winded from their plummet, trying to get their bearings. The trouble with that kind of juniper is that its many low branches seem to writhe along the ground, and it trips them further into its dark maze before finally spewing them, hot, scratched and pitchy, onto a flat rock.

"Oof."

"I gotta catch my breath. Let's stay here a spell."

* * *

(Unknown to Billy and Rich, that thump in the juniper is heard by the tall, shaggy creature. It flares its nostrils, catching a faint whiff of boy. It sighs a long, moaning sigh.)

* * *

CHAPTER 52
Lettuce and Bob

MEANWHILE, LETTUCE HAS WALKED down to Pete's house: still no one home, which she'd already supposed because of the absence of lights. Moozle's house is dark except for that blue glow in the living room window which so attracts the neighbourhood kids, like fruit flies to the chicken bucket. Lots of hospitality in that family, but no phone, no car. They know how to live. She needs someone with a truck to take a run up to Stooge's to check what's happening with Bob and the kids.

Lettuce tries to phone another friend, but the line is busy, has been busy almost non-stop all evening. Apparently a bear's been prowling around, and concern about that is competing on the phone with discussion about the upcoming boccie tournament. When finally Lettuce gets a turn on the five-party line, she calls a couple of people to see if they can help, but they're not home. Then another call about boccie takes over. Everyone on the line will soon be spreading word of her plight, but the trouble is, all the truck owners are at the Co-op meeting. Lettuce groans in

frustration. It will be a long meeting without Bob there to organize and delegate. Not much she can do about that. The meeting
hall doesn't have a phone. She considers running into the meeting
to get help. But that would create an awful fuss, which is not her
style. No. With her luck, she'd get half the town on its ear worrying about her family while Bob and the kids get home before her.
At least Hobart's hounds have quieted down. He must have taken
them in.

Lettuce tries to read. It's ten minutes before she admits the
pages might as well be blank, for all the sense she's getting out of
them. Not even suspense in the Amazon can distract her now.
She adds some water to the stew and puts it in the warming oven.
She makes a stab at sorting out the sewing room. It's too bad the
National Theater runs on a small budget and there's never extra
yardage. But the girls will be delighted with the scraps she's sorted
into a box for them.

Lettuce paces from the porch to the upstairs windows to
the veranda. She can hear the high-pitched gibbering of Mr.
Horkalinki's guinea fowl rushing up the alley. For a change, her
boys can't be blamed for letting them out. Most of the neighbourhood windows are still dark. Darn that meeting everyone seems
to be at.

She goes inside, checks on supper. Her life seems like an endless
stew. The phone jangles. It's Bette at the dairy, Moe's wife.

"Moe told me to tell you, Bob's going to be late. Well, I don't
rightly know, Moe just told me now, he's been out in the barn
for quite awhile. He's been tending the newborn, making sure it
suckles. No, no, Sweetgrass's calf. Bob helped Moe with the cow
up the mountain. She was in labour in the middle of the road. The
first hairpin. Moe said I should phone you that Bob will be late.
No, I don't know how long ago he saw Bob. Sometime after dark,
I take it. Moe's going to bed with a busted toe, that gol-darned
Sweetgrass stomped on it. You know how men are, have to go to

bed at the slightest thing, ha ha, and I have to go out the barn, now, keep an eye out Sweetgrass don't stomp on the Babe. Moe will be snoring when it's his turn, but I'm not staying out there all night. That Sweetgrass is his pet, not mine. Anyhow, he said to call you. Won't use the phone his-self, says it's an instrument of the devil, meaning women. Ha! Well anyhow, I'll let you know if I hear more but I might be in the barn, so I won't hear the phone and Moe won't answer it. What he'd do without me, he'd forget to wake up in the morning, that's what, ha ha. You're most welcome, I'm sure. Ta ta, Dear."

Lettuce shakes her head in consternation. The first hairpin turn? That's miles up the mountain. All she really knows for sure from Bette's call is that Bob will be late. He was late two hours ago. She adds water to the stew. The table has long been set. She washes the kettle and soaks out the orange Jello petrified in the bottom back corner of the fridge.

Lettuce tackles the haphazard shelf of recipe books, sorting out the flotsam and jetsam. She carefully re-copies some of the recipes which are sticky with frequent use, such as the kids' favorite, uncooked chocolate oatmeal drops. She decides to whip up a gingerbread cake, which is one of the smudgiest recipes, and soon has a big cake ready for the oven. She sets the timer for forty-five minutes. Then she puts her feet up and finally loses herself in her novel until the timer makes her jump. Good thing she set it, or she might have been lost in the mysterious mists of the Amazon while the cake burned.

CHAPTER 53
The Fright Sisters Continued

WHAT'S BURNING IS A campfire that's slowly getting bigger on the pitch-dark mountain.

Impatiently waiting for Billy and Rich to return from their plumbing expedition, Hazel and Fern practice Girl Guide semaphore. They've taught some of the others the alphabet of hand and arm positions, but only Fern and Hazel can transmit and receive a simple message in anything under twenty minutes. It takes immense patience, especially with random arm movements while slapping mosquitoes.

Brick dozes fitfully. The football tucked under his neck vibrates when he snores. Julie and Pink giggle, "It sounds like an insect orchestra."

Brick groans. His sisters scurry to him. "Brickle? Are you alright?" Hazel asks.

"Aarg. I was asleep. But I'm not sure…"

Herald helps him sit up. Fern feels his forehead. It's hot.

"Big ball, little ball," he rasps."...you know... rolling toward you, getting bigger and bigger... and running right over you? Then it gets smaller and smaller... gets too small and you feel like you're disappearing?"

"A fever dream," says Fern.

Alvin stares at Brick and Hazel, open-mouthed. "I've had big ball, little ball. I hate it."

Pink and Julie describe the big brown bugs coming at them when they had chickenpox and they kept kicking each other in their sleep.

"And Dad said, 'we'll see how you are in the morning,'" says Alvin.

"But though, you ate Cream of Wheat and Jello and that was it," adds Fern.

Herald admits to having bad nights where he can't tell if he's asleep or awake and ends up getting lost in his closet. Which gets a laugh out of everybody. He's good at that.

"Since when do you have a closet, Heron-ald?" teases Hazel.

"Well, you know, those stacks of apple-boxes with a rod between them to hang things on? And by the way, whoever's been taking my books better start putting some back, or that whole side of the room's going to cave in."

Alvin feels lighthearted when he realizes he's not the only one who can feel adrift and twilight-ish. He looks around at his brothers and sisters and feels warmer. They have a way of making a person feel alright about the world. Plus, he'd be dead if not for them. He takes Brick a cup of water and patiently holds the cup as he sips.

Herald, Hazel, and Ron give up on a game of Hearts. Pink and Julie burn neon-writing sticks. Fern stands vigil outside the ring of firelight. "Did you hear that thump a while ago?" she asks.

"What kind of thump?" asks Herald,

"I don't know; I thought I heard something," says Fern. Her ears have followed Billy and Rich much further than her eyes could.

Sedge joins Fern, accidentally kicking a branch and sending up a shower of sparks.

"Oooh, pretty," chirps Pink.

"Whoa," rumbles Brick, "Don't burn the mountain down!"

"Holy crap. My sleeve's smoking," Ron yelps. He sticks it in the water bucket. "Bucket's almost empty."

"Pink and Julie, please move your pinecones before they all catch at once," says Herald. "We better douse the edges. Come on, Ron, let's go fill the buckets."

That leaves only seven of them rubbing smoke from their eyes. Julie and Pink hover near Brick, chanting gibberish in solemn voices as they fan the smoke away from him. Alvin is scrounging wood, edging out of the ring of light. Hazel, Fern, and Sedge look anxiously into the forest for Billy and Rich.

In the gully where they lie, winded from their plummet into the juniper, Billy and Rich take awhile to get their bearings.

"Oof."

"I gotta catch my breath. Let's stay here a spell."

Lying on their backs, Billy and Rich gaze through a black hole in the clouds to a spangle of stars that are so bright they look close enough to touch. The boys talk about space and UFOs. By the time they've counted five shooting stars, the clouds have blotted out the sky again and their backs have gotten cold to the bone from lying on bare rock. Time to go back.

"It's sure quiet. I can't even see the fire."

"I didn't think we'd gone so far."

"Maybe they've all been teleported to Mars."

"Jeez. Oh, there's the fire, way over there."

Billy and Rich finally straggle back to camp, just as Herald and Ron are passing around mugs of fresh water.

"Hey you guys, what took you?" asks Ron.

"Well, we tripped on a great big juniper bush. Took us ages to climb out. Ate a few juniper berries. To remind us they taste like pitch," answers Billy.

"Those junipers are sure prickly," adds Rich. "The way they crawl along the ground, we kept tripping back into them." Neither of them mention they'd had a jolly good yak while staring at the sky. It's different by the fire. They can't see anything past it.

"Well anyhow, it's a good thing you're back in one piece." Fern wishes she hadn't bothered worrying about them, they seem so nonchalant.

There's a lull once everyone is resettled. Their mother would have been proud, if only she could have seen her Eleven momentarily so peaceful in each other's company. Sedge and Rich are crouched close to the fire, squinting at *Gyro Gearloose* and *Outer Limits*. Julie and Pink pretend Sedge and Rich are mountains, walking their matchbox dolls up and down them until one of the mountains shrugs, which sends the dolls tumbling. Pink and Julie go on a giggling rescue mission. Ron scrounges a tattered *Green Lantern* and leans against Rich to read it. They're reading by memory more than sight. Alvin and Billy play Snap.

Herald and Brick gaze into the fire, talking quietly. Herald is explaining how he really wants to go to Victoria for teacher's training. Brick encourages Herald to make a run for it, because there'll be a better chance of him getting away when he graduates if Herald breaks trail. Herald doesn't mention his hopes about the parsing competition in Toronto for fear of jinxing his chances.

Julie breaks the lull with, "Hey, Billy! We're waiting for the rest of your story!"

"Story?" he asks, knowing perfectly well.

"Yeah, Billy! Your chicken story!"

"Oh. Fright, Frightella and Egglantine Hilda-Garble? Oh yes, it was the day they walked into Aunt Molly's kitchen.

The Fright Sisters (Concluded)

It takes quite a while for the hens to get past their gate—one step forward, five steps back, the way chickens do—but eventually, they have a delightful picnic of worms and slugs in the damp grass. And then, with an excited "Eeeerrrrip eeerrrip," Fright spies a sunflower seed. Garble grabs it and they play keep-away until they find a trail of seeds leading right to the porch stairs. There's no one to shoo them away because the kids have all gone on a spur-of-the-moment overnight hike and the parents are busy in the garden on the other side of the yard.

Garble, Fright, and Frightella excitedly follow the seeds right up the stairs, one step up, two steps down, two steps up, one down. (Sort of the way huckleberry pickers walk, taking sharp glances to the side every step or two.) Eventually they make it to the top step. Garble sticks her neck out and shakes her head to get her brain back into the middle of her head, because sometimes it does get a bit over to one side when she's excited. She looks out the eye on one side, then out the other side. She can see that the kitchen door is open. Uttering a long, slow errrrreerrreeerrr of ambitious uncertainty, Garble lurches forward. She doesn't notice that she does a big mess right on the doorstep, but it gives Fright a fright and she squawks. Garble irritably garbles at her, "Shut up, you wing-nut; stay out of my way and don't be such a chicken," etcetera.

The doormat keeps the hens busy for several minutes, trying to peck off the coconut fibers. Then they have a delightful time with the small bag of sunflower seeds carelessly left open on the hallway floor. Soon they're messing about in the kitchen, pecking at crumbs and the squiggly pattern on the linoleum. Their claws keep slipping on the smooth surface, startling Fright and Frightella. They scuttle noisily under the table. Egglantine Hilda-Garble immediately starts scolding her sisters about being so neurotically and ridiculously panicked when they are so close to the source of all good things to eat, the chance of a lifetime.

Of course, they don't understand a thing she's saying, but it doesn't matter because right then, Aunt Molly comes stomping into the kitchen with an enormous bowl of shelled peas. Frightella, Fright, and Garble all screech. Molly jumps out of her bloomers. The peas go flying. You can imagine the commotion.

Billy stands up, stretches, yawns, rubs his eyes.

"Is that the end, Billy? Billy Bridge!"

"You haven't even told us the moral yet."

"Well," he says, "there's more than one moral. It's a deep story. One: It's easier to let hens out than to get them in... except when you've let them in and you have to get them out."

"Two: Never jump out of your bloomers if you have a bowl of peas in your hands... except if you want a chicken kitchen klatch."

"Three: Always fasten the chicken gate. But if your head hen is chicken, she'll never get far from the coop."

Billy bows, with Sedge catching his muddy blue fez just before it lands in the fire. There's stomping and shouting, guffawing and clapping.

"We'll be laughing about that one for a long time," says Fern. "Hooray for Charming Billy!"

Herald claps Bill on the back. "How long've you been working on that tale, Bill?"

"Oh, half an hour."

"How long honestly?" asks Brick.

"A few days."

"No wonder you're like in a trance half the time, Bill. With your lips moving but no sound coming out?"

"My lips moving, Brick? Oops. Must've been memorizing. Or pretend broadcasting. I make a lot up as I go along... but only when it's a story, not a documentary."

Hazel laughs, "It reminds me of Nestly. Remember our chick from Auntie Anne?"

"The cute little yellow fluff ball!" says Fern.

"She was everybody's pet until she started pooping all over the house. Remember making that house for her behind the stove, Brick?"

"Those cardboard boxes hacked up and taped back together?"

"Yeah, and Sedge, you kept sitting in the boxes," says Hazel. "Too bad Nestly was messy. Paper training didn't work with little poopy bloomers. She just tried to peck the letters off the *Times*, and pooped wherever she wanted to. And we had to clean it up."

"Bleh! That didn't last long. So we made a bigger house, bigger boxes hacked up and taped back together," says Brick.

"Nestly still got into the house, though, but mostly when Mom was sewing," reminisces Fern. "She followed you everywhere, Sedge, 'cause you fed her popcorn. A trail of popcorn and poop everywhere you went."

Alvin sighs, like letting the air out of a balloon. "Seems like all the good stuff happened before I was born."

That gets a screech from Pink and Julie. "What about us? And what's so great about a dumb chick pooping all over?"

"I don't mean little things like that, Julie. Being youngest brother seems like... It's like Billy, Brick, Rich, Ron, and Herald, they got this whole totem carved full of wings and beaks and antlers and stuff. Where do I get to carve?"

"Whoa," says Brick. "There's a big space for you at the top Alv. You can climb over the rest of it and get first dibs up there.

And there's that part near the ground too, we been saving for you and Billy."

"Thanks, Baloo."

Pink says, "Anyhow, me and Julie got whole big worlds you don't even know about."

"A zillion little worlds, too," adds Julie.

"Yes I'm sure you do," says Hazel. "But back to Nestly. She got so bold, she jumped right on the table when Mom was making pies. Mom near had a fit."

"Sometimes she does get fussy about things," drawls Ron.

"Out to the coop with little Nestly to live with the old biddies," says Herald. "Anyhow, by that time, she had nasty gray pinfeathers poking through her pretty yellow fluff."

"Yar, just like cute little human babies when they get old and ornery," says Brick. "Out of the cradle, into the coop."

"If we could train a chicken not to poop, it'd sure be handy," broods Rich. "Scraps could go straight to the chicken under the table."

"No more chicken bucket," Ron enthuses.

Fern says, "You guys never take the bucket out before you dump the scraps in, so they half end up under the sink."

"Oh, go wash the soap. You girls and your rules."

"Don't bicker."

"We're not bickering. We're nickering. Snickering. Slow clock tickering. Can you see what time it is, Brick?" asks Rich.

"Nope. If I move my arm, my other arm's going to fall off."

"Good grief."

CHAPTER 54
The Storyteller: 2005

FIFTY YEARS LATER, JULIE heaps up her bucket in a profuse berry patch under murmuring poplars. After five miles of zigzagging she has ended up across the creek from where she started in the morning. Holding her bucket with both hands, she wrangles her way through soopolallie and devil's club to a spot where she can cross the creek on a jumble of slippery rocks.

Her day has been what she and Pink would have called a balloon walk, a lopsided circle that begins and ends in the same spot. Now Julie just has to follow the long, winding string to her doorstep.

Though bone-weary, the day spent in her brothers' and sisters' old territory has been refreshing. She feels more united with Pink now. They had quit trying to understand their "magnetic connection" years ago. They simply know when they need to be together, and when to stay apart. Gradually, a feeling of gleeful anticipation has come to Julie, a knowing that Pink will be fine. The mantle of revelation that her twin had so generously shared with her all those years ago falls softly over her shoulders once more, a weightless eagerness.

In unhurried haste, Julie continues homeward. She can't help but run her hands over bushes along the trail. When the berries are a sickle of light in the dusk, a mere roundness to the fingertips, they are especially delicious.

Rules 33X, Y, and Z: Your berries will always shake down, making room for more. The smallest berries automatically jiggle to the bottom, pushing the large ones to the top. So don't hide those beauties. Eat your fill from the bushes on your way home, saving only the whoppers.

Rule 41D: Feel for stinkbugs as you fill your mouth. They're flat with lots of wiggly legs. You probably won't notice the inch-worms.

Julie savours the drift of dusk into darkness, of shadow into deeper shadow. The slivers of light along the rims of leaves disappear. The sky is night-indigo. Listening on the forest's edge, she sifts through the events of her day. How long has an owl been asking her that quiet question, over and over again?

The Huckleberry Chronicles bubble through her mind. She pushes them onto the hob to simmer. The trick is to cook them just enough, so they're digestible but still juicy.

Home at last, her bucket full to the brim, she rushes up the steps.

No sooner has she got inside and pulled off her boots than there's a knock at her door. A heavy cough. Scraping feet. Julie's heart sinks. It must be Turkle.

She detours to the biffy.

More knocking, a snort, a tapping foot. Julie hastily throws a towel over her berries and before she has the door half-open, Aggie Turkle has shoved a foot into her kitchen, eyes gleaming.

"Hello Aggie… I just… uh… Cup of tea?"

Aggie Turkle's eyes dart around the kitchen. She takes a long look at the sink and noisily pulls a chair to the table, smirking. Aggie had watched Julie leave the house hours ago with her bucket. All afternoon, her knitting needles have click-clacked over a long gray snood while she's kept a lookout for Julie, leaning on her counter, peering through dusty ropes of ivy, within easy reach of her phone. Aggie had yakked to all and sundry that afternoon, seeding rumours about Julie, out there all day when there's bears on the rampage. She might have her scalp torn off by now, an arm in shreds.

Now Aggie's eyes are riveted on the sink as Julie fills the kettle. Julie can feel Aggie lusting after her berries, hankering to scoop her mouth full. Julie hovers in front of the sink while waiting for the kettle.

Aggie coughs, loudly chews her cud, and sniffs.

While Julie is busy with the teapot, Aggie reads the note which Julie hasn't had time to notice on the table. So that's who came. Her curiosity satisfied, Aggie shoves the note off the back of the table as she reaches for the *Daily Times*. She reads the headline out loud: "Bears Cause Havoc in Haversack's Meat Shack!" Then she proceeds with an interrogation that Julie skirts around the best she can.

"Yes, a bit of a hike. Well, yes, I did see a bear. No, hardly a berry out there (not any more). I guess the bears got them all. Yeah, it was a big bear. Must have weighed two thousand pounds. Well, yeah, I was startled, but so was the bear. I think it was more scared than I was. (It ran away before I'd gotten my feet back under me.)

The mound under the thin yellow towel sits mute as Aggie sups her tea. Julie wills Aggie to go home, a long, weary sigh escaping her. Finally, with a last slurp and jabber, Aggie Turkle heaves herself out the door.

As soon as she's gone, Julie hauls out the hook scale and weighs her berries. Fifteen pounds. Not bad, one pound off for the bucket. She runs her hands through the glossy fruit. At last, a chance to gloat.

CHAPTER 55
Tempers Flare

WHAT ABOUT THOSE ELEVEN urchins, stranded up the mountain, waiting for their father? How are they faring? Well, they're far from content. Tempers are short. Alas, it's a far from perfect world.

In the flickering were-light, everyone's dodging the smoke sent out by a chunk of wet cottonwood on the fire. It's hard to tell who's saying what, but it doesn't sound good. Foul words are spoken. There's a low growl of thunder.

Rich, quietly whittling by touch, is getting irritated with Pink and Julie, who are leaning on his arm to see what he's doing. Being Rich, he doesn't say much, just stuffs his whittling away. He pulls out his harmonica and starts a whiny version of "Annie Laurie," to the complaint of Fern and Hazel.

Ron is whittling too, but he has a hatchet and a pine log to work with, almost outside the circle of light, chopping like a demented woodchuck. Luckily, his aim so far is good. When he takes an armload of wood to the fire, though, everyone has to shift out of his way. Smoke billows, there's general coughing and burning of eyeballs and that's when the arguments flare up, loud and cranky.

"Asinine arse ant!"

"Bloody bastardo!"

"Don't kick my foot, you moron!"

"I didn't, donkey dung."

"YOU DO THAT ONE MORE TIME, I'M GOING TO STAB YOU IN THE GULLET WITH MY FLENSING KNIFE!"

"Oo, wow, a flensing knife. Good thing I'm not a whale."

"Yeah, but you got blubber for brains!"

"Come on, you guys."

"We're only kidding. Can't you tell?"

"No, I can't tell."

"Toad barf!

"Save your energy," warns Herald. "If Dad's not here by morning, some of us'll have to walk home. And some'll have to stay here with our berries."

Brick says, "Leave me at camp with Pink and Julie. Nothing can harm me with the poltergeist twins on guard."

"Ha!"

"At least we've got fruit for breakfast, lots of water, and lots of wood. And it's not raining anymore," says Fern. "And we're all together. So let's cheer up."

"Yes, Ferny. But it's kind of skithery out here."

"Pinky, Ju Ju, why don't you snuggle with Sedge, she's just about asleep. Come on, I'll tuck this mackinaw over the three of you."

"Mmm, thanks, moo ma."

Then a lot of things happen at once.

There's the flapping of the mackinaw, the crash of thunder, the crackle of pitch, startled cries; a gust of wind, the burst of sparks, the leaping away, the explosion of flames on a cedar bough; the torching of canvas, the struggle to tear it aside and stomp it out, the choking smoke, the un-aimed throwing of water, the rush for more water, the quenching of flames, the billows of acrid steam; and then a dismal, wet group is huddling in the dark.

"Whew."

"Now what?"

"I'm cold."

"We'll have to make another fire."

"Everything's soaked. How can we? "

"Patiently, that's how."

"This jacket smells like a singed rat, but it's still dry."

"No wonder, the way you were smacking out sparks with it."

"The comics are wet! Help!"

Julie is soaked through. She slings off her clothes and burrows into the mackinaw with Pink. They look like they crawled out of a troll cave, both of Julie's arms in one sleeve, Pink's in the other.

Gradually, the kids wring themselves out and reorganize the fireplace. Wet debris is pulled away and the ring of rocks is made smaller. There are a few handfuls of dry whittlings around Rich, which he gathers on a piece of birch bark. Over this they make a wigwam of small sticks and hemlock cones. Now all they need is a dry match.

"My matches are wet."

"So're mine. My pockets are soaked."

"I think there's a jar of matches in Brick's pack."

"And fish in the sea."

"Wait a minute," shouts Alvin. "Here's my bug! I've got at least two matches inside it." He holds out a jam can that's fitted with a wire handle and a stub of candle firmly stuck into a hole inside. He pries loose the matches. Ron finds him a dry rock to strike one, but it goes out before he can reach it into the can. They gather around him to keep off the breeze and, on the second try, Alvin lights his make-shift lantern. They use it to ignite pieces of birch bark. A thin blue flame devours a curl of the bark. Bigger wood is made handy.

"Let's bank this wet muck around the edge," says Billy.

They feed their prodigal pet one stick at a time so it doesn't outgrow its bank of red coals. And still they wait, all eyes on the steady, low flame.

* * *

(That includes the glint of two dark eyes, mournfully watching the eleven children from behind a cedar bough. The shaggy creature has been eyeing them for some time, sniffing and salivating. It shied away when the fire exploded, retreating under a rocky ledge. But now, it takes a shuffling step forward, long face twitching. They can't hear its tongue make dry sucking sounds on the roof of its mouth as it settles down to wait.)

* * *

CHAPTER 56
Bob

LONG BEFORE BOB APPROACHES the dairy for the fourth time that night, the rich aroma of cows is heavy in the wet air. Most of the lights are off at Moe and Bette's house. Moe has just come in from the barn. He's supping ice cream without his dentures and soaking his squashed toe. "That dang-blasted Sweetgrass trod on me when I was settling her with her bairn. I'm not going nowheres else tonight; sorry, Bob. And my truck's got a flat. Go ahead and try the phone if it's any use."

But the party line's busy. Bob waits. And waits. Taps the mouthpiece, clears his throat, but they keep talking about their infernal boccie teams and the lost horse that's finally been taken back to its owner. He could use a horse right now. He narrowly refrains from yelling something rude into the phone. He thanks Moe anyhow and Moe says that when Bette comes in, he'll tell her to call Lettuce again. (But Moe falls asleep before Bette comes in from the barn.)

As Bob heads out the door, he can hear Sweetgrass lowing softly, the indulgent sound of maternal bliss. Dear ol' Sweetgrass. Ha.

Bob trudges yet again up the hill to town. Last trip, he was simply driving Crick to the hospital. Now, with the worry of the broken car heavy on his shoulders, he's bone-weary from his scramble down the mountain. He'll ask the first person he sees with a truck to give him a lift back up to Stooge's.

But it looks like the town is deserted, except for a lot of vehicles around the meeting hall. He pokes his head in. Oops. It's the Co-op Regional meeting, raucous as a rooster caucus. Before he can duck out, he's been spotted. "Come in, come on in, Bob, you're just in time to break a tied vote."

* * *

Half an hour later, the meeting is droning on but the important issues have been solved or shelved and people are drifting to the refreshment table. Bob catches sight of Sid heading that way.

"Hi Bob, glad you made it after all. You sure speeded things up through that folderol. Should've been done an hour ago."

"Yeah, well, they needed to re-word the motion and get it settled in one vote instead of two votes that contradicted each other."

"Same old story, four people tryin' to open the door, five people tryin' to shut it."

"Or vice versa. But hey, Sid, can you give me a hand?"

Bob gladly accepts a glass of lemonade pressed on him by the refreshment crew and swallows a handful of sandwiches while he explains to Sid about his eleven kids up the mountain and the dead Hearse. "Could you help haul them down—not the Hearse, just the kids? And probably a few buckets of berries?"

"Sure, let's hop in my pick-up and we'll go right on up and get them, no problem. I'll just have to stop and tell Marge I'm going."

But Sid's truck coughs when he tries to start it, coughs again, and shudders. "Out of gas. Seems like I just filled it. Damn, the station closed at eight."

"I just filled the Hearse. A lot of good that is."

"I guess I'm not much help after all, Bob, I can't even drive myself home. Tell you what though, my nephew Burt's got a good truck and he'd be glad to get out of helping Alice serve up the coffee. I'll run get him."

Bob waits in Sid's truck while Sid finds Burt. He leans his head against the window and closes his eyes, feeling like a bedraggled creature in some kids' bedtime story... He went along and he went along until he came upon a... Bob dozes, dreaming of Lettuce reading aloud to the children.

Sid disentangles Burt from an after-meeting confab with the coffee klatch and quickly explains to him about the situation. "You remember Bob, our neighbour? With all the kids? Well his car's broke down, see, and I'm out of gas, and he needs a lift. For his kids, see, they're all stranded up the mountain, twelve or fifteen of them. So can you maybe run up there and haul them down with Bob? You're always looking for an excuse to run that big rig of yours!"

Back outside, Sid thumps on the window and Bob jumps awake. He stumbles out of the truck, trying to figure out where he is. Sid introduces Burt. Burt's a cheerful looking young fellow, shaking Bob's hand with enthusiasm. "I'll be glad to help out, sure, I just got to dump this sluice box off at home to make room for your kids. They can all climb in the back. Might be a bit rough, but kids usually like that sort of thing. How many are there, fifteen?"

"No, no, only eleven. And the big ones can even walk home with me if you don't want to bother unloading your equipment. Or I can give you a hand with it, if you want."

"Actually, that would be great, I have to unload it anyhow. Alice wants me hauling parakeets to the Provincials in the morning, and there's sure not room for my junk and sixteen bird cages, never mind all her boxes and bags."

First, they drop Sid off at his place. Marge is just getting home from bingo and she goes right in to phone Lettuce. Bob looks towards the distant arc of light across town at his own house and thinks wistfully of his dinner. At Burt's acreage out of town, they unload a jumble of mining gear. Bob turns down Burt's offer of tea but asks if he's got a spare cardboard box to put some berries in, so buckets won't be tipping all over the truck. His kids have probably picked fifty pounds today.

"Holy cow! That much? I'll just dash in, tell Alice what's going on, see what I can find for boxes."

He's soon back with Alice, who gives Bob a bag of cookies and an armload of blankets for the kids. "They'll be tired and cold to the bone. But sorry, all our cardboard boxes are full of parakeet paraphernalia. Will this old galvanized tub be alright to keep the buckets steady? That road's rough as a rhino and you sure don't want to spill any precious berries."

Eventually, Bob and Burt are back on the road.

It's long after twelve when, for the fifth time, Bob casts an eye over the dairy. All the lights are out, even in the barn. Good-night, Sweetgrass. Good-night, Moe, and good-night, Bette.

Up that consarned rocky road again, this time with Burt discussing parakeet plumage, zinc oxide, and feather mites. Bob is content to let Burt ramble on, grunting occasionally to make up for not really listening. Burt doesn't seem to mind. He likes to talk.

"When I'm not hauling parakeets to shows for Alice, I'm usually out prospecting gold. One of these days I'll hit it rich. I can feel it sure as I can feel my nose, known it since infancy I'll strike it rich someday. My dad was the same; mind you, he sold Rawleigh Products off and on. I'll keep my job at the Co-op long as I have to. Anyhow, you have no idea how much paraphernalia goes along with parakeets. Itty-bitty boxes of itty-bitty bits of what-all I have no idea, eyedroppers and tinctures and feed pellets of a hundred sorts and then for the performances, ribbons and tiny-teeny bells that weigh the birds down a bit, you see, so's they can't fly away soon's something startles them. Oh, it's a lot of fun in its way, but fluffy bits are always floating up your nose. Last time I unloaded the cages, I near blew my schnoz off. Yessir, give me the wide-open spaces anytime and a truck load of mining gear and I'm a happy man. Just don't call me Bird. Mind you, the birds are real pretty, and I don't know what Alice would do without them to fuss over, us having no kids and all. No sirree Bob, not every man's lucky to have a brood like yours. But one of these days, mark my words, I'm going to hit a gold lode so rich it'll keep us in shiny leather boots till the end of our days."

As Burt enthuses, Bob shuts his eyes, the better to concentrate on his worries. It's nighttime, it's cold, and the kids are alone in the wilds, doing God-knows-what, while their mother is stranded at home alone, doubtless stewing her head off. Bob hopes she's gotten some kind of message about his whereabouts. Images loom and recede in his weary mind in lockstep with Burt's monologue. He envisions the children alternately waiting safely for him all together in one spot, and the children scattered across the mountain in all sorts of dilemmas. He pictures the Hearse sitting nicely, far enough off the road that Burt can easily drive past it, and then the Hearse sticking a bit too far out so that even by ripping the bumper off, Burt won't have room to pass. If Burt can't drive past the Hearse, then what? He sure as heck won't be able to turn around on that steep switchback. He'd have to back down. How many rocky hairpins can a truck back down without getting off kilter and rolling over? Could they shove the two-ton Hearse off the cliff? Bob pictures the rusty lummox flipping, horn croaking piteously, a thin voice of reproach growing fainter and fainter as it tumbles end over end, finally hitting the bottom of the abyss with a reverberating crunch.

Bob jolts awake with the realization he's been snoring very loudly. Burt is shouting, "Whoa! Arrragggggg?" He swerves the wheel, slams on the brake, and the pick-up shimmies to a stand-still. The engine judders, the lights go out.

A huge black shape looms in front of them.

"What in tarnation?! Holy cow! What is it?"

They're on the downhill side of what, in the dark, looks like a stalled brontosaurus. It's not a cow.

It's the Hearse.

CHAPTER 57
No Point Starting a Panic

A STRANGE THING HAPPENS at the campfire while Bob and Burt are gaping at the prehistoric six-door sedan.

The Eleven are trying to get comfortable in various stages of sleep, just-about-sleep, trying-not-to-sleep, and never-going-to-sleep-again. Julie and Pink share a dream and giggle. Brick snores and startles, yawns like a grave, snores and startles. He mumbles that he can't sleep and he can't stay awake, and then he snores. Fern and Hazel have dozed for a while and are having a whispered conversation. They collapse in muffled laughter. On the edge of their encampment, Herald is stretched on his back on cold concrete, listening for the Hearse. Unable to hear what they're talking about, Herald finds the girls' sibilant voices irritating, like the rustle of turning pages when you're trying to sleep. To Alvin, sitting with his arms wrapped around his knees, mesmerized by the fire, the whispering sounds like Deady-White-Eye rustling. He struggles to stay awake.

Billy has hiccups. He drinks some water backwards, holds his breath, hiccups in his sleep. Ron is sitting collapsed forward with his football under his chin. He's dreaming that he's changing his bicycle tire and the new tire's gliding on fine until the tube gets in the way. For some reason, he's blown up the tube before putting it on the rim.

Who's still awake? Sedge? No. She dreams about shards of coloured light falling around her, tinkling to the ground. She parts tall grass to look for the red, blue, emerald lights. The grass itches her legs; she wakes up scratching.

Rich dreams that he's working on his bird carving, shaping long, iridescent feathers and bright eyes that can see what he sees.

Fern dreams she's snug on the living-room couch and adjusts her head on a rock, sleeping peacefully.

Herald is dozing off when it dawns on him that a loud slurping noise has been going on for a long time. Way too long and too loud. He cautiously rises on an elbow to peer around the fire. Alvin is sitting bolt upright, staring over Herald's head with a look of disbelief. Hazel, too, is looking that way and moves a finger across her lips, "Shh."

Herald slowly sits up and turns to see a black shape moving amongst the trees, setting the branches swaying. It's something big and darker than the night. What?

Hazel creeps to Herald, whispering, "I don't think it's a bear."

"A bear?" Suddenly Alvin is standing beside Herald.

Herald doesn't want to alarm the others. No point starting a panic. Yet. So he puts his arm around Alvin and the three of them perch on the slab of concrete, staring into the dark. They can hear whatever it is shifting its weight from foot to foot, hidden in the trees. Hazel and Herald whisper back and forth:

"It sounds heavy."

"It sure was thirsty."

"Why don't you think it's a bear?" asks Alvin.

"It seems too tall," says Hazel.

"I couldn't see it properly," says Herald. "I could just tell where it was."

"I'm glad I'm not the only one who heard it," says Hazel.

"It must have been drinking from our fire bucket," says Herald. "Why was the bucket so far from the fire?"

Hazel whispers, "That's where I left it last time I filled it. Couldn't see where else to put it with everyone sprawled out, dead to the world."

"Shh… listen."

They listen intently, trying to hear what they cannot see.

"It's eating. Crunching something."

"Shouldn't we holler and scare it away?" asks Alvin.

"No. Then we'll never know what it is," says Hazel.

"And we'll wake everyone up and they'll be scared," says Herald.

"I'm not scared," says Alvin, wedging himself between Herald and Hazel.

The three continue to stare into the night, leaning on each other. They can hear occasional thumps of heavy feet and quiet munching.

"Bears eat grass."

"So do cows. Do you think it's a stray cow?"

"Can you hear it swishing its tail?"

"No."

"Then it's not a cow."

"Bears don't swish their tails."

"Maybe it's a Sasquatch."

"Sasquatches aren't real, Alv."

Alvin's pretty sure some aliens are real.

With a murmur, Hazel suddenly rises and steps forward. Herald reaches out to pull her back, but already she's slipping into the shadows, hands outstretched.

Herald gestures to Alvin to stay put and, with one stride, he, too, disappears into the bushes before Alvin can even croak, "Hazy... Herald, come back."

Suddenly alone, Alvin freezes. His voice no longer seems to work. Although he's no more than fifty steps from the campfire, all he can see in that direction is a wavering glow. He can't see his brothers and sisters huddled around it, dead to the world. When he looks back to where Hazel and Herald have disappeared, the darkness is darker. Alvin's chest is drumming.

After what seems like an hour and is less than ten minutes, Alvin hears branches rustling and noisy footsteps. He's astonished to hear Hazel and Herald laughing. Huh? Now he's glad he didn't cry out. He'd have felt like an idiot. As Hazel and Herald slowly approach, Alvin can see they're holding onto something big, very big and black. And tall. As they come closer he can see their hands on opposite sides of its wide back. It looks like it has big, white eyes. It's a... a horse!

By now those around the fire are waking up—except Ron, who is still working on his bike tire. Fern stirs up a flame so she can see what's going on. Billy and Rich clamber to their feet, stopping in their tracks when they see Alvin, Herald, and Hazel leading a black horse into the flickering firelight. It has a white patch on either side of its forehead.

Pink and Julie jump up and tentatively stroke the long, dusty nose. The horse pushes past their hands, stretching his muzzle towards the nearest bucket. "No, no, horsey, not our berries!"

"I think she just wants more water," says Sedge. "Look, she's ignoring the berries. Here's some more water, girl... there you go, girl."

But she wants something else. The horse keeps sniffing and looking around expectantly at the one person still sleeping. Good old Ron's as thorough about dreaming as he is about everything else, and he just about has the new inner tube wrapped around the wheel rim when Rich gives him a nudge and the bike falls over. Finally Ron wakes up with a groan and is startled to see a horse looking straight at him. The horse looks at each of them searchingly, as if counting them, looking hopefully into one face after another with eyes that are round and black and shining.

"Let's call her Huckleberry," says Pink.

"She sure is shaggy," says Sedge. "Her mane and bangs are all frazzled out with burrs and twigs."

"She must be a stray, way up here by herself," says Ron.

"Can we keep her?"

"I don't think so, Pink."

"We don't have a field," explains Billy wistfully. "Or a barn."

"He couldn't fit in the chicken shed even if we put the chickens somewhere else," says Alvin.

"And the veranda would be no good." says Fern.

"Anyhow," says Brick, "We can't just turn up at home with a horse. You can't pretend you didn't know a horse was following you home, same as you can with kittens."

"He's still sniffing for something. Anyhow, we need fresh water."

Herald and Hazel stumble to the creek to refill the bucket and canteens, puzzling about their visitor.

"It's so weird, that horse coming. Kind of eerie… like an omen."

"Oh jeez, you don't believe in omens, do you Hazel?"

Hazel flicks a handful of water at Herald but lucky for her, she misses his glasses and he doesn't have to pull her hair. "I don't… but it's weird. The nearest farm is miles away. And why did she come up here? And why tonight?"

"A messenger, like? But what's the message?"

"Who knows," says Hazel, "But she's sure friendly."

When Hazel and Herald get back to camp, the horse is happily licking the salt off some pretzels. Then she awkwardly lies down with her back to the fire. She seems quite at home, like a tired old friend staying the night. Several hands pat her as she heaves a sigh and settles herself for some serious shut-eye.

"He seems like a family pet, but what's he doing way out here?" Fern says.

"Search me," says Rich.

"Poor thing's exhausted," says Brick.

Ron says, "She must have got lost and followed our voices. Seems to like being near people."

"You know what?" Herald says, "I think I was hearing that horse for quite awhile before I realized she was there. I thought it was just the trees creaking or someone rummaging around trying to find a square inch without a rock to lie on."

"I wonder how long she was standing in the bushes before she got up her courage to drink our water," says Alvin.

"I don't know, but she sure made herself right at home once she did. Just as if she knew us," says Hazel.

"Mmmm, she's warm to snuggle against." Pink and Julie are cozy, leaning against the horse's back. Soon they too are soaking up some serious REM.

Alvin yawns, "It feels a bit safer with the horse here."

"Hey Alv, us oldies will look after things," Herald tells him. "Why don't you sack out by Ron and have a nap until Dad gets here."

Alvin doesn't need coaxing. He slumps down by Ron and falls instantly asleep. Ron listens for a while to the others nattering, then tucks his arm around Alvin and nods off, looking for his dream bike.

"Moe doesn't have a horse," muses Rich. "No one does in our end of town, unless they just got it."

"Maybe she's our guardian spirit," says Fern.

"But I never thought of angels being old and dusty," says Brick.

"If she is an angel, too bad she didn't bring her chariot," says Hazel.

CHAPTER 58
The Storyteller: Julie, 2005

WHILE JULIE CLEANS HER huckleberries, she thinks about the social intricacies of berry picking. There's no one more generous than her once she's picked the berries, but until then, they're all hers, and she's particular who she gives them to. Instinct and courtesy don't always match. Protection of territory cannot always be friendly.

Was that impulse to hide her berries from Aggie Turkle the same one that prompts her to duck out of sight when someone drives by where she's picking? If one doesn't want to fight tooth and claw for one's berries, surely the best defense is secrecy.

Julie laughs as she makes an entry in her "Chronicles of Huckleberry Picking" called "Turkle Rules":

Hardcore huckleberry picking is rife with rules like 12b, 14C, and 21F: Never tell the location of your berry patch, so you won't have some poacher's demise on your conscience when you're forced to protect your territory.

You should never admit that it's a good year for berries. If anyone asks, say the crop is meager.

Don't look enthusiastic when the subject comes up. Downplay the season. Say, "From what I've seen, the bushes don't look promising." (Of course not, after you've already scalped them).

If someone else picks where you usually pick, that's plundering. That's invasive. But if you stumble into a good patch on the edge of someone else's property, that's another matter. If the berries fall into your hands when you gently touch them, isn't it your responsibility to pick them? Waste is a terrible thing.

It's pitch dark by the time Julie has cleaned her berries. The feeling of happy anticipation which had grown over the afternoon is turning into restless fatigue. She munches bread and cheese, a few berries. She runs a hot bath, sets up *Amazon Intrigue* on the over-tub rack, and has been relaxing for several minutes when there's another knock on the porch door.

"Gad, what now?" she thinks.

Julie zips into her robe and is hurrying to answer the door when it bursts open. She shrieks.

CHAPTER 59
Lettuce at home

NINETY-NINE PERCENT OF WORRY is useless. But worry is what tired minds do best, especially when they're keeping vigil.

Lettuce puts down her book. When all her family is making a commotion around her, she can lose herself in the magic of lore. But not tonight, in this empty silence.

Terrible images flash through her mind: children cold and wet, lost on a cliff in the dark, too close to a creek to hear the others, or to be heard. Mine shafts. Tunnels. They're all explorers. Lettuce paces, hopes they're together, at least. They have talked about it often enough, the importance of sticking together, especially on hikes. When the going gets tough, they know they have to help each other.

But they're all so darn independent and half of them think they're super heroes.

Lettuce takes a flashlight and a box outside. Might as well collect some windfalls. It's murky dark. She follows the glow of tall white phlox along the side of the house. A bruise of fragrance fills the night.

At the transparent tree, the air is acid-sweet with ripe apples. She fills the box, then sits under the veranda light to peel and slice enough to make a big batch of sauce.

Lettuce had been glad when Marge and then Alice phoned, but all she really knows is that her family is still "out there" somewhere. It's reassuring that Burt has a good truck to bring them home. But it's ages since Alice phoned.

Lettuce washes more canning jars, then ranks-and-files them along a clean shelf on the porch and covers them with a tablecloth. They'll be glad of the empty counter space.

She tries not to glance at the clock. Its hands are clearly not moving. The only way to make time pass is to keep busy.

By one in the morning Lettuce has a nine-egg gingerbread cake cooling alongside a bowl of applesauce big enough to drown in. The kitchen is redolent with ginger and cinnamon. When she lifts the lid from the stew, onions add their pong to the medley, like the tuba having its say amongst the piccolos.

"Let them eat cake tonight and fill up on stew tomorrow," she thinks. Lettuce plunks herself at the table. She's done everything she can. Now's her chance to jot down some thoughts. But does she have the energy to find paper and pen?

The trick is to have inspiration when she has time and energy to do something with it. Too bad she has that addiction to reading. The thing is, when she's reading she can be pretty much aware of whatever else is going on in the house, and she can bookmark her place and easily find it again. But writing takes uninterrupted quiet, a rare thing in a busy household, so difficult to pick up where she'd left off.

Sometimes it's like drawing on snow.

She often jots mental notes over the course of a day; these flutter into her thought-garden like leaves, like tousled birds, like seeds, like compost. Brilliant lines may come to her when she's up to her eyebrows in mashing potatoes or wrenching bind weed out of the red currents, but when she's staring at the ceiling in the middle of the night, trying to sharpen an image, she's too tired for words. She glimpses green and scarlet feathers drifting away from her.

Now her thoughts fly again into a vortex of worry: children calling in the dark, lost to each other, plunging down mine holes, stung by wasps, mauled by bears, playing with fire. Fighting. Are they acting like fools right now, laughing on the edge of disaster? Shoving?

A flash-crash sends Lettuce to the veranda to see lightning forking every which way. She counts to fifteen before the thunder rolls away. "Keep moving away, storm. Keep off my family!"

She tugs on her gumboots and steps into the green-black void. The valley is eerie with mist. She can't see the mountain. There is no view except a few stars fleeting through cumulonimbus. For a moment Lettuce feels far from everyone, even herself, cut off from reality, powerless, anxious.

Gradually the rain-hush calms her. The night sounds are soft. Water trickles from cedar boughs, brushing over leaves. Evening primrose and nicotiana sweeten the air; their yellow and magenta petals are vibrant, though unseen.

Lettuce shakes off her panic. Her children are likely not having a fun time, but they'll be alright. Bob might even be with them. She's cooked supper, she's scrubbed, the house is warm and reasonably organized. There's nothing more she can do. She just has to wait for her family to come home.

In the quiet house, Lettuce rummages in a deep pantry drawer. She pulls out a bundle of papers held to a ledger by a rubber band cut from a defunct hot water bottle. She heaves the bundle onto the table. It's labeled, "Sewing Business and Egg Sales."

Her family knows there's more to her ciphering than tallying finances, but no one's ever had more than the scantiest glance at her papers, even from across the room. They know better than to pry. She has the look of a wild creature clutching her young to her heart when they get too close.

Amid, amongst, and betwixt her busy practical life, Lettuce tries to capture the ballad of her days, to give firm meaning to the ephemeral. But often it seems like trying to stuff mist into a bottle. Will the bottle drift onto an ocean shelf, opened, message obscured?

Lettuce often feels that life makes sense only one line at a time. She sharpens a pencil and rounds up some paper.

(Her alchemy will not be revealed until the children are grown up. Then "The Song of Years" by Lettuce Claire is published, to the excitement of her family and an enthusiastic public. Bob and the kids are delighted, but not entirely surprised, when they read her bright, clear lines, distilled from her life's musings.)

CHAPTER 60
Rescue At Last

THE FOUNDLINGS PERCHED AROUND their fire are getting colder and damper by the minute. Fern has long since doled out the cookies and raisins. Nerve-wracking lightning and thunder have given way to a steady drizzle. Perth would have hated the thunder, but they all wish their old dog was with them. The horse whickers in its sleep. The Eleven hunker down in gloomy silence. The fire-light casts odd shadows and highlights over their faces, elongating their noses, hollowing their eye sockets, glistening their teeth. They look haunted.

Herald, from time to time, paces the edge of the clearing, listening for any sound from down the mountain. Occasionally, the wind shifts and the roar of the creek gets louder, the eerie yip of coyotes closer. But now he hears a different sound. A rattle and bang, and a different kind of roar. Suddenly, he shouts, "Someone's coming! I hear a vehicle!"

"Lights!"

Sleepy faces peer from behind rocks and stumps.

"Doesn't sound like the Plymouth."

"No farts, no groans... not the Hearse."

"Told ya the Hearse prob'ly died."

"It's a truck!"

"Wahoo! We're rescued!"

"At last!"

Burt and Bob swing two large battery lamps as they approach the campsite. They see what looks like a bunch of stick figures clambering out of the shadows... figures which become plumper in the lamplight, with a full-colour pelage of coats and hats, rosy cheeks, and luminous eyes. The kids don't mind being blinded by the light. Light! Beautiful light. They've never seen such wonderful light. It's as if they're almost transported home already. All of them talk at once.

"Dad! Dad! We're all here."

"Did you forget when you told us to meet, Dad?"

"You bring any grub? In the truck? Yay!"

"Where's the Hearse?"

"We knew you'd come sooner or later."

"Me and Julie were playing Hansel and Gretel," shouts Pink, "abandoned in the forest."

"...with no crumbs to make a trail. But we kept dropping bits of silver foil that we just happened to have with us."

"I thought they were silver trinkets, Jule!"

"We were poor, remember."

"Did you have trouble with the flambulator, Dad?"

Burt is flabbergasted by the racket. It seems to him there's at least two dozen kids jumping around him. Bob laughs, "Okay gang, slow down, slow down. Shake hands with Burt, who's kindly volunteered to haul us all home."

As the Eleven swarm Burt, shaking hands and introducing themselves, Bob sees that Brick is hurt and having a hard time keeping up a brave face. He sizes up the situation quickly and tells

Brick he'll have to ride in the front of the truck, and the sooner he gets away from the rabble, the better. The others watch solemnly as Bob gives Brick his arm, grabs a lamp and a bucket of berries, and leads him away, talking to him quietly.

Burt enthusiastically holds up his lamp while the rest of them burst into action. It takes them quite a while to get organized, they're tripping over each other they're so excited, and it's not until they're making a last sweep of the foundations that, with a jolt, it hits all of them at once: "The horse is gone! Where is she?"

"He can't be gone far."

They'd been so busy they hadn't noticed the tall, shaggy form shuffling quietly into the night. Julie and Pink start to cry, though they haven't cried all day, no matter what. The others try to comfort them, but they, too, feel troubled, as though wakened from a spectral world into a reality they're not quite ready for. They haven't said goodbye to their new friend. They still don't know the horse's name, though the horse has certainly learned all their names.

"We'll come back and look for her, won't we, Haze?"

"Of course we will, Julie. We'll all come back and find her."

Bob nods at Burt. "Must have been the horse the party line was yakking about. Several people saw it wandering along the highway this evening but then it headed into the forest."

"Very strange. Last I heard, it was back home. I can't imagine Big White coming way up here. They figure some kids on a lark let her out last night."

"Big White?"

"How long ago did you kids see the horse?"

"We didn't see any Big White. Our horse was entirely black except for a white patch on each side of his forehead! He was here just a minute ago. He must have got shy and wandered away during all the fuss."

Pink and Julie look at each other tearfully, trying to be brave, clutching each other's hands. "We were going to call her Huckleberry because her eyes are like big, shiny huckleberries."

"That's a weird coincidence, two horses loose in one day. Dogs loose, okay, and kids loose, but not horses," mutters Burt, sweeping his lamp around the edge of the clearing. But no horse can be seen.

"Well, we can't spend the rest of the night looking for her," Bob says. "I hope she gets safely back to wherever she belongs. You can call around in the morning and see what you can find out. We'd better get home before your mother sends out a search party, if she hasn't already."

After one last look around, they squelch the fire and stir up the wet ashes. A steaming cloud of soot follows them as they plod to the truck.

After a very rough trip down the mining road, which involves some touch-and-go drama getting past the stranded Hearse, Bob, Burt, and the Eleven eventually make it home.

CHAPTER 61
Everyone Home

TEN TROGLODYTES STORM INTO the house, swooping Lettuce half off her feet as she meets them at the door. Bob helps Brick a few steps behind, followed by Burt. They all talk at once.

"Mom! We're home, Mom! Did you miss us? Mom! Brick's hurt!"

"Brick! What happened? Easy, easy. Give him some room, kids. Can you make it to the couch?"

They stand back, fluttering and cooing as Bob and Burt help Brick onto the couch. Lettuce gently fluffs pillows at his back, behind his head, and under his arm. "Oh, my dear boy. Someone make tea. And a hot water bottle. Oh, thank Providence you're all here at last."

"We ended up together, at least." They all jabber: "You dyed the curtains, Mom! Lemon-lime! Chartreuse! I love them, Mom. Mmmm, ginger cake. We got a lot of berries, Mom. What time is it? Only two o'clock? The windows look like sunlight, Mom, from outside. It looks like a whole new kitchen. Were you worried? We weren't. Except about Brick. And, well, about everybody at some point. Wait till you see all the berries, Mom! We better help Dad, he's unloading the truck."

Lettuce bustles. "Come in and sit down, Burt, you've done enough already, have something to eat. You can all eat soon as everything's brought in. Here, Burt, at the table. Julie and Pink, please take Brick his tea and help him hold it."

Before long, the kitchen is a welter of buckets and packs and the stew is being devoured as well as the cake. Burt is given a big slab of cake to take home. They try to give him a gallon of berries, but he'll take only a capful. (His cap is black, so no worry about stains.)

"Thank you, Burt... Thank you for helping us with your truck... Thank you for everything!... Thanks!... Thanks!" They crowd around the doorway to see Burt off and before Burt's down the driveway, Bob is already phoning the hospital about Brick's arm. No waiting till morning this time. Anyhow, it's already morning.

Nurse Legghorn answers the phone with a squawk. "More quills? Not another quill call! Doc just got back! Cutta-clack, cutta-clack!"

Bob holds the receiver away from his ear and speaks gently. Eventually Dr. Brundy comes on the line and says he'll be at the house in half an hour. He has to drop a young lad off on his way. He might be a bit longer. "Don't let your boy eat anything in case we have to operate."

Too late for that; Brick has wolfed down a bowl of stew. He sits in quiet misery. His brothers and sisters cluster around him, trying to cheer him up. They compare fingers to see whose are the most stained and have the usual argument about who squashes the berries and that's why their fingers are purpler. Rich, who has purposely squashed some berries to get the requisite colour, stays mum. All their hands are black, if not from berries then from soot and dirt, but you can easily tell that Rich and Julie have the purplest tongues, no contest. Fern's hair is so matted with pitch, she bravely hands Hazel the scissors and ends up with a short shag that suits her quite well. Sedge delicately clips a lump of pitch from

Brick's top knot. He grins shakily, "Thanks, Sis. Hey, this is great, lots of attention. Our Billy, have you built a new riddle lately?"

"I just got a new one nailed," he grins. "What did the farmer say when he saw the huge green oval thing in his field? Can't anyone guess? It's easy. When he saw the huge green oval thing in his field, the farmer said, 'What a melon!' Get it? 'Wata-melon'?"

"Oh, I get it, watermelon, except he didn't pronounce his 'ar'."

"Ha ha. Good one, Billy Bridge!"

"Have you finished your limerick, Bill? Can we hear it?"

Billy happily obliges. With his bright blue fez firmly on his head, and using his husky radio voice, Billy spiels off the words he's been practicing all day. "Ladies and gentlemen, I have a limerick to lick your gimmicks, the one and only,

Melon-imerick

There was a bright fellow named Melon

Who got cross when his boss called him Hellion;

It was a sight quite lurid

When he knocked his boss on the gourd,

An event called the Melon Rebellion!

When the hooting and groaning subside, Rich quietly hands Brick the bird he's been carving, saying, "I still have to work more on the feathers, Brick, but you can take it to the hospital. It's a get-well-fast bird."

Tears prickle Brick's eyes as he tucks the smooth shape into the palm of his hand. "Ah, Rich."

Not to be outdone, Ron presents Brick with the latest *Mad Magazine* he'd traded with Chuckie Moozle. Brick's grin is as wide as Alfred E. Newman's.

"Easy does it, Sis," he mutters to Fern as she starts washing his face, well-meaning as Kanga with her lathery flannel. He tolerates Hazel dabbing the worst of his insect bites with calamine, but he draws the line at having his hair brushed. Pink and Julie have patiently teased the knots out of his boot laces. Lettuce catches her breath as she gently pulls off his fuming socks. Herald gets Brick a bucket of warm soapy water to soak his feet in. First he dips his glasses in and spends ten minutes trying to clean them. When Brick's finished soaking his feet, Alvin towels them off and Bob gently tugs on clean woolen socks.

At last Brick stretches out, gratified by all the kind attention but wishing he could fast-forward his life on their Woolensak tape recorder. Finally left to himself, he's able to concentrate on the word, "operate… operate"…which has rattled through his thoughts since his dad's call to the doctor. He wonders why he isn't supposed to eat and wishes he hadn't. He wishes Doc Brundy would hurry up and get it over with. And he wishes the Doc would never arrive. Doc Doom. Doc Doom. Doom. If this is the kind of thing Mrs. Hortense says builds character, he'll have one heck of a lot of character, if he lives.

You can't sculpt character with a feather.

Fern and Hazel and Sedge drag the younger kids upstairs, nudging them toward their beds, some in pajamas, some not, one or two teeth brushed. At least no one goes to bed with shoes on, although Alvin's feet are so dirty, he pulls on socks before crawling between his sheets. Billy's thumb is throbbing and Fern binds it up with a glob of Raleigh's ointment.

Meanwhile, Lettuce is getting the kitchen reorganized. Herald and Bob are still hauling buckets from the driveway to the porch and from the porch to the kitchen when Doctor Brundy arrives. Keeping on his coat and hat, Doc strides through, pulls up a chair, and puts his hand on Brick's forehead, saying, "Humph… fever. We'll have to get that jacket off. I hate to cut it, but. Look at that sling! Good job, whoever made it."

Doc carefully unwinds the filthy blue scarf and the candy-pink and pumpkin-orange striped tie. "Hmmm… uhum… whup… don't like the look of that arm. Green-stick at least. Maybe worse. It'll heal, lad. Don't worry. This'll be cold; I'm going to swab it. Hmmmm. This smooth branch made a pretty good splint. But how about a wooden spoon? Hold steady, lad. That's the way. Some nice clean gauze to wrap it. Now then, what seems to be wrong with that knee? Yes, your knee. You're flinching every time I get near it. Let's have a look. Easy now. Hmmm. That's one swollen joint. We'll have to x-ray it and the arm both. Tell you what, we'll leave you here till the hospital gets going in the morning. Try to get some sleep. You'll be okay, lad."

"Nothing to eat, mind," the doctor instructs as he makes his way to the door, munching the cupful of huckleberries thrust on him by Lettuce. "Only sips of water til we read the x-rays. Can you bring him in about six-thirty? No car? What happened to your Hearse? Hmm… umm… umph… You've had quite a day. Tell you what, I'll call our technician. Arlo can collect Brick on his way to work in the morning. I'll call him at six, before he leaves for the hospital. He's got a station wagon, should be room for Mom and Dad too, if you want. About six-thirty, then."

And so arrangements are made for Brick to meet his demise. The hospital. Brick shudders. Oh yeah, he'll be in good hands with kind and skillful Doctor Brundy. But when a doctor tells you not to worry, of course you worry.

Excited messages are being relayed upstairs and down about the doctor's visit. Compassion flows through the house. But one and all, his wide-eyed brothers and sisters are glad it's not them, while Brick faces the tough reality that if you need to be doctored, nobody can take your place. He glumly listens to the background clatter of activity in the kitchen.

"We might as well get going on these wet berries," says Lettuce.

Herald, Hazel, and Fern have geared up, almost reluctant to end their longest day. They work alongside their parents until Fern collapses in a chair with her head in her hands and the others shoo her off to bed. Hazel spills a handful of berries and bangs her head when retrieving them from under the table. She, too, stumbles away to bed. Herald stays to mop the floor and chat with his parents, then he, too, is off.

CHAPTER 62
Bob and Lettuce in the Kitchen

IT'S FOUR IN THE morning. Twelve quarts are cooling, twelve more boiling. Lettuce looks around at the bowls and buckets of huckleberries waiting. She grins at Bob, "What a haul!"

Bob stuffs wood in the stove. "But how much more of this jamming and jarring can you stand, Let?"

"The kids can help after a good sleep-in. We need a few more quarts. We ran out in February this year. Last summer, we canned eighty quarts only. Twenty more would have seen us through."

Bob topples into a chair. "But it's still July. If we all go picking a couple more times, we'll have plenty. If it's a wet summer, they'll be ripe further up the mountains in September."

"That's a lot of 'ifs.' We can't count on the weather. If it's dry, this could be the main crop. But. The Hundred Quart Rule could be bent a little, I suppose, Bob. Those kids sure worked hard… just staying alive up there."

"I feel quite proud of them," says Bob. "You should have seen their camp. Quite the home away from home."

Lettuce nods. "They'd been plotting this trip since their first day off from school. I tried my hardest to talk the younger three out of going…"

"And there they were, everyone ready at six am," Bob laughs.

Lettuce adjusts the damper, rattles the grate. "Herald was rummaging at four, getting organized. He'd been awake for twenty-four hours by the time he just went to bed… feeling responsible for everyone. You know, Bob, he blamed himself for Brick's accident, letting him use the broken pack-board. Why did we keep that wreck of a thing?"

"Because the longer we keep something, the longer we have to keep it? Maybe we saved it for a mythical everything-gets-fixed day. Maybe things from the past help anchor us in the present?"

"Like the One Hundred Quart Rule, Bob?"

"Well. Isn't the Rule more an ideal than reality, Let? It's not as if we're going to starve if we don't can a hundred quarts. There's all the other fruit you put up."

Lettuce scrubs at the sink. "It isn't just about the berries. It's a family goal. Something to work towards for everyone's benefit… keeps the kids from falling into idle ways… teaches them to value hard work and accomplishment, and so on and so forth. But you're right, I don't take the Rule totally literally. Still, you never know, next year there could be a crop failure. Too much rain during pollination. Or tent caterpillars!"

"That's why the good old One Hundred Quart Rule has been etched into your family cranium for generations, like footprints in concrete. Hey, don't throw that dishrag at me, Let!"

"Okay, Bob, okay: the kids can sell the rest of the berries!"

Lettuce and Bob clink coffee cups. "Here's to wealth and charity! And a hard-working family!"

Lettuce topples into a chair. "But I'm never again letting the kids go off alone like that. From now on, I'm going with them."

"Uh huh. I can imagine explaining that to their dates."

"You know what I mean. I was so scared. Deep down, I knew they'd survive, but even now I'm still scared just thinking about it."

"I know. The whole thing's been a nightmare, worrying about them, trying to reach them. I should never have trusted that car. If I'd had a reliable vehicle, Brick's arm could be in a cast by now. Anyhow, I might as well put more coffee on. You want some, Let?"

"Yes, please. No point trying to sleep now. Although that's one thing can put me out fast, sitting down with a coffee when I'm exhausted and have to get up in a few minutes. We have to get Brick ready for the hospital pretty soon. Might as well dry-sort berries while we sit here." Lettuce pulls a bucket up to the table. "But, Bob, what was that you were saying about the Hearse?"

"Ah, pushing the Hearse over. It was the wee gidgets who gave it the last ounce we needed. When push came to shove, it was either the Hearse or us. You see, when I finally got up the mountain, I got stuck on the last hairpin."

"But I thought Marge said you were stuck at the first switchback?"

"Oh, that was my first time up, when the cow was on the road, after I'd taken Crick to the hospital. Yes, Crick. More about that later. But see, after I finally got going again, the Hearse broke down on the last hairpin. Blown tire, bent axle, mangled oil pan, the works. So I had to walk all the way back to town to get help. Which is one of the many reasons we were so late getting home."

"Of all my dire imaginings, I had no idea the goings on."

"And that's only half of it. I had to dig Sid out of the Co-op meeting and of course I got hornswoggled into the meeting for a while. And then Sid had no gas so he got Burt to drive me. Nice guys, both of them, all too glad to help.

"On the way up the mountain, Burt managed to squeak past the Hearse by driving up the bank a bit, but on the way back down, his truck slid a bit cock-eyed. We tried clearing rocks so Sid could pull further up the bank, but more rocks kept sliding down. We had to move the Hearse! It seemed impossible, but we had to do it. So we all piled out of Burt's truck, except Brick, of course. He would've made a big difference, too, but it's a good thing he could keep a foot on the brake, because Sid's emergency's not too dependable. Anyhow, I sent Pink and Julie up the road, out of harm's way. That sure made them mad, I'll tell you. The rest of us heaved on that tyrannical tyrannosaurus until our guts hurt and all we could do was get it rocking slightly.

"Then Pink and Julie came hollering down that they had to help. You can probably guess what happened. As soon as they leaned their midget weight on the bumper, even before the 'one-two-three-heave,' the Hearse started to groan, way deep down in its innards. I swear, as soon as those imps laid their hands on it, it started to move. One more push, and with an enormous belch it rolled, end over end, hood over tailpipe, like an avalanche of bolts into the abyss."

"Gone! But you had always managed to fix it, Bob."

"Not this time. Nope. Our long-suffering Hearse is no longer part of our family."

"I feel quite sad."

"Me too. But it's sort of like getting rid of a bunion. You're sad about losing part of your foot, but it has to be done. It's a relief there's no hauling the old hulk back this time. No more cutting belts out of old tires, no more holding it together with wire and bicycle chains and binder twine, no more kids teasing me about a broken flambulator. No more getting stranded on back roads with eleven kids. Not in that vehicle, anyway."

"Imagine it taking five-year twin power to move the immovable. That's frightening. Those girls are a force to reckon with, no two ways about it."

"May we have the strength! I'll tell you, I was sure glad when I saw everyone on solid ground after the Plymouth gave way. We weren't expecting the funeral to be over so suddenly. And then everyone had to take one last look over the edge. All you could see was mist creeping up the cliff like out of a crypt. So help me, it felt like I was using every ounce of will power to get the kids and caboodle back into Burt's truck. Thanks to Brick, the truck stayed put, but the second he let his foot off the brake, it started to slide, with Burt still trying to get his door shut. That Burt's a wizard in the driver's seat. What a trip. It was lucky the heavy rain held off till we were just about home."

"I wonder if the kids will ever finish talking about it. It might take years. The bucket walk to beat all bucket walks. The Eleven's Day on the Mountain. Seventy chapters and still counting. Eleven viewpoints to disentangle—not to mention yours and mine, Bob."

"At least they don't have to figure it out in one night, like us at Co-op meetings. I'm going to set the alarm for one hour, in case we fall asleep."

But when Bob leans back in his chair and tries to relax, he sees five thousand jigsaw pieces spinning around his head. So he keeps his eyes open. He glances at Lettuce. She has her head propped on one hand, staring at the table. "Remember the time up north when we took that raft down the river?" he asks. "Tonight reminded me of that trip... Five miles from the nearest road, on the wrong side of the river."

"Oh yes," Lettuce giggles. "We trusted rusty nails and rotten rope... under-estimated the current... that raft fell apart just as we got to the far side, in the dark. But we had fun, once we got used to the idea of camping with nothing but a few matches and some bread and cheese. And wild raspberries. And we knew how to keep warm."

"We were so young," sighs Bob. "We didn't care. Until the next morning when we noticed the cougar scats not twenty feet from our fire, so fresh they were steaming. We'd be pretty mad if our kids crossed a river on a half-wrecked raft. I've never told them about that trip. Have you, Let?"

"Not yet. Because of setting a bad example. I always figured, if we worked hard and were honest and loved our children, what could possibly go wrong?"

"Nothing… Nothhwip. Thnuk. Shnup."

Snore.

Brick, listening to his parents from the couch, has given up trying to catch their words. It's comforting to hear their quiet voices, steady as a murmuring stream. Until they stop talking.

Though he had slept on the mountain, with a rock for a pillow and ten brothers and sisters making a racket, Brick can't sleep in the quiet house, though the plump couch is snug as a warm lap. Every time he nods off, an echo of the crashing Hearse clangs in his head and he feels himself pitching off the cliff, falling and falling. The beast gnawing his arm grips tighter. As his parents' voices fall silent, the fever dream skulking at the edge of his consciousness takes over. Big ball rolls closer, closer, swallowing him, then suddenly it's little ball, pulling him further and further away from himself into nothing, then, clang!, the hearse crashes, clang! Clang! He jumps. And groans when he jolts his arm.

Lettuce and Bob are slouched over the table. Bob has fallen into a fuzzy void. Lettuce dreams that someone has dumped rusty nails on her new curtains. She's glaring at the rust stains on the lime green cloth when, clang! The alarm clock startles her awake. "Huh?"

"What the… oh. Lord love a duck, it's six o'clock."

"Agh… Time to get Brick to the hospital, Bob. The morning shift should be just about ready for him."

"I'll see if he's awake. It's okay, Brick, did that blasted alarm startle you too? It's time to get going, son. Let's get some light in here."

"Nmph."

His dad's arm feels like a life preserver. Morning. The endless night is over at last. Bob helps Brick sit up and brush his teeth.

Hooray, Brick thinks, he won't have bad breath when he dies. His mom folds her woolen shawl over his shoulders. Jeez. He's not an old woman. His dad pulls his own slippers over Brick's knee-high woolen socks. With a quirky half smile and his red hair sticking straight up like a pileated woodpecker's, Brick is ready to go.

Lettuce has gotten Hazel up to resume her role as second-mother-in-charge. They speak in hushed voices so as not to rouse the others, who will hopefully sleep a few more hours.

Hazel grins at Brick, "You'll be okay. Heck, by this time next year, you'll be good as new."

"Hmph. Thanks a lot, Sis."

She follows him, thrusting a wad of comics under his good arm. He chortles. "The new ones you traded? I love you, Haze."

"Bye, Brickle."

Arlo the x-ray technician is patiently waiting, as planned, station wagon backed up to the steps. Bob helps Brick into the front, then climbs in back with Lettuce. Hazel watches the red glow recede into mist. A robin chirps.

Hazel was shocked at how glad she'd been to get home, she who dreams of isolated summits, though in the hubbub of arrival, the walls had soon pressed in on her. She knows with certainty her soul will always live outdoors, though her heart needs a home. Whereas Fern, happily crowded in the commotion of homecoming, is assured that's where her heart will always be. But something about the look of Billy's thumb last night has cooled her ambition to be a nurse.

Fern joins Hazel now on the doorstep. Arms entwined, they watch daylight coalesce in a silvery green shimmer on the edge of lawn.

"I think he'll be alright, don't you, Fern?"

"Of course he will, Haze. Aren't we sending him our get-well spell?"

"Full force… I'm hungry."

"Me too, but though, I could sleep another ten hours."

"No one's hollering yet. Let's have a nap."

The girls are soon curled up on opposite ends of the couch, under Brick's quilt, munching apples.

"How was Brick this morning, Haze?"

"Like a zombie, but you know Brick, not complaining. Just his freckles standing out like dirt on a plate of blancmange. And his eyes bugged out and his hair sticking straight up like Mr. Ego-Evanomalosovitch's, only red. Looked like he'd hatched backwards."

"Good ol' Brickle," Fern sighs, "ummmm."

"Umph. Snuff." They sleep.

CHAPTER 63
Getting Ready for Brick

THREE HOURS LATER, FERN and Hazel are roused by thumps overhead, giggling, and a hollering plum-rush for the bathrooms.

Gradually everyone wanders into the kitchen. "Where's Mom and Dad?" ask Pink and Julie

"Gone to the hospital with Brick. "

"Oh yeah. The hospital," says Alvin with a gulp.

"I wonder what they're doing to Brick right now," says Billy. "Do you think he'll need an operation? Dr. Brundy said he might."

"'Cause he didn't like the way Brick's arm was hanging," adds Julie.

"We'll have to wait and see," says Hazel, brushing Pink's hair out of her face.

"They'll put him to sleep," Julie shudders. "That was the creepiest part when I got my tonsils out."

"Poor lil' Julie. Poor old Brickle," says Ron. "He's going to hate not doing anything. How's he going to blow off steam without chopping wood?"

"Good thing it's his right arm, him being left-handed," muses Rich. "Like when I lost my brakes on Ralph's hill and no cars came… there's always something lucky about bad luck."

"Like lucky it's him and not you," Ron teases.

"I'm starving," says Herald. "Mom said save the cake for later, Billy! Let's make flapjacks."

Soon Fern has Julie and Pink stirring the dry ingredients.

"There's no way we're wasting huckleberries on these pancakes!" says Rich. "I'll gag if I eat one more."

"Give you a couple hours." Herald looks like he's walking in his sleep, but he's getting three fry pans ready while Ron stuffs the stove with chunks of pine. Hazel's bringing in more wood when the phone makes them all jump. Fern grabs it.

"Mom? I can hardly hear you, Mom. Surgery? Oh no. When will we get to see him? Tomorrow? Jeez. When will you be home, Mom? When he wakes up? Ether. Okay, Mom, we'll keep organized. But wait! Mom! Should we can the rest of the berries? But… what about the One Hundred Quart Rule? Really? For real? Okay, let us know when he comes out. Say hi to him. Bye, Mom."

"Brick has to have an operation," sobs Fern. "His ulna is broken and displaced. The ether might make him sick, like it did you, JuJu. They're staying till they know he's okay. But hey! Mom says seventy-five quarts is enough for now! We can sell the rest! Dad says we deserve something for our hard work besides berries."

"How many are left? A couple pounds? Looks like they're already all in jars," says Ron.

"She said to look on the porch."

"Holy kryptonite, the soup pot's still full! You mean we can sell all these?" yells Billy.

"Yes!" says Fern. "And they even look clean… on top, anyhow."

"Wahoo! I never thought she'd break that cast-iron-fry-pan rule!" chortles Pink.

"How much should we charge for them?" Alvin wonders.

Ron is all business. "Depends who we sell them to. Let's go round to the church ladies! They always feel sorry for us. We can take the berries in the wagon, in three-pound buckets with a couple pansies on top. They won't be able to resist that."

"Three pounds minimum order? We should charge eight bits a pound." says Billy.

"Fat chance. Anyhow, let's get these pancakes going," says Hazel. "Alvin and Billy, could you get the eggs? We need at least three more. And take out the chicken bucket, pleee-ease."

Gluttonia, Dorcas, Gusset, and gang are brooding on their eggs (even though it's hopeless with no rooster), puffing their feathers, cackling and pecking. But the boys triumphantly return with five eggs. They start right in helping Pink and Julie haul plates to the table, they're so anxious to get on with the eating.

"Hey, I didn't see you guys wash your hands," says Hazel.

"We washed outside at the tap."

"Yeah? Maybe you looked at the tap, but your hands are dry! Get in that bathroom and scrub."

Good thing, because the first pancakes are devoured out of hand near the stove. A second batch and part of a third are eaten at the table, smeared with peanut butter and jam and mustard and washed down with a jug of powdered, non-instant milk which Rich and Ron have just concocted.

"Yuk," Pink says, "it's solid lumps."

"Just chew your milk," says Ron. "This is the smoothest we could get it with that ratchety old eggbeater. It's ready for Herald's contraption."

"Hey! You guys didn't throw any bone meal in that milk powder, did you?" asks Herald.

"Shoot, why didn't we think of that when we still had lots on hand?" laughs Ron.

"Lucky for you, we put all the gristle in the porridge yesterday," scoffs Rich.

Hazel swats him with the dish rag. "Let's clean up! Before Mom and Dad get home!"

"They're going to be famished," Fern says. She puts the remaining pancakes in the warming oven and tackles the mess at the sink with Sedge and Rich. Ron wipes the table and Hazel splits kindling. Then they start getting the living room ready for Brick. "He'll have to sleep on the couch for quite a while, especially now he's got a busted knee, too," says Alvin sadly.

Herald groans, "He sure didn't admit anything about his knee yesterday. He's too tough for his own good. Seriously, everyone, carry your own junk from now on!"

Fern mournfully picks up Brick's cut-open jacket, slumped behind the couch like a molted pelt. "Doc cut it along the seam, at least, so it won't be too hard to mend." (Brick will have outgrown it by the time his cast's off.)

Ron sets up two backless chairs for a night table. "He'll need a lamp," Rich decides. "It's dark in this corner."

"We should trim the honeysuckle," says Billy.

"Don't open the window, it'll grow over the piano in no time," warns Sedge. "Do you think Dad needs this lamp by the puzzle table?"

"Yes! We all do. We've got to finish that ocean so we can start a more exciting puzzle," says Fern. "But Dad won't miss his bed-lamp, will he? It'll fit just right."

"Brick can use my transistor radio," offers Billy. "I'll get it tuned up. He won't let anyone else fiddle with it. Hint hint."

Pink and Julie come in with flowers and raspberries. They help Herald and Alvin sort the newspaper box for the *Star Weekly*'s full-page comic strips, and puzzles hardly glanced at all summer.

"I'll get his books by his bed," says Rich, "his *Robinson Crusoe* and *Treasure Island*, to make him feel at home."

"And I'll bring down his box of comics," says Ron.

"No!" Sedge cries. "He hates you moving his stuff!"

Ron and Rich stop in their tracks. Herald gives them his sternest teacher look. "Keep your cotton-picking paws off Brick's stuff. And off everybody else's stuff. Brick can tell you if he wants you to get something of his."

Ron and Rich try to hide nervous grins. They feel like they're being Miss Hortense-ified. Now Hazel and Fern are glowering at them too. Sedge looks worried. "I didn't mean to start a fight, Herald."

"It's not a fight, it's just time Ron and Rich stopped teasing. You think it's funny to meddle with Brick's stuff, and keep taking books from my shelf when they're holding up another shelf, and rearranging my invention so I don't hardly know what it is anymore, not to mention that whole debacle yesterday. Smarten up, once and for all!"

"Okay, Herald. Cross our hearts and hope to die."

Herald waits till Ron and Rich look like they mean it, then he gives them a boa squeeze. "Good, that'll save me hauling buckets of water up the maple tree."

The girls shake their heads.

CHAPTER 64
Salesmanship

BRICK HAS REACHED CELEBRITY status by the time he gets home and, with a great deal of fuss, he's led to his corner of the living room. He can hardly believe his eyes at the welcoming arrangement: the covers turned down, a sandwich waiting, the Meccano box where he can reach it.

Brick can't do much in the way of one-handed mechanics, but he obligingly sorts and finds Meccano pieces for the others when not working on the space mazes and word jumbles which Pink, Julie, and Alvin have clipped out of the papers for him. He also has a stack of new books which the others have brought from the library. Brick contentedly thumbs through them, trying to decide which to read first. A huge bouquet of delphinium and tiger-lilies sits in view and fresh raspberries are within reach.

Luckily, the weather is cool and the huckleberries are keeping well on the veranda. But once Brick is settled, selling the berries is the next order of business. Herald has a full week at the factory and Hazel has to help with the cherries and raspberries, but the nine younger kids head out with a wagon of berries and great optimism. Unfortunately, the pouring rain makes door-to-door sales difficult, even with an umbrella over the wagon. No one wants to open their door to the wind and rain, or what look like drenched rats seeking a home.

The kids worry when Lettuce, eyeing the empty jars on the counter, says, "Too bad this rain is splitting the cherries."

"Yeah, but good thing we ate most of them before they got ripe enough to split, eh Mom?" teases Billy.

"Please give us another day, Mom," pleads Alvin.

"Okay, but pretty soon the berries will only be good for jam."

"Mom," says Billy, "don't you want to help sort that two thousand piece carousel puzzle? It looks really colourful and fun."

"You rascal, trying to distract me. Tell you what, you get those berries sold and I'll help you make fudge for the Co-op Fun Fair. But why bother dragging the berries all over town? How about you leave them here and just go out to take orders? You won't have to jar them around so much."

Hazel hoots, "The berries are going to get jarred one way or another no matter what you do. But that's a good idea, Mom."

"But we'll all have to go together, won't we?" asks Ron. "Or how are we supposed to know who's sold what?"

And so they palaver. They'll do it in relays. They'll all go to the first place, then someone can run back to the house for berries if they get an order. Then on to the next place. "Holler if you can't see where the rest of us are... Let's start in this neighbourhood and work our way out... But we've already done this neighbourhood..."

Finally Brick says, "Hold on you guys, I can't go with you, but I can sure help you get organized... ..buzz... buzz... keeping the runners going to the right place... buzz... I can write it all down."

"Okay, so let's start the top of Ralph's Hill," says Billy.

"Nah, why way up there?" objects Ron.

"'Cause it's better to go downhill on the way home."

Quibble. Squabble.

Half an hour later, they've worked out a system, more or less, and headed out in slickers, mackinaws, and gumboots. Brick is with them in spirit every inch of the way, although it takes a long time for the first runner to get back from the top of Ralph's Hill with a three pound order. Why they had to start way up there... Then, bingo, a five-pound order on the other side of town, another three, and another three. The kids are running back and forth like crazy, with Brick keeping track in a notebook. And then things aren't going so well. Ron comes home with his pants half-torn off. Then, finally, a one-pound mercy order from Mr. Horkalinki, although he still suspects Ron and Rich let his guinea hens loose on the one night they had a cast-iron-fry-pan alibi.

It must be because of the rain that their sales are off. And maybe because they look more like a gang than a family, by the time Chuckie and Clem Moozle are traipsing along with them, plus Betty, Velma, and Luke, Pepper and Annette, and then Buddy and three of his sisters, everyone laughing and shouting and shoving with nothing better to do on a rainy day.

Anyhow, with not half the berries sold, it's a dejected Eleven who mope around the house that evening.

Until the phone rings.

It's a kind of a miracle they even get a call, half the lines being down with the wind. Their one phone, on the wall near the couch, has made three false rings, anxiously answered by Brick each time, this being his new job. The fourth time, it rings properly and Brick's right on it, with most of the kids crowding round.

A loud voice booms out, so clear they can all hear it, "Calling from the Jam Factory... We want to make a run of specialty jam... huckleberry jam. There's no cherries. All split and gone to mold in the orchards. Rain at the worst time. Don't usually bother with wild fruit, not enough of it. But we've got a contract for small specialty orders. We heard you're selling huckleberries? We'll buy fifteen pounds minimum. How many you got? Forty pounds? We'll take them. And anything over fifteen pounds you can bring in. Cash on delivery. Thank you, Sir. Nice talking to you lad." Click.

Pandemonium.

They'll be rich! New bikes, swim goggles, vats of Friendship Garden. A crystal chandelier!

"Just a minute," says Herald. "Did he say how much he'll pay for them?"

"Uh oh. We'd better call back," says Brick."

"Let's ask twenty-five cents a pound," says Ron.

"And don't go lower than fifteen," adds Herald.

But the phone is dead.

The phone stays dead. Trees have blown down.

The Eleven sleep on an uncomfortable nest of unhatched eggs that night while dreaming of fluffy chicks. Outside, the wind howls.

In the morning, the phone lines are still down.

Ron and Rich run to the factory with Herald when he goes for his five am shift. They return pell-mell, gasping for breath.

"Twenty cents a pound! Clean. Minimum fifteen pounds. We have to get them to the factory before seven each morning, starting tomorrow. Which is perfect, because Herald has to be at work by five, so he can help carry."

The news runs through the house like electricity.

Jubilation!

But the factory won't need the berries until next morning. Will they keep? More cardboard boxes are torn up to insulate them.

Before breakfast, Ron, Rich, and Alvin check out the yard for storm damage: there's a big maple branch down, a ladder keeled over, a clothesline in the gooseberries, a rug on the roof. Nothing major. Except for tons of wet raspberries and battered cherries to bite the good parts out of. A full table of red-cheeked troglodytes eats four dozen flapjacks that morning before buckling down to two hours work, canning, jamming, cleaning and clanging.

Technically, the berries are sold, all but the money in their hands. So as promised, Lettuce hauls out the fudge pans and aprons.

Soon, pots and pans and wooden spoons are flying into action. A sack of flour is dumped into the bin and kids skate on a film of flour as they measure, melt, and stir. Brick becomes an expert at judging soft-ball stage. Some of it is and some of it isn't, but whether toffee or fudge, it's all good. If you're going to mess up the kitchen, you might as well have something to show for it, right? Amid slurping and sampling, four double-batches of candy are made and the kitchen is once again scrubbed. They have ten packages for the Co-op Fun Fair and a plateful of seconds for a dinnertime celebration.

At dinner, Bob mentions that he'd talked to Crick when he'd seen the boy limping through town. Initially, Crick had hidden under his mop of hair and wouldn't say a word, but when Bob sympathized about the porcupine quills, Crick had shared a few scary facts about Pink and Julie. Bob had invited the boy to come over for a Friday night feed of buttered popcorn.

"You what?" screeches Ron. "Crick? Coming here?"

"He'll kill us," says Rich.

"We ain't gonna be here," says Ron. "Let's go to Moozle's."

"You'll do no such thing," says Bob. "Crick's an unfortunate lad without your advantages in life. It's time you heard his point of view for a change."

This is met with silence, but there's a lot of disgruntled muttering later, upstairs.

For his part, Crick's scared to go to the Eleven's house. He can't possibly go. They'll kill him. But he's curious, and he hasn't tasted buttered popcorn for months. He kind of likes Bob. But all Bob's kids hate him and he's pretty sure he hates them. There's way too many rules wrapped around that bunch. And they're sissy book-brains, spoiled rotten just by having Bob for a dad.

But. Buttered popcorn?... They may be sissies, but they're sure good at swearing and acting like maniacs, and they can spit like stink. They can't be all bad. Crick decides to go for the popcorn, but he won't tell his brothers.

It turns out that after a couple of popcorn evenings, with everybody making a ruckus but not getting hollered at, Crick feels alright sitting at their table. Though he can't look at Pink or Julie without a glint of terror in his eyes.

CHAPTER 65
Housebound

THE RAIN CONTINUES. There's much activity indoors revolving around the couch corner. Brick enjoys being in the thick of things, with free entertainment swirling around him. His cast is autographed to the last inch and the wall behind him is layered with cards and drawings. Brick grows adept at one-handed work on the two-thousand-piece carousel puzzle. (It's a colourful relief after the gray-on-gray ocean, which was mysteriously schlepped back into its box, one dark and stormy corner still undone.)

But tempers are eventually worn ragged by the wind and rain. Lettuce has to assign housework, three to a floor, until even the high cupboards are spic and span.

During breaks in the weather, Brick splits kindling while the rest of them make forays up the mountain, even Herald after work. But they pull in only a meager fifteen pounds, including the five pounds Pink and Julie have the gall to snag under the sumac and hawthorns in the empty lot in the middle of town. That fills another order. A thin stream of coins jingles around town, but the second week of wet weather is colder.

"Well, it figures the berries would peter out, just when they're worth something," the kids grumble. "You can pick the same hillside only so many times." The clothes-racks are overloaded with soggy clothes.

On his days off, Herald attacks the piles of papers on his door-on-saw-horses desk. He's filling out applications and resumes and practicing his parsing skills. He doesn't get much time for his contraption on the back porch, but now that everyone's convinced to keep their hands off, it's starting to look like it might work. For what, no one is sure, until Herald hunts down the box of dried beans that weren't shelled last fall. It works so well at separating the beans from their pods that they dub it the Free Beaner at his family demonstration. It speeds up a job that's tedious and hard on the hands.

Ron rolls a log into a handy spot for Brick to pound spikes into when he needs to blow off steam. Sometimes captive to long family piano recitals, Brick is glad of the hammer and nails. He sighs. It's not his arm that's slowing him down. Heck, it was only broken, and no more annoying than the heavy plaster he has to drag it around in. His knee is his nemesis: torn, strained, sprained, pulled, pained, and useless. He can't walk more than ten steps without agony. The others wince to see him.

One evening, Bob unearths his hoard of geographic and historic tidbits he's clipped from letters over the years and hands Brick a tea-box full of postage stamps. He stands back and grins as Brick's eyes pin-wheel with philatelistic glee.

"THANKS, Dad! Julie and Pink! Come help me sort these stamps." Black mouse fluff, pink frizz, and pileated woodpecker bend over the stamps until the twins are hustled off to bed an hour late. The next day, the Couch Corner Summer Philately Club is born.

When Pink and Julie aren't soaking stamps from envelopes, they're working on a secret project that involves scurrying from attic to mountainside with bags and paint-boxes. The others notice that the twins are spending longer and longer times apart. In a spirit of daring exuberance, they've worked up to spending forty-five minutes solo. Only Pink and Julie know they're working on their magnetism skills.

Sedge and Fern bring their appliqué quilt and sewing boxes to the couch, and Brick learns to blanket-stitch. He kindly stitches whatever the girls throw at him, but in the nick of time, just before he has to learn feather stitch, he gets his cast removed. He graduates to sculpting clay and, when he can pass kitchen-boss Hazel's clean-hands inspection, he kneads vast batches of bread. No bone dust. His arm recovers with no sign of permanent damage. Now, if only his knee would smarten up. No more Atlas act for Brick. He'll gladly haul food and a hatchet, and even a tent, but only one harmonica. Comic books and dolls, no. When the winter's coal is dumped by the back door with a roar that shakes the house, Brick gets to oversee the shoveling. Har. Sometimes that transverse displaced ulna fracture pays off.

CHAPTER 66
Ron Makes a Find

THE WEATHER FINALLY CLEARS. No one has mentioned Alvin's shoe-less state... the others have tactfully kept mum. And it's been gumboot weather. But Alvin knows sooner or later, the whole embarrassing story's going to hit him in the face like a mugful of sour milk. So, one day, he parks himself beside Bob and helps hold the chair his dad's fitting with a new spindle.

"Dad?"

"Mph?"

"Dad, I lost my shoes."

"Oh?" Bob darts a look at Alvin's solemn face. "Well, I guess that's not the end of the world, Alv. I lost my school bag once, and I'm still alive."

"But Dad, it's just... Well, they were those nice shoes Pepper traded me... for my old ones, for his brother? But Dad. It's the way I lost them. Down a mine hole, Dad."

Bob puts the chair down and looks at Alvin.

Then Alvin's whole story spills out. "I was pretending, Dad. And I know that's a baby thing to do, but. About gold. And I fell through some rotten boards in a mine tunnel… almost to China, feet first. And I could hear my shoes falling and falling, knocking rocks down and more rocks, and I hollered and hollered until Billy came, and Ron, and Hazel, and she was like a wire spider stretched across the rotten boards and it was lucky they didn't all fall through… and… Don't tell Mom, please, Dad, she's upset enough about Brick. I didn't get hurt. Just those scrapes on the back of my legs. And belly. But Ron, Hazel, and Billy, they got me out."

Bob's hands have tightened on the chair back. His knuckles are white, his face is white. He says, "Alvin Bartholomew, I think you'd better make Ron, Hazel, and Billy a thank-you-for-saving-my-life card. And give it to them at suppertime. Okay, Alvin?"

"Yes, Dad."

So he does. His rescuers accept the card with surprise and watch silently as Alvin turns to Lettuce and blurts out his mine story to her.

Tears well in her eyes. Lettuce shudders and whispers, "Come here, Alvin. And the rest of you. I need you to hug me to death."

Surprised at their mother's mushy response, they nevertheless pile on and hug her to within an inch of her life.

Some days later, Ron runs into the house and charges upstairs, shouting. "Alvin! Alvin, come here, I got something for you!" Alvin hesitantly crawls out from a stack of encyclopedias. Ron's grinning, rattling a paper bag behind his back. "Hey Alv, choose a hand. Any hand."

Laughing, Alvin chooses both hands and Ron tosses him the bag. Ron's as excited as Alvin, watching him open it. And what does Alvin see? A pair of shoes! Beautiful, sturdy shoes. His size. The fanciest shoes he's ever had in his own two hands. He tries them on, wiggles his toes. Perfect! He strides up and down the room in them. Comfy as anything.

Just one thing. They're pink. And they have mermaids on them. Ron is obviously expecting Alvin to be very happy. And Alvin is happy, and he knows it shouldn't matter. But he can't stop staring at those mermaids.

Ron sizes up the situation. "Oh, yeah, well, I didn't think it'd matter. Once you muddy them up, no one'll notice. See, what happened is, you know the charity that sent all the dolls to Luke's house when he doesn't have any sisters? Well, they got their wires crossed again and sent him a ton of girl's shoes. He has to haul them over to Buddy's house for his sisters, but I was there and he gave me first pick!"

"Ron, they're great. My feet feel so good. I already got this one mermaid half picked off and like you said, a few days mucking around, they'll look perfectly normal. Hey, thanks Ron!"

Ron bops him on the head with the wadded-up paper bag and Alvin whacks him on the back with it as they run downstairs. They head out to the back yard to use the wad of paper for a football and get the mermaids dirty.

CHAPTER 67
A Pet At Last

BURT COMES OVER ONE afternoon, carrying a bulky item under a blanket. Lettuce has been expecting him and smiles, "I have just the spot." She ushers him into the living room where five or six kids look up from playing cards. She shows Burt a bracket near the window.

"Shh, now," Burt tells them as he carefully unwraps a circular cage and suspends it from the bracket. They crowd around, whispering.

A lovebird greets them with an inquisitive eye. It has soft green and yellow feathers and pink cheeks. A communal hum fills the room. They can't believe it.

Burt beams happily at their awe-struck faces. "Her name's Lila. She's got an odd bit of fluff, see, at the back of her head, you'd never notice, but that keeps her out of the beauty league. But she thinks she's a queen. She'll have a good home here, because she likes lots of attention. She's been raised by hand, see, so you can handle her after a few days, when she's gotten used to the place. She'll be watching and listening every minute she's awake. Mind, cover her cage at night, she needs her rest. She likes to nibble my fingernail, see, when I pet her under her chin. Sometimes these lovebirds get a bit nippy when they're older. But when they're handled from hatching like Lila's been, they can be very nice pets. If she ever flies away, just leave her door open and she'll come back when she's ready. This is an awful big house, though. But good thing you have no cats."

So much for playing cards. Lila is now the focus of the household, which takes some of the pressure off Brick, who's starting to feel like an old sock. It takes Lila about three weeks to assert her own ideas about where and how she's going to live. The wisp of lovely feathers will lead them on a merry chase, cutting strips of paper for her nests from any books she fancies.

Effusive thanks follow Burt to the door.

Before he leaves, Burt remembers the other reason he called round. He's wondering how they're getting along without a vehicle. He wants to drive up the summit some day soon, get some berries. Do any of them want a lift up?

Well! Lettuce puts the kettle on.

Brick is determined to go on the trip, and decides he needs a cane. The town is scoured for one, until an unexpected call comes from Mr. Nitmust. It turns out that for several years, he has cared for an elderly uncle who's now confined to a wheelchair and no longer needs his cane. The kids feel bad for their unkindly thoughts about their teacher when they hear this, although they examine the gnarled, black oak cane with suspicion. But Brick finds it's just what he needs. He gets a laugh out of rapping on the floor when he wants something and using the crook for a handy ankle grabber.

Then, amid the daily hubbub, Herald gets an official-looking manila envelope in the mail, postmarked Ontario. He runs into the house, waving it over his head.

"It's the results of the provincials," he hollers. "I've won! I'm in the Parsing Finals. And here's a bunch of instructions for flying to Ottawa, for the National Parsing Competition."

Hazel whoops, "Way to go, Hare!

Sedge says, "Nouns modified by the adjudicative adjective?"

"Ha ha, in your dreams, Hedge."

"But how can you afford to fly there?"

"It says here, Fern. They'll pay my trip. I just have to get to the airport."

Lettuce takes the papers in her hands and scans them until her eyes smart. Between the lines, she sees her first-born dashing away from home into a wide, jagged universe, the other ten scurrying pell-mell after him. She blinks and sighs. "Well, I guess that's what your dad and I have been working on all these years, getting you ready to fly the coop. Surly we can get you to the airport."

Brick looks at Herald long and thoughtfully. He pictures his brother blazing a trail that will widen in reverse perspective, getting wider and wider in the shining distance. He sees them on interconnecting pathways, trekking toward a glowing future. "We'll get you to the airport, Herald, even if we have to put you on a horse!"

Herald laughs, "Thanks, Brick. Hey! Speaking of horses, it turns out that black horse was Mr. Dorsey's."

"The one at Stooge's Mill?" squeals Pink. "Why didn't you tell us?"

"Because this letter put it out of my mind, and I only just found out."

While Herald was waiting for Brick at his appointment that morning, Mr. Dorsey had been waiting to talk to nurse Legghorn. (She was flapping and cutta-clacking like a mad hen, what with the specialist there for Brick and all.) Mr. Dorsey hadn't talked to anyone for weeks. He was like an over-wound clock, with his main-spring about to break loose if he didn't unwind a bit. Herald had been just the sort of kind, good listener he needed to talk to.

Herald takes a breath. "One night a few weeks ago, Mr. Dorsey's horse, Satan, got loose and wandered off. His dog brought him limping back two days later. His dog's named Respect."

"Weird," says Hazel, "sounds like *Pilgrim's Progress*. Mr. Dorsey's life must be one big allegory."

"Yeah, sure, Haze," mutters Herald. "Anyhow, Satan and Respect were covered in burrs when they got home. Mr. Darcy figures some boys let his horse out, same night as that 'hooliganism' around town."

"The broken window and tipped garbage cans?" asks Ron. "And the pea patch snatch? I heard that was Dick and Hodge. Good thing we were up the mountain and no one could blame us for a change."

"Yeah," says Rich, "and good thing we'd already stripped our peas."

"Anyhow, Mr. Dorsey said by the time he got out to see why Respect was barking so much, he only glimpsed some shadows high-tailing it up the road and Ol' Satan disappearing up the mountain. He was too stove up to go after him."

"I suppose the party line was busy and worse than no help," says Lettuce. "Seems like the whole town's on one line, or there's no line at all, since that last storm."

"Mr. Dorsey said Respect came back the next morning and dropped a pant leg at his feet," continues Herald. "Then the dog took off again, and it wasn't till the next afternoon he led Satan down the bluff... said they looked like walking bushes, they were so full of sticks and burrs."

"Aw, poor things," murmurs Sedge.

"So," says Herald, "I told him about the horse we saw when Satan was loose. It must have been Satan!"

"Why does he call his horse Satan?" asks Julie. "She's not a mean horse."

"No, it's because he's pure black except the white spot on each side of his head, like horns," says Herald.

"The horse is a boy?" asks Pink.

"I guess so. Whoever heard of a girl called Satan?" laughs Fern.

"I could think of a few," says Billy.

Fern gives Billy a shove. He gives her a bear hug... oof.

"Anyhow, Mr. Dorsey said his horse is really gentle from being brought up with kids, he used to go camping with the Dorsey boys all the time. But Satan has gotten shy the last few years... not enough company... and especially shy of women. Just like his owner. Satan was happy as a jay bird while Mr. Dorsey's sons were home, but they have their own farms and families now. They come out often as they can, but it's not the same."

Pink and Julie are already packing lunch and grabbing their sweaters, "Let's go visit Mr. Dorsey and Satan!"

"Hang on, you have no idea how far away they live," says their mom.

Alvin asks, "How come he's always Mr. Dorsey, but we can call Burt and Sid their first names?"

"It's because he's older and he was a Scoutmaster," explains Lettuce. "Like teachers and doctors, you show them extra respect because they spend most of their time looking after other people."

"Doctor Brundy? I thought his first name was Doc," says Pink. "Maybe Mister Dorsey's first name is Mister."

"I thought no one still lived at the old Dorsey place behind the mountain. It always looks deserted from up top," says Brick.

"Well, that just goes to show," says Herald. "Anyhow, Mr. Dorsey said Satan must have smelt the smoke from our campfire, leaking down through the mine holes. Sometimes Mr. Dorsey can see smoke curling out of the rocks behind his barn. He just prays he'll never see sparks. And sometimes he can hear shouting... but he can't make out the words... and drums throbbing in the ground."

"Creepy. Prob'ly when a bunch of us are messing around up there."

"That's what he thinks too, Ron. He said Satan hadn't had his supper yet and he must have thought he'd get something to eat at our campfire, so he followed the smoke all the way up to us."

"Isn't that against basic instinct, not to run away from smoke?" asks Hazel.

"Well," explains Herald, "When the Dorsey boys took Satan camping, his favorite treat after they unloaded his saddlebags was a hot dog. But Satan wouldn't gulp his down whole like Respect would: he'd make it last, and lick his lips for ages to get off the last bit of mustard."

"I knew that horse was kind of different," muses Sedge. "She seemed so happy to be with us, once she got over being shy. No wonder she seemed comfortable at our campfire."

"I still think that horse was our guardian angel," says Fern.

"Then its name shouldn't be Satan," laughs Hazel.

Herald continues, "Mr. Dorsey says he can muddle along on his own, but Satan needs company. They sound lonely."

"Let's go visit them tomorrow!" says Rich.

"Not till next week, I'm afraid, kids. There's too much to be done around here, getting ready for your trip with Burt. The food. And we'll have to get a few dozen wide mouth masons hauled up from the basement and washed and ready."

"But Mom!" Billy stammers, "Didn't we already can seventy-five quarts? How come we need a few dozen more jars?"

"Just checking your math. Anyhow, there's more plums coming on and more transparents. It'll soon be time to make apple butter. You'll all have to pitch in around here for a few days before you go gallivanting again. And now Herald's trip is coming up, too. Not to mention, I go for the costume selection in Montreal this fall."

"Couldn't some of us go with you?" pleads Julie.

"Some day. But the National Theater can barely afford my flight. I'm lucky they feel they need me there."

"You deserve it," says Fern. "They pay you peanuts, Mom."

"I love the work."

"You and Herald are both flying the coop," sighs Hazel.

"And there's so much to do beforehand. You'll have to start getting organized, Herald."

"Mom, my trip isn't until the end of August. And you don't need to worry about it, I can get my stuff ready. I won't need much."

"You don't have much, Herald. Your gray pants have a hole in them and your brown ones are about six inches too short."

"Thanks for pointing that out to me, Fern."

"Well, they're fine around here, but you can't go to Ottawa looking like Li'l Abner. We could make you some new pants, hey, Hazel?"

"No thanks, Daisy Mae, I'll mend my gray pants myself, and I won't have rats and daisies embroidered on them. I do have some standards."

(Little does Herald know how his standards will alter at college, when he looks into the blue eyes of someone named Cynthia.)

After the news gets in the local papers about Herald winning the Provincial Parsing Competition, people are phoning for two days to congratulate him and offer him rides to the airport, although they have him winning at everything from water witching to basement fixing.

In the meantime, the huckleberry trip with Burt is very successful, but a bounteous harvest means slavery in the kitchen. After three hot days of clatter and bumping elbows, Hazel happily pings the lids on the last canner load. One Hundred Quarts sealed!

That leaves eighty-five pounds to clean, weigh, and pack for the jam factory... wahoo!... Plus enough for a massive cobbler to celebrate.

Huckleberry Cobbler
(Serves 15)

Blend in saucepan 6 tablespoons flour, 3 cups water and 1 cup sugar.
Cook until bubbling. Stir in 6–8 cups huckleberries and pour into large
Pyrex pan.

Cover with sweet-drop biscuit dough:
Blend 4 cups flour, half a cup of sugar, 9 teaspoons baking powder, 3/4
teaspoon of salt.
Cut in 3/4 cup of shortening, 3 eggs, and 1 ½ cup milk.

Bake in moderate oven for 45 minutes. Serve hot or cold.

CHAPTER 68
The Family Expands

A CORNUCOPIC SPILL OF community events unfolds because of the Eleven's long night on the mountain. First is the emergence of Mr. Dorsey into their lives, after his conversation with Herald. Next thing, Satan is being curried and walked every day by Crick in exchange for all the hot dogs the boy can eat and a modest wage. It's just like the good old days for Satan.

Soon Crick's younger brothers and then the older ones, Squat and Yellow-Mane, are following the tantalizing odour of hot dogs straight to Mr. Dorsey's doorstep. He can hear them laughing, swearing, and carrying on long before they come into view. Does he mind? Not a bit. He hasn't had so much fun since his own boys left home. And since Bell died. He'd forgotten he missed the shouting and jostling around the crowded kitchen, when there was always something cooking besides porridge, and boys and girls had free run of the place. Bell had been the heart of their home, her laughter ringing through the rooms… Bell singing while she worked… Bell chatting with the boys. Mr. Dorsey has missed the kids and he's missed his wife. He's missed the fun. He'd had to let go of Scouts when Bell got sick. Is he too old now to get back into things? He can sense a troop gathering around him and he stretches his legs towards the fire, contentedly thumbing through his Audubon.

He's careful not to mention Scouts to the boys, sure they'd shy away from any goody-good organization. He's careful not to instruct them in any obvious way. When they get too rowdy in the house, he gives Respect a signal, and Respect makes one sharp bark. That bark is the kind that puts your teeth on edge; you don't want to hear it again. Respect then watches the boys for a few minutes, following their every move with solemn brown eyes, until he decides it's safe to curl up at Mr. Dorsey's feet again.

The boys gradually get over their outcast act. Mr. Dorsey greets them by name, as far as he can keep them straight, and they're friendly, especially once their bellies are full. Squat is the most easy-going and talkative. He says he doesn't mind that his nickname is short for Sasquatch. He likes that better than his real name, which is Sylvester, which is okay because it's in honor of his Mom, Sylvia. But shortened to Syl, it's a sissy name, and he won't put up with it. Just try it.

Mr. Dorsey makes sure he gets food on the table as soon as they show up, then quietly and matter-of-factly goes about whatever tasks are at hand. He'll mend his coveralls, clean the ash grate, peel apples, read, all the while seeming to ignore the boys unless they talk to him.

Mr. Dorsey's motto is: Feed the Kids.

After the third visit, he lets them get the food out themselves and go at it, insisting only that they clean up after themselves and they never use his porridge pot. When they burn the bean pan beyond redemption, he plants parsley in it and puts it out with the other herbs, where mint long ago escaped its bucket and took over the yard with its sparky fragrance.

The boys naturally take to Satan. Truth be told, when they had let the horse loose, it had been a botched attempt to steal her. At first, they overwhelm her with attention and she shies away. But when they take turns brushing and walking her without shoving and shouting, she offers her nose for scratching. The gleam returns to her huckleberry eyes, the strut to her step.

The gang starts hauling Mr. Dorsey's groceries and what-not back from town for a small wage, and it sure beats him coercing his jalopy into making the trip. When they prove they can make their shortcut across Dorsey Bluffs fast enough that the milk won't sour, they're permitted to guzzle it along with most of the groceries they haul. As for Satan, he's smiling half the time now, whiffling traces of mustard off his chin.

Without them realizing they're being taught and not just messing around, the kids learn from Mr. Dorsey how to use an assortment of tools and take care of them. And especially how to put them away. He shows them useful knots. He teaches them first aid. They fill his wood shed and replace a broken window. By filling his house with noise and cooking, the young people turn his house into a home again.

Mr. Dorsey soon has a stream of company—not only Crick and his brothers, but also Herald and his brothers; Chuckie and Clem Moozle; and Joe, Dan, Luke, and his lot.

Even Dick and Hodge turn up occasionally and initiate games of poker. They're different, those boys; a little put on, a bit too full of themselves, nosing around a bit too much. Yellow-Mane keeps a sharp eye on them. They think they can play hardball. But no one is going to mess with Mr. Dorsey.

Before long, Hazel, Sedge, and Fern find they, too, enjoy the hike up to Mr. Dorsey's, bringing homemade cookies and armfuls of wildflowers. He welcomes them, learning their names and interests. They like "comfortizing" his house for him, making a new cushion for his reading chair, replacing the torn curtains, visiting their friends. Fern, especially, is glad for the chance to play hostess to some boys who aren't her brothers.

One day a crew of boys helps Mr. Dorsey replace his stove-pipes. There's soot and creosote over the whole kitchen by the time the shiny new pipes from Sears are in place. The more they try to clean it up, the worse the mess gets. And then who should meander up the driveway, shrieking and laughing, but Fern, Hazel, Sedge, Velma, Annette, and Liz, loaded down with fresh baked bread and jars of damson jam. The girls are quite happy to spend the afternoon cleaning. They marvel at how fun it is, doing housework when it's not your own house. They're giggling as they wash the floor all the way to the rock wall along the driveway, and hysterical as they swoosh buckets of soapy water into the bushes, narrowly missing a pack of boys straightening nails and banging boards together.

Sedge often escapes the racket to explore an ever-widening swath of the countryside, taking stock of birds, plants, rocks, mosses, rodents, fungi, snakes, butterflies, and newts. When the house is quiet, she makes Mr. Dorsey tea and retreats into his shelves of nature books, scouting manuals, Gerald Durrell, Twain, and the heaps of *National Geographics*, which she and Alvin are gradually sorting by year.

In one afternoon of rambling, Sedge, Billy, and Hazel discover that the Dorsey and Kludge properties join on a rear flank of the mountain, linked by what Mr. Dorsey says is an overgrown mining trail. Over the summer, that trail is gradually cleared and frequently used.

In the ebb and flow of Satan's fan club, there's one constant and that's Crick, seeing to the horse's needs and giving him a warm hand to nuzzle every day. When Mr. Dorsey is seized with the lumbago again, he can relax knowing that Crick will be there at least once between dawn and dark. Crick takes his job seriously.

When Julie and Pink and friends start making all-day treks out to the farm, the horse enjoys being scratched and nuzzled to oblivion, but poor Crick says to himself that he's "jabbed with quills of fear whenever the hexing twins are near." He'll vamoose, coming back only at dusk when he knows the girls will have scuttled away home. Then he'll gently remove the daisy chains and release the tight braids in Satan's mane.

Two softball teams evolve that summer from the scrappy games in the Kludge and Dorsey fields. The teams are a shifting mix of old and young, whoever shows up on a Saturday afternoon; players, dogs, on-lookers, and bettors. As summer starts to wind down, Mr. Dorsey suggests they have a softball tournament. He's game to have it at his place, as long as everyone brings food and helps clean up afterward.

And so the round-about result of the Eleven's horrific night on the mountain is a coming together of the whole community. One thing leads to another, the party-line spreads the word, and a gigantic hotdog roast and picnic take place along with the ball tournament.

Brick gets a ride to the farm and, for the first time, meets Satan and Respect. He has a delighted ramble with his cane before he finds his niche umpiring the games. What with four dogs chasing through the field, running off with the cardboard bases, there's an argument to this day about which team won the tournament. But there's so much good food, even before supper, that nobody has room to carry a grudge. Buttered popcorn is made by the bushel in an assembly line master-minded by Pink and Julie, who buzz like hummingbirds here, there, and everywhere.

When Crick sniffs that popcorn, he tells himself he's not really scared of Pink and Julie: he just can't stand being near them. He needs to stay close to Satan, to look after the horse and make sure no one tires her out too much. But his nose twitches and his mouth waters as the smell of his favourite food drifts his way. Hot, buttered, salted popcorn. Satan, too, stretches his neck out, sniffing. The twin witches come skipping down to the barn and Crick stands his ground by Satan's side, watching their every move with suspicion. When they offer him a bag of popcorn, he can't say no. Buttered popcorn is buttered popcorn. Eventually, Pink and Julie start feeding their popcorn to Satan; Crick is overcome and has to run away.

Moe supplies the picnic with seven huge watermelons that are devoured that day. He lugs the first one from his truck to the kitchen, cradled on his paunch, his arms barely meeting around it. He snaps off a button in the process. Puffing, he asks the older girls to haul in the rest of the melons, knowing they won't drop his pride and joys—and won't run off into the woods with them or any tomfoolery like that.

Yellow-Mane's eyes bulge when he sees those watermelons. Dusty and sweaty from dragging around old doors and saw-horses to make food trestles, he can hear those melons calling him. They croon to him, they yell at him. He can't keep his eyes off them as he sets up folding chairs. Yellow-Mane imagines eating a whole melon, smashing his face into it and not coming up for air until he's sucked it dry. Watermelon. When was the last time he tasted one? Last summer, and then only a slurp shared twelve ways. But this looks unbelievable. Lots of watermelons. Holy mackinaw. He stands frozen in wonder. He pictures himself grabbing a whole watermelon and high-tailing it down the ravine.

Moe wipes sweat from his face with a vast hanky and looks around the field, thinking to himself that it sure is a busy place. Must be the whole town. Even Sam, with his pet sheep, Mandy, is strolling up the road. Moe looks to see if Mandy has a chicken brooding on her back. There's Mr. Horkalinki fetching up with a big roasting pan. And who's that big lad who has been working so hard setting up tables? Looks like he's in a trance. Yellow-Mane, isn't it? He sure has his eyes on the watermelons.

Moe shouts, "Hey, you! Yellow-Mane! That's you, isn't it, big fella? You and your crew look like you could use some refreshment. I know I sure could. Come on over here, let's have us a slab of this here watermelon."

Next thing Yellow-Mane knows, he's being handed a lengthwise wedge so big he has to hold it with both hands. Soon he and his buddies are guzzling and there's still lots more. And that's only one melon! Yellow-Mane makes the shocking discovery that he can't eat even half one of those beauties by himself. Although the day is still young.

Moe likes nothing better, after his cows and, of course, Bette, than sharing his watermelons with people who really enjoy them. No one grows watermelons like his anymore: glossy green, as long as your arm, juicy red flesh liberally sprinkled with shiny black seeds. At that picnic, no part of the fruit goes to waste. The rinds are gnawed down to the white, then tossed into a box to be fed to Mrs. Broom's hogs, except those rinds that are carefully washed and trimmed by Bette for candying. Even the slippery black seeds are put to good use. Squeezed between thumb and forefinger or ejected from lips, they can be squirted quite a distance and kids compete to see whose can go the farthest. Clem and Chuckie Moozle arrive with a handful of brand new, white-striped red, green, and blue plastic peashooters, which they share around. Watermelon seeds make perfect projectiles.

The pea-shooters are soon confiscated by Mrs. Moozle after Buddy's sister's doll gets hit in the eye and its head falls off. Ron and Luke split a gut laughing when darling Toddy Amegrotto scoops up the doll's head and toddles around with it tucked under his chin, its one eye hanging by a string, and Mrs. Amegrotto cooing, "What a cute baby."

In a tub of running water in the shade, jars of Jello have been set to chill, fanned out in magical hues of lime, cherry, orange, and lemon that glisten invitingly. Now is decided to be a good time for everyone to have a refreshing Jello break. The volume of talking and laughter grows.

Burt wonders, "Have we all been together before like this in one place, with the whole fandamilies?" No one knows. Maybe at some school event? But this is different. As far as the kids are concerned, they don't have to be on school behavior and they have more fun than a riot. Luckily, through wild play over the summer, even the roughest have learned that reasonable give-and-take is usually better than a black eye. Around the home of the old Scoutmaster and the watchful gaze of his dog, Respect, they've gotten half-civilized in spite of themselves.

Some of the adults get to know each other for the first time at that picnic. A horseshoe pitch is resurrected and a tournament takes place along with the ball games. Dr. Brundy and Hilltop Ralph are soon in tight competition for the most ringers, to thunderous applause from the sidelines. Nurse Legghorn kicks up such clouds of dust in her excitement that everyone is left wheezing, and Miss Prizz has to go home just when she's starting to see the fun in it.

As the dust settles, the adults gather in groups, chatting. Young children run rampant. The teens play Ante-i-over at the barn. The men gather at the trucks, talking about all the work they need to do: fixing roofs, mending fences and septic systems. Nasty kinds of jobs, too much for one person to tackle alone, especially if there's health problems or no "man of the house."

"Trouble is, we're a lot of independent cusses. Even though we all belong to the Co-op."

"Sure. We're great when it comes to doing community jobs at the arena or the Bingo Hall. But at home, if someone lacks a ladder, a drill, or a strong back, the job's put off."

"There's some jobs can't be put off much longer. We've got to band together. Get things done."

While the talk gets serious by the trucks, the Scouts have been taming the bonfire into campfire proportions, hosing the area around it. Mr. Dorsey gets into a water fight with Squat and Rich and the others; they all get sluiced off and half-dry by supper. The old troop leader is quite at ease with the commotion. He grins as he walks around with his dripping hat, tweaking proceedings here and there to keep things running smoothly.

Finally, Moe clangs a cow bell. "Cooooome and get it! The soup's on." Nurse Legghorn claps her hands as Dr. Brundy bellows, "It's time to eat!"

Mrs. Hortense is, as usual, expected to say a quick welcome and grace when everyone settles down. She'd thought of getting everyone to join hands and leading them in a choral verse, but as soon as she stands up, her students cheer, "Happy birthday, Teacher Hortense!" She's so surprised, she almost sits down again. Amid laughter and applause, she's too overcome to say more than four words, with perfect enunciation.

"Thank you and welcome."

The crowd is nonplussed, having expected at least a half-hour speech, but a rollicking rendition erupts of, "For She's a Jolly Good Fellow." After five rounds, someone hollers, "Rub-a-dub-dub, thanks for the grub! Yea God! Let's eat!"…and the laden tables are plundered.

An hour and a half later, the feast is starting to wind down. Everyone is full to busting and feeling drowsy. There's a replete hum. And then there's hubbub as the young people are herded into the kitchen, arms loaded with dishes. The food is gradually reorganized onto trays for snacking. When the last dish is wiped and stacked, ready to return with its owner, the youth move to the campfire and the barn. Adults regroup around the tables, chatting and sharing anecdotes. When the topic of work comes up again, they launch into a heated discussion.

"Seems like the town needs a lot of ship-shaping. And I don't mean the arena. I mean our own places."

"I know what you mean. Our place is looking like Lower Slobbovia.

"Our fences are falling around our ears. There's just too much to keep up with."

"Let's get some work parties organized."

"The problem is, not enough men. There's not enough fathers since the mine accident. And what fathers there are, they're overloaded, like Bob here, helping everyone, with not enough time to get things done at home." A few baleful glances fall on Bob from neighbours who, on second thought, wish they had bought huckleberries from his industrious children.

"Some men are also struggling with disabilities from the explosion."

Ajax Kludge growls, "Hear, hear."

"What about the big lads, why aren't they pitching in more?"

"They're mostly working at Phoenix Jam to pay family bills. Or leaving for work elsewhere, now the mine's done. We can hardly blame them wanting to run wild a bit, when they have time off from responsibilities."

"And from despair."

"I think they'll pitch in when they see we're pulling together. Once they see things improving around their own places, they'll take some pride in helping. Get a crew of teens going and the rest will want to join in."

Before the month is over, Mr. Dorsey, Bob, Sid, and Burt have organized a crew to gather up the lumber and electrical and plumbing supplies left over from the arena renovations. These are hauled to various places around town, where projects are planned. One of the first stops is the Kludges'.

Ajax Kludge is taken aback when a crew lands at his place. He hauls himself on his wooden leg to scowl at the men, checking for religious pamphlets, but when he sees only tool boxes he says, "Oh, it's you blokes," and shows them the chairs by the back door. He clomps inside to call Sylvia; could she rustle them up some tea? He's like a terrier trying to pat his bristles down. He feels less at a disadvantage once Sylvia is so nicely passing out the tray with her precious china teacups, and he settles back to hear what the men have to say.

Once Ajax sees they mean business with no shenanigans, he pulls his weight, which is considerable, and in little over a week, there's an electric wringer washer agitating merrily in his shored-up wash-shed. The week after that, the upstairs is wired for light. Only one ceiling bulb, mind you, but it makes all the difference.

Of course, life isn't a bag of marshmallows from then on, but there's a new, hopeful feeling in the air. Under Sylvia's direction, the boys give each other haircuts. Her hands are too riveted with arthritis to use scissors, so she tells them to get on with it. No one wants a hatchet job, but that's pretty much what they all get. Trying to even it up is the main problem. With duck-tails in mind, they end up with hack-saw crew-cuts, but it's still an improvement. And some learn the hard way that it's never a good idea to sass your barber.

To everyone's amazement, after a bit of practice, Yellow-Mane discovers a natural talent with scissors. He quickly becomes professional when Buddy's sister donates her old salon chair to the cause, and before long, half the town has paid him four bits for a cut. Even Fern gets a stylish cut, though Yellow-Mane will succumb to no more than a trim himself. He has a reputation to uphold.

More than one face loses its pinched look that summer; dried tears are washed away. Work crews move from house to house, setting things to rights. Before the snow flies, Lettuce and Bob have a reinforced back porch and a mighty double clothesline, thanks to hard work from their own tribe and the strong shoulders of

Yellow-Mane, Squat, and their cousins. Crick has shown amazing ability with a measuring tape and level.

The mending of Mr. Dorsey's barn roof is a more dicey affair, with teens hauling buckets of melted tar up the ladder and splitting shakes all over the yard. But hammered and mauled, the job gets done with nothing worse than bruised knuckles and a mashed fingertip, thanks to Mr. Dorsey and his dog Respect keeping a quiet but commanding eye on the proceedings.

A new doghouse, thickly lined with newspapers and cardboard and complete with a porch, is also knocked together on the knoll behind Mr. Dorsey's barn. Respect can now sit in comfort while keeping watch over the whole hillside. He can study *National Geographics* to his heart's content by his master's chair in the daytime, but there'll be no more raccoons nesting in the wood shed or horses roaming wild at night.

The ball field is scythed to provide Satan with enough vetch and grass for the winter. Things are good and getting better for the famous black horse with white horn spots. So well groomed she's hardly shaggy anymore, Satan smiles while dreaming of hot dogs.

As summer winds down, Herald is dispatched to Ottawa, not for water witching, parsnip pickling, or cement mixing, but for the National Parsing Competition. Most of the family ends up going to the airport in a neighbourhood cavalcade.

Six long days later, Herald returns with his eyes bagged halfway to his cheekbones, his glasses lopsided and his face one big grin. He has won a year's tuition to Victoria College. Which just goes to show, even something as boring as grammar can get you a long way if you put your mind to it, and if you're determined not to get stuck in a jam factory the rest of your life.

CHAPTER 69
Moving On

AS HERALD RAMPS UP his plans for winter in Victoria, it feels like the house is breathing erratically, trying to hold on to him at the same time as preparing to let him go. The ark is shifting.

About that same time, Bob's contract with the chemistry lab finishes with a cash bonus. "Do you want a new wringer washer or an electric sewing machine?" he asks Lettuce. She chooses an electric Singer. "The wash will always be a chore," she says. "Sewing is pleasure; let it be joy." Bob buys new glasses for Herald and himself. Their outlook on life has never been so bright. The kids aren't thrilled with their dentist appointments, but.

Bob gets two weeks' holiday before he starts as a pharmacist in the Community Drug Store. Two weeks! Reminiscing about that rafting expedition with Lettuce has gotten Bob thinking. Lettuce and him, having fun. Why not? "Let's go camping, Lettuce! You and me for a couple nights?"

"On our own? When can we leave?"

If the Eleven can survive in the wilds, they should be fine at home, right?

After three days' preparation and a four in the morning hug from their eldest son, Lettuce and Bob fly out the door. By suppertime, they're at a sub-alpine lake, a smooth, silver in the evening light. They feast on brown bread and cheese and huckleberries just coming ripe. Looking into fold over fold of mountains washed with pastel mist, they unroll their sleeping bags and fall into them, laughing. Under the stars, they dream quiet dreams.

The next day, Lettuce and Bob climb to the alpine on that best sort of hike where you start out half-way up the mountain. Though tired to the bone, the years fall away as they stand on the summit. From that lofty perspective, the trials and tribulations of home seem insignificant.

On the third day, Lettuce and Bob wander homeward, grubby and radiant. But the nearer they get to home, the more parental worries assail them.

What awaits them by the steps is not encouraging: a box of broken glass. The porch window is boarded up.

No one meets them at the door.

The kitchen is uncannily tidy. It's as if everything's been lifted up and put back a bit differently. Even the welter around the couch looks sifted. Brick's cane is hooked over the edge of the table and he's nowhere to be seen.

Home always looks strange after a vacation, though, doesn't it? Things you're used to suddenly pop out. Was the fridge always that robin's egg blue? It must have been, and that dog-eared mess of notes stuck around the phone. But, to Bob and Lettuce, everything looks shifted.

Bob picks a sliver of glass out of the door jamb. Lettuce notices a smear of blood on the edge of the counter. "Hello! Kids! Where are you?"

There's distant thumping overhead, then, finally, the herd thunders downstairs. Alive and boisterous.

The window? A bear tried to break in. The second morning! Looked like a grizzly. Scared off soon's they all stampeded to the porch. The blood? Oh well, Pink got a little cut. She waggles a huge wad of gauze wrapped around one finger. "It doesn't hurt anymore," she smiles.

Gradually, the story comes out. No sooner had Bob and Lettuce gone, than Brick discovered Lovebird Lila missing. Who left the cage open? They blame each other. There's shouting and recriminations, eyes darting frantically for that flash of green.

It's only after twenty-four hours of noisy search, when the Eleven have fallen into the glum silence of defeat, that a persistent, small sound is noticed. It seems to come through a vent in the livingroom ceiling. The sound of paper tearing.

The girl twins spring into action, fingers on lips, freezing the others in their tracks. Totally focused and inter-coordinated, Pink and Julie quietly track the sound to their attic dormer, and there's Lila in the pixie diorama, working on a three-storey nest of shredded Bobbsey Twin books. (All still readable, praises be.) Seeing them, she takes a break to have a sip of water and snack on the birdseed the girls had scattered for the pixies.

It's soon discovered that the green-winged Houdini can, by dint of stealth and rapid navigation, make it from her cage back to the diorama in less than an hour. Julie and Pink fetch her more water, seeds, and a stack of magazines to shred... although she will occasionally sample more high-brow reading.

It's decided that Lila can live in the diorama dormer, provided Pink and Julie take responsibility for watering and feeding her, and cleaning the area daily. They're the only ones who haven't been nipped by the little love. At last the girls have a real pet, and this opens the way for discussion of a family dog to replace Perth. Ron and Rich have a friend with puppies.

Now that Brick can manage the stairs, the couch corner gets thoroughly reamed out. This takes two days of shift-work and a coat of paint which has just enough time to dry before the Aunties Ben, Anne, and Hilarity arrive.

Full of sass and vinegar, the three aunts whirl through the house for several days, noticing everything, talking to everyone, spinning plans for next summer's Hilarity Art Camp. In Billy's words, "It will be for all shirttail and whole-shirt relatives."

The aunties rock the ark from alcove to attic, which helps distract everyone from Herald cheerfully packing his boxes for Victoria. When the aunts leave, it's as if one corner of the house slumps.

As the dreaded moment of Herald's departure draws near, he notices Ron and Rich moping. He swoops them into a bear hug, and they have to dash outside to hide their tears. They'll actually miss his heart-to-heart talks. Without the challenge of out-witting him, though, their behavior does improve, especially when Hazel and Fern press-gang them into taking more responsibility for the *housework*. With Herald leaving, Brick laid up, and Lettuce whirring through her fall assignment, second and third mother need reinforcement. Sedge is increasingly her mother's dedicated assistant, honing a flare for design which will lead to great things in her future.

As for Billy and Alvin, they're building a two-room cabin out back when they're not glued to Brick, who is teaching them to sculpt. Julie and Pink help with the cabin... when they're not smoothing precious candy foil onto sun-warmed pebbles and adding to their hoard of small painted objects.

Herald eventually tunnels through the family gauntlet of fare-wells, wearing the decent brown trousers that Hazel and Fern have sewn him. After twenty hours on a bus he reaches Victoria and steps into the arms of his Auntie Ben and Uncle Al and throng of cousins. Sadly they live too far from the college for him to live with them, but they've secured him room and board at a friend's house.

When he unpacks, he discovers four pounds of colourful foil-covered pebbles surreptitiously scattered throughout his luggage, along with many tightly folded notes and painted thread spools. He doesn't care that these had added to his freight expense, as he delightedly distributes Pink and Julie's gifts around his garret.

CHAPTER 70
The Storyteller: Julie, 2005

LEAPING FROM HER TUB and zipping on her robe just as her porch door bursts open, Julie shrieks.

It's Pink! Pink in her turquoise coveralls, her red frizz tied up in a yellow bandanna. They leap into each other's arms.

"Pink! Here? I was expecting you later. How? With a pail of huckleberries! But it's been dark for ages!"

"My night vision is good as ever, Jule. Anyhow, didn't you see my note? On the table? I went for a bucket walk when you weren't here. I love your moxie robe… turquoise and yellow… zow! And that pixie cut suits you!"

"But how in the heck? When?" Julie spies the note under the far end of the table…"Turkle must have shoved it… But, Pink!" Between hugs and exclamations of disbelief, Julie gets the gist of Pink's story and puts the kettle on. A strong cup of pekoe is called for.

Pink's operation had been yesterday. "I got a cancellation, Julie! I only needed a laparoscopy after all! Everything's perfect! I got a standby flight… caught the shuttle. I wanted to surprise you!"

"You rascal, Pink. You rapscallion! Yesterday I baked. Today I worried. But then… I knew everything was alright."

"It is alright, Ju Ju. I am alright. I just need two-month check-ups. Can we have some huckleberries? Or are you sticking to the One Hundred Quart Rule?

Julie laughs, "I've already canned the twenty quarts I need. Yes… let's eat huckleberries with pound cake and cream and… Pink! We can go?"

"Yes, Jule! I brought some maps!" Pink drags out a satchel stuffed behind the porch swing.

They laugh and plan far into the night, giggling as they reminisce about how they and their nine siblings bungled their way through childhood. It didn't seem like bungling at the time, of course. Not for the most part. They had gradually evolved individual and interconnecting pathways which they had followed by fits and starts, into what Brick had envisioned fifty years earlier: a trail in reverse perspective, getting wider and brighter in the shining horizon.

The Eleven are still interconnected in myriad ways. Lettuce and Bob will always be in their songs, their tears, and their peals of laughter, as Pink and Julie reunite with their siblings around the world.

But first, one last semester of teaching at the Chagall Art Academy, one last extravaganza of creative hilarity, and a firm promise to return in one year. Then Julie and Pink will fly the coop, traveling the world for a year to celebrate their fifty-five years of twin-dom.

Concluding Recipe: Huckleberry Buckle
(Serves 15)

Mix 3 cups brown sugar, 1 cup margarine, 5 cups milk and 6 or
more eggs.
Stir in flour to right consistency (5–6 cups) with 2 tablespoons baking
powder, 2 teaspoons salt.
Add 9 cups huckleberries.

Spread in pan.
Sprinkle top with mixture of flour, sugar and margarine.
Bake 50 minutes or until top is golden brown.

Printed in Canada